Praise for *The Second Home*

One of *Good Morning America*'s "25 Novels You'll Want to Read this Summer"

"A riveting family saga that fans of J. Courtney Sullivan, Cristina Alger, and Maria de los Santos will devour, Clancy's debut novel is a delight. With nostalgia as thick as the scent of coconut-scented sunscreen, *The Second Home* explores the consequences of emotional decisions and the strength needed to set things right."   —*Booklist* (starred review)

"Transporting . . . Clancy's beach-ready debut is sure to be a favorite with book clubs."   —*Publishers Weekly*

"With its fond descriptions of Cape Cod's land and seascapes and an evocation of a historic house layered with love and secrets, Clancy's debut clearly has its eye firmly set on the summer-read market."

—*Kirkus Reviews*

"Warm, absorbing, and thought-provoking."   —*Shelf Awareness*

"Witty and compassionate, this is the page-turning saga, unfolding in several voices, of two sisters, their estranged adopted brother, and the dispute that arises fifteen years after their parents' death."   —*Naples Daily News*

"Christina Clancy writes with warmth, wit, and wisdom about fantastically human characters. A novel of family and place and belonging for fans of Ann Packer and J. Courtney Sullivan."

—Rebecca Makkai, Pulitzer Prize finalist for *The Great Believers*

"I gobbled *The Second Home* in a matter of days, fully invested in the history, hurt, and hopes of this very human family. Christina Clancy writes with empathy and rich detail: to read about the Gordons is to smell the pine and oak of Wellfleet, to tread the well-worn rooms of their eccentric summer home, and to learn all sides of the explosive rift that sent them hurtling in different directions."

—Chloe Benjamin, *New York Times* bestselling author of *The Immortalists*

"*The Second Home* shows us how families are knit together and how they unravel; how a place—a geography, a house—can act as the repository for our best and most important memories. And that even the most damaged past can be reclaimed, a hard-won wisdom that shines through on every page. A compelling story, beautifully told."

—Jean Thompson, *New York Times* bestselling author of *The Year We Left Home* and *A Cloud in the Shape of a Girl*

"Christina Clancy's debut novel is about the ways we build walls with secrets. Clancy imagines her complicated characters with such empathy and precision that every questionable choice, every mistake, feels like the only option. *The Second Home* is a big, sprawling, smart, beautiful story about love and betrayal, home and family, and the foundations of forgiveness." —Lauren Fox, *New York Times* bestselling author of *Send for Me*

"Christina Clancy writes with an arresting vividness and a nuanced understanding of her characters, who are buffeted by a storm of conflicting desires. *The Second Home* is a poignant but also a very entertaining novel—full of startling detail, humor, and above all, an abiding sympathy for its beautifully drawn characters." —Christina Sneed, author of *Little Known Facts* and *The Virginity of Famous Men*

"This deeply moving and heartfelt book explores what makes a home—and how homes make us. It's deftly plotted, sensuously told, and incredibly smart about the secrets that pull families apart and the love that knits them back together." —Liam Callanan, author of *Paris by the Book*

"Every Wellfleet sand dune, every breeze and beach and pond, came alive for me in this beautiful, heartbreaking debut about a Milwaukee family's complicated history with their summer home. Clancy's characters are so real and flawed, so caught between the darkness and the light, that they step right off the page, and you won't rest until you know what becomes of them."   —Meg Mitchell Moore, author of *Two Truths and a Lie*

"From the first pages of *The Second Home*, it's abundantly clear that Christina Clancy has an abiding love for outer Cape Cod, which she conjures in all its bluster and beauty. But as this compelling novel progresses, it also becomes obvious that Clancy has a keen awareness of how secrets can tear apart even the closest of families. Drawn in by the exquisitely rendered setting, I was riveted by this stirring family drama."
    —Karen Dukess, author of *The Last Book Party*

The Second Home

Christina Clancy

ST. MARTIN'S GRIFFIN
NEW YORK

Published in the United States by St. Martin's Griffin, an imprint
of St. Martin's Publishing Group

THE SECOND HOME. Copyright © 2020 by Christina Clancy. All rights reserved.
Printed in the United States of America. For information, address
St. Martin's Publishing Group, 120 Broadway, New York, NY 10271.

www.stmartins.com

An excerpt from the poem "Vaporizer" from *An Algebra* by Don Bogen,
(University of Chicago Press, 2009) was reprinted with permission.

The Library of Congress has cataloged the hardcover edition as follows:

Names: Clancy, Christina, author.
Title: The second home / Christina Clancy.
Description: First edition. | New York: St. Martin's Press, 2020.
Identifiers: LCCN 2019051878 | ISBN 9781250239341 (hardcover) |
 ISBN 9781250239600 (ebook)
Classification: LCC PS3603.L3514 S43 2020 | DDC 813/.6—dc23
LC record available at https://lccn.loc.gov/2019051878

ISBN 978-1-250-23962-4 (trade paperback)

Our books may be purchased in bulk for promotional, educational, or business use.
Please contact your local bookseller or the Macmillan Corporate and Premium
Sales Department at 1-800-221-7945, extension 5442, or
by email at MacmillanSpecialMarkets@macmillan.com.

First St. Martin's Griffin Edition: 2021

10 9 8 7 6 5 4 3 2 1

For my family, my home

I walked past a house where I lived once: a man and a woman
are still together in the whispers there.

—YEHUDA AMICHAI

The house of childhood sold,
or razed—
not lost but
softened, distended:
diaphanous linked chambers springing from
a lightshaft or a varnish smell,
the way a floorboard aches,
a scrap of wallpaper
tunnels the heart.

—BY DON BOGEN

Prologue

Ann had never been to Wellfleet in February. Each fall her parents emptied the water heater, shut down the well pump, flushed antifreeze down the toilets, threw some sheets over the furniture, pulled down all the shades, and closed the house. Cape Cod felt like a hazy dream the rest of the year, a place suspended forever in beach days filled with sunshine and warmth.

But there she was, alone and cold in a house that felt both familiar and now strange because it was the off-season, and because her parents were gone, although she could feel them there. It was as if they were sitting behind mirrored glass during a focus group like the ones Ann participated in at work, watching and listening to everything Ann did and said. Even now, half a year after they'd died, she kept waiting for some magical door to swing open, and for her parents to walk out from the other side of the glass to tell her they'd been watching her this whole time.

She felt her parents' radiant energy in everything she saw as she paced the house to stay warm: in the chipped wineglass left in the sink, the sloppily folded beach towels and stained pillowcases, her mother's cookbooks, her father's telescope, even in the bulb digger where they'd always hidden the heavy iron key that unlocked the back door. Their possessions seemed ready to be put to use again and again, and made the house feel like it was less a place they'd left behind than a place they'd planned to return to.

Ann shivered and took a sip of her now-cold Starbucks coffee. She checked her phone to see if Carol, the Realtor, had tried to contact her to say she'd be late, but she had weak cell reception out here on the Outer Cape. Maybe she'd gotten lost. You couldn't see the house from Route 6, and the mouth of the long driveway, tucked in a thicket of brush and oak trees, was easy to miss.

Ann didn't want Carol to think she was someone who could be talked into a low asking price, so she'd dressed for their meeting in her most serious work suit, a chocolate-colored alligator jacquard jacket and matching pencil skirt. Not wanting to diminish the impact of her outfit, she left her wool coat in her car, but the house wasn't heated and she was freezing. It was better this way, she thought. She'd need the sharpness of the cold to get through this.

A strong breeze blew so hard that the house seemed to moan and the door flew open. Ann jumped, as though the ghosts of her parents had breezed in and scolded her for what she was doing. She rushed over to the door and shut it firmly. She needed to list the house before she lost her resolve, and before summer arrived along with all the tourists and their naïve dreams of owning a place on the Cape. She already hated the buyers (whoever they were) who would love the house differently than her family did, free of their complicated history and conflicting personalities, unburdened by all the stuff they'd accumulated across three generations. It felt oddly intimate and wrong to imagine strangers living there, like she was letting them wear her own skin.

She tried to focus on logistics. She and her younger sister, Poppy, would split the proceeds. If they got a good price, Ann could use her share to put some money in Noah's college fund and move into a bigger apartment in Boston than the cramped two-bedroom they shared in the South End. She was tired of living paycheck-to-paycheck; it would be nice to put some cartilage between the bones, especially since her job was now on the line. Noah had pleaded with her not to sell. She tried to explain to him that it made no sense to hold on to a house for sentimental reasons, although that was an argument that was easier to make from a distance.

Ann opened the door to the "blue room," the bedroom she'd always shared with Poppy. The twin beds, covered in the ancient crochet bedcovers, stuck out from the wall like piano keys. The room had once been a parlor. When they were kids and they'd finally arrived for the summer, Poppy would bolt out of the station wagon, run inside, and throw herself on her creaky old spring mattress, clinging to it like a life raft. "We're back!" Ann's great-grandmother had died in this room the same day she was born, which was how she had escaped being named after a flower herself.

She could glimpse Drummer Cove through the wavy lead glass in the window. After the railroad dike was built in the late 1800s, the cove began to fill in with silt deposited with every high tide. When the tide emptied out, it left a mudflat with the consistency of quicksand. *Real* quicksand, the stuff of fairy tales and nightmares. The cove was a place where boats had been marooned, deer got stuck, and dolphins were stranded. Dead horseshoe crabs littered the edges. Ann hardly ever visited the cove now that she was an adult. The tall beach grass was thick with ticks, and the damp hay path was always squishy from the last high tide. She wouldn't dare swim in that muck. Still, Ann thought the cove was pretty to look at. It smelled like rotten eggs at low tide, but that was a smell she loved in the same primal way that she'd loved the smell of Noah's sweet bald head when he was a baby. She'd roll down her car windows as soon as she got to Blackfish Creek and wait for the odor to hit her. When it did, every molecule in her body seemed to change. That's when she knew she was really there, on the "real" part of the Cape.

She walked back into the living room and pulled down the writing desk of her late grandmother's beloved antique secretary. She rummaged through the contents of the delicate little drawers, finding only yellowed cash register receipts, nail clippers, and kite string. She lifted the piles of paperwork in the larger cubbies—just old *New Yorker*s, bills from the plumber that could have been thrown away years ago, and there, on the bottom, some old crayon drawings Noah had made when he was little, the words "I love you Nana" in his sweet, sloppy capital letters. It amazed her, all the fresh new ways her heart could break.

She stuffed the papers back where she'd found them and, more gently this time, closed the desk back up, remembering how her grandmother would scold her if she was rough with the furniture. She looked around the room with a scavenger's eye. Surely there must be a will—how could her father, who'd spent hours preparing detailed notes for substitutes in his classroom—not have one?

An old framed family photograph on the mantel caught her eye, perhaps because it was strangely free of the veil of dust that gently shrouded everything else in the still house. The photo was almost too painful to look at. After everything that had happened with Michael, she was surprised her parents had kept it on display—how had she never noticed it before? That was his first summer with them, when she and Michael were sophomores and best friends. He hadn't been adopted yet. Michael stood between Ann and Poppy, all of them about the same age, still about the same height before Michael's growth spurt the next year. Ann's hair was pulled back, but Poppy's whipped wildly around her face. Michael was smiling like he'd just won the lottery.

They all looked so happy, so innocent.

Pilgrim Monument loomed behind them. Ann and Poppy always had to beg their parents to take them to P-town. They complained that the traffic at the tip of the Cape was terrible and there was nowhere to park. They didn't want to be mistaken as tourists with their fudge-stained lips and boxes of saltwater taffy stuffed under their arms, gawking at the friendly drag queens who stood outside bars in giant wigs, stuffing postcards for drag shows into the hands of passersby. Her parents had only agreed to that excursion because it was Michael's first summer on the Cape. The next summer, Ann would miss the trip to Provincetown, because she'd spend all her days babysitting for the Shaws.

Oh God, the Shaws. She couldn't think about them without hearing an explosion echo in her ears.

Ann was holding the photo when a car crunched toward the house on the broken oyster shells her father scattered on the driveway.

The Realtor.

Suddenly the picture burned in her hands. She furtively stuffed it under the old Popeye-themed sheet that covered the couch, grateful she'd hidden the evidence before Carol arrived. Michael looked nothing like Ann or Poppy. He could be any random kid, a cousin or friend. Even if the Realtor saw the photo, why would she suspect he was their adopted brother, an heir?

CAROL MADE ANN FEEL EMBARRASSED about the house. She touched every surface, ran her fingers along the window casings, setting free so much dust that it flew loose in a cloudy puff. "Needs a good scrub-down," she said. She wiped her hand on her vest, leaving a gray smear. "I'll give you a list of cleaners. They do an excellent job."

"I can take care of it," Ann said.

"I'm sure you can."

Carol was younger than Ann thought she'd be, maybe thirty-five, about Ann's own age, and she was ruggedly attractive. She was cool, even for someone who chose to live on the lonely outermost Cape year-round, a coolness that Ann thought was wasted here. It would serve her better someplace more hip and urban, like Boston or New York. Ann thought Carol's beauty was wasted here, too, with so few people to appreciate it. She had big, watchful eyes and a heap of curly blond hair piled on top of her head. She wore an artsy purple A-line skirt made out of thick sailcloth material that looked heavy and uncomfortable and swished when she walked. Unlike Carol's thick wool tights, Ann's hose were sheer, and her frozen toes were stuffed into black, pointy pumps with straps around the ankles. Ann followed Carol from room to room, the sound of her stupid heels like pickaxes digging into ice when they clicked against the hardwood plank floors. It was an odd sound in a place where everyone had always gone barefoot.

"So, what do you think?"

"About the price?" Carol paused to lean into the fireplace to look up into the flue. "Well, it's hard to say. Houses like this don't usually come on the market."

"It's one of the oldest on the Cape," Ann said, feeling a tingle of pride combined with sadness. "It's one of a kind."

Carol said, "Actually, there are plenty of antique saltboxes in Wellfleet."

"They say the house was made from the wood of a merchant boat that was stranded in the cove. It's old. *Really* old." Ann looked around at the historic putty-colored oil trim that was thankfully untouched, just like the flinty woodblock-print wallpaper sagging against the walls. Until that afternoon, seeing the house through Carol's eyes, she hadn't noticed how stained and worn it looked, as though it had been exposed to a fire. She was so familiar with the house that she didn't even see it anymore, the way she could listen to an old song she'd heard a thousand times on the radio and not really hear it.

"Oh, I'm not disputing that the house has an interesting history," Carol said. "I'm sure your buyer will want to learn everything you know about it. What's unique is that it's coming on the market in the first place. Out here, old houses usually stay in the family." The way Carol said it made Ann feel like she was being judged, like her whole family had failed. And they had.

"So, tell me," Carol said. "Why are you selling this treasure?"

"Treasure" sounded good, or maybe Carol was mocking her? Ann couldn't tell. This bothered her, because she liked to think she usually *could* tell these things. "My sister and I think selling makes the most sense."

If only Poppy could hear Ann speaking as if they were a united front.

We. They hadn't talked about what to do with this house, not yet. Poppy said she wanted to spend her summer here, and who knew, she might want to keep it, but she didn't have a practical bone in her body. Besides, Poppy couldn't afford to buy Ann out, not with the money she made teaching yoga and waiting tables in Puerto Rico, South Africa, wherever. She flitted from beach to beach, chasing STDs and waves. She didn't even check her email regularly, which was why she didn't hear about their parents' accident until two weeks after it had happened—the loneliest two weeks of Ann's life.

"Does your sister also live in Boston?"

Ann shook her head. "She's a bit of an itinerant. She lives all over."

Carol nodded as though this was perfectly normal. Wellfleet was filled with artists and outsiders like Ann's parents.

"She's back home now," Ann said, thinking about how strange the word "home" sounded. What was home anymore? She tried to clarify: "At my parents' house. In Wisconsin." Ann pointed at the Green Bay Packers potholder hanging from a hook near the oven as if she needed supporting evidence.

"Wisconsin?" Carol said "Wisconsin" the way most people out East said it, like they'd just heard the name of a high school classmate they'd long forgotten.

"That's where we, where *they,* lived most of the year. We have to sell that house, too. My parents were in the middle of a remodel when it happened."

Carol didn't seem particularly interested in what "it" was, and Ann was grateful. She didn't think she had the strength to talk about the semi driver who had crossed lanes and hit her parents' car head-on while they were headed back home from the Cape last August. Talking about the accident here, in this sacred space, would only make it real again.

"My sister and I, we aren't any good at houses and now, suddenly, we have *two* to sell, and they both need work."

"Divide and conquer."

"That's my plan," Ann said. "My sister is getting the Milwaukee house ready to sell, and I'm taking care of this one. We'll both be in real estate hell."

"It's like childbirth," Carol said, although Ann suspected Carol was childless. "You'll forget how awful it is as soon as you get the check at closing."

"Closing": Ann suddenly appreciated what a nice word that was. Ann wanted closure.

"It's good that you and your sister are in agreement about selling," Carol said. "Houses, even houses that aren't special like this one, well, they often make people sentimental." She talked about sentiment with anthropological distance. "The ones that are hardest to let go of are places that are passed down generation to generation."

Ann's great-grandfather had initially come from Ireland to the Cape to work for the Pacific Guano Company in Woods Hole, a business that imported bat shit for fertilizer. When the company went bankrupt, he moved farther up the Cape to Wellfleet and tried to start a farm here. Her father, an only child, eventually inherited the house and wouldn't think of selling, even though he lived halfway across the country. They could have sunk the money into a much cheaper cottage in Door County or Waupaca—it seemed everyone had a lake place in Wisconsin—but her parents loved it here. They let the Cape house dictate their lives. Her parents never earned high salaries; they were teachers because they adored kids, but mostly because their jobs allowed them to spend their summers in Wellfleet.

Carol said, "In my experience, the deeper the roots, the harder the sale."

"We're fine." This was a lie. Ann didn't feel at all fine. She was racked with guilt, because she knew, even with a missing will, that her parents would have wanted her to make whatever sacrifice was necessary to pass their beloved family home down to Noah. And then there was Poppy, who had already turned her entire life into one long summer vacation. And Michael—no, no. She didn't want to think about Michael. She couldn't.

Carol sat down at the Formica kitchen table and gestured for Ann to join her. "This might be hard to hear, but I wouldn't be doing my job if I didn't level with you. A house like this, as charming as it is, can be hard to move. Old homes require special owners." Carol talked about the house like she was a doctor talking with parents about a child with a tragic congenital defect whose future would not be bright.

"Your home is wonderful. It's in relatively good shape, for its age, and the lot is nice. But you're right on Route 6, so there's road noise."

"But you can hardly hear it."

"True. The problem is the address. Some of my clients, they won't even look at a house on the state highway. And I should tell you that the first thing a buyer will see is what *I* saw when I first got here: the shingles aren't in great shape and the roof needs to be replaced. The problem is that your home looks *old* instead of *historic*. You've only got one small bathroom, and any buyer will want another one upstairs. The fixtures are dated. The oil boiler—you know that will scare people. And the kitchen . . ." She looked around. Ann had to agree: the kitchen was a nightmare, complete with sticky-looking cupboards, and the funky pink and brown mushroom wallpaper her mother had put up in the seventies. "Kitchens sell houses."

"What are you saying?"

"I know this is hard to hear, but it might be easier for you to set a low price to reflect the deficiencies."

"'Deficiencies'?" Ann felt deflated by that word.

"Given the lot size you can probably get a larger septic system, and that's a good thing, but it's expensive to upgrade, I'm guessing about twelve grand. And you'll need a new well. Water is a problem in this area."

"What do you mean it's a problem? We've always had water."

Ann walked over to the kitchen sink and flipped the faucet on, but nothing came out; worse, the handle fell off, clattering when it hit the bottom of the metal sink. "Well, it's turned off in the winter. There's water. There's always been water."

Carol shook her head. "It's a known problem."

"Great," Ann said. Her stupid suit did nothing to make her feel more in control.

"People want to swoop in for a few days, unwind, drink, play in the sand, whatever. They think about how much they can get for rent in the summer, and a place like this is hard to rent out until it's fixed up. The house is very special, it is, but it's easier to rent a cleaner-looking, more generic space. And it's on the water I guess, but you're set too far back to get a good view of the cove."

"You're saying it's hopeless."

Carol's smile was as unexpected as it was refreshing. "Of course not! I just want you to be realistic. You'll find a buyer who's into history, who gets into the old hardware and square nails, the big fireplace, the bean-pot cellar. For those people, the smell of an old house is like the smell of a baseball glove for a baseball player. You're looking for a romantic." The way Carol said it, she might have said, *You're looking for . . . a hopeless loser.* "But a more likely scenario is that your buyer will want to tear it down."

"But it's, it's historic. They can't."

"It's not in the historic district, and it's not listed on the National Register."

Ann felt like cleaning out her ears. Did this Realtor just talk about the house being torn down? Out loud, in the light of day, practically within earshot of Ann's dead parents? Selling was one thing; bulldozing the house was something different altogether. It would be like killing a living thing.

Ann said, "Can we make it so that whoever buys it can't?" She paused. "Can't tear it down?"

"Maybe you could put a restriction on the deed, or impose a short waiting period, but that'll drag down the value. If you want to sell, and it sounds like you do, I suggest you try to set your emotions aside. I understand that can be difficult with a family home."

No, Ann thought. Carol didn't understand. Carol didn't have the slightest idea what Ann was going through. Carol wouldn't want to know.

"So how would you price it?" Ann tried not to sound desperate. Maybe she could finally start her own business, something she'd dreamed of doing since she got her MBA. She wanted to advance out of her old life and into a new one. No matter how bad things got, Ann always believed she could start fresh.

A low number: she could tell by the way Carol looked around and bit her lower lip that that was what she was thinking. Before Carol arrived, Ann thought the house was special and valuable. Now? She felt like she'd have to pay someone to take it off her hands.

"I need to run some figures, look at the comps. What about the title? I'll need a CYA to be sure you have legal authority to proceed with the sale."

"A CYA?"

"I'm sure it's not a problem, but we don't want to get into a legal snarl with heirs. Happens with houses that have been in the family a long time. I'll need to know that the title is clear."

The word "title" made Ann's stomach twist. She thought about Michael. She couldn't help but see him here: his thick, dark hair that always hung over his intense brown eyes. She could hear his footsteps on the creaky stairs, see his sandals on the mat by the door, smell the Old Spice he insisted on using because that was what her dad wore, imagine him curled on his side in the twin bed under the eaves in the attic. She felt him here, present to her in a way he hadn't been in years. She swore she could almost feel his breath. Who knew where he'd gone off to? She wasn't about to try to find him—certainly not now, even though she knew she probably should.

"The title is all clear," Ann lied, the same way she lied to the probate court officer when she filed to be the administrator of her parents' estate. She felt bad about lying, she did, but she was beaten down, desperate. "It's clean as a whistle."

Part One

1999

ONE

Michael

Ann ordered Michael to drop his bag next to a long, skinny door that had an iron lever for a doorknob. "Your room will be upstairs," she said, although there were no stairs he could see. Michael struggled with the handle, and Ann, impatient, pushed his hand away. "Everything here is old and weird. Here—"

She showed him how it worked, pressing the lever with her thumb and tugging the swollen door from the frame, revealing a staircase unlike any Michael had seen. It was so steep it was almost a wall, with only enough room on each narrow step for the balls of his feet, and the pine risers were riddled with scuff marks. "These are the captain's stairs," Ann said.

He lifted his leg to begin his ascent, but Ann pulled him back. "Later. We need to get going." She swung the door shut with a disheartening thud.

Michael wanted to explore the house, but the girls explained that they'd stay only long enough to change into swimsuits and head straight to the beach. This was a family tradition, the first thing they did after their annual drive halfway across the country from Milwaukee to Wellfleet. But Michael wasn't ready to leave.

The house had seemed peaceful and dark when they'd first walked in, as if it were sleeping. It wasn't like any home he'd ever been in. It even smelled different, because it sat closed up all winter long. Now the house was already buzzing with life. Connie pulled the sheets off the furniture. Michael walked to the couch to help her, but his mind was still on those stairs. He wanted to know where he'd sleep—no, he *needed* to know. He'd spent too many nights not knowing.

Ed walked with purpose to the window and pulled up the heavy wood blind with a hearty yank of the yellowed cord. Dust rose and lingered like confetti in the abrupt sunlight, revealing four playing cards, all aces, nailed to the wall above the door to the sunporch.

"What are those?" Michael asked.

Ed smiled. "Oh, that's the stuff of legend. My grandfather Cullen, he won this house in a game of poker."

"He won a whole house in a game?"

"They were gambling out here. The homeowner, Hopkinson, he'd built the newer house next door to be closer to the cove. At the time, this was just the back house—his man cave. Anyway, Cullen was way up. Hopkinson was low on chips but he wanted to stay in for one last game. He had a winning hand, and you know what he did? He bet the house."

"The house?" Michael couldn't imagine being so reckless.

"Well, at that time it wasn't worth a plug nickel. And Hopkinson, you know, he didn't think he'd lose. He had four kings. But that was Cullen's hand." Ed pointed at the playing cards, pinned unevenly to the wall and stained from the long, rusty nails. "He'd tell that story to anyone who would listen."

Connie playfully swatted Ed on the behind with the dust rag she was holding. "*You'll* tell it to anyone who will listen." She wiped down the top of the bookcase. "The little room next to ours is a birthing room, where women had their babies so they could stay warm near the fire. And this room we're in, this is called a *keeping room*." She was happy to show off the old house, and clearly happy to finally be there. "See these tall, thin doors? They called them courting doors because of the tiny windows above them." She pointed up. "For spying."

Poppy opened a cabinet on the side of the large, squat fireplace that dominated the room. "They used to bake bread in here," she said. "Check this out. This is the best part." She walked over to a bookcase on the other side of the fireplace and gave it a push, revealing a hidden compartment one or two small people might fit in if they huddled together. "A hiding place."

"To hide from what?" Michael asked.

"Well, as you can imagine, back in the day the natives weren't too happy with the colonists." Ed's statement was innocent enough, but it hit Michael sideways, heightening his awareness of insiders and outsiders, natives and impostors.

Still, he was happy to be there. More than happy. He found the house, with its leathery smell and unexpected spaces, even more magical than he'd anticipated—as magical as he found the Gordon family with their traditions, games, inside jokes, Sunday dinners, and summer vacations "out East."

Ann emerged from the bedroom. He looked beyond her and saw her clothing already scattered all over the twin beds in the room she and Poppy shared. She adjusted the shoulder straps of her suit with a snap. "Let's go. I'm dying to swim." Ann dabbed some Coppertone on her cheeks. The room smelled suddenly of coconut. He wished he could reach out and smooth out the glob of lotion next to her nose that she'd missed.

"You go ahead," he said. "I can wait here."

"Don't you want to see the back shore?"

He did, he supposed, but he hated the idea of leaving. "I want to unpack."

Ann walked toward the door. "You've got all summer to unpack. Come on, get changed."

"I'll just wear my shorts," Michael said.

He didn't want to tell her that he didn't own a swimsuit.

MICHAEL RACED DOWN THE DUNE behind the girls, so intent on staying steady in the deep, rust-colored sand that he didn't look up or ahead as he followed their winding tracks around beach blankets, Frisbee players, coolers, sandcastles, and the lifeguard stand. They stopped just short of the surf. Michael stood next to Ann and stared in awe at the limitless expanse of blue sky and churning gray water spread out in front of him. His lungs and legs burned. He'd seen Lake Michigan plenty of times. The lake was just a puddle compared to the Atlantic. The ocean was as frightening as it was beautiful. He felt as if he were standing at the mouth of a massive and hungry living thing.

Poppy squealed with delight when a wave broke against her leg. She was always in her own world, daydreaming and doodling palm trees on her folders and the textbook covers she made out of old grocery bags and Scotch tape. She changed when she got near the water. It was as if he could see her snap into herself, become her own person.

"It's even colder than I remembered." Poppy's smile was broad, her shoulders glistened, and the thick rope of her braid hung over one bare shoulder. He'd always been so preoccupied with Ann that he felt as if he was only now seeing Poppy. Her looks were more rugged and outdoorsy than Ann's. Poppy didn't seem like she'd just arrived at the beach; it was as if she'd been there all along. "Put your foot in, Michael."

The girls watched Michael expectantly as he took in the rise, curl, and crash of waves against the shore. He couldn't move. He was overwhelmed by both the power of the surf and the girls' intense focus on him. He began to feel there was something pressingly selfish about their interest, as though they didn't really care if he connected to Cape Cod; what they wanted was for him to recognize *their* attachment to the place.

"C'mon," Poppy said in her dreamy voice, splashing the water like a dancer. "It's amazing."

"It's cold at first," Ann said, "but you'll get used to it."

He didn't know what to do. He couldn't shake his fear that the Gordons could still change their mind about him. During the drive out, he was convinced they'd leave him stranded at a gas station or rest stop. He couldn't believe they'd asked him to come along to this place Ed called "the outermost Cape." "Outermost" was right: it seemed about as different and as far away as he could possibly get from Milwaukee.

He thought he'd known what to expect. Poppy and Ann had shown him their scrapbooks stuffed with pictures of Wellfleet. The photos made the place seem quiet and peaceful, and he looked forward to going there the way his mother had talked about going to heaven. He hadn't anticipated the wind ripping in his ears, the ocean roaring like a freight train, and the girls staring at him.

"Don't you want to swim?" Poppy asked. It was as if she thought the ocean could change him, and she was right. It could. The ocean could change him from hot to cold, change the air in his lungs to water, change him from living to dead.

Michael looked down at his feet to anchor himself but got dizzy watching the small pebbles crash against each other, roll forward, skitter back, forward, back. They were powerless, grinding down to nothing against each other.

The air tasted like salt. Gulls swirled overhead and the wind ripped at his hair. Children misbehaved and their parents in plaid swim trunks and polo shirts scolded them in their strange East Coast accents. *Daniel, I tooold you not to put sand in your brotha's eyes* and *Whea's your noodle?* They were the kind of people who belonged here, people who set summers aside from the rest of the year, people who had money and families, who knew how to swim and thought nothing of it. People who thought this beach was *relaxing*.

Ann reached for his hand, and her touch sent a familiar shock through him. "Isn't it amazing, Michael?"

It *was* amazing and it was *theirs*—the roaring ocean, the old vacation home, their nice parents, everything. The girls thought they were sharing it with him, but he felt like they were rubbing their perfect lives in his face, saying, *This is ours, ours, ours—we know all about it, we come here every year. You have no history, you know nothing, you have nothing, you are nothing.*

Ann's hand was nestled into his own, warm and soft compared to the cool ocean spray, but just as dangerous.

On the drive out, she sat next to him in the cramped backseat and pressed her thigh against his. It made him crazy, and he had a feeling from her faint smile that she knew it would. He'd tried his best to concentrate on the family game they called "Anibitz." Ann and Poppy said they'd made it up and played it since they were little. Someone would name an animal, like a sea lion, and someone else would name another one, like a tarantula, and whoever was "it" had to draw a combination of the two and come up with a combined name, like "sealantula." Or they'd draw a creature and everyone else would try to guess what it was made out of—a roach, a monkey, a polar bear: a "romopobear."

By the time they reached Cleveland they could mash together three, four, five creatures into one, and they added real people into the mix, like Prince and Mrs. LaSpisa, the guidance counselor from school who gave him a beeswax candle when she'd heard his mother had died. Michael thought the game was stupid and funny and charming. He was excited to see Cape Cod, and the ride out there—with all of them close together, playing games like a *real* family—would have been perfect if he hadn't been so distrustful of his good fortune to be included, and so skeptical that his luck would last.

After their stop in Syracuse, Ann fell asleep with her head on his shoulder. He couldn't help it: the feeling of her breath on his neck and the fruity smell of shampoo in her long, straight hair made him hard. Of course she turned him on. She was pretty, but there was more to his attraction to her than that. He'd heard kids at school say she was stuck-up, and he supposed she could be, but he admired her confidence and drive. Plus, she'd allowed him to see a side of her that other people didn't see. He'd be forever in her debt for taking an interest in him when nobody else did. If it weren't for Ann, he'd be in some foster home or out on the street.

He could practically taste her, smell her, feel her soft hair in his hands. He studied everything about her: the dimple on her cheek, the bump on her nose, the way she frowned when she did homework and tapped her fingers against her leg when she was bored. He couldn't explain it; it was as if she'd been imprinting herself on him.

The waves kept smashing against the shore, and the wind whistled in his ears. Couldn't everything just stop for a minute? Couldn't there be quiet? He didn't know what to do; he only knew that Ann's hand felt like an anchor. He wanted her to keep holding on as much as he knew she should let go. He wasn't her boyfriend.

"Let's swim," Ann said. A strand of her hair had gotten caught in the bubble-gum-scented lip gloss she always used, and it was all he could do not to reach out and pull it away for her. In the sun, her hair looked as golden as the tinsel on a Christmas tree, while Poppy's hair had a copper cast to it. They were both wearing one-pieces, the kind of modest suits girls wear to swim meets, but it was cold near the water and he couldn't help but notice Ann's nipples poking through the fabric. Michael looked away, embarrassed.

Ann stepped closer to the water and tugged on his arm. "Come on. Don't you want to swim?"

"No," he said. "I don't. Go ahead."

Ann, as usual, caught on quickly. "Oh my God, you don't know how, do you?" Her reaction might not have been so devastating if she hadn't dropped his hand when she said it.

Michael had been so anxious about this moment that he didn't know what to say. He didn't know how to swim. He never spent his summers in a place like this. He didn't know anyone who would have bothered to take him to a pool or Lake Michigan and teach him. Besides, he hated water, because it was his mom's boyfriend's favorite form of punishment. When he was little and he got in trouble over what seemed like nothing, Marcus would make him sit in an ice-cold bath, or in water so hot it burned his skin.

"It's OK," Poppy said. "I can show you how. But you should learn in the ponds, not here, not with the riptide."

Michael didn't know what a riptide was, only that it sounded terrifying: *rip*.

"I've never met anyone our age who couldn't swim," Ann said.

Michael's mother had told him that it's the people who think before they talk that you should worry about. Because she was so confident, Ann usually just said whatever was on her mind. But that afternoon her words hurt him deeply. He wanted to throw up.

Poppy might have been a space cadet, but she could see the pain in Michael's face. He couldn't hide anything from her; she was alert when it came to emotions, a human tuning fork. "God, Ann," she said. "You didn't have to say it like that."

"I just meant that he'll learn. It's not hard, nothing to be embarrassed about. Even little kids can swim." Ann pointed off in the distance at a little boy playing in a pool that had formed between a sandbar and the beach.

"Ann!" Poppy said.

"It's really not a big deal," Michael said.

That was a lie. It was a big deal. The stakes never felt higher than they did now. He couldn't make sense of the recent dizzying turn of events. Six months ago, he was hiding out in the storage locker in the basement of the building near the Marquette campus where he and his mother had an apartment until she'd died. He'd showered at school and slept with his shoes on because he was afraid the rats would bite his toes at night.

That's when he got to know Ann. They were at a track meet in Wautoma, at one of those hotels with a dome over the pool. Everyone else had a room to sleep in. But Michael couldn't afford one, so he told his coach he had family in town. He went to sleep in the lounge chair by the pool. Ann found him there. She said she couldn't sleep because her roommate snored. She sat next to him in the watery green light and they started talking.

Before he knew it, Ann told him about the long history of tensions between her and the girls at school, the false rumors her old boyfriend Nick Maddox had started about her "putting out" when he was upset she wouldn't sleep with him, the difficulties of attending a school where your father was a teacher, how she thought her mother favored Poppy and her father cared more about his students than he cared about her.

He told her that his dad, a boxer, got hit in the head too hard in a fight and ended up in a home. "He can't even spread peanut butter on a piece of bread or say his own name," Michael said. "After my dad, my mom had this boyfriend. Marcus. He worked at the Red Star yeast factory. He smelled like a moldy piece of bread."

Ann laughed—until Michael lifted up his shirt and showed her a dark brown stripe across his abdomen. "This is from when he hit me with an extension cord. And this?" He pointed at a lump on his shin. "This is from when he kicked me so hard I couldn't walk for a week."

"I'm so sorry," Ann said. "How could anyone hurt you?"

Michael shrugged. "People hurt each other all the time."

He couldn't believe that he'd confided in her, and he couldn't believe that Ann, Miss Popular, was so sincere in her concern. He'd always thought of her as someone who was totally inaccessible. She was confident and pretty. He saw how the boys tried to get her attention and the girls tried to keep up with her. He'd heard girls talk shit about her, like she thought she was all that, but he found her to be sincere and direct in a way other kids weren't, which was why, that night, he'd told her more than he'd told anyone else when she asked him about his mom.

"She was a partier. But after Marcus left, she swore she would change. She did. She got a job, cleaned up. But then she got sick. She was tired all the time, had these pains in her gut. At first, I was happy. Her being sick meant she was home with me, and I could take care of her. I thought she'd get better, but remember when that bacteria got into the Milwaukee water?"

"Cryptosporidium? Sure. Everyone in the city got it."

"Well, because my mom was already sick, it made her even sicker. I didn't know what to do. She wouldn't go to the hospital. She hated doctors. I thought that I could take care of her myself, make her better. But I couldn't, you know? Turns out she had AIDS."

Ann gasped.

"See why I don't tell anyone? I say cancer and people are sorry for me. I say she had AIDS and they do what you just did. I don't have it. I'm not sick. Don't worry."

Ann put her hand on his arm to demonstrate her concern. "I'm not worried, Michael." She said his name out loud with particular care and kindness. She reached for his hand and held it.

They fell asleep like that, at three in the morning, with hotel towels covering them instead of blankets. The shimmering, hazy light from the pool reflected on the glassy dome, the atmosphere safe, womblike. That night, he'd had Ann all to himself. It was perfect.

The next day, he ran his fastest 200 meters. She was right there at the finish line, cheering him on. After that, she started bringing sandwiches and snacks to him at school. Soon her parents invited him for dinner. The next thing he knew, he was sleeping on their couch. One day, Ed told him that he'd converted the office upstairs into a bedroom, and he gave him an extra key to their house. Ann became his constant companion. They walked to and from school together, and they ran along the lakeshore in the late afternoons. He wasn't part of Ann's social circle, but at home they were inseparable. They watched old movies, folded laundry together, and sat at the kitchen table doing homework until they lost focus and shot rubber bands at each other. Even though Michael didn't have the best grades, he was a whiz at math, and he helped Poppy with her geometry homework. Connie took Michael to the dentist and bought him some new clothes at Kohl's. He and Ed played pickup games at Riverside Park, and Ed asked him to join his bowling league at the Polish Falcons.

Michael had been so thrilled by this new arrangement that he hadn't thought of how strange it must have seemed to other people—that is, until one afternoon when he'd stopped by Ed's classroom and overheard Mr. Frederickson, the chemistry teacher, warning Ed about him. "He's staying with you? Kid had a tough ride, I get it. Shit happens to all our students. You take on one Oliver Twist and pretty soon you could have half the high school living in your house. Michael doesn't have to be your problem."

"He's not a problem."

"Not now. Just be careful. Your girls are only what, a year apart? Irish twins? Beautiful girls in full bloom."

"He doesn't think about them like that."

"Whatever you say. You know, I heard about a couple who woke up from a nap to find their foster kid standing at the foot of their bed with a hunting knife in his hand."

Mr. Frederickson's words were always in the back of Michael's mind, especially when Ed and Connie asked him if he'd like to join them on "the Cod," as Ed called it. Michael said yes, although the trip filled him with as much anxiety as excitement.

And now here he was.

He turned back and looked at the steep sand dune he'd just run down, and the dark, jagged path the beachgoers had cut into it. The parking lot was up there, and Ed and Connie. Why hadn't they come down yet?

He had to leave. He needed to escape the girls with their long, knowing looks, and the ocean, and all those strange people dotting the beach who were nothing like him. Nothing.

He made a run for it.

Where are you going? The girls' high voices were drowned out by the wind and surf. Where was he going? He had no idea. He only knew they couldn't keep up, not even Ann. She had good endurance and could hold her own against the guys on the team, but Michael was a sprinter. He'd set the school's record for the 100 meters. He could run fast to a finish line, but he ran even faster when he had something to run away from.

When he got to the top of the dune he was exhausted from his intense burst of effort uphill through the deep sand. He could see the heat hovering over the parking lot as if he were looking through a veil of sheer plastic wrap. The asphalt was hot as molten lava. Aside from the thump of his heartbeat and the sound of his bare feet hitting pavement, it was suddenly quiet, an eerie peacefulness he found both welcome and disconcerting.

He headed straight for Ed, who was pulling beach towels and tattered folding chairs out of the back of the Buick wagon. Ed didn't look anything like Mr. Gordon the history teacher from Riverside High. At school, Ed wore polyester shirts with wide ties and kept his hair pulled back into a scraggy ponytail. But here he was, a family guy on vacation in his old Marquette Warriors T-shirt and ratty sandals. His curly salt-and-pepper hair, what was left of it, whipped around his head. They'd left Milwaukee two days ago and already his scruffy black beard was beginning to show. He said he never shaved in the summer. Michael thought about giving up shaving for the summer, too, but puberty hadn't kicked in all the way; it took him weeks to establish anything thicker than peach fuzz.

"Forget something?" Ed asked.

Michael shook his head. His lungs felt the way they did at the end of a race, like they were filled with broken glass, and his spent quads twitched.

Ed looked at him with concern. "Hey man," he said, doing his best to blunt a crisis with casual talk. "What's wrong?"

What's wrong? Michael didn't know where to start. He was a thousand miles from everything that was familiar to him. He missed his mom. All of the Gordon rituals and inside jokes and easy familiarity made him feel even more alone. The girls didn't know how good they had it with their two parents and two houses. He was jealous and angry. He didn't understand how the cosmic scales could get so tipped. *What's wrong?* He'd never been good at putting his feelings to words. He wanted to lash out when he felt like this.

"Speak your truth," Ed said.

His truth? He wanted to be with them and he wanted to leave. He wanted to *be* them, or rather, he wanted to live the way they did, free of dents. But he couldn't trust the happiness he felt with the family, couldn't believe anything good could ever last.

The parking lot was packed full of cars. Michael looked at the little shack in the distance where a teenager in a red tank top checked for beach stickers. Beyond that was the road they'd taken to get here, lined with scrubby pine and oak trees. Michael thought about taking off. The problem was that he had no idea how to get back to their house.

"Michael," Ed said. "Talk to me."

"I think I left my Discman in the car," Michael lied. He loved his Discman, and the KMD, Massive Attack, and Sonic Youth CDs that he listened to constantly. He could tell by the look on Ed's face that he was suspicious. Teachers had built-in bullshit detectors. Michael opened the passenger-side door so he could pretend to look for his stuff while he thought about his next move. That's when he saw Connie in the front seat with a burning joint between her fingers. She was startled when she saw him. He heard the *pfft* of the lit end being snuffed out in her can of Diet Rite.

"Forget something?" she asked, trying hard not to exhale in front of him.

"You guys are getting stoned?"

"Just a little," Connie said. Smoke trickled out of her nose. "It's relaxing."

It seemed to Michael that she should be more embarrassed than she was. Teachers always expected kids to explain themselves, but when they got busted? No big deal.

Ed came over to him. "Did you find it?"

"The joint? No, Connie wasted it. She didn't even offer to share."

"Very funny."

"Everything's funny because you're high too, right Ed? Everything's a fucking blast."

A young family walked by toting beach bags and an inflatable-giraffe inner tube. The mother hustled her kids past when she heard Michael swear.

He knew he should drop it, but Michael felt like picking a fight, even if it meant proving Mr. Frederickson right. Ed and Connie weren't supposed to do this stuff. They were supposed to be perfect, wholesome, clean, boring.

"So, this is what you do. You act like you're so good, but you're . . ."

"We're just people, Michael," Ed said. "And this is the first day of our vacation after a long school year and a very long car ride."

"Yeah, right."

"Look, I can see why you're upset, but this is purely recreational. We don't have a problem."

"You don't have a problem like my mom? Is that what you mean? You think you're so different from her, but you're not. You're all the same."

Michael could feel people staring at them, all the perfect families with their beach bags and goggles and coolers full of food.

"I never said we weren't screwed up in our own way."

It hadn't even occurred to Michael until that moment that the Gordon family could have problems or issues of their own. The idea that the Gordons could be screwed up floored Michael. He couldn't even consider it.

Ed always talked about how important it was for Michael to express himself, face his pain and be *real*, but it was easy for Ed to say shit like that. Ed hadn't choked on a bar of soap or heard the *fliittt* sound of a belt slicing the air, followed by the crack of the metal buckle against his collarbone. Ed hadn't taken care of his dying mother in a hot apartment with one window and a broken fan, hadn't been surprised by how much shit could come out of a person after they drank the city's bad water, hadn't seen the purple spots on the insides of her eyelids and the white spots on her tongue, hadn't put damp washcloths on her clammy skin, felt the ridges of her bones as she shrank like a piece of dehydrated fruit, hadn't held her bird claw of a hand, hadn't heard the grating sound of her breath, hadn't wanted someone, anyone to walk through the door to tell him they could help, they'd take care of her, she'd be fine, everything would be all right. Ed hadn't pleaded with someone not to die, just don't die. Stay here.

"Everything is going to be OK." Ed's voice was kind, but Ed didn't know shit. He thought the whole world could get better with one big "Kumbaya"—or one long suck on a joint. What did Ed know about how it felt to have nobody, to be totally, utterly alone? What did Ed know about being *real*?

Michael wanted to throw a punch at him the way his father had taught him to land a right hook when he was a little boy; he wanted to feel something break inside Ed. He felt his fists ball up at his sides like knots and every muscle in his body grow tight. He wanted Ed to look at him in disbelief and ask, "Why'd you do that?" He wanted Ed to feel betrayed the way Michael had felt betrayed so many times. He wanted to challenge Ed's supposed devotion and give him a painful, bloody reason to change his mind. He wanted Ed to reject him sooner rather than later.

Connie emerged from the car wearing her vintage cat-eye sunglasses and a yellow polka-dot bathing suit that had lost its elasticity and sagged around her chest, stomach, and waist. Ann and Poppy inherited Ed's height, high cheekbones, and square chin, but their softness came from Connie. She was still youngish, still pretty in a puffy sort of way, but Connie didn't care about her looks. She let her long hair turn white and wore it hanging to her waist. She was nice but distracted in the same way Poppy was.

"Jump!" she said.

That's what Connie told him to do when he got angry: jump up and down, release it, move the energy in a different direction. Connie was super smart, which made it hard for Michael to accept her weird interests and beliefs. He didn't understand where they came from until Poppy explained that Connie had lived in Nepal when she'd served in the Peace Corps. Poppy told him that Connie had a secret name that had been given to her by a shaman, and she'd witnessed the sacrifice of a black goat in a healing ceremony. She'd had to rub kerosene on the legs of her cot to keep the bedbugs from crawling into it. On her way back, she almost died when the landing gear on her small airplane from Kathmandu to the Delhi airport had failed. The wheels flopped up and down and wouldn't lock in place. They flew back and forth over the tower for over an hour to lessen the fuel load before the emergency landing. "She'll never fly again. She says Cape Cod is all the adventure she needs now," Poppy said. "I wouldn't let one bad experience in an airplane keep me from traveling. Someday, I'm going to go *everywhere*." It was the one point on which mother and daughter differed, Michael noted. Otherwise they were two peas in a pod.

He saw now that her time in the Peace Corps had been formative for Connie, and it was why she believed that everything was about *energy*. She even wore a string with a crystal on it that hung from her neck. When Poppy and Ann fought over space in the backseat on the ride out, Connie told them they were making her crystal turn cloudy.

Poppy was alarmed, while Ann rolled her eyes and groaned.

"Come on, Michael," Connie said. "You need to change your energy. Please. I'll jump with you."

Jump? He didn't feel like jumping. That was the bullshit for crystal-wearing ex-hippie teachers. Connie jumped, and her giant breasts rose and collapsed with her. She started laughing, and before Michael could help it, he laughed a little, too, and his anger crashed like a wave.

Suddenly he was deeply sad. It was all too much. "I want to go back," Michael said, afraid his voice would break and he'd start to cry.

Ed said, "Back where? Milwaukee?"

No, no. That wasn't what Michael was thinking. He shook his head violently. Milwaukee? He'd be fine if he never went back there, not ever.

Michael was so pent-up he could hardly open his mouth to speak. "The house," he said. "I want to go back to the house."

Ann suddenly appeared next to him, followed by Poppy. They came to an abrupt stop, sweaty from the run. The sun glinted off their foreheads and cheeks.

Connie said, "Michael tells us he wants to go home."

Ed said, "What the hell is going on?"

"Why are you looking at me?" Ann said.

"Oh, Ann," Connie said, as if she'd been frustrated with Ann a million times before. Mother and daughter were nothing alike—or as Connie would say, their energy was different. Ann liked to stir things up; Connie liked to smooth them over.

"He's embarrassed because he can't swim," Poppy said.

"I told him it was no big deal and it totally isn't." Ann spoke about Michael the way the counselors and social workers did, like he wasn't even standing right there in front of them, covered in sweat.

Ed put his large hand on Michael's damp back. Michael tried to step away, but Ed pulled him into a tight embrace. This threw Michael off, because Ed rarely touched him; he said he respected his "borders." Michael could see that holding back was hard for Ed, who was affectionate and open. But now, he couldn't seem to help himself. "Don't you know we don't care that you can't swim?" Ed's voice broke.

Michael freed himself and took a few steps back. He was in the center of the circle. All eyes were on him. He felt trapped.

Ann looked at Ed. "Can we tell him, Dad?"

"Now?" Ed said. "I thought we were going to wait."

"Please?"

"Tell him what?" Poppy asked.

Michael braced himself: they were about to tell him he'd have to turn around and leave. He knew it, he just knew it.

Ed looked straight into Michael's eyes, serious. "We're thinking we'd like to adopt you, Michael."

Poppy put her hand over her mouth and gasped. "Seriously?"

Ann said, "Isn't it great?"

"Yes, but . . ."

"But what?" Ann said.

"Nobody ever tells me anything."

"What's your problem?" Ann said. "We knew you'd be OK with it. We all love Michael."

The word "love" threw Michael even more off balance. "You want to what?" Michael asked. He'd once seen a bird fly into a window at school—this was the same kind of shock, of not knowing that plate of glass was right there, right in front of you.

"Only if that's what you want," Connie said. "Nobody is forcing you to do anything."

"We started the paperwork, that's all," Ed said. "When we get back to Milwaukee in the fall, if you're game, we can make it official."

Connie smiled dreamily. "Don't you feel we're already related? The first time you walked through the door I felt we'd been together in a past life."

Michael didn't believe them. This couldn't be real. Past life? They were high.

Ann said, "It was so hard for me not to say anything. It was my idea."

"Everything is Ann's idea," Poppy said. She looked almost as stunned as Michael felt.

"Aren't I too old to be adopted?"

Ann said, "You're never too old to need a family."

"Sixteen is nothing," Ed said. "You still have two years of high school. Those are two important years. But you have to give consent. The whole thing is totally up to you."

Poppy brightened. She took his hand. "You'll be my brother."

Until that moment, Michael hadn't realized he already felt like he was Poppy's brother. But then Ann said, "And I'll be your sister."

Ann? His sister?

That was a harder idea to process. It reminded him of that optical illusion his psychology teacher had shown him, the ink drawing where you see either two faces or a vase; you can see it only one way at a time. The faces or the vase.

That entire summer in Wellfleet and all through the next school year, when his adoption was made final, he tried to see and think of Ann that way: just a sister. Only a sister. He tried.

TWO

Ann

Wellfleet
2000

Ann lined up a babysitting job her second day back on the Cape. Some lady named Mrs. Shaw had called the house after she'd seen the flyer Ann posted at the Wellfleet library. She had two boys. More importantly, she offered to pay Ann more than double what she made back home in Milwaukee.

Ann babysat every summer since she'd become Red Cross certified—well, except for last summer, because her parents had wanted her to spend time with Michael. She didn't mind. She cheered him on at his swim lessons; they ran together on the sandy soil in the fire lanes, looked for shells at Mayo Beach, and ate soft serve on the town pier. Ann had always loved Cape Cod, but last summer, seeing the place through Michael's eyes, she became newly aware of how special it was, and how much Michael meant to her—more than she should feel for a "brother."

Michael loved their Cape house. Ann felt badly that he had to sleep in the bedroom in the attic, where it was hot and stuffy, and the ceilings were so slanted that he would bump his head when he woke. She tried to make his space nicer by wallpapering it with some old, yellowed newspapers from the thirties she'd found in the basement, and she covered the armrests of her grandfather's favorite chair that sat in the middle of the room with electrical tape where the mice had chewed the upholstery.

That first summer, the prospect of Michael's upcoming adoption made everything seem new and exciting. But now, a year later, everything was different. Ann realized that absorbing another person into the family, even someone she cared about as much as she cared about Michael, wasn't as easy as she thought it would be. All her parents seemed to care about lately was the idea of *family*. They talked about being together like it was some sort of higher calling.

Money was tighter and her parents were busy. They'd always had a lot going on, but now they had all the appointments with lawyers, social workers, and therapists that legal adoption required. Ann noticed that Poppy and Michael had grown closer in the past year, so close that sometimes Ann felt like a third wheel around them, a feeling that was uncomfortable and disarming.

Unlike Ann, neither Poppy nor Michael was part of a big clique, both of them preferring to hang out with the granola crowd at the Coffee Trader on Downer Avenue. They made knotted bracelets out of embroidery thread, shared inside jokes and secret handshakes, and liked to make each other disgusting potions with milk, syrup, and turmeric in the kitchen. Michael seemed loose and comfortable with Poppy, but when Ann walked into the room he'd freeze up, and Poppy would act like she was interrupting them. All her life, Poppy had followed Ann around like a lost puppy, wearing her clothes, imitating her gestures, wanting to hang out with Ann and her friends instead of making her own. Ann was used to shrugging Poppy off, only now Poppy didn't seem to care if Ann lived or died. She missed Poppy, but she was too proud to say so. Instead, she slammed doors and walked around in a huff, expecting Poppy to understand why she was upset, hoping Poppy would care.

She didn't. She had Michael now.

Something was off with Michael, too. She felt him pushing her away. He wouldn't sit on the same couch with her, or come into her bedroom to talk late into the night the way he used to. He'd started running with some of the faster guys on the varsity team, and when he wasn't chumming around with Poppy, he'd sometimes hang out with them. He'd grown taller, more muscular and lean, more confident. His thick brown hair stretched to his shoulders. Suddenly Ann's friends wanted to spend a lot more time at her house so they could be around him. She could understand why. Truthfully, she felt the same way they did. Michael—her *brother*—was so good-looking that Ann sometimes felt shy around him. She averted her gaze, afraid of his intensity, afraid of the way he made her feel, afraid of the closeness they once shared, but missing it all the same.

Ann was still happy that Michael was part of the family, but by the time their car pulled into the Cape house driveway for the first time that summer, she felt so frustrated by her siblings that she thought she might burst. She needed some space, and she wanted to make some money for college, which was only a year away. So, when Mrs. Shaw asked her to start babysitting the very next day, Ann jumped at the opportunity.

WHEN SHE WAS YOUNGER, ANN understood her parents' concern about her prospective employers. Now that she was seventeen, their supervision felt unnecessary and annoying. They insisted on driving her to the Shaws'. She sat in the backseat, feeling like a little kid. "I told you I can ride my bike. It's not that far."

"We just want to know where you'll be." Her dad was driving slowly, looking carefully at the addresses on the mailboxes, pissing off the drivers who were stuck behind him, not that he ever cared what anyone else thought. They were on Chequessett Neck Road, north of Mayo Beach, in a fancy area somewhere near the yacht club. This was the way they drove to get to Jeremy Point, their favorite picnic spot.

"This is so embarrassing."

Her mother said, "We're your parents. Someday you'll have your own kids and you'll understand."

"You always say that."

"Because it's true."

"How are they going to trust me to watch their children if you guys show up? It's not dangerous here, like in Milwaukee." Oh God, why did she have to say that? She knew any reference to Milwaukee and crime would lead her mother to think about serial killer Jeffrey Dahmer. Ann was still in elementary school during his trial, but she remembered Connie volunteering as a court comforter to provide support to the victims' families. She brought them food, coffee, and tissues, and held their hands while they listened to gory testimony about how he'd drugged and tortured all those young men.

Her mother never spoke much about what she'd heard, although Ann noticed that the experience had changed her. Because of her easy nature, her mother was still more laid-back than most of Ann's friends' parents, but after the trial she seemed more suspicious of people, warier. Ann sometimes wondered if that's why her mother was willing to move forward with Michael's adoption. Dahmer had lived near the Marquette neighborhood where he'd found his victims. Michael was young and vulnerable—he could have easily been in danger.

"Mom," Ann said. "Really. You know nothing bad ever happens here."

"That's not true," her father said. "A woman was murdered in Truro a few years ago, remember?"

"Ed!"

"I'm not scared. I'll be fine," Ann said. "Next year I'll be in college. What will you do then?"

"We'll never let you go." Her mother reached back and squeezed Ann's knee like she meant it literally. Ann swatted her hand away and frowned, even though she wanted to be nice to her mother, because her mother was always nice to her.

"Tell you what, Ann with a Plan." That was her father's name for her, because she'd always been so determined, and so focused on her next steps. "How about we just drop you off and leave. We won't lurk."

"Yes!" Ann said. "Thank you."

"We wouldn't think of embarrassing you in front of *Mrs. Shaw*." It was Ann's mother who had taken her call while Ann was at Gull Pond with Michael and Poppy. Michael could swim about as well as both of them now, and he could outpace her both on the land and in the water. When Ann called back, Mrs. Shaw sounded breathless. "I was just *thrilled* to see your sign on the bulletin board. I'm positively *desperate*. You know how it is with two rambunctious boys and a household to manage, and my husband is hardly ever around and we have all these visitors and activities. Exhausting!"

Her father whistled when he pulled up to the house—not an appreciative whistle, but the kind of whistle he'd make if he passed a bad car accident, a whistle that seemed to say, *Look at that disaster.* The Shaws' house was huge, dwarfing the still large but comparatively smaller houses next door. He double-checked the address. "I guess this really is the place," he said. "Geez."

"Oh dear," Connie said. "Look how it blocks the view of the bay. I'll bet their neighbors hate them. It's so big . . . and so brown."

Her dad said, "That's a 'fuck you' house if I ever saw one."

Ann thought the house was awesome *because* it was so massive, and so different from the homes she was used to seeing in Wellfleet. It reminded her of one of the big, new houses she saw in subdivisions in Mequon, a wealthy community north of Milwaukee where some of the kids she'd met in the Model UN lived. The Shaws' house was neither charming and old nor sleek and modern; it was the kind of house that was simply meant to impress. It was newer but not original, massive but not grand.

Ann said goodbye to her parents quickly and slipped out of the car. She walked down the long, curving driveway in the shadow of the enormous house. Her father's car engine was still idling. She turned around and mouthed *Go away* until he backed off and drove away in the same direction he'd come.

MRS. SHAW GREETED ANN AT the door. She was attractive in a severe, weatherworn way, tall but slightly stooped. Her thick, red hair looked like it might have been curly if she hadn't blow-dried it into submission. She'd pulled it back into a ponytail so tight that it tugged at the sides of her eyes. Her skin was dark and freckled, and a stack of gold bracelets jangled against her thin wrist. She wore a belted Izod polo dress that hung slack off her bony shoulders.

"You must be Ann. I'm so pleased this worked out. I'm Maureen." She pushed her tortoiseshell eyeglasses higher up the bridge of her nose. "I enjoyed speaking with your mother. She sounds lovely. She says you want to make a little *mad money.*"

Money might have seemed like a trivial matter to someone like Maureen, but Ann needed it. Back home, Ann took as many babysitting jobs and shifts at Lisa's Pizza as they'd give her. Her parents told her she'd need to pay for part of college, and she had every intention of going to a school out East, even if it was more expensive. She had her heart set on Boston College and Amherst, maybe even Harvard if she could get in.

Maureen ushered Ann inside, to the center of an airy great room. The dining room, living room, kitchen, and family room were all part of one huge, uncluttered space, not unlike the lobby of a megachurch. Just beyond the giant picture windows was a mound of lush, green lawn, the kind of lawn Ann wasn't used to seeing in sandy Wellfleet, where the grass grew in patches at best. Beyond the yard, the water sparkled in the bay, a view quite different from her family's view of the cove. There were no scrappy pitch pines or cacti in sight, no mulberry or beach grass. The water in the distance was seemingly always at high tide, while the cove her family's house fronted was a mud pit half the time. She looked out the Shaws' window and saw a different Cape than the one she thought she knew, a Cape that was placid and tame instead of rustic and wild. It made Ann jealous of this big house and their perfect, organized life.

Achingly bright pillows in turquoise and orange punctuated the white expanse of drywall and bleached hardwood floors. A buoy hung from fishing line above the couch. Big navy letters spelled out SHAW on the top and COTTAGE on the bottom. Ann figured they must be important to live in such a big house and to broadcast their name like that. It must really mean something to be a Shaw.

"I love your house," Ann said.

"Do you?" Maureen asked. She seemed surprised.

"It's so impressive."

"Too many bathrooms to clean if you ask me. I actually spent my summers in a sweet old house that sat on this very spot. It was leaky and creaky and filled with bats."

"Sounds like our house."

"Oh, you're so lucky! I absolutely loved our old place."

"Did it burn down?"

"No, no. We had it razed." Maureen gestured with a flat hand, sweeping across the air. "There were problems with the foundation, although that could have been fixed, but don't mention that to the town preservationists, promise?"

Ann liked Maureen right away, the way she made her feel like she was important enough to gossip with.

"My husband calls them the preservation*istas*. They had a fit when we demolished the house. They made us dig around in the yard for Indian artifacts and they hit us with zoning bylaws and challenged every permit. It took over a year just to get the plans approved. Anthony—my husband—he wanted something new. He grew up poor. He said he couldn't understand why we'd want to live the way he had, with old two-prong electrical outlets that sparked when you put a plug in, and a well pump that always seemed to break. Old houses aren't for everyone, I guess. Certainly not for Anthony. And now, after everything we went through to get into this house, he's hardly ever around." The giant, pear-shaped diamond in Maureen's wedding band twinkled under the recessed lighting.

Maureen walked toward the hallway and shouted, "Toby! Brooks! Come meet Ann."

Maureen rifled through her big bag and pulled out a car key. The chain had a Jaguar logo. "Your mother says your driving record sparkles."

"Well, I just got my license."

"Of course, you don't need me to tell you to be careful, but the people out here drive like the sun is in their eyes. It gets worse every summer. I need you to shuttle the boys to Chatham this afternoon. Their friends are having a party. You can just drop them off and meander around town— Chatham is so lovely, don't you think?"

Ann was about to say that yes, she did like Chatham, until Maureen said, "I personally avoid the town because every third person I see there is from Marblehead, where we live. What's the point of getting away when you're surrounded by the same awful people? Funny, I find myself wondering what vacations are even for lately. What's the point? I'm just as stressed as ever with this house and the kids. Vacation from *what*, that's what I want to know."

It wasn't really a question, but Ann felt Maureen looking at her as if she had answers. Vacations made perfect sense to Ann; she lived for vacation, even if this one was off to a rough start.

A boy walked into the room. He must have been ten or eleven years old. He had Maureen's frizzy red hair and freckles. He was also tall and thin like Maureen, but he had a very large head and big joints that seemed out of proportion to his frame, suggesting he still had a lot of growing to do. The boy looked Ann up and down.

"Brooks, honey, this is Ann. She's going to help us out this afternoon."

Brooks? Ann thought it was a rich name, like the rich house.

"I told you I don't need a babysitter," he said. His tone wasn't much different than the one Ann had used on her own parents just a few minutes earlier.

"Well, perhaps not, but Ann can get you to the party at Max's house that you wanted to go to. I can't, because I'm meeting with a contractor. Ann is in charge while I'm gone, understand? Now go tell Toby you need to get moving. And change, please, into a shirt that doesn't have a stain."

Ann couldn't see a stain on the boy's polo shirt. It practically glowed white. Everything he wore looked like it was brand-new.

Brooks glared at Ann and ran back down the hallway. She heard his feet thud down the carpeted stairs to what must have been the lower level.

"I'm afraid we're entering the throes of adolescence. You know how boys are."

Ann smiled. "I do now. We just adopted a boy."

"A baby!" Maureen clapped her hands together, and her bracelets jangled. "How wonderful."

"No, we're the same age."

"You mean to tell me your family adopted a teenager?" She said it as if Ann had brought home a bird with a broken wing.

"It was my idea," she said in her "Ann with a Plan" voice.

"Do you mind if I ask, and I certainly don't mean to pry, but why?"

Ann went with the easy and honest answer: "He had no place else to go."

Her parents were the kind of people who always tried to do the right thing, and they often accused Ann of being self-absorbed. Actually, "myopic" was the word her mother used. But she'd gone and done just the sort of thing they'd wanted her to do, even if, deep down, she knew her motives weren't entirely selfless, and her benevolence gave her cover for the truth: she wanted to be around Michael. How could they refuse?

Maureen seemed stupefied by this. Her mouth hung open, and she leaned forward with her hands on her hips. "That's incredible! Your family sounds very special. And *you*, Ann, sound very, very special indeed."

Ann loved this kind of praise—the way her advocacy on behalf of Michael helped her parents, teachers, and friends see her as more than just a popular girl.

Maureen looked at her watch and frowned. "I want to hear all about this later. But Ann, I can already tell you're a remarkable young woman. I'm sure you have a lot to teach my boys about generosity of spirit."

She gave Ann a quick hug. Ann liked how Mrs. Shaw made her feel validated and special.

"I'm so pleased we found you!" *We.* "What a gift you are."

Ann looked around the breezy home and wondered what it would be like to be a Shaw instead of a Gordon. Ever since Michael had moved in with them, she thought a lot about what it was like to enter other people's families.

THREE

Poppy

Poppy woke to an unusually silent house. She didn't need to look at a clock to know she'd slept in; she could tell by the dusty light streaming in through the old wood blinds. She'd always slept her hardest and best on the Cape, as if she were double-sealed in her dreams under the perfect weight of her great-grandmother's handmade quilts. She loved to sleep, loved the heaviness of it, the ability to lose herself. She'd dreamt that her teeth were falling out, although she hadn't realized it until a stranger, a nondescript nine-year-old boy in a hunting cap, opened his palm and showed them to her. They'd crumbled, and looked like piles of sand.

She saw Ann's empty bed and wished she were around so she could ask her sister what she thought the dream meant. Poppy consulted the dream dictionary she kept under her pillow: it said teeth are used to bite, tear, gnaw. Losing your teeth in a dream represents a fear that you are losing power. If her teeth had dissolved to sand, she'd never get her power back.

She found her mother sitting in the living room with her twisted ankle propped on the hope chest. She'd tripped on a lobster trap on the pier a few days earlier, and seemed perfectly happy to have an excuse to take it easy for a while. On the table next to her were a stack of plastic-covered library books, a cup of tea, and the stationery she used to write to her friends and relatives back home. Her mother loved to stay in touch with everyone she knew. She had a million friends: other teachers, her former students, parishioners at the Unitarian church, the old lady down the street she made meals for, her book group, and the feminists who joined the potluck salon she hosted in their house once a month. Back home, everyone in town knew Poppy as Connie's daughter. But here on the Cape, her mother retreated into a more private, less social life. Well-fleet was a place where she could nurture her introverted self, as if storing energy for the social whirlwind that waited for her upon their return.

"Where's Ann?" Poppy asked. All her life, this was the first thing she needed to know each day. *You set your clock to Ann,* as her father said.

"She's off babysitting for the haute bourgeoisie, as usual. Today she's taking the boys all the way to Plimoth Plantation for an ancestor role-playing workshop or something."

"God, that sounds totally horrible."

"I know, doesn't it? Those boys aren't going to know what to do with themselves when they're set loose in the real world."

"What's Dad doing?"

"He took Michael to the Historical Society."

"He's taking *Michael* to the Historical Society?"

"I guess the poor guy is getting dragged into your father's 'research.'"

He and Poppy used to visit the Wellfleet Historical Society with a pile of yellow legal pads, taking notes and stuffing them into the accordion files with folders labeled HOUSE, LAND, COVE, LORE, and RANDOM BULL-SHIT in his distinctive block handwriting. Her father was always asking questions: Why did they stop farming on the land? Why'd they dredge the pond and turn it into a cove? Was it called Drummer Cove because that was the local name for a type of flounder, or was it named for the traveling salesmen who used to stay at the old inn on the property next door, who were called "drummers," as in "to drum up business"? And what about the house? The Barnstable County Courthouse had burned down sometime in the 1800s, so there was no way for him to confirm the date it had been built. There must be documents to authenticate the age, he said. There must be.

Poppy wasn't that interested in his research—or rather, she was, because she loved the house and the cove, but it was summer, and the last place she wanted to spend her morning was in that dark building filled with old ship captains' relics, whaling gear, and dour black-and-white photographs in chipped mahogany frames. She preferred to practice tai chi with her mom in the yard. Before she messed up her ankle, they'd gotten better at memorizing the movements, and at moving gently—*as if with the wind and the water*, as Lu, her mother's instructor, had taught them. Poppy had even gotten to the point where she could still her mind when she was deep in her practice, or find *jing*.

Poppy found the serenity amazing, the integration of the mind with the body. Ann thought it was all a joke. She made fun of them when they practiced. She'd sneak up behind Poppy and yank down her shorts, or spray water at her through the hose when she was most absorbed in their poses, laughing her infectious laugh.

Now her mom couldn't do anything and Michael was monopolizing her dad, as usual. The other day she'd found them in the barn together, her father introducing him to all the old tools Poppy and Ann had never gotten excited about. Her father put his arm around Michael's shoulder and said, "Makes me feel good that you'll know how to use this stuff. After I kick the bucket, these tools will be yours, and trust me, they'll come in handy. An old house like this doesn't take care of itself." It hadn't occurred to Poppy until that moment that Michael's adoption meant that the tools, and even the house, would also be his. Michael beamed from ear to ear.

She loved Michael, so why did she feel so selfish? She wanted to tell Michael that the house was *theirs*, and summer was *her* time with her father, because during the school year she had to share him with his beloved students. They all thought Mr. Gordon was the epitome of middle-age coolness. He swore and told inappropriate jokes. When students raised their hands to answer a question, he'd call on them and say, "Speak your piece." He showed his students how history is complicated and biased. He taught in a game show format, had his students analyze the lyrics to Bob Dylan and Woody Guthrie protest songs, arranged field trips to tour ethnic neighborhoods, and invited Holocaust survivors and former socialist mayors to speak to his classes. Until she started high school, she had no idea how much everyone loved him: jocks, preps, and geeks. They high-fived him when they passed him in the halls. "Yo Gord-O!"

Poppy stomped into the kitchen, angrier than she felt she had a right to be. Her niceness didn't get her anywhere. It made her as invisible as her sister's occasional bitchiness made Ann stand out. Ann, the queen bee, had the power to make everyone, including Poppy, feel both incredibly small and hugely important, depending on her mood. Ann was driven, hungry for a bigger life. Poppy, on the other hand, was usually agreeable and easy. She was the person teachers always paired with the new kids. She never got upset, never got angry, or at least she didn't let her anger show unless it built up.

And it had been building up for a while now. She loved Michael. That wasn't the problem. The problem was that nobody had bothered to consult her. They figured she'd be fine.

Only she wasn't, not lately.

Poppy threw the cabinet door open and slammed a mug on the counter. Michael was great, he was. He was! She poured the leftover, burnt coffee into her cup, and stirred in several tablespoons of sugar.

Poppy returned to the living room. Her mother was reading poetry—she always read poetry in the mornings, and recited it out loud in her annoying poetry-reading voice, like she expected whoever heard the lines to listen and gasp in wonder. Poppy couldn't focus on the words—something about a house and Russia. "So what am I supposed to do today?"

"Anne Sexton. Isn't it lovely?"

"I'm *bored*."

"Only boring people get—"

"Just don't," Poppy said. She adored her mom. She'd memorized her, right down to the way her hair parted down the middle and the shape of her fingers. But sometimes her mother was too familiar, too predictable.

Poppy ran into her room, grabbed her tote bag, and did something she'd never done before: she went to the beach alone. The flame of her anger cooled into self-criticism. Who was she to complain about Michael? She was in the judge's chambers when Michael signed his adoption papers, tears of happiness streaming down his face—they were all crying. She didn't even want to go to the Historical Society. Her dad was great—why shouldn't Michael want to hang out with him?

Poppy sat on the beach, alone, gazing at the families under their beach umbrellas and the kids playing together in the surf. The tide was going out. Everything felt like it was draining away.

A girl her own age walked up to where Poppy sat with her legs tucked under her. The girl's hair was blond but dirty from the wads of seaweed that got stuck in it. The seaweed was all over her, clinging to her tanned skin and sticking out of her bra top. This was the summer of the red tide, when the usually clear, ice-cold water turned into a junky stew of slick ocean fauna, like boiled red cabbage.

The girl's surfboard was twice as tall as she was. She held on to it loosely with one arm, like she was resting it around the shoulders of a dance partner. She had a long, lean torso and short, strong legs. "You surf?"

"No," Poppy said, although she wished she had a different answer, because she'd always watched the surfers and wished she could join them. The closest she ever got to catching a wave was riding the Styrofoam boogie boards they bought at the junk souvenir stores that dotted Route 6. Real surfboards were expensive, and besides, she didn't know anyone who could teach her. Surfing was out of the question, like charter fishing, regattas, and visits to Nantucket—all the stuff she'd heard Ann saying she wanted to do ever since she started babysitting for the Shaws.

The girl reached out her hand. Her fingers were short and stubby and covered in silver rings, even her thumbs. The rings looked like they were cutting off her circulation. "I'm Kit."

"Poppy."

"Like the flower. Gotcha." Kit's grin was crooked and revealed front teeth that were a shade yellower than the rest. Caps. Poppy figured she'd broken her front teeth on her board or a rock. Kit stared at Poppy with eyes that seemed to be in a perpetual squint. "Why are you alone?"

The way she said it implied that being alone was unnatural. "Everyone else in my family is busy."

"Screw your family."

Poppy smiled. That was *exactly* what she needed to hear.

Kit gestured at the orange dunes and the great big ocean. "You got good balance? You skateboard or ski?"

"Does cross-country skiing count?" She and her mom liked to ski on the trails through Riverside Park.

"Your name is Poppy and you fucking cross-country ski. God, you kill me. Where are you from?"

"Milwaukee."

Kit let out a snort that made Poppy laugh. "That's fucking rad. Of course you're from Canada."

"No, Wisconsin. Milwaukee is in Wisconsin."

"Whatever. May as well be nowhere if there's no ocean."

"We have Lake Michigan."

Kit snorted again. "A lake is no ocean."

"You can't see the other side when you look across it. It's big."

"You *kill* me, flower girl."

Poppy liked Kit immediately.

"Not a lot of girls who surf out here," Kit said.

"I've always wanted to try."

"OK already, so I'll teach you."

"Seriously?"

"Sure." She shrugged. "I brought my long board. It's easier for beginners.

The surf is ankle busters today. Waves are shit. They almost always are this time of year unless there's a storm. But good for learning."

Poppy looked out at the ocean. The waves were gentle bumps lumbering toward shore, nothing like the waves that scared Michael when they'd first taken him to this very beach last summer, when she found out her family was about to change forever.

"Follow me," Kit said, walking toward the ocean. "Your gremlin days are over."

FOUR

Ann

Brooks and Toby were easy. Too easy. Mostly they ignored Ann. She wasn't of much interest to them, just the hired help, one of many in a long string of au pairs and nannies. Toby was right: he didn't need a babysitter and neither did Brooks. What they needed was a chauffeur—one who could tolerate listening to their Backstreet Boys CD on constant repeat. She'd rather stuff tinfoil into her ears.

Ann was told to drive the boys in Maureen's silver Jaguar to the Chequessett yacht club for sailing lessons, to Highland Links golf course in Truro, to the tutor's house in Orleans, all the way to Plimoth Plantation for classes, and again and again to their friends' fancy houses in Chatham on Fox Hill Road. She'd never spent so much time in a car and, after only a few days, was already tired of driving around rotaries, and getting stuck behind lost tourists, or cars slowing down to admire the occasional water view.

Once, Ann drove past the driveway that led to her house, and pointed it out to the boys. "That's where I live," she said.

Toby sounded surprised. "I thought you said you live in Wellfleet."

"I do. This is South Wellfleet."

"I thought there was only *Wellfleet* Wellfleet." He sounded disapproving.

Brooks, who was awkward and sweet, and addicted to his Rubik's Cube, looked away from his toy and out the window. He said, "You mean you live right on Route 6?"

He said it with such disdain that Ann was embarrassed she'd mentioned it in the first place. After that, every time she drove past her family's home the rest of that summer—and she drove past it at least twice a day, it was unavoidable—she could hear his words in her head.

Ann's parents had old-fashioned ideas of summer fun that involved walking across Uncle Tim's Bridge, flying kites, making grave rubbings on the old tombstones with charcoal and tracing paper, catching frogs, picking wild blueberries, going for hikes, reading library books, and whittling the sticks they found in the yard with a Swiss Army knife. They'd introduced all these things to Michael the previous summer, and he'd loved every second of it. Once, when they were standing in line for ice cream at P.J.'s, Michael had said, out of the blue, "I'm having the best time ever."

These boys knew nothing of that sort of best time. They didn't ride rusty, ill-fitting bikes or eat sandy peanut butter and jelly sandwiches on the beach. Maureen was so panicked about her sons' schedules and fearful of their boredom, it was as if she feared that a single idle moment would cause them to grow listless and die.

It would be great to be rich, Ann thought, but also exhausting.

Maureen signed the boys up for an afternoon sailing camp the second week Ann worked for them. She didn't really need Ann to hang around the house while they were gone, but Ann didn't feel she could leave.

Alone and bored in the Shaws' silent, sterile home, Ann missed the fun she'd had with Michael and Poppy the previous summer. If only Poppy and Michael had jobs, too, maybe she wouldn't feel like she was missing out so much.

She tried to focus on *The Pelican Brief*, a book Maureen had told her she just loved. "I'm crazy for courtroom dramas," she'd said. "I have a law degree, believe it or not. I used to have a brain before it got trash-compacted by my kids and the minutiae of everyday life."

Ann didn't know what those minutiae were, or why Maureen felt she had to put herself down. She was clearly bright. When she wasn't reading the latest thriller, she completed crossword puzzles or had her nose in a book about natural selection or an article in *The Boston Globe* about the HIV epidemic. Then again, for someone so smart, Maureen could act like any stupid girl from Ann's high school. Earlier that day, before she left for Marblehead, Maureen ran into the living room in a sleeveless pink Lilly Pulitzer dress that she said she planned to wear to dinner at the Wicked Oyster that weekend with her *husband*. She acted like she'd just gotten invited to the prom.

Ann quickly discovered that Maureen was one of those women who used the word "husband" too much. My husband this, my husband that. If she cared so much about her husband, why didn't she stay in Marblehead with him and get some action? Ann couldn't believe Maureen was so giddy over someone she'd been married to for a long time. It made her even more anxious to meet this mysterious *husband*, which was why she agreed to babysit the next night, even though the last thing she wanted was to spend more time in the Shaws' hermetically sealed home. Maureen offered to pay her overtime, and that was nice, but Ann babysat because she was curious: What kind of man could make his own wife so insecure? What was it about him that made Maureen so jumpy and eager to please?

All she knew about him was that his name was Anthony, and that he had large feet, based on the worn leather boat shoes that sat outside the back door. She liked to imagine him as a real man, strong and confident like the characters in the Harlequin romances she read. A man with secrets. Men, she thought, should be different from her father, inaccessible and mysterious.

Maureen twirled in front of Ann like a little girl in a beauty pageant. "So, be honest. What do you think?"

"It's nice," Ann said, although she thought otherwise: that pink wasn't a good color for Maureen, not with her burnt-red hair and freckly, coral complexion. The silk clung to all the wrong places.

Maureen put her hand on Ann's shoulder and smiled. "Gosh, it's so nice to have another gal in the house."

Gosh? A *gal?*

Maureen could sense Ann's disapproval. "You think I'm too old for it, don't you?"

"I don't think you're old," Ann lied. She thought Maureen was ancient.

"You're so young and beautiful. What would you know about losing your looks?" Maureen shook her finger at her, which made Ann feel like she was being scolded instead of warned. "It happens just like that, you know. Like someone flipped a switch. You'll see, my dear. Sooner than you think. One day you're beautiful, the belle of the ball, and the next day you're—well, you're me."

Ann set the book down. The plot of *Pelican Brief* was too confusing. She looked around the living room and groaned. Maureen's decorating was so self-conscious that Ann felt like she was in a museum. Every object was on display as if it were meant to be observed and learned from, like the framed photos of Toby and Brooks that Maureen had blown up and tinted sepia to make them look timeless. The photos hung in the dining room and were framed in gold and lit from above as if they were real art. The boys' necks looked like they could snap under the weight of their abnormally large heads. They had small eyes, big noses, thin lips, and their mother's ruddy freckles. The strange combination of features was a study in big and little, delicate and thick, and their expressions were of kids who didn't like to have their photos taken. Ann felt restless for the boys, as if they were trapped inside those frames the same way she felt trapped inside their sealed house, where Maureen's hovering attention to the home was evident in every detail, like the polished decorative seashells that Maureen had scattered thoughtfully on the coffee table and across the mantel. Ann had never seen pink shells on the Wellfleet beaches that were anything like the ones Maureen picked out. She suspected they'd been bought in Bermuda, a place that sounded especially rich, and where Maureen told her they owned another home—or "a little place," as Maureen called it.

Ann looked out the window to make sure nobody was around before she walked down the plush white-carpeted hallway that led to the Shaws' bedroom. She opened Maureen's closet and found the dress hanging on the door in a sheer plastic bag. She carefully pulled the raw silk off the hanger and set it on the bed, the pink standing out against the dizzying Waverly floral print on the coverlet.

Ann had poked around in the master bedroom before. She loved to discover things in the intimate spaces of the people she babysat for. Back home, she'd discovered a completed marriage quiz in the green pages inside the Johnsons' *Ms.* magazine. Mrs. Johnson had answered "No" to the question "Do you still love your husband" and "Yes" to one that asked if she fantasized about other men.

In the Shaws' nightstand drawers, she found a *Reader's Digest*, a half-used tube of K-Y jelly, and a container that looked like the one she'd used to store her retainer, only it had a rubbery, flesh-colored disc inside. A diaphragm. She recoiled in horror, as if she'd seen a jellyfish swimming around in the bedside table.

Maureen's room was huge. In the corner was a full-length three-way mirror complete with big round vanity lights. It belonged in the dressing room of a fancy department store instead of a summer home. Ann flipped on the lights and inspected her outfit: a Boston College T-shirt she'd gotten when they'd stopped to tour there on the drive out, and a pair of loose athletic shorts. She kicked off her shorts and T-shirt and stood in front of the mirror in her bra and underwear, a matching set with little red hearts on them. Usually she'd be tan by now, but she'd spent so little time in the sun that her skin was still as pale as it was in February back home in Wisconsin.

She wasn't used to seeing her whole body so completely, front and back, side to side. She unclasped her bra and let her breasts loose. She had a large chest for someone so tall and thin, almost a D cup—breasts that slowed her down when she ran. One of her nipples was inverted. She rubbed the soft, pink flesh between her thumb and index finger until it got hard to match the other one. Pleased with the result, she turned around and focused on the spot where her thigh met the soft curve of her ass. She didn't have any dimples or cellulite to worry about, no flaps under her arms, not yet. She could hear Maureen's voice in her ear. *One day you're beautiful, the belle of the ball* . . .

She cupped her butt cheek with her hand and remembered when Tommy McNair had done the same thing when they danced together at junior prom, his sweaty hand greedy and impatient. He'd just snorted an eight-ball of coke and was jacked up and distracted. "Let's get out of here and *do it*," he'd said, burying his oily face in her neck. She looked across the room and saw Michael staring at her with an expression of concern.

"No," Ann said. "Let's not."

At the after-party, he threw up all over the pool table. Boys were idiots. Well, not all boys. Not Michael.

Yesterday, when she'd come home from babysitting, she found him working in the garden, shirtless. He'd stopped to smile and wave to her. She swore he must have grown almost a foot since he'd moved in with them, and he'd become more muscular, but still lean. His dark hair had some wave in it from the humidity. She couldn't believe how handsome he was—and how wrong it was for her to even think of him like that. She looked at her reflection and thought of his golden-brown skin, and the trail of dark hair below his belly button that led—no, no, *no*!

She shook her head to clear away the thought the way she might shake an Etch A Sketch. He was her brother now, for real. The papers were signed.

The door swung open.

Mr. Shaw.

He wore an expensive-looking black suit that looked small on him, as though the seams were about to pop.

She was so surprised she couldn't even scream. She reached for her T-shirt and held it against her naked torso.

"Well," he said. His voice was so deep the walls practically shook when he spoke. "Hello there." He sounded amused instead of angry. So much was happening she couldn't think straight.

"So, you're the new girl. Ann."

Ann nodded. She could feel her face burn from embarrassment. Why was he speaking to her so casually?

"I hear you're from the Midwest," he said, looking her in the eyes, which made her feel even more naked. What was he talking about? Why was he engaging in a normal conversation with her?

"I'm—" She felt so stupid.

"I've been to Chicago a few times. Some great blues bars there. You like the blues?"

The blues? She did, actually. Her dad was a fan of the old stuff. Ma Rainey. Lightnin' Hopkins. Curley Weaver. She couldn't tell him this. She just nodded.

Anthony took his tie off.

"I know I shouldn't be in here," Ann said.

"Says who? This is my house. I say it's just fine. More than fine."

"But I—"

"My wife is right."

"Right about what?"

"She says you are *darling*." He said it like they were sharing an inside joke. "Although I might have chosen a different word." He looked at her hip. " 'Darling' doesn't do you justice."

"I'm sorry. I should—"

"Don't be embarrassed. We're both grown-ups."

Ann didn't feel like a grown-up. She snuck a longer look at Anthony in the mirror. She'd expected him to be preppy, like the grown-up dads in yacht club shirts and madras shorts she'd met when she picked the boys up in Chatham. They had receding hairlines and potbellies. He was nothing like that. He was sturdy and strong. He wasn't very tall, probably shorter than Maureen, but he took up space as if he were a bigger man.

He had dark brown hair and a clipped, manicured beard that accentuated the bluntness of his features. His nose was short and thick and looked like it had just been punched, and his chin was perfectly square. His cheekbones were so pronounced that they were practically shelves for his eyes—eyes that stared appreciatively at Ann's reflection in the mirror.

"Is that yours?" he asked, pointing at Maureen's dress on the bed.

She shook her head no. Of course it wasn't hers. He knew that. "It's your wife's."

The word "wife" hung in the air between them, awkward and even a little sexy. Ann tried to convince herself that the wife wasn't Maureen, but the idea of a wife.

"Tell me, do you like it?"

"Like what?"

"The dress."

"I guess so." What did it matter what she thought of it? "Look, I should go."

"No, no. You like it. You should try it on. That's what you were going to do, right? Don't let me get in the way. Let's see it on you."

"I can't."

He unbuttoned his suit jacket and loosened his tie, revealing a prominent Adam's apple. "I told you, it's fine."

"I shouldn't have come in here."

"Leave it to me to tell you where you should and shouldn't be in my own home. Look, I understand. You were bored. Tell you what: I get bored here, too. Bored senseless." He slurred the last word, so it sounded like a blur of *s*'s. She wondered if he'd been drinking.

"I should go get the boys. Their lessons will be over soon."

"You have time. Go ahead, try it on. It'll only take a few seconds. Come on, indulge me. Let's see if you're as pretty in pink as I think you'll be."

"Can you . . . can you look away? Please?"

"No, Ann. I honestly can't." That was the first time she'd ever heard her name said that way, or the ache of desire in a man's voice, a real *grown* man's voice. It scared her, but it also turned her on. She felt like she'd gained access into a world that had previously been forbidden.

He grabbed the dress by the skirt and passed it to her. Then he let his finger graze the top of her hand when he tugged the shirt she'd been holding so it would fall free and drop on the floor. "Boston College, huh?"

Perhaps if she'd corrected him things might have gone differently. But she liked being thought of as older than she was.

"Just let me see," he said, smiling. "I'm not asking you to *un*dress."

He sat down on the edge of the bed with his chin on his hands. She looked at him through his reflection in the mirror—three sets in the vanity, from three angles, his eyes all over her. "C'mon," he said, and smiled.

She'd screwed around with boys back home, "mashing" under the bleachers at football games or in her friends' wood-paneled basements at parties, but she'd never let it go too far. She was usually comfortable saying no, pulling a boy's hand away from the hem of her shirt and the snap of her pants.

She decided to think of this as a game, one in which *she* had power. Emboldened, she smiled. She pointed her toe through the dress, and shimmied the delicate fabric over her hips. It felt like a whisper against her skin. She slipped her arms into the armholes. The dress was meant to be cute, not sexy, but it might as well have been lingerie, the way Ann felt wearing it. She reached behind her for the zipper and struggled to pull it up.

Anthony stepped off the bed and approached her. "Let me help." He did nothing at first. She could feel the heat off his body, and she wanted badly for him to either walk out of the room or to touch her, but she was also worried about either scenario.

His breath was heavy and warm on her shoulder. It ignited something in her, a hunger that felt suddenly hot and urgent—and wrong.

He reached for the zipper at the small of her back. He dragged it up slowly, one tooth at a time, until his fingers made electric contact on the base of her neck, lingering there, warm and insistent, his fingers callused and hard and masculine. He gently tugged at the rubber band holding her ponytail and set her golden hair loose. "There," he said. "All you need is matching polish for your toenails."

She curled her bare toes deep into the thick pile carpet.

He backed away and stood in profile, doing nothing to hide the hard-on that bulged pointedly through his slacks like a drawn sword. She knew he was proud and he meant for her to see it.

He stared at her for a while, his gaze intense, direct. "I think I'm going to have to start spending more time out here on the Cape, aren't I?"

Ann didn't realize she'd been lost in a spell until Anthony cleared his throat. "Well. I hope you'll forgive me. This is entirely inappropriate, Ann. My work has been stressful—incredibly stressful—and the drive out here was long. Horrible traffic at the bridge. When I walked into my room and saw you, what could I do?" He paused. "What could any man do?"

"It's—it's fine," she said.

"No. It's not. I let this go too far. It was my good fortune to see you in all your glory. Now if you'll excuse me, you should change. Mo would be upset if she knew you were rummaging around through her things. She likes to keep things separate."

Keep things separate? What did that mean, she wondered.

"But don't worry, I won't share your secret."

"My secret?"

"I wouldn't think of it." He walked to the door and winked. "It was so nice to meet you, Ann."

He lingered over her name before he walked out of the room and gently clicked the door shut behind him. By the time she'd taken off the dress and hung it back up she could hear his car engine turn over, followed by the sound of his wheels rolling backward.

FIVE

Poppy

Kit taught Poppy all the parts of the board: nose, tail, deck, rails.
Before they even got in the water she lectured her about safety,
which made Poppy think Kit was a little less cool, because safety was
something only adults were supposed to care about.

Poppy's parents took the ocean seriously. Over the years, Poppy and
Ann had frequently lost track of the shore while they were swimming.
Depending on the direction of the wind, the gentle pull of the tide
would slowly and imperceptibly tug them north toward Truro, or south
toward Orleans. They'd get caught up in their bodysurfing, and when
they looked at the beach for the lifeguard stand and the familiar yellow
umbrella marking their parents' encampment, they'd see only a blank
expanse of sand. Suddenly, they would swim to shore and race down the
beach, finding Ed and Connie frantically calling out their names. They
knew that the pull of the ocean could take their girls away into unsafe
waters, farther from the main swimming areas, where the seals swam and
the sharks followed.

Safety was just as serious for Kit as it was for Poppy's parents. She
had a kind of reverence for it, barking out what sounded more like com-

mands than bits of advice. "Never let your board get between you and the wave. Always hold the nose up. Don't ever think you know where your board is when you pop. Cover your head no matter what. If it's behind you and a wave is coming, the board'll smash you in the head or crack your nose. Hurts like hell, trust me. That's why my nose whistles when I breathe."

Before they even got in the water, Kit taught Poppy how to paddle on dry land. She also made her practice lifting up her chest, bringing her right leg forward and planting it sideways on the board while her other leg dragged behind it. She practiced squatting, arms down. "Don't look at your feet. Look at the horizon. Imagine the water is rushing around you. Squat. Bring down your center of gravity."

Poppy, anxious and tired of imagining surfing, finally got into the water. It was cold and exhilarating, and the board was huge and hard to manage. Kit sounded like a drill sergeant, and Poppy internalized Kit's voice.

"Get on your board when the water is waist high. Paddle to the sandbar. Use your shoulders! Now go to where the waves are breaking. Turn around and face the shore. Look behind you for the wave. OK, here it comes. You're going to need to learn how to watch for waves. OK now paddle, paddle, lift up your chest, feel it, feel it, now *go*!"

Poppy stood up her very first time. She loved the feeling of the water under her board, loved the energy of the surf, loved the rush of adrenaline. This was way better than researching history or babysitting rich kids. And it was way better than what she was before that moment: Gordo's daughter, her mother's sidekick, Ann's pesky younger sister, Michael's coffee shop buddy. She was always somebody else's something; never anything special on her own. She didn't stir the pot the way Ann did, she didn't tug at anyone's heartstrings like sweet Michael. Everyone thought she was just a space cadet, quiet and dreamy. And now here she was, on top of the ocean.

"You got it, girl!"

Poppy didn't ride her first wave for long, maybe ten seconds, just long enough to know she'd never had more fun. It was as if the moment she stood up on the water she'd finally become her true self. She'd heard of people who knew they were alcoholics after their first sip of whiskey. Poppy was addicted to surfing after her first wave.

SIX

Ann

Ann showed up to babysit that weekend, nervous. She'd fantasized about that scene in the bedroom a hundred times since it had happened, and in her fantasies, Anthony grew more and more handsome, their conversations more and more intimate.

Maureen answered the door with a bright smile. Ann startled when she saw the pink dress on her. "You look nice."

"Aren't you sweet," Maureen said. "I thought about returning this silly dress. I could tell you didn't like it on me, but my *husband* insisted I keep it. Positively insisted, which is unusual. He just loves it. Speaking of . . ." She turned around and called out, "Tony? Come meet Ann." She smiled. "I can't believe you two haven't even met yet."

Ann did not correct her.

Maureen waited expectantly while Anthony and the boys wrestled on the floor. Maureen walked over to them and began to act more like a parent than Ann was used to seeing. Maureen told them to stop in her faux-stern voice: *please, boys, please now, that's enough.* They didn't listen to her and that was fine with Maureen, who didn't seem to care. Anthony's hair was tousled, and he appeared refreshingly lighthearted, laughing when Toby tried to put him in a headlock. "Who do you think you are, huh? André the Giant?" It was the first time Ann noticed an accent in his voice. It wasn't like Maureen's more refined Boston drawl; this was more working class and rough. Anthony stood up and twisted Toby around so that he was slung across his broad shoulders like a blanket. Toby weighed almost as much as Ann, but when Anthony picked him up, he could have been as light as a loaf of bread.

Toby laughed so hard he couldn't speak.

"Anthony," Maureen said. "Could you take a break? Ann is here." As if he'd snapped out of a spell, Anthony slid Toby off his shoulders and onto the couch. He was flushed and breathless. The boys looked at Ann, clearly disappointed that their father would leave soon.

"No shoes on the davenport," Maureen said, pointing disapprovingly at Toby's sandaled feet. Ann had never heard anyone call a couch a "davenport" before.

"Fine." Toby tagged Brooks, and the boys ran outside onto the deck.

Anthony wore a pair of pressed khakis and a light blue golf shirt, although, like his suit, the ensemble didn't seem to fit him right. He seemed out of place in Maureen's domesticated world, energetic where Maureen tried to impose order, dressed in an outfit he probably wouldn't have picked for himself.

Ann tried not to smile. "I'm Ann." She reached her hand to her employer and looked him in the eye. He smiled—a cordial smile that gave nothing away. He shook her hand. His grip was firm and forceful, sweaty. His middle finger reached toward her wrist. She tried to shake her hand loose but he gently tightened his grip and held it a few seconds longer, long enough for her to remember the feeling of his callused fingers on the back of her neck when he tugged her ponytail holder loose, long enough to linger without Maureen, who busied herself straightening up the cushions, taking no notice. "I've heard you're a terrific babysitter," he said, and smiled.

Maureen walked away and applied another coat of lipstick in the hallway mirror. "Caged animals, that's what they are. Especially this time of night."

"You need to let the tiger out of the cage," Anthony said.

"Our reservation is in ten minutes," she said. "I just need to get my purse." She practically skipped down the hallway that led to their bedroom.

"Ah, nice color," Anthony said, pointing at Ann's toes. She'd painted them with the closest shade of pink she could find, given the limited selection at the General Store. She looked at him, feeling both bold and embarrassed, and smiled.

Anthony turned his attention to Brooks and Toby, who had run back into the family room. "You'll behave for Ann tonight, right?"

"Right," they said in unison.

Anthony walked over to the couch and picked up a needlepoint pillow with the word COTTAGE stitched into it. "This is new," he said. "I wonder what my father would think of it."

He tossed it to Ann, who caught it.

"He worked third shift in the Enlow Fork coal mine."

"Where's that?"

"Pennsylvania. Coal country. He supported us on twelve bucks an hour. Every day, he went six hundred and fifty feet underground. It was dark. Machines with teeth as big as you are chewed a hole in the ground. At any moment, something could explode or collapse. He came home looking like the earth swallowed him up and spit him back out. When he was my age, his eardrums were ruptured, his kidneys shot. His spine was a zigzag. He died of black lung."

"I'm sorry."

"I am too." Anthony's voice broke. "He was a great guy. The best, and he pissed his life away trying to provide for us. And now here I am, just a coal miner's son, with a pillow that says 'cottage.' If we had a pillow like that in the house I grew up in, it would say 'shithole.'"

All this time she'd thought of herself as the poor intruder into Maureen's tidy world. Now she felt, well—not rich, but fortunate.

"My wife," Anthony said. "She's a wonderful woman, but she was born with a silver spoon in her mouth. She doesn't know hardship."

Ann saw Maureen standing in the doorway clutching her purse, looking hurt. Suddenly Ann ached for her: it wasn't her fault that she was born into money. It wasn't wrong of her to try to make their home nice, and everything she did was for Anthony. She didn't seem to know what else she was supposed to do with herself. "I'm ready," Maureen said, looking hopeful and anxious. She walked toward the front door and jiggled the handle. "You said you wanted to let the tiger out of the cage."

"My date with the zookeeper awaits." He opened the door for Maureen, but before he ushered her out, he looked at Ann and said, "Don't you think this is a terrific dress my wife is wearing?"

Ann nodded, afraid her blush was obvious. "It's great."

"Tell me, would you ever wear a dress like this, Ann?"

"Yeah," Ann said. "Sure."

Maureen seemed genuinely touched and even more grateful for Anthony's attention. "You're so dear," she said, and her words made Ann feel that she was caught up in something complicated and awkward.

Maureen stepped outside and Anthony stalled at the door. He gave Ann a little wave. Just like that, Ann become part of a secret—an adult secret.

SEVEN

Michael

The Shaws were all Ann talked about when she was home, although she was hardly ever home. He couldn't give a shit that Maureen—*Mo* now—drank basil-and-lemon-infused water and ate cucumber sandwiches without crusts, or that she'd let Ann drive her *Jag*, or that she was the kind of person who made sure her napkins matched the colors of the flowers in her bouquets, or that her kids' allowance was fifty bucks a month for doing absolutely nothing.

And then there was the dad, who sounded like a real number. Ann said his name, *Anthony*, with a certain lilt in her voice that made Michael squirm inside. It was as if she'd been on a first-name basis with the guy her whole life. She said he was very busy, as if not being around your family was a sign of success. Ann said he ran the *family business* as if she were a Shaw herself. She didn't even know what their *family business* did. She just loved the idea of a *family* fucking *business*.

Anthony this, Anthony that. Anthony drove his Jeep on Nauset Beach. Anthony chartered fishing boats. Well, guess what? Ed chartered a fishing boat, too, only Ann didn't know that, and Michael wasn't about to tell her. Besides, he was sworn to secrecy. Ed told Connie that they were out conducting "research," but really, they were fishing, spending money Ed said he really shouldn't spend.

But then, a few nights ago, Ann suddenly directed the golden beam of her attention back on him. She returned home from babysitting and found Michael in his room in the attic. He was bored because Poppy was gone again, hanging out with her new surfing friends, and Ed and Connie went to bed early. A few minutes after they'd shut their bedroom door he heard the bedsprings squeak and the headboard bang rhythmically against the paper-thin wall. He figured he should get lost.

Before he could leave, he heard the kitchen door swing open, followed by the fast tap-tap-tap of Ann's feet on the steep stairs. He knew it was Ann; he knew the sound of her footsteps, her breathing, her sneezes.

She didn't bother to knock first. She sat on the end of his bed and smiled. "I have exciting news! *Anthony* said Jason, his landscaper, needs help this summer, and I told him you could do it. I guess it's really hard to find workers here. I told him you love to garden. You want a job, right?"

He was having fun without a job, but Michael liked to work, and he liked the idea of making his own money. He couldn't get used to Ed and Connie paying for his stuff; he saw the way their brows furrowed and their expressions changed whenever they held out their credit card. Michael figured he'd pay them back someday, help them when they were old, something to make them feel like he'd earned his place in the family.

"I don't know much about gardening out here," he said.

"Don't worry about that. He'll train you. You'd probably do more of the basic stuff anyway. Jason is desperate. I've met him. He's nice. You'd like him."

Michael resented Ann for assuming that he'd say yes. What was he, Ann's own private lawn boy on demand?

"We'd practically be coworkers. You'll be at the Shaws' all the time. Maureen said Jason is going to help them build a stone patio. Please, Michael?"

Ann's eyes were gray-green. She had little baby hairs that curled around her forehead where the rest of her hair was pulled back. Her cheeks were red from running up the stairs. Her hand was on his calf. She was on his bed, he could feel her weight, her heat. He wished he could reach out—

"Sure," he said, closing his notebook.

"Awesome!"

He agreed because he missed Ann, and this was a way to get close to her. Ever since they'd first met, that night under the green light of the Holidome, he knew one thing: he wanted to be wherever she was.

JASON PULLED UP THE GORDONS' DRIVE at six o'clock in the morning. Michael guessed he was about Ed's age, maybe a little younger. His face was leathery from the outdoors. "Climb on in," Jason said, pointing at his rusty orange Toyota pickup truck with rakes, hoes, and a wheelbarrow in the back. A big black Lab sat waiting in the cab. "That's Flip. She's a good girl."

The cab smelled like dirt and dog breath. Flip stood to lick Michael's face, then turned to lick Jason, and her tail swatted against Michael like a windshield wiper. Jason slipped his Red Sox cap on his head and took a drink from his thermal mug. "You got your pruning shears on the dash, rain jackets behind the seats, work gloves all over. Do me a favor: try harder than I do to keep them in pairs." *Fay-vah. Pay-as.* His accent sounded so thick to Michael that it was almost a speech impediment. "You have problems gettin' up this early?"

"No," said Michael.

"You're in this for beer money?"

"I actually like working with plants."

"Look, all I care about is you show up when you say you're going to show up, you work hard, keep it honest. And you need to learn quick because I'm so goddamn behind I don't know my ass from my elbow. Weather this year is kicking my ass. Shaw is riding my keister about his goddamn *yaah-d*. He's the type who wants his grass mowed in a checkerboard pattern. Too rich to do his own yard, too poor to hire a property manager. So here we are."

"Is he a bad guy?" Finally Michael had someone to ask.

"He's money, that's what he is, and money is what I need right now. I'm running my business from my backyard and my neighbors aren't happy. I'm trying to buy some land in an industrial park in Eastham. Bigger crew, space for my tools. Speaking of money, I pay shit, but you work hard and I'll see you get your due at the end of the summer. I got you on manure duty today. You'll go home smelling like you crawled up a cow's ass."

MICHAEL LIKED JASON. He was demanding and rough, but also creative and patient. He loved what he did. He showed Michael how to nurture hearty Cape Cod plants so they'd survive the high wind, salt air, and sandy soil. He taught him how to make planting charts, explained how lavender, bee balm, and citronella deter pests, and showed him how to use stakes and string to trim the hedges. Michael loved how Jason talked about plants and gardening—breaking buds, deadheading, air layering, double-digging, scarification. He treated Michael as an equal, not some kid who'd once been an orphan.

Michael loved gardening, even the grunt work of spreading manure and mulch, moving stones and digging holes. He liked the feeling of having earned his fatigue at the end of the day. It was good to be outside, good to be in control, good to have Jason press a wad of cash in his hand at the end of the week, good to hear the girls make comments about him when he was on pruning duty in town and worked shirtless. Mostly, it was good to be on Cape Cod with Jason, who ended each day at Indian Neck, where he picked the ticks off his legs and went for a swim while Michael sat on the shore. He could swim now, but he only liked the ponds. He was almost too reverent about the ocean. It seemed too mysterious, too deep. It struck him that he felt the same way about Ann.

Jason kept a small cooler in the back of his truck and gave Michael a can of Sam Adams without concern that he was underage. The beer tasted good. They watched Flip chase the gulls.

"How about coming back here next summer?" Jason asked.

"I could come back here forever," Michael said.

"Uh-oh."

"What?"

"You've got sand in your shoes."

The sun turned the water gold. The sailboats dotting the horizon chased the wind. It was perfect. Michael never wanted to leave.

EIGHT

Poppy

Poppy went back to the ocean again and again to meet up with Kit. She didn't tell her parents she was surfing because they'd worry. She said she'd made a new friend at Long Pond and she was going to her house, although she had no idea where Kit lived.

Instead, she met up with Kit at her friends' houses on the ocean side near Cahoon Hollow. Most of them lived on a private road marked with a tree trunk at the entrance covered in bright buoys and wooden planks with the names of the residences painted on them: Witt's End, Lynch Lodge, Nolan's Nook, Ma and Pa's. The long, sandy drive led through the pine forest to the ocean, where their houses were low-slung, sleepy sixties-style shingled ranch homes with big windows overlooking the water. They all had some stylish variation on short leather couches, teak furniture, massive paintings, and rag rugs to catch the sand before it scuffed up the pine floors. Expensive, sporty cars sat in their driveways.

The kids had unconventional names: Skip, Collins, Evie, and Rye. They were golden and loose, comfortable in their skin, as familiar with each other as siblings because their parents had gone to Harvard and

Yale together. They'd all grown up in wealthy suburbs of Connecticut and New York, and spent every summer on the Cape. They slept at each other's houses as though their families were interchangeable. It seemed to Poppy that the parents wanted lots of kids around so the kids could keep each other company, leaving the adults free to have their own fun.

Their sheds were stuffed with surfboards and wet suits. Before, a surfboard seemed out of reach to Poppy. Now, her new friends told her she could borrow one anytime. She'd had a feeling there was a right way and a wrong way to vacation here, and she'd finally tapped into the right way.

Evenings, they went from house to house. Poppy wished Ann could be there with her, because they'd always experienced the Cape together. But Ann was always at the Shaws', and the more time she spent with them, the more distracted and stuck-up she became. Poppy had visited Ann a few times when she first started, and thought she'd die if she had to spend ten minutes in that house. She felt sorry for those loser kids, too. They seemed miserable, like trained poodles. When Poppy thought of Ann sealed up in the Shaws' house, she imagined a figure trapped in an air-conditioned snow globe.

The surfer kids were competitive fun seekers. Drinking was no big deal. Their refrigerators were stocked with beer and their cabinets filled with gin, bourbon, and whiskey. Back home, Poppy occasionally had some shots of Jim Beam, Rumple Minze, and Jägermeister. On the Cape, her new friends could mix her a Manhattan or a Rusty Nail. They were experts at picking seeds out of pot and rolling fat joints the size of cigars. If the parents were gone (and the parents were almost always gone), Kit and Poppy and a loose, interchangeable gathering of siblings and friends would sit outside on the wood decks, drink, take hits, and watch the sun set behind the pitch pines, comparing notes about that day's surf. Everything was surf: whether it sucked or it was awesome. They predicted where and when they could catch the best swells, where and when the storms were coming, how big the tide would be based on the fullness of the moon, whether the wind would be offshore and perfect (the way it almost never was), or whether the waves would crumble. A storm could move the breaks, because there were no piers or moorings to hold the sand in place on this side of the Cape. Unpredictability was what made surfing so intoxicating.

No piers, no moorings, good pot, unpredictability. Poppy felt herself coming loose with every wave, every toke, every shot, every pill.

NINE

Michael

Michael and Ann rode their bikes to the Shaws' house on Michael's first full day of working on their lawn. Michael was nervous, because Jason had made such a big deal of the Shaws' yard (he called the Shaws' home "the Shaw Mahal"). He had a key to the house. Jason had showed him where he'd hung the keys for all his clients. In summer, he worked on their lawns, and in winter he checked in on their empty houses, leaving tire prints and footmarks in the snow to ward off possible intruders.

Jason told him he'd meet him at the Shaws' with the Gravely and some tools, and detailed instructions about how to mow exactly the way Shaw liked. "You can't fuck up," Jason said. "I need him."

Ann seemed excited that Michael would be at the house with her, and it made him happy that she felt that way. They snapped on their bike helmets, although as soon as they turned on LeCount Hollow Road, beyond Ed and Connie's view, Ann stopped to take hers off and hung it on her handlebars. "I don't want helmet hair," she said, which seemed strange, like a lot of things lately. She dressed up to babysit, and took a long time in the bathroom before she left, emerging with mascara and lipstick. Her hair was usually wavy. Michael loved the way it looked when it was a bit messy, but before she went to the Shaws' house she ironed it with a flatiron. "Let's take the long way," she said.

They biked along Ocean View Drive, stopping at White Crest Beach to look down the bluff at the ocean, where a group of surfers paddled around in the water waiting for waves. Then they passed Long Pond. The water was so clear he could almost see to the bottom at the deepest part. Here, away from the back shore and the cove, the air smelled like pine and oak, a scent Michael found intoxicating.

By the time he got to the Shaws' house on the bay side, that scent was diluted. The haze was beginning to burn off. Michael looked at the big brown house. It was too big. Too brown. The rolling lawn that surrounded it was too lush, too green. It was a yard that looked unnatural, a boob job of a yard.

The house was surrounded by healthy bushes bursting with pompons of big, blue hydrangeas. "Cape Cod clichés" was what Jason called them. Light pink roses bloomed on the trellis. Earlier that week Jason had taught Michael how to prune, a task he enjoyed from the start. "For roses," he said, "you have to hack the shit out of it. Take it down hard. Don't be kind. I'll know you did a good job if they look ugly."

"That's him," Ann said, propping her bike up against the garage. "Hi, Anthony!" She stood on her toes and waved, a shy smile on her lips. What was with the wave and the smile?

Mr. Shaw waved back, but not before looking her up and down.

Ann seemed nervous and excited, her face red from biking up the hill, her breathing deep and heavy. "I'll see you later," she said. "Have fun." She straightened her shirt and ran into the house, leaving Michael with a funny feeling, like he'd walked into a party he hadn't been invited to.

Mr. Shaw stood with his hands on his hips, staring off into the distance, his expression serious.

Here he was, *Anthony*, the real deal, live and in person. Michael walked to where he stood. He stuck his hand out to offer a handshake, but instead of accepting it, Mr. Shaw pulled up the hem of his sweat-stained Penn T-shirt and wiped off his damp forehead.

"I just got back from a long run," he said, as if this should impress Michael. It didn't. This Anthony guy was fit, sure, but he didn't have a runner's body. He was a bulldog of a man, squat and strong. Michael could outpace him no problem.

Anthony eyed his property as if he thought Michael was there to take it from him. He seemed like the kind of person who believed everyone wanted what he had.

"Is there something wrong?" Michael felt like he'd already done something to piss the guy off and he hadn't even started work.

It seemed everyone on the Cape was good-natured. They were on vacation, so why shouldn't they be? But this guy's expression was dark and brooding, like he'd never had a good time in his life. He gave Michael the feeling he was about to whip a knife out of his pocket.

"I'll tell you what's wrong," Anthony said. He gazed out at the vast expanse of emerald-green grass in front of him, and the twinkling bay in the distance. "My lawn looks like hell."

"Looks nice to me," Michael said.

"Then you should go home. If this looks nice to you, you aren't the right person for this job. I need someone with standards."

Michael actually *did* have standards. He appreciated the Gordons' long-neglected lawn (was it even a lawn?) on the cove, even though it was mottled with patches of fusarium, creeping Charlie, prickly pears, and bayberries. The vegetation gave it color and interest. It looked natural, like it belonged there. The Shaws' lawn might as well have been a putting green. The smell of lush grass was almost strong enough to make Michael forget he was next to an ocean, surrounded by bogs and marshes. It made him glad he wasn't back in Milwaukee, where it seemed everyone wanted a boring lawn like the Shaws'.

Anthony crossed his arms tightly over his thick chest. He gazed at the vast slope of his grand property and sneered. "Jason's last guy didn't know a lawn mower from a toaster oven. Look." He made a wide, sweeping gesture with his arm. "You can see he didn't set the casters on the mow deck evenly. See how there are lines on one side? It looks like he was planning to plant corn here, not mow a lawn. He didn't get close enough to the trees or bevel the edges by the road. And the leftover grass cuttings, just look at them." He reached down and grabbed a fistful of grass in his hand. "Don't even get me started on the cuttings. Unacceptable. Entirely unacceptable."

"I'll take care of it."

Jason had warned Michael about using the Gravely on Shaw's yard. He said you steer with the handles, and no matter what, you have to maintain a perfect line. "I don't care if a horsefly is chewing up your arm, you don't stop, you don't swat it away. You keep the lines straight."

Off in the distance Michael saw a tall, thin lady lean over the porch rail. "Anthony! Let's go!"

"She wants us to look for furniture for the patio you're going to build for me. Then she's dragging me to a play."

"The play sounds like fun." Connie had already taken Michael to two plays in the little theater by the town pier. One was based on *Death of a Salesman,* but it was told from the mistress's perspective. The other one was *Three Sisters.* He liked them both, or maybe he just liked having Connie to himself since Ann and Poppy were always busy.

"You're young. You don't have the first idea of fun yet. Tell you what, Michael: enjoy your youth. I used to be young like you, and now here I am, worrying about my yard, going to a play followed by another insufferable dinner with Janey and Bill Bingham. You know what she said the last time we went to dinner? She told me she makes a list every morning of all the things she thinks she should worry about. A goddamn worry list. She says it gives her control. That's what we talk about. And Bill's golf swing. Sometimes, at these dinners, I feel like I'm a character in one of those James Bond films who gets trapped in a room and all four walls move in on him. You say that sounds fun? You're lying to me, and that's OK. I respect that. You *should* lie to me, because you want me to keep you on the job so you can make some money, and I appreciate your work ethic. Tell me what you think I want to hear, that's a good strategy."

"I'm not lying," Michael said. "I don't lie."

"Yeah, you seem like a straight shooter. Look, I know what you're thinking," Shaw said. "I've got a beautiful house, a beautiful life. Who am I to complain? It's not that I don't appreciate it. I do. But tell me, Michael, what's all this for?"

How was Michael supposed to respond? He said nothing. He wasn't a therapist. He knew nothing about this guy's life. He didn't want to know.

Michael looked down the road to see if Jason's truck was anywhere nearby. He said he'd be there around nine o'clock to drop off the rake and mower. He'd spent enough time alone with this guy.

"So how about that sister of yours," Anthony said, lingering on the word "sister," like it was the punch line of a joke.

"What about her?"

"She's something to look at, huh? Must be hard to sleep under the same roof."

"It's not."

Anthony slapped Michael on the back. "Oh, come on."

"I don't look at her that way."

"Sure you do. I saw the way you just looked at her, just now. You're the bug, she's the windshield. It's OK. You look at her the way any man would."

Michael felt a heat rise up in him. Then he thought of Jason: *Don't fuck up. I need his business. Don't fuck up!*

"I know she's not your real sister. Anyone could tell you're not related."

What had Ann told Shaw? Had she felt sorry for Michael—was that why he was here? Because Ann said he needed the money? Had her parents asked her to find work for him to get him out of the house, out of their hair?

"I'm just here to work, all right? I don't want to talk about Ann."

Anthony winked. "She ever put the moves on you?"

God, Michael wanted to land a punch right on this guy's nose. Judging from the looks of it, he wouldn't be the first person to break it. *Don't fuck up.*

"Look, I think of her like she's my sister. She thinks of me like I'm her brother."

"Whatever you say."

"I just want to get to work."

Sometimes, after a deluge of rain in Milwaukee, the pressure would build enough to pop three-hundred-pound manhole covers into the air. That was how Michael felt, like at any moment he might blow. Who the hell did this guy think he was, looking at Ann the way he did, talking about her like she was a piece of ass?

"Hey," Anthony said, his voice softening. "No offense. I thought we could be honest with each other. We're not so different, you know, you and me."

"We've got nothing in common."

"Oh, come on." He nudged Michael and laughed as if they were at a bar, joking around. "Lighten up, sport. I helped you get this job, you know. I'm not out to get you. I know what it's like to need to earn your own keep. Those new parents of yours, they did a great thing for you, and you know it never hurts to claim another dependent come tax time."

"What?"

"Big deduction. I'm sure they care about you, but don't forget that they get something out of the deal, too."

It never occurred to Michael that the Gordons could have selfish reasons for adopting him.

"We're the kind of people who like to pay our own way in life. Let me give you some advice, Michael: never turn down an opportunity to make an honest buck. I've got plenty of work for you to do here. I told Jason that I can keep you busy all summer long."

All summer? Michael hadn't even started and already he wanted to quit. This guy wasn't worth the shitty pay Jason offered him. But then he thought of Ann. He thought of her smile and the way the sunlight glinted off her hair, and the way she'd asked him to take this job. He'd do it, mostly because he didn't want to leave her alone with this guy.

TEN

Poppy

One thing Kit didn't teach Poppy soon enough was that you never dropped in on another surfer's wave—especially a local's. That's what she did one morning. The surfer didn't see her coming. When they got to shore he popped up and she joined him. He was older, maybe even as old as her dad. He lifted his arm to reveal a gash across his torso. He'd been sliced by her fin.

"Look what you did."

"Oh God, I'm so sorry. I didn't—"

"You didn't pay attention to what the hell you were doing. You *should* be sorry. Hurts like hell, you stupid washashore." He inspected the gash. It was clean-looking, at least. "You people, you and your little friends, you think you own everything. Go back to Manhattan."

"I'm not from Manhattan."

"OK, Connecticut."

"Wisconsin."

When Poppy told Kit she was from Wisconsin it was a joke, but somehow this revelation redeemed her in the leather-skinned surfer's eyes. "You a Packers fan?"

"Of course."

"Super Bowl champs! How about that? The green and gold. Nothing but Patriots fans out here. Tired of 'em. I'm Dirk."

"Poppy."

He slapped some seaweed on his cut and swore when the salt stung.

"Takes years to learn to surf. Years and years. You're off to a good start. I watched you. You've got good balance and you're quick. Watchful. And you're a girl. Not a lot of girls out here."

"I noticed."

"Show up at LeCount before sunrise tomorrow. I'll introduce you to some people who can help you work your board. *Real* surfers."

"That's early."

"That's the best time of day."

"I'll be there."

RYE AND SKIP COULDN'T BELIEVE Poppy had dropped in on Dirk and survived. He was one of the outer shore's resident surfing legends, one of the old guard who got started in the seventies. For the old guys, surfing was as much a spiritual thing as it was athletic.

Poppy didn't tell Kit about her meeting with Dirk, because it was like discussing a party only she'd been invited to.

It was tough to get up before sunrise the next morning, but she woke early and went to LeCount Hollow, where he told her he'd meet her. She sat on the bench where the parking lot met the steep bluff that led down to the ocean. The sun was beginning to rise, and a layer of yellow like a line of highlighter shone at the crease of the horizon. The wind pushed the cold off the ocean to shore and made her hair whip around her head. She could taste the salt on her lips. She liked being there early. It made her feel like she had the world all to herself.

A few minutes later a caravan of trucks drove into the lot, led by Dirk. His truck was white and covered with bumper stickers her dad would approve of, like the Grateful Dead marching bears, RELAX, a mustache, a Greenpeace logo, RALPH NADER FOR PRESIDENT OF OUTER SPACE. A series of doors slammed and a group of guys close to her own age gathered around her. The last person to approach was a girl.

"Kit?"

"You didn't know I'm a local? I guess you are too, now, Wisconsin."

UNLIKE THE "WASHASHORES" WHO started surfing in the afternoons and evenings—after their hangovers began to lift—the locals got started first thing. Their days began with a sacred ritual of coffee at sunrise. Then they'd check the breaks to see where the surf was best. They'd cruise the coast from Truro to Orleans chasing swells.

"You have to be gnarly to surf with them," Kit said, and Poppy soon learned what that meant. Dirk taught Poppy that surfing with the locals meant peeing in your own wet suit. It meant shitting in the dunes. It meant staying in the cold waters of the Atlantic as long as the swell would last, because it might be another tide or day or week before you'd hit a good one again. It meant keeping up with the guys, some of them about her age, some as old as Dirk. They felt like a family of brothers who were different than Michael. Poppy felt protective of him, while these guys looked out for *her* safety, taught technique, and let her drink and get high with them.

Sometimes they went to Dirk's. He was such a hippie, he made Poppy's dad seem like a WASP by comparison. Dirk lived on a plot of land deep in the woods near Cole's Neck. He slept in the back of a caramel-colored International Harvester Travelall parked next to a giant boat hidden under a tented tarp. He'd proudly rip it off when he showed it to his guests, like the host of a game show revealing the contestant's prize. The wooden boat was beautiful but far from seaworthy. The boat was what Dirk worked on when he wasn't surfing or taking on odd carpentry jobs. Poppy had a feeling that Dirk, like her dad with his local history and house projects, put a lot of work into things he would never finish.

Dirk loved it when Poppy and the other surfers came to visit him. He liked being the center of attention, and railed about Marxism and capitalism and the evil war machines and NAFTA. He told Poppy that he was a typical old-school "Fleetian." He didn't follow anyone's rules, didn't care about the countless citations the town slapped on him when the neighbors complained about the mess in his yard. He seemed so right about everything and so cool and wise that when he passed around sheets of LSD, Poppy didn't hesitate to set one on her tongue.

Why not? Nobody seemed to care what Poppy was up to. Michael and Ann were always at the Shaws' dumb house, and her parents, whom she'd seen get high plenty of times, didn't seem to notice. This past year they'd been so focused on Michael's adjustment and so busy with the logistics of his adoption that sometimes Poppy felt overlooked.

She didn't say a word about Dirk and Kit and Mickey and Nick and Paul, her new best friends. Her parents seemed pleased that she wasn't bored anymore. She'd crawl into bed after the end of a long day and feel like she'd just experienced the whole world—a world that felt bigger and more expansive.

Poppy felt herself change between waves and bonfires and drunk kisses with her new friends—the boys and even Kit. She couldn't tell if she was losing her former self or becoming the person she always thought she was. It was exciting and fun and scary, like catching a wave just before it crested. She rode straight into it the way Dirk taught her. She rode into it until it rode her.

ELEVEN

Ann

Ann stood on the porch and watched Michael work. She'd only seen him this focused when he ran—he had a sort of zen concentration she admired. He cut the grass in a perfect diamond pattern, cleaned up every clipping, and snipped away all the stray grass that grew around the base of the trees. Maureen joined her on the deck and offered her a glass of water with a wedge of lime hanging off the rim. "Anthony thinks your brother isn't bad. High praise coming from him. You've probably noticed that my husband isn't easily pleased," Maureen said. "It drives me crazy sometimes, but that's why he's so successful at running the business."

What was this "business" Maureen referred to? She liked to imagine they worked on something really important and interesting, like a blood test that could detect cancer, or a computer chip, or some dot-com business like GeoCities.

Maureen took a drink out of her own glass. "Tony says 'Jump' and his workers say 'How high?' He's really got a remarkable gift for leadership, for encouraging people to do well. Of course, like any of us, he has his vices." Maureen's voice trailed off.

Vices? Ann wanted to know more; she was dying to get inside their marriage, figure him out.

"Your brother is a sweetheart," Maureen said, gesturing for her to join her at the bistro table. "I think it's wonderful what your family has done for him. It's gotten me thinking that maybe we should look into adopting a needy child. We tried to have a third, you know. I wanted a daughter, someone I could talk to the way I talk to you." She pressed her hand on Ann's knee and smiled. Her fingers felt long and cold and hard, like the chilled shrimp she'd left on the kitchen counter for guests earlier that day. "Then I had female problems. Cysts, fibroids."

Oh God, no. No! Ann wished she could put her fingers in her ears. She didn't want to hear this, didn't want to know, didn't want to be Maureen's female friend. Her *gal*. Especially since she'd been daydreaming about Anthony.

"I have this theory," Maureen said, "that women should be born with zippers, and once we're done having babies we should just unzip ourselves and get rid of all that stuff we don't need anymore."

"That would be cool," Ann said. She stood up. "I should go check on the boys."

"Look at them, they're fine." Maureen pointed at the patio doors that opened to the family room. Through the glass, Ann could see the boys sitting on the couch, absorbed in whatever it was they were watching on the television. "There are so many children who need homes. I was thinking we could adopt a child from Nicaragua or Vietnam, but then again there are children just like Michael right here in our own backyard." She looked out at the rich green landscape and conveniently saw Michael bent over a pile of cedar chips. "Everything is so out of balance in this world. I mean, look at me, here in this huge house. Your family has really gotten me thinking about my own family, Ann. About how we can be better, do more."

We. That word sounded funny to Ann.

"Do you know," Maureen said, "that I sent a note to your mother and father telling them what lovely young people they are raising?"

Oh God, now she was sending notes to her parents?

"Your upbringing seems so simple. So good. I'm jealous of you Gordons, all of you. So wholesome, like a television family."

Ann thought of her dad's bong hidden in the linen closet, the way he swore like a sailor, her mother's stash of Valium, the way she felt when she'd barged into Michael's basement bedroom back home and caught a glimpse of him without his clothes on, and the secret, forbidden fantasies that moment had produced. "We're just like anyone."

"No, no. That's not true. I hope Toby and Brooks turn out to be half the young people you and Michael are. Tony thinks it's because you're from the Midwest."

She thought it was both shameful and exciting that there was so much that Maureen didn't know. The other day, while Maureen was out, she was cleaning up after the boys in the family room. When she looked up, she saw Anthony in the hallway, watching her. He was headed to the beach, and wore just his swim trunks and a towel around his neck. She stood up straight, blushed, and pulled her shirt down, because it had slid up while she was bent over to pick up the LEGOs. "You have great legs," he'd said.

"You're so dear," Maureen said.

Their conversation made Ann feel like she'd entered into the kind of fake friendship that she had with some of the girls at her high school. Maureen tucked her wild burnt hair behind her ears. It was hot and still. Her forehead and nose were beginning to glisten with sweat. She shook her head, as if to shake an unwelcome thought out of it. "You have such a nice family, which is why I feel so terrible asking you to spend more time away from them. But I'll be busy the next two weeks. Shhhh!" She put her finger to her lips and winked. "I'm taking an acting class in Provincetown, isn't that something? Please don't breathe a word about it to Tony. He thinks actors are kooks. Despite his flair for drama, he has zero appreciation for the stage. And next Saturday we have an oyster party to go to. Could you—"

"Sure," Ann said. She knew her parents would be upset if she missed out on another weekend with them. "You're more of a nanny than a babysitter with those hours," her father had said. "We don't haul ass halfway across the country so you can spend time with someone else's family." But with Anthony around, the Shaws' house was a lot less boring. His presence was as intimidating as it was enticing. Her memories of that afternoon in the bedroom were on autoloop and took on a fantasy life of their own.

TWELVE

Michael

Heat bore down on the Cape. It hadn't rained in weeks. The bluestone Jason ordered for Anthony's patio still hadn't come in. There was little for Michael to do in the Shaws' garden aside from watering. Mowing was pointless—dusty and dirty. He tried to stay busy. He snipped away the dead blooms, pulled some weeds, and waited for rain, tending to the garden the way a security guard might watch over a business that had closed for the night.

Jason told Michael he could go home, but he stuck around. Even without pay, it was nice at the Shaws' with Maureen out of the picture. Anthony was gone, too, in Los Angeles for business. Michael was temporarily free of worry that he'd drop in the way he did—unannounced, hovering at the edge of the yard, critical of every little thing.

With just Ann and Michael around, he felt like he and Ann were playing house, as if they were married. He imagined that the garden he tended was for them, and the Shaws' nerdy boys were *their* nerdy boys. Maureen had become so preoccupied with her acting classes that she hadn't made plans for them. Suddenly the boys were always underfoot, bored, seeking Michael's attention.

"I don't know what to do with them," Ann said.

"Let's take them to Mayo Beach."

"No," Ann said. "Anthony is worried they'll get stung by a jellyfish or cut their feet on the razor clams. He thinks Mayo is dirty."

"Dirty? It's the ocean. Why do they even bother to come here?"

"How about we go to the park across the street from the beach?"

The boys tied the laces on their perfectly white tennis shoes and followed Michael and Ann like ducklings to the playground. They played flag football and Frisbee with the boys and taught them how to improve their time in the forty-yard dash.

"Want to play horse?" Michael asked.

"What's that?"

"It's a basketball game." He tousled Brooks's hair. "Don't you poor little rich kids know how to do anything?"

They played horse for hours.

The heat persisted. They went back to the playground the next day and the next. The boys' awkwardness seemed to melt away. They started meeting other kids their age. Michael had Ann all to himself again.

ONE AFTERNOON THE BOYS were in a pickup game, darting around with the grace of ostriches. After an argument over a foul Brooks called, they started taking jabs at each other.

"Did I ever tell you my dad was a lightweight champ?" Michael said to Ann. They sat on the bench outside the court, watching.

"Just that he was a boxer."

"He traveled a lot for matches. He'd come around every few months and take me to the gym, or to watch his friends fight—but I never saw him compete. He'd never let me watch him get hit."

The wind blew off the water, filling the air with the pungent, salty smell of the bay. Seagulls came ashore and dipped down to pick up bits of fries and picnic food the tourists had left between the benches and the basketball court.

"I wanted to be just like my dad," Michael said. "He was cool. Real cool. He wore snakeskin shoes and he had a big cross on his neck, and he had two gold teeth replacing the ones that got knocked out in a fight. One year he gave me a punching bag for Christmas. I couldn't make it budge. I was like those boys, skinny and weak. My dad, he taught me how to land a right hook. It was like he was dancing and then pow! He'd hit the shit out of it. All I ever did was hit that thing. After he got hurt and my mom hooked up with Marcus, I got so good the sand came out of it. I hated that guy so much. I don't know what I would have done to him if it weren't for the bag."

Ann's sunglasses reflected the cloudless sky. "What was your mom like?"

As close as they were, Michael hadn't said much about his mom to Ann. It was painful for him to talk about her.

"She was tough. I saw her run after my dad with a knife once. One time she hit him in the kidney with the heel of her shoe so hard he had to go to the hospital."

Ann laughed.

"It was actually kind of funny to hear her scream, saying 'Oh no you don't, Macho Camacho!' She loved my dad. They had something. But they liked to party. They'd disappear for days, weeks, months at a time when I lived with my grandmother. When my parents were gone I'd sit at the window and wait for them all night. Only one time, it was just my mom who came back. She said my dad got hurt. She took me to see him in the hospital. He didn't move when I called his name. Didn't squeeze my hand back. He didn't even know I was there. I said his name over and over till I started screaming it. Nothing. He just drooled and stared at the wall.

"My mom cried all the time. She kept saying he'd come back, but he didn't. He went to a home. Then Marcus entered the picture."

Michael thought he could forget all about Marcus. He had a new family now. A new life. But Marcus was always there at the edge of his thoughts.

"Most of the time he didn't want me around, so he made me stay in my room. I had nothing to do in there but read books or draw. All weekend long I'd sit on my bed, staring at the door, waiting to get out." He stared off at the distance. "But you know what, it's because of Marcus that I like to garden."

"Why Marcus?" Michael didn't like hearing his name on Ann's lips.

"He started locking me outside in the backyard like I was a dog. I'd bang on the door and beg to be let in. Then I wised up and realized it was better out there, out of sight. Things change outside, you know? I studied the way the grass grew, dug up the roots of plants, put my fingers in the soil to see how much water was in it. I'd collect seeds from plants I found in the park and keep them in ziplock bags in my pockets. At school, I read books about edible plants and perennials and hybrid varieties. I started a whole garden. Hollyhocks, peonies. One day our neighbor, this old lady named Darlene, she gave me a bag of tomato seeds. The next week she left me a starter basil plant. Then sweet peas. She showed me how to plant them. My plants grew. My mom got into coke, heroin. Darlene bought me more stuff. Peppers, oregano, cucumbers. The more my garden grew, the worse my mom got. The garden was the only place I had any control. I thought—" He paused.

"What? What did you think?"

He looked down at his basketball shoes. "It's stupid, but I thought, with my garden, that Marcus would see that I was more than the worthless little shit he thought I was. That's how Anthony makes me feel. Like I want to work on his yard and do a good job because *he* thinks I'm a worthless little shit."

"He's nothing like Marcus," Ann said. "You don't have to prove anything to him."

"I feel like I do."

"Anthony's not so bad. He's nice, actually."

Michael couldn't stand to hear Ann standing up for that guy. Why couldn't she see what he saw? "He's not nice, Ann."

"He is! He tells me things. His dad was a coal miner. He said he gets bored."

"That doesn't make him a good guy. I don't like the way he looks at you." Michael couldn't even look at Ann when he said it. He knew what it was like to look at her that way. He knew. "Be careful."

"He's fine. He's just rough around the edges."

"He's rough all over."

"Don't take this the wrong way," she said, "but maybe you don't see him clearly. Because of Marcus."

"I see him clearly all right." He sat forward and did a few triceps dips on the bench. Ann joined him. Her arms were lean and strong. She had a cowlick where her hair parted. She was beautiful, he thought—so beautiful and perfect that looking at her twisted something deep inside him.

He felt overwhelmed with these strong feelings of wanting her, and wanting to protect her. He'd spent almost a year trying to snuff his feelings for Ann, trying not to look at her, think about her. *Sister,* he told himself. *She's my sister.* But at that moment, she was just Ann, and her face was right there, leaning closer to his. He couldn't help himself. He did the most natural thing in the world: he kissed Ann on the lips, or she kissed him, he couldn't tell who started it. He kissed her the way he'd always wanted to kiss her, and she kissed him back, she did. She tasted good and sweet. Perfect. This kiss felt like completion, like tying a knot. It felt like they were acknowledging a deep and boundless connection. He let his hand travel to the back of her neck. He'd wanted to touch that downy, golden hair and now, finally, he could. He wished that honest, perfect kiss could last forever.

But it didn't. Ann pushed Michael away and pulled back. "You love me." Her voice broke. "You love me, don't you?" It sounded less like a question than an accusation.

Michael looked at his basketball shoes. He wanted to say yes, but he said nothing.

Ann stood up and wiped the sweat off her forehead with the back of her hand. Just then Toby snuck up from behind Michael and giggled. "Gross! You kissed your sister. We saw you."

"You didn't see anything," Ann said.

Brooks said, "Yeah we did. Isn't that against the law? You can't kiss your brother."

Michael sprinted away, turning the corner by Captain Higgins, running as fast as he'd ever run.

THIRTEEN

Ann

Ann fell asleep on the Shaws' couch and slipped into a dream about Michael and that kiss. His lips were soft but insistent, his hand resting gently on her shoulder. She worked so hard to suppress her feelings for Michael and deny her attraction to him that it felt good to let go in her dreams, where she could indulge all of her pent-up emotions and guilty thoughts.

But then Michael started morphing into Anthony. His features became blunt, his scent musky. He was saying her name: *Ann, Ann.* She felt the grip grow tighter. It was Anthony's hand—had it also been his lips on hers, or had she dreamt it? *We're home. Wake up.* She opened her eyes and saw him leaning close to her, his hand still there, his face just inches from her own.

"You were out cold," he said. "I enjoyed watching you."

"Sorry," she said, wiping the drool off her cheek. She wondered if she'd fallen asleep with her mouth open—how stupid had she looked? "I can never make it past the music part of *Saturday Night Live.*"

"Did the boys behave?"

The boys, the boys . . . it was hard to focus. "They were fine."

"Now, that was a party!" Maureen said, pulling a big gold bangle off her wrist and tossing it on the kitchen island, where it dinged against the granite.

"A miserable one," Anthony said.

Ann didn't think Maureen looked like she'd had fun. She looked sad, worn out, with smudged mascara under her eyes and sweat marks in her shirt under her armpits. Anthony was clearly agitated, his face also grim. Ann could tell they'd been in an argument, and that the argument would have continued if she weren't there.

Maureen reached into her purse and jiggled her keys. "I need to get you home."

"I'll drive her," Anthony said, snatching the keys from her hands.

"I'm fine," Maureen said.

She didn't look fine to Ann. She was wilting in her espadrilles. It was hard for Ann to see Maureen like this. It made her feel guilty for fantasizing about Anthony, but wasn't it better than how she thought about Michael? Her brother? That was wrong, and dangerous, and look what it had already led to. Imagining an encounter with Anthony was fun and harmless. He was a grown man, married, a dad. She liked to imagine she was married to him—they'd drop the boys off with Maureen so *she* could be their babysitter, while Anthony took Ann to restaurants and ordered her wine and filet mignon and the waitstaff fawned all over them. In her fantasies Maureen was the competition—the wife who didn't understand her husband, who didn't meet his needs.

In reality, and at that moment, it seemed it was Maureen who was misunderstood.

"My wife needs some sleep," Anthony said to Ann without looking at her. "And some water and aspirin."

"I need *many* things," Maureen said. "Sleep is far down the list. A husband who cares about my personal aspirations? That would be right at the top."

Anthony walked into the kitchen and poured her a large glass of water.

He grabbed a bottle of aspirin off the shelf and shook a few into his meaty palm. "I do care. Here," he said. "Take this."

"Isn't he putting on a good show for you?" Maureen said to Ann, her words running together. "It's always a show."

"You know all about shows," he said. "This house, the parties, and now I find out you're a budding actress . . ."

Maureen winked at Ann. "I let it slip."

Anthony spoke in a low, frustrated grumble. "I work night and day so you can have this wonderful life, and now you're paying a sitter to go off to—"

"Ha!" Maureen said. "You *married* into this wonderful life, Tony. This wonderful life was *my* wonderful life. My father gave you your job."

Ann didn't want to be in the middle of their argument. Her parents hardly ever fought. "I should get going," she said.

Maureen pushed her hair behind her ears and straightened her dress. "Good night, my dear. I'm sorry you saw me like this. You come from such a sweet family, I'll bet your parents never fight."

"We're normal."

Maureen smiled a crooked smile and touched the side of Ann's face with her skinny hand. "Normal. Listen to you. Don't you know that 'normal' is so lovely and so sweet?" She wobbled backward. "We're so lucky we found you. You've saved our summer. You and dear Michael." Maureen's expression changed, like she'd just remembered something. "I've been meaning to talk to you about that. Brooks said he saw something peculiar. You and Mich—"

"Brooks loves to make up stories," Ann said.

Anthony put his arm across Maureen's shoulders and tried to lead her to their bedroom. He was so wide and strong and solid, while she was tall and thin. "You need to sleep." He led her down the hallway and she tipped, knocking a framed photo collage of the boys off kilter. Anthony looked over his shoulder at Ann. "Back in a moment," he said.

"I'll wait outside."

Ann felt the shock of leaving the air-conditioned house. Outside was dark, the heat as pressing as it was in the middle of the day only it seemed even hotter now with the humidity. The moisture held the smell of the ocean in the air.

The security lights by the garage lit up as she walked past, revealing a furious cloud of gnats. She walked into the yard, unaware that Michael had set up a timer on the sprinkler by the garden to go off at night. It startled her when it turned on and the water shot out, sounding like a pack of hissing snakes. She screamed in surprise and ran to the paved driveway as fast as she could.

"Cooling off?" Anthony said. He had seen the whole scene from the deck. His eyes settled on the damp shirt clinging to her chest. The eerie outdoor light sharpened his already-sharp features.

She looked down. She could see the tiny heart print of her bra through the fabric.

"I was going to suggest another way to cool down."

"What do you mean?"

"You'll see." He pointed at the green Jeep that sat in the driveway. "My wife won't ride in it because it's too rough, but you won't mind a rough ride, will you?" His question wasn't a question.

"A ride in the Jeep sounds fun," Ann said.

He was clearly pleased. "Oh, Ann. You are so uncorrupted, so fresh. I love spending time with you." He ran his hand down her arm. "After the night I had with Mo's sorority sisters from Smith and their boring husbands, you're just what I need."

Ann smiled. It took so little to please him. She just needed to be who she was. He walked over to the passenger side and put his hand over her hip to help her step in. "Up you go." He let his hand linger even after she was seated. She liked the warmth, and that electric tingle that shot through her.

When he got into the driver's seat, Ann said, as if to absolve herself of all her forbidden daydreams, "Is Maureen OK?"

"You're kind to be concerned."

"She seemed tired."

"She can't hold her liquor. She's not a hearty Midwesterner like you. I'll bet you can hold your own." Anthony sat next to her in the driver's seat and stared at the windshield. He didn't put the keys in the ignition right away.

Ann decided to take advantage of the pause and the silence. "Are you happy with her?" She felt emboldened by the warmth she could still feel from his hand, and their previous closeness.

He didn't seem to mind the bluntness of her question. If anything, he seemed to appreciate her directness, her willingness to take him on. "What does it mean to be happy with another person?"

"My parents are happy with each other." She regretted mentioning her parents. She thought this made her sound like a little kid. But they *were* happy together, she knew it.

He turned the key in the ignition and the Jeep roared to life. "Good for them." Anthony's voice changed. "I mean really, good for them. That's great. Marriage can be a tricky business."

He drove through downtown Wellfleet. During the day, the town was bustling with tourists buying ice cream, visiting galleries, and shopping in the little stores that lined the main street, buying their Wellfleet sweatshirts at Abiyoyo. This late, it settled back into a limp quiet. The flag sagged from the flagpole in front of the town hall. Next to it sat the cannon, immortalized with a plaque and surrounded by stones. "You know that cannon?" Ann said. "It was dug out of our neighbors' yard." She loved their neighbors, a nice couple who kept busy entertaining their grandchildren.

"Is that so?" Anthony's smile was distracted, insincere. This disappointed Ann. Nervous, she told him the story about a rivalry that once existed between Wellfleet and South Wellfleet, and how they'd had their own cannons that they shot from their respective hills on the Fourth of July. One of the cannons was destroyed when, as a prank, some locals filled it with wet sand. After that, the young men used to steal the remaining cannon and shoot it off wherever it ended up. This went on for years, until the final cannon disappeared. Nobody knew what had happened to it until 1976, when it was unearthed. "There's supposedly a curse on it," she'd said.

"Hmmm . . ." Anthony said, disinterested. He turned onto Route 6 and picked up speed. They passed all the landmarks she knew so well: the Stop & Shop, Brownies Cabins, J.P.'s, the yarn and quilting store on the hill, and the water tower. Before that night she knew this strip of highway the way a kid would, from looking at it from the backseat of a car, watching it go by in a blur. Now, sitting close to Anthony with the warm breeze rushing over her, everything looked different.

Anthony reached over and yanked the ponytail holder out of her hair and left his hand on the back of her neck on the same spot where Michael had put his hand just before she'd pulled away. He said, "That's more like it. The whole point of a Jeep ride is to get your hair messed up." All this attention from forbidden men! Between Michael and Anthony, Ann felt desirable in a way she'd never felt before. It was intoxicating, as if she were at the center of the world.

Anthony took a left turn just past the red Citgo sign onto Old County Road South.

"But I live—" She pointed farther down Route 6, toward the General Store, the post office, and the apothecary.

"I told you I was taking you on a little adventure."

Ann couldn't have been more pleased. Time with Anthony all to herself? As far as she was concerned, the evening could go on forever.

Old King's Highway was winding and hilly. Anthony took the curves so fast she had to hold on to the dash to keep from being thrown out of the side of the doorless car. When he descended a hill she felt the sensation of an elevator dropping down the shaft.

Just past the sleeping RVs and tents in Paine's Campground, he switched off his lights, slowed down, and turned onto the unmarked dirt road. Ann was surprised Anthony knew about Duck Pond, a pristine kettle pond tucked into the National Seashore property. The pond was technically public but there were no signs—the locals made sure of that, removing them as quickly as the town could put them up. To get there meant following a bumpy dirt road for almost a mile, and crossing the sandy telegraph road before heading back into the woods.

Anthony expertly maneuvered over the potholes in the compacted sand. "I love it back here," he said.

"Me too. We come here all the time."

"See, that's your life, and that's beautiful. Me, I've got two lives. A Jaguar life and a Jeep life. A Chequessett Neck Road life and a dirt road life. Don't get me wrong, the Jaguar life is nothing to complain about, but this? This is real. You make me feel real, Ann."

Michael was wrong about Anthony, she thought. Here he was, opening himself up to her, revealing how conflicted he felt. He was mysterious. Interesting. Torn. And he thought enough of Ann to share those thoughts with her.

He accelerated into a dip in the road. He smiled at her. "That's how I feel when I look at you." He reached across her for the glove compartment.

He pulled out a silver flask and set it on her bare thigh, just below the tattered hem of her jean shorts. He let his hand rest on the seat next to her, his fingertips grazing her skin, setting something off, a feeling so warm and overwhelmingly good and big that she thought she could die from it. Ann loved not knowing what would come next, loved that Anthony was in control, loved the heat and the way her body felt, lean and alive, loved that he didn't think of her as a kid but as someone worthy of sharing thoughts with about his marriage and his two lives. His marriage. Maureen!

"I should probably go home," she said.

"I'll take you, don't worry. First just have some fun. You've been working all summer. You deserve some fun, don't you?"

She took a gulp.

"Go ahead. Have another. Enjoy it. The scotch is casked. Only two hundred and forty bottles, twenty-five years old. The good stuff. I grew up drinking moonshine. Life's too short to get drunk on cheap whiskey."

Anthony drove over another bump. Half the contents went into her mouth, while the rest spilled down her chin and all over her already-damp shirt. The alcohol burned her throat and shot up her sinuses. She coughed.

Anthony laughed. It was the first time she'd heard him laugh. She liked the mellow sound of his voice, and the way his eye squinted at the corner. The moonlight picked up the stray silver hairs in his beard. He seemed so grown-up. So manly.

"That's about thirty bucks' worth you just spilled all over yourself."

"Sorry," she said again, still coughing.

"You may as well finish it off." She did. The liquid landed like a burning torch in her gut.

He stopped the Jeep. "Now, how am I going to take you home to your parents smelling like a distillery?"

Ann didn't want to think about her parents, didn't want him to mention them. She wanted to keep Anthony and her parents separate.

"It's a perfect night to look at the moonlight on the water with a beautiful young woman. Let's walk down to the pond."

Ann pulled off her sandals and tucked them under her seat. She always left her sandals in the car when she came here with her family.

The path was sandy, the only danger the tree roots.

He led the way down the long, sandy footpath. His shoulders were broad, his calves firm. There was a butterfly-shaped sweat stain showing through the back of his linen shirt.

It was impossibly strange for her to be in this place with Anthony. Because the pond was walking distance from their house, she'd been there a thousand times, mostly with Poppy. It was their favorite escape when their parents were napping or bird-watching and didn't want to drive them anywhere. This is where they collected pinecones and ate the wild blueberries and beach plums. She and Poppy looked for tadpoles in the shallows and chased the sounds of the giant bullfrogs. If a childhood could be defined by a place, this was where Ann's resided.

When they got to the small beach she looked around to see if any campers from the campsite were there, or a hobo, or an insomniac. The shoreline was miraculously empty. There was no wind. The water was as still as a Jell-O mold. Warm yellow lights lit up the windows in the single house on the far shore, like a pair of eyes watching them. That was Ann's favorite house in the world. She'd always envied the people who owned it. When she and Poppy swam across the pond (it was their ritual to swim across all the Wellfleet ponds each visit, yet this strange summer they'd only made it across Gull and Great Pond), they felt funny getting close to the property. They'd squeal when they touched their wooden raft, and sprint back to the opposite, public shore, feeling as if they'd invaded a foreign territory. The house, tucked into the National Seashore, seemed to have dropped out of the sky. Ann and Poppy had tried without success to find the driveway on the fire roads. She wondered if it was even real, or part of a dream.

Anthony led Ann away from the public beach, walking barefoot through the crystal-clear water to a smaller beach tucked behind scrub pine and oak trees on an inlet a few hundred feet away. He reached down and splashed some on his face. "God, this feels good on a hot night," he said. "I sweated all through that miserable dinner."

He seemed more relaxed than she'd ever seen him. She noticed little things about him: the way his hair curled behind his ears in the humidity, the droplets of water that got stuck in his beard, that the skin on his face seemed soft while the rest of him was so solid and hard.

"The water is perfect." He splashed her and smiled a mischievous smile. She could imagine him as a naughty little boy, full of sneakiness and tricks.

She smiled back and took a step into the water, then another. "Did you know there's a tile medallion of a mermaid somewhere on the bottom of this pond? My parents said that people from the campground set it on the bottom. My sister and I, we try to find it every time we come here. Poppy swears she's seen it, but I don't believe her."

"What about you? Have you seen it?"

"I feel like I have. Like I can picture it in my mind's eye."

"You can only see it on magic nights like this, in the moonlight. Someone put a spell on it, just for people like us, a couple of fools who still want to believe." Anthony walked closer to her. "Can I kiss you, Ann? Just once, before summer is over?"

Once sounded safe. Fun. Interesting. Just enough. And she'd wanted him to kiss her all summer even though—no. She tried to convince herself that nothing else was real but that moment. "Sure, I guess."

He grabbed her chin between his thumb and forefinger and tilted her head up. He wasn't much taller than she was. He leaned forward and she felt a strange tickle from the softness of his beard, followed by his lips pressing against hers. She thought of Michael, the perfection of that kiss, how it had sounded like an accusation when she asked if he loved her, when she meant it as a question. If she hadn't been so surprised, and if he hadn't run away, she might have told him that she loved him, too. Why was she thinking about Michael when Anthony's tongue darted into her mouth, thrusting and urgent—too much. She pulled away.

"You have no goddamn idea how beautiful you are." He shook his head and started unbuttoning his shirt. "You're ripe."

Ann soaked up his flattery, every word, even though she'd always known she was pretty. The boys at school asked her out, but they were just boys. She'd fool around with them sometimes when she was drunk. She was curious about sex, but she never went too far.

Anthony began to unbutton his shirt. "Swim with me."

"I don't have a suit."

He shrugged. "You have the one you were born in. Besides, you're already soaked."

Ann laughed for no reason. She was nervous, and at the nervous edge of desire.

Anthony stripped his shirt off. His chest was covered in a mat of thick, black hair. His body wasn't perfect the way she'd imagined it would be. He looked older without his shirt on, more like a middle-aged dad. Even in the dark she could see the dim outline of the farmer's tan on his thick forearms. His stomach bulged a little over the waist of his shorts.

He smiled as though he was proud of what he had to show her, proud to be in this situation in the first place. He threw his shirt on the sandy area next to a tree a few feet away. Then he unbuckled his belt, his eyes trained on her. She could have sworn that the metallic ripping sound his zipper made when he unzipped it could be heard for miles around, as loud as an airplane crossing in the sky.

"Well," he said. "I guess it's my turn to be looked at."

Ann felt suddenly shy, unable to bring herself to watch him continue to undress. It was strange, how her desire could come and go so quickly. She looked at the water gently lapping the shoreline behind him and thought about home. Were her parents starting to wonder where she was? Did Poppy go out with her new friends again? Her mother had complained she'd hardly seen either of her girls.

"You know, I've often thought about that afternoon in our bedroom." The word "our" unsettled Ann, the way it invoked Maureen. She'd been trying hard not to think about her. "That was so damn erotic. I'd had such a hard day at work and there you were, it was like finding the mermaid medallion. The last thing I expected. Glorious."

Ann could feel the whiskey kicking in, dulling her nerves. Her thoughts were starting to bump into each other. She tried hard to be clearheaded.

"Besides, you need to rinse the smell of whiskey off your clothes before I take you home," he said. "Come on."

"But then I'll have to explain why my clothes are wet."

"They were wet when you walked into the sprinklers. What do you think your parents are going to do, hire a detective? I can't take you home to your father smelling like whiskey."

Her father. She could just picture him on a public beach right next to where she stood, reading the mystery novels he only read on vacation, his floppy hat on his head, one hairy leg crossed over the other, his Birkenstock hanging off his callused foot.

"Let's find that medallion," Anthony said. He dashed into the water. She saw his bare ass in the moonlight. It was round but muscular, a shocking flash of vulnerable white.

Alone on the beach, Ann drunkenly weighed what to do next. She wanted to swim. She loved swimming more than anything, even running, and it was still so hot. She decided that Anthony was right about needing to get the smell out of her clothes. She took off her shirt and dragged it around in the water, then hung it on a branch to dry. She saw Anthony's head about twenty feet away, far enough to feel he couldn't see her too clearly. The alcohol mellowed her nerves, and so did his admiration. She liked being watched.

Why not? She slipped off her shorts and rinsed them off, too. When she turned to look for Anthony she saw that he was gone, already half-way across the pond. When Anthony's head slipped back under the liquid black water, she took off her underwear and ran in, completely naked.

Never had the cool liquid thickness of the kettle pond felt so erotic, like she was swimming through silk scarves. The heat and her nakedness made the water seem thicker, like it embraced her. She went deep and felt the temperature grow colder, then warmer again as she surfaced. Her hair fanned out around her shoulders.

Anthony quickened his crawl and swam toward her. He was a strong swimmer. When he got close enough he went underwater and circled her. She knew his eyes were open. She could feel him watching, the water clean and clear in the moonlight.

He surfaced and moaned. "Good Lord. You're naked. Oh, Ann. You have no idea what you're doing to me."

Anthony put his arms around her from behind. His hands were on her breasts. She could feel his beard in the crook of her neck and the soft hair of his chest on her back. The water wasn't deep. She leaned against him and put her feet down, shocked and grateful for the solidity of his body and the earth. Ann was turned on, but she was also scared and struck by the wrongness of what she was doing, a wrongness that was dulled by the alcohol. Was this even real?

She knew it was when he moved one hand down to her crotch and rubbed it with his fingers, slowly, deftly. Ann could tell this was a part of a woman's body he knew well. Desire began to erode her fear. This was natural, right? It was what people did all the time. Half of her friends had already lost their virginity, and they lost it to dorks who didn't know what they were doing. Anthony was a man. He had children. She was almost eighteen, after all. She was old enough.

She turned around and slid against him, pressing her mouth against his, delighting in the sensation of his soft whiskers against her face. Then his tongue darted into her mouth again. He tasted like garlic and wine, while Michael's kiss—why was she thinking about Michael? He'd tasted sweet and fresh.

She ran her fingers through his hair, because that's what lovers did in the movies. His hair looked like it would be coarse but it was wonderfully soft. She thought this was a show of tenderness, but she hardly knew him. He pulled her hand away—was she doing something wrong?—and moved it to his penis, thick and hard. She held it and marveled at how solid it was. It turned her on to feel him, but what was she supposed to do? She just held it the way she might hold a softball bat while waiting for the pitcher to toss the ball.

"Like this," he said, and he put his hand over hers. Then he moaned. The sound was so animalistic, so loud, it broke her out of her spell. She looked at the beach to be sure nobody was there, but then again, she wished someone would show up. She wasn't turned on anymore. She felt sick, sick! How could she do this in the pond her parents took her to? She imagined Maureen standing on the shore in her pink dress, her hands on her hips, watching . . .

He grabbed her by the hand and led her to the private nook where their clothes waited. The sight of her shirt hanging in the tree made her want to put it on. The air felt cold against her damp skin. Her legs shook. She looked around in the trees hoping someone would show up and interrupt them, give them a reason to flee.

She stopped, suddenly sober and scared. "I need to go home."

Home, home. She'd never wanted to be home so badly, never even understood what home meant to her until that moment.

"No, this is where it's at." He picked her up like she weighed less than a sack of flour and set her down on the sand. It felt cold, hard and damp. He knelt over her and stared at her breasts. He dragged his fingertip down her breastbone, down her hard stomach, and let his hand rest over the soft patch of pubic hair. She had so much she wanted to say but she didn't have the words. "We can't go. It would be like waking up from the best dream ever."

"But you're—" He put his hand over her mouth. "I'm—"

He hovered over her with his elbows next to her ears, pinning her down. She could feel the damp warmness of his skin, smell his musk. He reached between her legs and with two fingers he made a part. His finger dashed inside. "Oh Jesus, you're dripping. See? You want this."

"I didn't mean to lead you on. I'm sorry. Please. Maureen wouldn't want us to—"

"Shhh, don't worry about her. We haven't touched each other in months."

"But I don't want this." She thought of what she'd learned in health class. They made it seem easy to make good choices, easy to say no, like declining the green beans when they are passed to you at the dinner table. Her gym teacher never told her about situations like this. His rubbing became more insistent. "No. Please, stop." She tried to twist away from him, but he was stronger than she was. She should have listened to Michael when he'd warned her about him.

"Why are you acting this way? Don't deny yourself pleasure."

"I don't want it. Let's go, can we—"

He put his hand over her mouth. "Don't ruin this." She bit his fingers. "Stop!"

But it was too late. He pushed himself inside her, so far inside she ceased to exist. She was nothing but that deep feeling of hurt. She cried out in pain but he was oblivious to her discomfort. She swore she was being split apart. He pressed her shoulders down with his hands so she was pinned to the beach.

"Stop! Don't."

"Oh, good Lord. Oh man. I . . . can't."

His lips covered hers and his tongue, like a giant sock, filled her mouth. Tears dripped down the side of her face. His movement became more hurried and urgent until suddenly he let her loose and shuddered.

The entire weight of his body came to rest on top of hers. He was heavy, hot, suffocating. She could see beads of sweat on his back. He rolled off to the side and ran his hand over her hip, a gesture that would have seemed erotic a few minutes ago but now she thought he did it to show that he owned her. She'd seen him touch things around the house like that, like he couldn't believe his good fortune.

"You shouldn't have done that." She was surprised to hear her own voice.

"Your skin is like velvet."

"I asked you to stop," she whispered.

"Oh come on, you wanted it too."

"No."

"This is disappointing. I didn't take you for a tease, Ann. Do you tease that 'brother' of yours the same way you tease me?"

A tease? That brother? She was drunk and sober at the same time, trying to untangle his words from what just went on between them, trying to figure out what she was supposed to think and do, trying not to feel the burning of residual heat, the grit of sand and ache of pain in her crotch, the guilt for being so stupid, for getting in over her head, for betraying Maureen, for betraying Michael.

She thought that when she finally had sex it would open up something, reveal a new world; it did, but she didn't like this new world she was in. She felt dirty and guilty. Sad in a way she'd never before been sad.

"I was a virgin."

"Oh, come on."

Anthony stood up and went back into the pond to rinse off. When he got out, he shook his head like a dog to get the water out of his thick hair. She could see red dots like zits on his ass and a giant mole on his back. She rolled herself into a ball and stared at the roots of the oak tree that stuck up above the soil, wishing Anthony would just go away, and that she could rewind the evening, do everything differently.

"You gave me every reason to believe you wanted the same thing I did. It was fun. It was *hot*."

"I didn't want that."

"Really? I didn't undress you." His tone was warmer. "You kissed me back. Gave me all the signals. That's what I'll say if anyone asks."

Ann thought about other people finding out what had just gone on. No, no. She'd never tell anyone. She couldn't.

"You shouldn't have done that."

"You're a piece of work, you know that? You don't know what you want."

He was right; she was. She didn't. She dressed in silence, her fingers shaking, a cry or a scream pounding wordlessly inside her.

"Let's go," he said. He sounded irritated. This was the impatient voice she'd heard him use with the boys. Just fifteen minutes ago, she'd felt herself a woman. Now she was a child again.

She took one last look at the pond and saw that house, the lights off now, dark. She knew it wasn't just her virginity she'd lost; the pond would never be the same place for her ever again. She felt like a part of her drowned in that pond.

He led her back to the beach and up the long, sandy path to the parking lot. It was all a blur through her teary eyes. When she walked this trail with her dad he always walked behind her to make sure her footing was safe with all the tree roots and loose branches. Anthony didn't care that she could trip and that her legs were shaking—her whole body shook. She'd felt this way after her friend's car had been rear-ended at a stoplight and Ann was the passenger. At first, she was fine. Then she shook and shook.

Anthony walked ahead, twirling the key ring to the Jeep around his finger.

He turned on the engine and looked straight ahead at the forest of pine trees. Ann expected him to back up right away, because he was always moving from one thing to the next. Instead he put his hand over hers. "Let's forget this ever happened."

She yanked her hand away. She was sore and tingling and damp and filled with confusion. Forget it ever happened? Easy for him to say. *He* could forget. She would never forget this.

Anthony returned his hand to the wheel and threw the Jeep into reverse. She thought she might throw up with every bump on the long dirt road. When he got to her house, he didn't drive up the driveway but stopped right on Route 6. "Good night." He looked straight ahead.

She wanted to get out of the car and get away from him, but her body had grown stiff. She couldn't move.

"Look, you say one thing and do another. How am I supposed to know what you want?"

She stepped one foot out of the Jeep, but before she got out, he set his hand on her shoulder and squeezed it—hard.

"Don't you dare mention this. I mean it. Not to your sister, not that kid Michael, not your best friend, not your parents. Nobody."

These were so many words, like mosquitoes swarming in her ears. She didn't want to hear his voice anymore, didn't care what he had to say.

"You can do that, right? Keep a secret?"

Ann didn't say anything.

"Because if you tell anyone about this, I'll deny it. Life is simple for you. But it's not simple for me. You saw that tonight. One word about this and you have no idea what kind of shit will rain down on you. Besides, just think of what people would say if they knew you seduced me."

"*I* seduced *you*?"

He tapped his wedding ring against the steering wheel with every word. "We wouldn't want to hurt Maureen. You saw how unstable she is. Her problems are deeper than you know. If she heard about this, it would push her over the edge. You wouldn't want to do that, would you?"

She couldn't even think about Maureen.

Anthony opened the wallet he'd left on the dash and pulled out some hundred-dollar bills. "Here." He pushed the bills under her nose. "Consider it severance. We won't need your services anymore."

"I wouldn't ever come back anyway."

"Take it. Do whatever the fuck you want with it."

"I don't want your money."

"I know how you work. You say you don't want what you want. Everyone wants money."

"No."

"Take it."

"No!" The emotion she felt was outsized for her body. "I'm not a . . . a prostitute." She moved to step out.

"Remember." His voice was low, menacing. "Not one single word. You have no idea what I'm capable of, what I could do to you and your family. Where I come from, we take care of business the old-fashioned way. Understand?"

"You're such an asshole."

"Just take it." He thrust the money at her again.

"You think paying me will make you feel better? I told you, I don't want your damn money."

"You're fucked up."

"*I'm* fucked up? I'm your kids' babysitter."

She jumped down from the Jeep and fell by the road. She saw him throw the bills out of the window and speed away on Route 6. She thought about picking up the money, but no: that money was dirty.

She ran toward the house. Through the window she could see the unfinished jigsaw puzzle her parents had been working on all summer. She couldn't go in there, not with a wad of underwear in her pocket and her face blotchy from tears. She walked past the barn, past the hammock that hung between the two big spruce pines, and went down the path to the cove, lit by the blue light of the moon. She wished she could walk out into the quicksand and disappear. It was low tide. She could.

Instead, she turned around and looked back at the old house. There was light coming from Michael's room in the attic. He was probably reading in order to impress her mother, who took him to the Wellfleet library twice a week and forced all the books on him that she thought would complete his childhood, the same books Poppy and Ann had read years ago—old Edward Eager books like *Half Magic* and *Magic by the Lake;* the Chronicles of Narnia, *A Wrinkle in Time, The Prophet.*

She walked inside. The living room was quiet and still. She could hear the whirring of old metal fans in the bedrooms, fans that were so loud they allowed her to arrive home without waking up her parents. She stood there for a minute, staring at the grooves her parents' bodies had worn into the couch, the age spots on the mirror on the wall by the porch, the ancient needlepoint pillow on the rocking chair. It was a space she knew so well, but now the house seemed small to her, different, the same way her body felt different.

The door to the bedroom she shared with Poppy was open. Poppy wasn't home, and it was late. Where was she? Ann desperately wanted Poppy to be there. She missed the way they used to play go fish and war, missed fighting with her about things that didn't matter, missed looking through magazines together and talking with her about their futures— the jobs they'd have, the perfect men they'd marry, the children they'd name Austen, Reed, Rowan, Emily, Nicole. She wanted to confide in Poppy, but even if she'd been home, Ann wasn't sure she would have been able to tell her about what had happened with Anthony. For the first time in her life, she had a secret that was too big to share.

She couldn't stand the smell of Anthony on her skin, the taste of his tongue lingering in her mouth. She went to the outdoor shower and made herself vomit. She brushed her teeth and soaped herself, then stood under the stream of water until the heat ran out. She wrapped herself in a towel, still feeling dirty from what she couldn't wash away. She thought about going back into her bedroom, but she couldn't stand the idea of being alone. There were two stairwells to the attic, one by the living room and another on the front side of the house behind the big fireplace. If she went up the steps by the fireplace her parents wouldn't hear, so she lifted the metal thumb latch and crept up the narrow stairs.

Michael was surprised to see her. He sat up in his bed, his chest bare and hairless the way a young man's chest should be. It was nothing like Anthony's.

"Ann? What are you doing up here?"

"Can I just lie with you?"

"No way. Your parents."

"I don't want to be alone. Please, Michael? You're the only person I want to see right now. You don't know how much you mean to me."

He scooted over to one side of his twin bed. She rolled in next to him, grateful he was there. Maybe this was why she pushed so hard for her parents to adopt him; she knew she'd need him. He put his hand on her bare shoulder and she pulled away.

"You OK? What happened?"

"Can we not talk?" She turned out the light so he wouldn't see her weep.

"Is this about the other day? I shouldn't have kissed you."

"Just shut up. Please?"

"It isn't a good idea for you to be up here."

"I don't care."

Ann closed her eyes and listened to Michael's steady breathing. She longed to go back to a place that no longer existed, to a feeling she could never capture again.

A FEW HOURS LATER SHE WOKE to the sound of the door slamming and Poppy laughing maniacally. "Two hundred dollars! I found two hundred dollars cash right at the base of our driveway! Kurt Cobain left it for me. He's alive, you know. He's in Wellfleet!"

"Poppy," Ann's mom said, "you're high. What are you on?"

"I'm on life! Check it out, Mama! Two hundred bucks! I mean, it was just right there. The walls, the walls. Can you see them move? Did you know they did that? They're talking."

"Where were you? Who were you with? Where's your sister?"

The next thing Ann heard was her dad's feet clomping up the narrow attic steps. "Michael, have you seen Ann? I don't think she came home and Poppy's—"

Her father stood at the foot of Michael's bed looking at Ann's bare shoulder peeking out from under the sheet.

"No."

"It's not how it looks," Michael said, sitting up abruptly.

"No!" Ann's father bent over and held his stomach. "What happened?" he asked, his pain visible. "First Poppy, now this. What the hell happened to my family this summer?"

Her mother limped up the stairs and stood behind him, her hair wild from sleep. Ann wanted so badly to collapse into her mother's arms at that moment.

"Oh, Ann," she said. Ann was used to hearing the disappointment in her mother's voice directed at her. Usually she could deflect it, because it was because of something minor. This time it hurt. This time she wanted to push back and tell her mother that she was good. She was. Or at least, she used to be.

"Pack your stuff," her father said.

"I didn't do anything, I swear," Michael said.

"Pack your stuff! All of you!"

Ann saw panic in Michael's eyes, and she felt sorry for him in a way she hadn't before. He'd wanted so badly to fit into her family. This was all her fault.

"He's telling the truth, Dad."

"I don't want to know what happened. All I know is we're going back home."

"Milwaukee?" Michael said, confused and shocked.

"Good," Ann said. "I want to go home. I never want to come back to this place again."

FOURTEEN

Ann

In October, Ann was painting the homecoming window on a restaurant called Shahrazad on Oakland Avenue for the cross-country team. Their mascot was a tiger, and they were competing against the Whitefish Bay Blue Dukes. Ann was painting their tagline. It said, "It's a bad day to be a Duke." That was Nell Finch's idea, and it was OK, but not great. Usually Ann would come up with something better, but she'd been distracted. David Simons, her homecoming date, was painting a crown on the tiger's head. Keisha Brown drew the duke. She was a great artist, and had depicted a wimpy little duke standing in the middle of the field, looking terrified. "Do you like it?" she asked Ann and David. All Ann could do was nod. She was suddenly overcome with nausea and threw up right there, right in front of them. It splattered on David's Adidas.

"Oh gross," he said, while Keisha rubbed her back and pulled back her hair.

"You OK?"

"I drank too much at Evan's last night," Ann said, but that was a lie. She hadn't even gone to Evan's party. She'd been too tired. All she wanted to do lately was sleep. She wondered if she had mono.

But the next week, she threw up again when she ate one of the candy corns that Mrs. Brennan, her guidance counselor, kept in a bowl on her desk. They were talking about her college applications and SAT scores, and what a good shot Mrs. Brennan thought Ann had at getting into a good East Coast school, but Ann was calculating the best route to the bathroom, so overtaken with nausea she couldn't focus.

She tried to convince herself she wasn't pregnant. She went to the bathroom so often to see if she was bleeding that her classmates began to notice. She prayed she'd find blood in her underwear—God, she never thought she'd want a period this badly. She looked back through calendars and counted backward to that awful night. She couldn't remember when she'd last used a tampon.

She'd thought about taking a test but put it off. It was just one time, the first time. What were the odds? Homecoming was next week. She couldn't be pregnant on homecoming court—this sort of thing couldn't happen to school royalty. It happened to other people.

NOT UNTIL AFTER THANKSGIVING did Ann finally muster the nerve to go to the Planned Parenthood next to Shank Hall, the place where she'd heard that the girls from her high school got their birth control and had their abortions, and where the glassy-eyed protesters held up giant signs of bloody fetuses. She filled out paperwork, peed in a cup, read brochures asking "Is a seed a tree?," and looked around at the other girls in the waiting room. Were they also pregnant? Why did they all seem so calm?

The counselor confirmed her suspicion. "You're pretty far along," she said. "We need to perform an ultrasound to confirm the dates."

Was she too far along for an abortion? Ann thought about her alternatives: Drinking bleach. Throwing herself down the stairs.

He put some cold jelly on her stomach, and there, on the black-and-white television screen, she saw it: a baby, not just the idea of a baby but a real, perfect little child. It seemed so alone inside her there, so vulnerable. So alive.

The pregnancy reminded her of something Michael had taught her about gardening: that if you want a ripe tomato early in the season you can slam a shovel into the roots and throw the plant into a shock, enough shock to produce fruit before the plant would otherwise be ready.

Shock was what she suffered from after that afternoon appointment. It made her blurry and distracted, unable to focus on school, much less her plans moving forward. She didn't know how to process it all: the idea of this life inside her, and the end of the future she'd planned for herself. College out East. A great job. The kids at school would take gossipy delight in her situation. Now *she* was that girl: the one who got knocked up, the one who got in trouble. She was stupid and careless. She'd blown up her own bright future as if she'd dropped a hand grenade at her feet.

But that baby! That perfect baby. It was floating inside her, innocent. *Her* child, not Anthony's. He'd already taken too much from her. This baby would never be his. She'd never think of it as the product of that awful night on Duck Pond. She'd think of it as fate.

She started to resign herself to her new situation. *Not* knowing was hard. Now that she knew, she felt strangely focused. Ann always preferred certainty over ambiguity. She was amazed to discover that she was capable of tapping into a deep inner calm.

Somewhere in all the fear and ambivalence, she realized that she could do this. It would suck. It would be hard. It would throw off all the plans she'd made for herself, but she would be fine.

She knew it.

What she wasn't so sure about was Anthony.

She couldn't tell him. His threats, his voice, his clammy skin, the smell of whiskey on his breath, the way he moaned, the fiery pain between her legs, how she'd tried to bite through his fingers . . .

And yet. As wrong as Anthony was to do what he did, she felt that telling him was the right thing to do. Strange as it might sound, she also wanted to talk to an adult, someone who could see their way through the situation. Why would she think Anthony could offer her any kind of assurance? Mostly, she knew she'd need him to help pay to raise the child. She didn't make much money at Lisa's Pizza. Her parents would help. They'd be disappointed, but she knew they'd be cool about it. Well, eventually.

She still had the Shaws' "backup" number at their house in Marblehead. Maureen had given it to her in case of an emergency. If only Maureen had known the full range of emergencies Ann might experience! She called a few times, using the star-key combination to suppress her number, and Maureen answered the phone in her singsong voice. Ann hung up.

Finally, the next day, Anthony answered with his usual distracted gruffness. "Hello?" His voice set something off in her; her body flushed with adrenaline the way it did when her car hit black ice last winter, and for a few seconds—seconds that might as well have stretched into days—she thought for sure she'd end up in a ditch.

"It's Ann." Her hand shook as she held the receiver.

He paused, as if he had to mentally scroll through all the possible women named Ann who might call him. "Ann," he said. "Ann, Ann. How's Wisconsin?"

What a stupid question. "I'm pregnant." It was the first time she'd said those words out loud to another person. They sounded leaded. Permanent.

She could hear him breathing into the phone, saying nothing. His breath—she remembered the sound of it in her ear, heavy and wet. That night she'd tried so hard to forget might as well have been happening all over again.

"Are you waiting for me to congratulate you? It's not mine," he said. "If that's what you're getting at."

"It could only be yours."

"I don't have time for this."

"You don't have time? I told you I was a virgin. You are the only person I've—who's—the only one. Believe me, if I thought it was someone else's kid I wouldn't contact you."

"Oh, come on. You were no virgin." His voice lowered to a whisper. "Besides, I had a vasectomy."

"That's a lie!" Ann wished she could kick him. She'd never felt such rage. "You are lying, but I don't care. I know I can prove it."

Was Maureen within hearing distance? The thought made Ann feel sick.

"What do you want?"

What did she want? She wanted to feel less alone, less scared. For Anthony to be the man she thought he was when she first met him. To go back in time and burn that babysitting ad she'd posted on the bulletin board. She was so low at that moment that she even wished he could make it so she'd never been born.

"How much does an abortion cost these days?"

Ann was shocked by the coldness in his voice.

"It's too late."

Ann banged the back of her head against the Third Eye Blind poster on her wall. She looked at the track trophies that lined her bookshelves, the framed corkboard pinned with ribbons and concert tickets and photos with her friends on hayrides and waterskiing and late nights at Ma Fischer's. She looked at the pile of college brochures from Harvard and Boston College and Amherst, schools that wouldn't want her now, and even if they did, how could she possibly make college work, or at least college so far from home?

"How far along?" he said.

"Can't you do the math?" She'd been so angry since that night on Duck Pond that she felt she was manufacturing rage in her own body, when really, she was manufacturing his child; part of Anthony was inside of her, his cells wildly multiplying and dividing with her own. How could that be? She wished like hell that she'd never met him. She liked to think of Anthony as an apple core she could toss out of a car window, something that could be forgotten, left to rot into nothing.

"Do you show?"

"I'm starting to." She used a large safety pin to extend the waist of her pants, and wore long flannel shirts to cover her belly.

"And does anyone know?"

"Just you. You and the doctor at Planned Parenthood."

"Just keep it quiet. For now. Let me figure this out. I'll come up with a plan. Does Michael know?"

"No," Ann said. "Not yet." She wanted to tell him, and came close a few times, but she knew he wouldn't take it well. His feelings for her weren't exclusively brotherly, a fact he couldn't hide no matter how aloof he tried to act around her. She remembered Michael's kiss as if it had been exchanged between two people totally different from who they were now. That one perfect moment of sweet adolescence she hadn't known would, in a matter of weeks, dissolve into this shitty version of adulthood.

"I need to tell my parents," she said. "I'm telling them tonight."

"Not tonight. In a week. Give me a week to think."

"They're going to figure it out on their own."

"Just give me a week, Ann."

"I don't have a lot of weeks to give."

"Let me handle it. You're confused, this is a hard time. Look, you can't make good decisions right now. You normally can, I know, but you're under a lot of stress. Everything is going to be OK. I know you don't have any reason to believe me, but I'll make sure of it. Just hold tight."

This sounded almost reassuring. She started to think she might hate Anthony just a little less until he said, "And don't breathe a word of this to my wife."

The line went dead.

FIFTEEN

Michael

Thank God school was over for the holidays. In Michael's last class, they watched an Alistair Cooke *Letter from America* episode on pork barrel politics. Mrs. McCarthy must have shown that video a hundred times. He wasn't a big fan of school, but ever since that last night on the Cape, when Ed found Ann in his bed, he'd tried hard to focus and get back in Ed's good graces. Michael was pulling decent grades—passing, at least. He took the AP chemistry class Ed thought he should take, joined basketball, and started playing chess at lunch. Ed talked to him about college, and he'd sent an application to UW–Milwaukee, but he didn't want to go to college, at least not right away.

He and Ann had denied that anything had gone on between them, but Michael wasn't at all convinced that Ed and Connie believed them. They seemed distant and wary. It felt as if the spell had been broken, and in the four months since their abrupt departure from Wellfleet, the Gordons had gone from being a model family to being a bunch of people who shared a house. He'd been lonely before he met Ann, sure, but he felt even lonelier now, because he was so acutely aware of what he'd lost.

Michael had always done his best to keep his distance, but now Ann was totally off-limits; she might as well have been wrapped up in police tape. She was a different person, too, only her perfect grades weren't so perfect, and she'd become dramatically less involved, abruptly quitting the cross-country team and forensics. She even skipped homecoming, even though she'd been elected to the court and had a date. She was always in her room. She'd been distracted, not rude or mean. That is, until that morning. She'd been in the small bathroom they all shared for fifteen minutes. He worried he wouldn't get to school on time, so he knocked gently on the door. "Will you be done soon?"

Ann threw the door open and stormed out. "I can't get any privacy in this house!"

"What's your problem?" he asked. He sincerely wanted to know the answer. He felt like he didn't even recognize her anymore.

"My problem," she said, "is that there are too many people in this house thanks to you. You aren't the only person with shit to deal with. Take your shower and go. Just go away. Get out of my life." She ran into her bedroom and slammed the door.

Ann could have said anything, but to tell him to get out of her life? Nothing could have hurt more. He nursed that hurt all day at school, his stomach a mess. He walked home slowly, his backpack heavy from textbooks, his mood as low as the heavy clouds that hung over the lake. He used to be able to turn to Poppy, his former ally, but she was just as distant as Ann, stoned all the time and doing God knows what. She was never home. She'd finally found her group, a new crowd in his own grade that Michael didn't approve of: Chris Bonner, Priscilla Madden, Leah Bagnoli, people with runny noses and long pinkie nails. They hung out at Fuel Café instead of Coffee Trader, went to the Grateful Dead tape night on Thursdays at Thurman's, got high and played hacky sack on the UWM concourse. Poppy even dressed differently, in oversized burlap *harga* shirts, ripped jeans, and Birkenstocks. She snuck out at night, and snuck back in. She reeked, and her pupils were dilated.

The wind off Lake Michigan was strong and damp. He turned down Newberry Boulevard. The Gordon house, with its Victorian turret, was visible in the distance. A car with tinted windows pulled into a driveway just in front of him, practically rolling over his feet. The window rolled down slowly, like in rock videos on MTV when limousines slow down and musicians invite someone to join the party.

Only this was no limo, and it was no party. This was Anthony.

"What are *you* doing here?"

"Get in, Michael. Let's go for a ride," he said. "We need to talk."

THE CAR SLID THROUGH THE STREETS on the East Side toward Lake Michigan, where it turned south to head downtown. Stately mansions lined Lake Drive, huge Tudors and Colonials, homes that were bigger, nicer, classier, and more solidly built than Anthony's place on the Cape. Ann once told Michael that she thought it was a bad omen if the lake and the sky were the same color. On this day, they were the same flat dark gray.

"Milwaukee isn't bad," Anthony said. "Parks, the lake. Old houses. I expected factories, Laverne and Shirley. *Happy Days.*"

"Why are you here?" Michael asked.

"I'll bet this does seem curious."

What a pompous ass, Michael thought. "*Curious*"? More like *wrong*. To see Anthony in Milwaukee was about as normal as seeing the waves crash sideways. "What is this about?" Michael asked.

"It's sensitive. And it concerns you. Me. And Ann. Your *sister.*" He put special emphasis on that word. "It's important to her that we talk. But let's not discuss it now, not while I'm driving."

It didn't take long to get downtown, maybe ten minutes. By then, the insides of Anthony's windows were covered with moisture. Downtown Milwaukee could sometimes seem abandoned, aside from the few grim-faced workers on Wisconsin Avenue walking with their arms crossed in front of them, bracing against the cold. Wreaths with big red bows hung from the electrical lines on each block. With the holiday just a few weeks away, Michael had hoped against hope that the festivities of the season might bring the Gordons back together. Last year, his first Christmas with the family, Connie had put up the nativity scene even though they didn't go to church. It was a family joke to move Mary's figurine closer and closer to Jesus each day of Advent. Ed resurrected the model train set he'd used as a kid. He'd spent a lot of time showing Michael how it worked. Once they propped up the tree (they'd driven out to a farm and cut it down themselves, which seemed impossibly quaint compared to the Charlie Brown trees his mother used to buy at the gas station), Ed set the train in motion around the base. Christmas morning was like a scene from a cheesy after-school movie. It wouldn't be like that this year.

"Here we are." Anthony pulled up in front of the classic old Pfister Hotel. The valet opened Michael's door at the same moment he was about to open it himself. He almost fell out of the car, right at the valet's feet.

They walked inside. Anthony took off his camel coat and draped it casually over his arm. He was dressed in pressed khakis and a soft, expensive-looking beige sweater. His leather shoes were shiny, free of scuffs. His tan was gone and so was his beard. His face was pale, which only made his black hair and dark eyelashes all the more striking and blunt, more startling than handsome.

Everyone at the hotel, including Anthony, was dressed nicely, expensively. It made Michael wish he'd given his outfit more thought, but how would he have ever known that morning when he was getting dressed in such a hurry that he'd end up here, at the Pfister? He wore jeans and an open jacket over the T-shirt Poppy gave him for his birthday last October. It said CAPE COD but looked like the Coca-Cola logo. He felt like everyone in the hushed lobby was staring at him.

"Follow me," Anthony said, and walked to a mahogany table with plush gold chairs in the bar area, away from where most everyone else was seated. Michael walked several steps behind him. They sat down, practically hidden next to the base of the huge Christmas tree. The tree was as out of place as Michael felt; he was suddenly struck by the oddness of the grand piece of nature brought indoors. It was decorated with tasteful, classic ornaments, tinsel, and little lights that looked like old-fashioned gas lamps. There were gold foil gift-wrapped packages around the base of the tree. From a distance the gifts looked nice, but up close he could tell they were old, overused props. The foil was dented and there were small tears on the sides of the packages. Fake presents were the worst.

Anthony gestured at the waitress. "Bring us two red wines," he said.

Michael was too stunned to speak, so he looked around the lobby of the fancy old hotel. He felt like he was in a cathedral. The trim was gilded gold, and the ceiling was vaulted, and painted with red-faced cherubs, blue skies, and clouds. Everything was old here, even the bartenders. They seemed wise, knowing, like they understood exactly what was going on with Anthony, who cleared his throat, his Adam's apple like the stub of a branch that had broken off a tree. "I had business in Chicago. Thought I'd jog north for a bit to see you. And Ann."

"You've seen her?"

"She's upstairs. In my room."

"What's she doing in your room?"

"Resting."

"She's resting in your room?"

"She isn't feeling well."

"I want to see her."

Anthony held up his hand: *stop.* The waitress set the wine in front of them and left. Anthony held his glass a few inches from his face, closed his eyes, let his jaw go slack as if he were sleeping, and inhaled. "This is how you smell wine," he said. "Breathe in with both your nose and your mouth, taste and smell at the same time. Try it." He passed the glass to Michael.

"I don't care about wine." Michael pushed it back. Ann was in this guy's room!

"How old are you now?"

"Eighteen. What's she doing in there? She should go home." It was all he could do to avoid dumping it all over Anthony's expensive cashmere sweater, and smashing the glass against the wall.

"So, she hasn't told you."

"Told me what?"

Anthony looked around. "You'll keep this to yourself?"

"What gives?"

Anthony took another sip. He was stalling, or maybe he was nervous. It was hard to imagine that Anthony could feel that way. "This wine is from France. You should try to go to France someday. The Loire Valley is beautiful. The garden at Villandry—"

"I don't want to talk about France."

"This is a very delicate matter." Anthony was so intense that it was hard for Michael to look him in the eye. He gave Michael that feeling you get when you meet a street dog for the first time. It might act like it wants you to pet it, but as soon as you do, it bites your hand off.

"First, Michael, I want to tell you a story."

"I don't want to hear your story. I really don't." Michael hated it when adults started conversations like this. He'd heard plenty of inspiring life stories from teachers, guidance counselors, social workers, ministers. Anthony wasn't there because he wanted to shoot the shit. He wanted something. But what?

"Just indulge me for a moment, would you? Maureen . . ." Anthony said. He cleared his throat. "You like her?"

"Sure," Michael said. He did like Maureen. He liked her very much. He could picture her in her tennis dress, offering him cookies, asking if he needed something to drink.

"Maureen is not my first wife."

"So? What's your room number? I should get Ann. We should go home."

"Stay right there." Anthony's tone was forceful, threatening. He practically pinned Michael to his chair with his black eyes.

"See, I'm like you. I grew up with nothing. We actually have a lot in common. We're scrappy. Scrappy is good, it means we've got fight. I see fight in you. Or I should say, I *recognize* it." He pointed two of his fingers at himself, then at Michael and back at himself for emphasis. "There's a difference, you know, between seeing something and recognizing that it's there."

"I have no idea what you are saying."

"Someday you will. Straight out of high school I got a job at the mine where my dad worked."

Michael stood up. "I said I want to see Ann."

"Would you calm down?" Anthony grabbed Michael's arm and yanked it so he fell back into his seat. "See, I barely had hair on my chest and already I had a ring on my finger. Jackie, she wouldn't let me sleep with her unless we were good in the eyes of God, and what can I say? I was a red-blooded teenage boy, like you are now. You know how it is. Besides, in my shitty little town, I figured I'd have the same shitty kind of life everyone else had so I made the same shitty decisions. It was OK at first. I was making a paycheck, getting drunk with my friends and getting laid every night, but you know what? It wasn't enough for me. I had this feeling, you know? That someone could live and die and not know about me or my town or the mine or Jackie, and it wouldn't make a bit of difference. Real life happened somewhere else, that's what I thought. Everyone else I knew seemed OK with staying put, but me? I knew I was different. I knew I was meant to have a better life. A bigger life. I wanted what I did to matter."

"I don't know why you're telling me this," Michael said. "It has nothing to do with me."

"I'm telling you this story for your own benefit. You might not realize it yet, but you're different from other people in the same way *I'm* different from other people. We know we can choose between a shitty life and a big life. People like us . . ."

"You don't even know me."

"Sure I do. I've watched you cut my grass. You did a good job. Perfect diamond pattern. I was impressed. You showed up on time, did the job right, took on more than I asked you to. You're responsible, reliable. Ann says the same thing. She thinks the world of you."

"Ann talked about me with you?"

"We talk about everything. Almost every day, sometimes twice a day."

Michael couldn't believe it. He wanted to start the day over. Was this even real?

"I'm not a bad guy, Michael. You think I am, but I'm just older than you are, and I've got more than you've ever had. More stuff, but also more problems. And right now, I've got a hell of a problem on my hands. So does Ann."

"What's going on?"

"That's why I asked you here."

"You didn't give me much choice."

"See—" But before Anthony could say anything, a big family sat down at the table next to them, a mother and father and three kids, all dressed up for their big holiday outing. The mother ordered Shirley Temples, and she made a big point of telling the waitress that they were going to *The Nutcracker* at the Pabst Theater that night, a big family tradition. The waitress couldn't have cared less, Michael could tell. He paid attention to people in the service industry; they were more like him than jerks like Anthony. He wished this were any old day, and that he and the waitress could take a break together and complain about guys like Anthony who made a big show of smelling their wine, and families like The Perfects over there. The mother and her daughter wore matching headbands made of plaid silk.

Anthony watched them, too, although he was probably thinking about how poorly the wife had aged, how she was probably hot back in the day. He probably wondered how much money the husband made, or if he was, as Connie would say about some of the fancy houses on the Cape, "mortgaged to the hilt."

Once the family were talking among themselves, Anthony cleared his throat and snapped back to attention. "Where was I?"

"I don't care where you were. Look, why am I here? What do you want?"

"My story. So I started taking college classes at night. I didn't tell anyone what I was doing. When I finished, I wanted to find a job in a big city. Jackie—now my wife—she didn't want to go. Her mom and dad were in West Finley, and her sisters, and her friends, all the people she'd ever cared about. Jackie was a great girl. We had chemistry, we did. Maybe she was the love of my life, but that didn't matter—I couldn't let shit like that matter. I realized something hard, but true, and this is why I'm telling you this tale: sometimes you have to hurt people to get what you need. Sometimes you have to do what you need to do to get where you want to go."

Anthony leaned back in his chair, flagged down the waitress, and ordered another glass of wine. Beads of sweat formed on his upper lip, and his face was flushed red. "Your question: What does any of this have to do with you, right?"

The father at the table next to them pushed his son's arm and said, "Elbows off!"

"Ann has a rather large problem, Michael. A large problem that requires a complex solution."

"I don't know what this has to do with me."

"She's pregnant."

Pregnant? This felt like a body blow. She couldn't be. No, no, no. Not Ann. Pregnant? Why was this asshole making up stories about her?

Michael never drank, just sometimes with Jason at the end of the day. He took a drink at that moment, some wine to wash down what Anthony just said. "You don't know what you're talking about."

"She's too far along to take care of it. And, well, here's the thing: she wants to have this baby because she loves me."

"She does not."

"I was as shocked as you are by this news. Not that she loves me. She's told me that a hundred times. But about this baby. I care about her, I care deeply, but I'm afraid I'm not in a position to—"

"She doesn't love you." The bustling of waiters and clinking of silverware and twinkling of lights became a confused blur. Michael looked at Anthony and felt an anger rise up in him that he hadn't felt for a long time. "You got her pregnant?"

Anthony wiped his mouth with his napkin, leaving a red streak from the wine that had stained his lip.

This prick slept with Ann? Michael wanted to reach out and slam Anthony's smug face to the table. He must have inherited his father's fighting spirit. He wanted to pulverize him, reduce him to nothing, make him his sand-filled punching bag.

"I know this is a shock," Anthony said. Michael swore he saw a smile tug at the corner of Anthony's disgusting mouth, a mouth he'd pressed against Ann's mouth—no! Michael banged his fists on his thighs, jiggled his leg like a coke addict.

"You're making this up."

"Do you think I'd make up a story like this?"

"What about college? She's getting scholarship offers. She's smart." Connie and Ed would be so disappointed. Academics were everything. Both of their houses were stuffed with books. Connie had just put a bumper sticker on her car that said KILL YOUR TELEVISION. "You ruined her future."

"It was her own future she compromised. She told me she was on the pill."

"She was your babysitter!"

The woman at the table next to them looked at Anthony with disapproval, and shifted her body to block Anthony's view of her daughter.

"She was more than that. You know how special she is. Let's just say we'd grown close." That word "we" was what bothered Michael the most: *we* grew close. Ann wasn't even there and he felt he was being ganged up on. "It's hard to control your emotions when you're physically intimate with someone again and again. You think you can, but it's easy to get carried away. I'm afraid this is especially true for Ann."

Michael balled up his fists, and Anthony stared at them.

"We need to talk about this like men. Grown men. You don't want to punch me like you're some kid on the playground. Let's have an adult conversation about it, shall we? This is hard enough without all the tough guy bullshit."

The lobby seemed to go still. Michael looked around, trying to think about something, anything else. He focused on an old lady with her granddaughter, the doll the girl was holding, their waitress's black shoes, the busboy's big tray. He listened for the tinny Christmas music playing in the background. Ann was pregnant, Anthony was the father. *I am a poor boy too pa rum pa pum pum.*

"I've got nothing to say to you." Michael reached for his coat. "You're sick. A sick pervert." Michael pushed his heavy chair back and stood up.

"If you walk away right now, Michael, you'll be responsible for Ann getting nothing."

"You'd do that to her? She doesn't need you or your money. She'll be fine."

"That's not what she thinks. Give her some credit. She's smart enough to know she'll need financial support, and I want to help, I do, but I can only do so in the most discreet manner. Come on, Michael. Have a heart. You were raised by a single mother. You know she'll need all the help she can get."

"Her parents will be there for her."

"She's not at all convinced that will be the case. And even if they are, I'm guessing there's not a lot of money to go around."

Michael thought of Connie's coupon file, organized neatly by grocery aisle. He remembered the small arguments he'd overheard between Connie and Ed about spending, the way Ed had to sneak the expense of their fishing trips. How Connie had suggested that maybe they sell the Cape house to help pay for Ann's college, and Ed said no, never. The Wellfleet house had to stay in the family, it was for the kids and their kids and their kids' kids.

"Strange as it may sound, Ann's well-being is in your hands. If you really care about her, you'll sit back down and talk to me."

"What are you trying to say? You won't help Ann if I won't listen to you?"

"Sit." Anthony looked at Michael's empty chair.

Michael thought about leaving, but he wanted to talk to Ann. Thing was, Ann was upstairs. In Anthony's room. Resting. Pregnant. No wonder she'd been so distracted. She really loved this guy?

"I told you that story about myself because I've made sacrifices to get what I want. To be perfectly honest, I don't look back with regret. I've done what I had to do, and you are the type of person who can do the same. I told you that story because I want you to think about the kind of sacrifices *you* might also make, for others, sure, but also for yourself. See, Ann and I, we've been talking." God, it made Michael physically sick to imagine Ann talking to this guy, even sicker to think about what else they'd done together. "We've come up with a plan of sorts. Actually, it was Ann who came up with this. I need to give her credit. She's incredibly strategic in a time of crisis."

"I don't believe you."

"Please. Hear me out. I need—*we* need—well, now this is a hard thing to say: we need you to say you're the father."

"Me? No way. No *fucking* way. Are you kidding?"

The mother at the table next to them shot a severe look at Michael when she heard him swear near her children, like *he* was the bad guy instead of Anthony. "I don't want to be part of your plan. I won't lie about that. Are you nuts? Why would I do that? Her parents would kill me."

Anthony put his finger over his lips. "Keep it down," he said. "Please."

Michael noticed a vein bulge on the bony ridge of Anthony's big, Neanderthal forehead. His face was red and strained like he was in the middle of a bench press.

"Poor Ann, she was so certain you'd be willing to step up for her."

"Ann came up with this?"

"Just listen. I want to keep my family together, Michael. I slipped up, every man does, but I'm a family guy, you've seen that. I should have had more control, should have been a better man. But I screwed up and I'm sorry. The chemistry was too much. We couldn't keep our hands off each other."

"Bullshit. This is bullshit."

"I know you don't think much of me, and you shouldn't, but all I'm asking you to do—and all *Ann* is asking you to do—is to tell a little lie."

"That's not a little lie! That's like the biggest fucking lie I could ever tell."

Anthony didn't respond right away. He eyed Michael, assessing the situation, developing his strategy. He drank some wine. "Are you forgetting that Ann did *you* a big favor? She gave you a place to stay when you had no place to go; she gave you a family when you had nobody. You would have been a foster kid. You're fine now, Michael, just look at you. How about returning Ann's favor? Everyone knows you're in love with her. I could tell myself, the minute I saw you lay eyes on her. And my boys told us they saw you surprise her with an unwelcome kiss. Maureen was so concerned she called your parents to discuss it with them."

Anthony paused to let that sink in—and embarrass him further. So that night Ed found Ann in his bed—that was after Maureen had told them? No wonder he didn't seem to believe Ann and Michael when they insisted nothing had gone on between them.

"Ann told me how awkward she's felt around you, with you mooning all over her."

Michael wanted to die. He could hear Ann's voice in his head as if through a megaphone: *You love me, don't you?*

"So you have a thing for her, big deal. That's nothing to be ashamed of, she's the whole package. I've fallen for plenty of women I can't have. But she thinks of you as a, well, as a brother. Hell, man, she *made* you her brother. That's how it works sometimes. You'll learn that, like with me and Ann, there's this, this snap of electricity, this heat, this sizzle. Someday you'll know what I'm talking about. But whatever, she's your friend, your sister. And she needs you to help her out now."

"By lying?"

"Yes."

"But all she'd need to do is take one of those tests. It'll prove I'm not the dad."

This seemed to get under Anthony's skin. It seemed as if he'd anticipated every argument, the way a candidate prepares for a debate. "And if she takes that test, know what happens? My marriage is over. Let me put the pieces together for you: If my marriage is over, Michael, I won't have any money. And if I have no money, I can't support Ann. Ann knows this." Anthony took another big sip, so big you'd think he'd mistaken his wineglass for water. "Connecting the dots?"

Michael *was* connecting the dots—one horrible dot at a time.

"Ann, you know, she could go after me. Sure. She could drag me through legal hell. But why do that when what she really wants and needs right now, bottom line, is my financial support? What I'm saying, Michael, is that if word of this situation gets out, if the wheels come off my marriage, I'll be cut off, a pauper. Here's the plan: I've set up an account in your name at a bank here in Milwaukee, you just need to sign some paperwork. I'll be on the account, too, but it'll look like it's yours. Every month it'll look like it's you who sent money, and that's good for you, right? That way your parents won't think you're a deadbeat."

A deadbeat. Michael couldn't stand the idea of Ed and Connie thinking of him in those terms. He'd never get Ann—or anyone—pregnant, and then run off. Never.

"I can't," Michael said. He thought of the way Ed had looked at him that night when he'd discovered Ann curled up in his bed. He didn't ever want to see that expression of anger and disappointment cross his face again, couldn't stand the idea of it. "Her parents, they've been so good to me. I don't want them to think I'd ever—"

"Oh Michael, it's too late for you to worry about your reputation with them. They wish they'd never adopted you, don't you know that? That's what Ann tells me. You can have lots of reasons to hesitate to accept my offer, but that family isn't one of them. You've already let them down." Anthony wiped the rim of his wineglass with the corner of his napkin, staining it for no reason. "They were just trying to be nice. Liberal guilt, you know?"

"She told you that?" He thought of what Ann had said earlier that day: *Get out of my life!*

"But Ann, *she* believes in you. She knows that after everything she's done for you, that you'll help her through this."

"Why don't you just man up and be honest? Say you're the father."

Anthony sighed, as if this whole discussion was too tiresome for him. "You know I can't do that. What I can do, what I'm trying to do at least, what Ann is also trying to do, is come up with a creative way to support her."

Michael pushed his chair away from the heavy table and stood up. He threw his coat back on and started for the door.

Anthony followed him. "If you walk away right now, Ann will suffer."

"I want to talk to her."

"She's got nothing to say. This is *her* plan, remember? She thought this was a great idea. And it is. We can look shiny as diamonds. Hear me out."

Michael shook his head. No. He thought he might faint. He couldn't move, couldn't focus on anything but the carpet below his feet, the hum of voices and music.

"You don't think we'd ask you to do this for nothing, do you? There's something in it for you. Quite a significant something." He pulled out his wallet and unfolded a check written out to Michael, and pressed it into his hand. Fifty thousand dollars.

"Is this real?"

Anthony laughed. "Yes, it's real. I recognize this sacrifice comes at no small cost to you. I need to make it worth your while."

Michael had to look twice at the number, and read it spelled out in fancy script: *Fifty thousand and 00/100 dollars.* More money than he'd ever seen in one place. Anthony pulled another check out of his wallet. "And here's another check just like that one. You can go ahead, keep both of them. But if you do, Ann gets nothing. Or, if you love your sister, you pocket one, sign over the other, say you're the dad, and then you disappear."

"You're bribing me."

"Oh, I don't think of it that way. I'm simply making an unpleasant situation less unpleasant for all of us."

Michael fingered the edges of the checks, tempted to rip them in half. It was just paper, after all, yet in that moment, the checks felt like they were made of steel.

"I'm willing to pay to prevent this from destroying my life. Ann understands this, she does. I have the best lawyers, and I know the kinds of people who could screw Ann over, leave her with nothing. Screw both of you over. I don't want to do that, I really don't. You're nice kids. But I'll do whatever it takes to protect myself and my family. Just sign the paperwork and the check and let's get this over with."

Anthony led the way back to the table, and Michael grudgingly followed. Then Anthony slid some papers out of his leather attaché case. He seemed like the kind of guy who was always whipping out paperwork—making deals, talking people into doing things they shouldn't do, not giving them much choice in the matter while making them feel like all the choices were theirs. He set the papers on the table and pushed them toward Michael. "I need your signature here"—he tapped a line next to an X on the top piece of paper— "and here." He flipped the paper over. "And this is where you write down your social security number for the trust." He pressed a pen into Michael's hand. Not just any pen, but the fancy kind you get for graduation. Like a surgeon picking the proper tool for an operation. This pen felt heavy and involved, perfect for the task at hand.

"You can start a business," Anthony said. "You can be your own man. All you have to do is say the kid is yours—that's it. This is the easiest money that'll ever come your way. Go out West or something. Go to college. See the world. You're eighteen now. An adult. Nobody is going to chase after you. You're free to make your own life."

Michael knew it should be easy to sign his name, but his hand wouldn't move. He was signing the last two years of his life away, signing away Ed and Connie, Poppy and Ann, his life in Milwaukee. Cape Cod. Everything that mattered to him. Signing his name was more like erasing it.

"Like I said, it'll look like it's coming from you."

"Where are her parents going to think I got that much money?"

"Their only concern is that their daughter is taken care of. Look, my life is complicated, Michael. Complicated in ways you wouldn't understand. Your life, on the other hand, is simple. You can just tell one little lie, pocket a chunk of money, leave a family you were never really a part of, and the girl who never loved you back the way you wanted her to. Ann did a lot for you, I get it. But now her future is in your hands. Everyone will think you're the father anyway. Do the right thing."

Anthony was right: everyone would think Michael was the father. Everyone. But Ann—she really came up with this plan? She really loved this guy? Slept with him again and again? When she'd come to his bed that summer, was she upset because he wouldn't leave Maureen? He might not have believed what Anthony told him if he hadn't heard the coldness in her voice that morning, if she hadn't been so distant for the past few months. And now she was willing to use Michael to help Anthony? Couldn't she see what Anthony was? She *loved* this sack of shit? Then again, his mother had loved Marcus. He treated her terribly and still she'd loved him.

"I hate you," Michael said. He looked Anthony right in the eye.

"I get that. I'd hate me too if I were you. Just sign."

And that's what Michael did. He signed quickly, wherever he was told, before he could change his mind. And just like that, he became nobody.

Michael stood, put on his coat, and looked at the revolving door near the exit. He was overcome by a hot, explosive rage. He understood now why Anthony wanted to discuss this matter in a public place. He knew that Michael would want to hurt him. And he did: just like that he reached forward to strike Anthony, forgetting that Anthony was quick as a wrestler. He grabbed his wrist, twisted it so hard Michael could have sworn it broke, and let go. Michael yanked his aching arm back. Anthony stared at him, a stare that dared Michael to try again, a stare that was oddly calculated. Michael couldn't lead with his right hand, so he used his left, and landed a sloppy hook on the side of Anthony's nose. It couldn't have hurt him. The family at the next table gasped.

Anthony stood and addressed them. "Will you please ask the bartender to call security?"

His face was right next to Michael's ear. He whispered, "I'm going to press charges if you don't get the hell out of here. Get lost, Michael. Go away. Disappear. Nobody cares about you. Not me. Certainly not Ann. Just take the money and run, and don't you dare try to make contact with either of us. As far as you're concerned, you never saw me. I've never stepped foot in this tired industrial town. That other paper you signed? It's a silence agreement. Break it, and you'll be in debt for the rest of your life, I'll make sure of it."

Michael saw the security guard in the distance. He spit on Anthony and made a run for it. He burst through the revolving doors and stumbled onto the sidewalk. He picked himself up and ran away from the hotel, away from Lake Michigan, away from the Gordon family home. Breathless, a few blocks south on Broadway, he caught his reflection in the giant plate-glass windows of the Grain Exchange and saw what everyone else saw: just some horny, troubled kid living with two beautiful girls his own age, a lovesick "stray" who would take advantage of any situation. He was an opportunist. He could feel that check in his back pocket—proof.

He couldn't believe Ann would turn on him.

One thing was certain: he could never go back to the Gordons' house. That part of his life was over, ripped away from him. He walked to the Greyhound station with nothing but his backpack. He used the pay phone at the station to leave a message on the Gordons' voice-message machine. "Look, I'm sorry about what I did to Ann," he said. He couldn't bear to say he'd gotten her pregnant, couldn't bear to lie.

He hung up and looked at the bus schedule. He had so much money now, he could go anywhere. Anywhere at all.

SIXTEEN

Ann

How would Michael even know I'm pregnant?" Ann asked Anthony. "And how would he know it was *you*? I never told him anything."

"You didn't have to. He said he overheard you when you called me. You should have been more discreet, Ann."

"No." Ann couldn't think straight anymore. Nobody had been home when she'd spoken to Anthony, right? That was just a few days ago, and she could hardly remember it, couldn't remember what she'd eaten for breakfast that very morning, what homework she'd turned in and what was late, what her own name was. Her brain was too busy trying to make sense of the messiness of her life. She remembered yelling at Michael and feeling bad about it. She'd been anxious for him to come home after school so she could apologize, tell him she didn't mean what she'd said, she'd just been so alone, so confused, that she needed to lash out. She was building up the resolve to tell everyone, her parents, Michael, Poppy. Once Michael knew this secret she'd been keeping, he'd understand, right?

"He wouldn't do that. He wouldn't blackmail you. Not Michael."

"*Especially* Michael," Anthony said. His voice was so authoritative she felt as if he were in the same room with her. "What do you know about his life before you met him? He was a street kid, Ann. He learned to get what he wanted. Think about it. He lived with your family for what, not even two years? He just turned eighteen, doesn't want to go to college. He could work at a McDonald's the rest of his life or he could hit me up for a load of cash, which is just what he did. He called me at work. Last person in the world I expected to hear from at nine o'clock in the morning. I almost spit out my coffee."

"He called you? How did he have your number at work?"

"I gave him my card when he worked for me last summer. Told him to stay in touch if he wanted me to write a letter of recommendation. Thought I was doing the kid a favor and look how he repaid me. He had the whole plan figured out. He said he'd say he's the father and skip town if I'd give him money."

"No."

"It's time for you to open your eyes, Ann. You don't believe me? He even had a bank account set up. He said he'd keep fifty grand for himself, and then he'd deposit the rest of my money and the bank would automatically send you a check every month. If you don't believe me I can show you the paperwork he faxed over. Think about it: I can't set up a bank account for someone else. He needed to do this. It was his plan."

Ann stared at the dizzying jelly-roll pattern of the quilt on her bed that her mother had made for her as a present when she turned sixteen. They'd driven all over town looking for fabric. Michael set up an account?

"He had me in a vise, Ann. Kid like that, he's seen people in situations like mine. Part of me admires him, actually. But look: it's just money. I paid him, and I put money in his little account. You'll get a thousand bucks every month. That ought to help you get by. He's gone for good, off to who-knows-where. You won't see him again. Good riddance."

It was one thing to imagine never seeing Anthony again, but Michael?

He'd been such a constant in her life the past few years. Even though they hadn't been as close lately, she relied on him, cared for him, loved him in ways she could acknowledge, and ways she had to deny, even to herself. She couldn't digest what Anthony told her—all she could think about was that Michael was gone, and he'd betrayed her. Anthony kept talking, his words floating like the greasy scum on top of dirty water. Most of what he said was just posturing, but she snapped to attention when he said, "Let's face it, Ann. This situation is difficult enough. Neither of us want to get dragged into a custody battle."

"Custody": that was a word she hadn't even thought of yet. It made her stomach turn to think of this baby growing inside of her being ripped away, raised by someone like Anthony. "What did you say?"

"If the kid is mine, like you say, you bet I want to raise it. That is, if I didn't have to keep everything a secret. Practically speaking, I do."

"All I need to do is take a paternity test."

"Right. And you know what'll happen if I'm really the father? I'll drag you and your family through the mud, take the kid, do whatever I need to do. Listen good, Ann: if you come after me, if you take that test, I'll be a permanent part of your life, you can bet on that. There won't be a day you won't communicate with me."

Ann held the phone so hard she thought it could melt in her hand. She used to think she could handle anything, but this? This was too much.

"I know what Michael did is hurtful, but you don't see him clearly. You don't know the kinds of people I've known. He's had to look out for himself, do whatever it takes to survive. I think he thinks he's doing you a favor. You'll keep this a secret."

"I don't believe this."

"Here's what you do. When you tell your parents, you say Michael's the dad just like he worked out. He gets something in exchange for lying. Fair's fair I guess, as unpleasant as it is. He has a price, and I paid it. This sucks for me too, you know."

"My whole future just blew up. Don't tell me what sucks for you."

"I'm basically giving up any opportunity to get to know my child, and I don't even have proof that it really is mine. You think that's easy for me?" His cold voice softened for a moment. "Having a kid is hard, but it's not the end of the world. My boys, they mean the world to me. You saw that. I'd never go back in time and wish they hadn't been born. I didn't believe in God until I looked in their eyes. But look, Michael is long gone, and I can be long gone, too, if that's what's best. You just play along. You're independent, I can see that. That's why I liked you. You raise the kid the way you want. Your parents will help, you know that. Or you put it up for adoption for some nice family. The money in that account will still be yours, and you'll get it a month at a time so we don't raise any eyebrows."

"I don't know."

"What's not to know? The way I look at it, and probably the way Michael does, too, is that he's doing us both a favor."

All the rest was a blur. His insistence that this was simple appealed to her, it did. She needed a check to appear every month, just like Anthony had said it would. It sounded like there was so much money that it would never run out.

Ann still had so many questions about what Michael had done. It didn't feel right to her. But she needed a narrative, a story. So, when her father burst into her bedroom demanding to know what Michael had "done" to her, that was the story she told. "Oh, Ann," he said, racked with disappointment. "How could you let this happen?"

If he'd responded differently and said something less inadvertently hurtful, she might not have stuck to it with as much tenacity.

WORD SPREAD AROUND SCHOOL like a brush fire. Ann wasn't the first kid at Riverside to get pregnant, that was for sure, but she was Ed Gordon's kid, a straight-A student, the kind of girl who, a year ago, might have been the one to spread rumors about *other* teen pregnancies. The worst part was seeing that look on her teachers' faces, many of whom were her dad's friends. They'd been to the house for potlucks and barbecues, knew her mom, had watched Ann grow up. Such a shame, they seemed to say every time they saw her walk into the classroom, their eyes on her stomach. Even her mom's friend Dawn, who was like an aunt to her, seemed to disapprove.

Her pregnancy became public as her college acceptance letters arrived. She was waitlisted at Harvard, which, under normal circumstances, would have been a big deal—maybe it would mean heartbreak, maybe it would change her life forever. Now it was just a stone dropping through water. Only Amherst sent a rejection. She could have gone to college out East after all: Boston College wanted her. So did Northeastern and Vassar. Vassar even offered her a scholarship. Ann insisted she could still go. "How?" her mother asked. "Honey, a baby is a lot of work. You have no idea."

Poppy rallied to Ann's side. She called the admissions offices, pretending she was Ann. *Sorry,* she said, while tears streamed down Ann's face, *I'm taking advantage of other offers.* Ann grudgingly enrolled at the achingly familiar University of Wisconsin–Milwaukee. She had practically lived on campus her entire life. She'd even attended the day care there; now, in addition to her application, she was filling out forms for her own child to be taken care of while she attended classes.

This radical change in plans might have crushed her if she didn't have bigger worries than school. She worried her father might never look at her the same way again, worried that Michael might have gotten into some trouble (why should she worry about Michael?), worried when she overheard some girls talking about snorting coke with Poppy in Mike Lassiter's Pontiac Firebird during lunch. There was so much worry, and then she'd read she could stress the fetus, who'd already been exposed to so much of her anxiety that she was certain he or she was doomed to become a mental case.

And then, one day at school, between second and third period, just outside Mrs. Chalmer's door . . . what was that? She almost dropped her books. A flutter deep inside her. A literal flutter, light and quick. Her classmates rushed past her, late for class. Kathy Landuski put on lipstick. Ben Johnson gave Marcus Rose a high five. The bell rang, shrill and loud. There it was again. The baby! Before, the baby meant the end of her future, her youth, her life as she'd known it. Now the baby was more than an idea. It was real, alive and kicking. It was *hers*.

This gave her a new appreciation for her mom, wise now because she'd also once been pregnant and given birth. She took off work to drive Ann to her appointments, reminded her to take the horse-pill-sized vitamins, and sewed elastic panels into Ann's jeans. She and her friends had started a baby quilt. Connie held her hand as the technician spread the wand over the gooey junk on her stomach. There on the screen, like a black-and-white etching, she saw the round C of a spine. A skull. Fingers and toes. The technician measured the circumference of the baby's head, counted the ventricles of his heart. "I'm not supposed to say this, but your baby is perfect," she said. She confirmed what Ann intuitively knew: a boy. She was having a boy, and the boy was sucking his thumb. This news seemed to please Ed. He'd been supportive, although Ann could tell he blamed himself for not being more attentive to what he thought had been happening right under his roof. She could also tell that Ed missed Michael. Ann had heard her parents arguing about whether or not to try harder to find him. "He's eighteen now," Connie said. "He's not a missing child; he's not even a runaway. Ed, let him go. I can forgive him for getting Ann pregnant, but I can't forgive him for leaving. I just can't."

Now there was this new boy to focus on, growing so fast and so hard that Ann would sometimes double over from the pain of spreading muscles and stretching skin as she moved into her third trimester. Once the news settled in at school, kids watched Ann's growing belly with blatant interest. She'd liked being the center of attention before; now she wanted to escape all the sideways glances and outright stares, the classmates who dared ask if they could touch her impossibly swollen belly, the kid who sat next to her in chemistry who noticed a tiny elbow glide from one side of her stomach to the other and shouted, "Holy shit!" She didn't care anymore about being popular or admired. It was so freeing to care only about this constant companion twisting, hiccuping, kicking, and swimming inside her.

Her body was the bell, and the baby the clapper.

SEVENTEEN

Poppy

Bradford Beach was the perfect place to trip. There was so much to experience between the cloudless night sky, Lake Michigan, and the steep bluff across the bridge spanning Lincoln Memorial Drive. The campfire blazed, offering welcome relief from the biting wind that blew off the water. The sand was cold under Poppy's bare feet. It was late April, just warm enough to smell the promise of the approaching summer. Usually, this meant that a trip to Cape Cod was in the offing. Not this year. Poppy's parents told her that they'd stay in Wisconsin because Ann refused to go east, and they couldn't leave her back home alone with the baby. The baby, the baby, the baby. Everything was because of the baby.

Poppy made some new friends from Ann's year. Kurt Schwartz sat across from Poppy, his face nearly impossible to see under his ashy blond dreadlocks. Angie Dols, who worked at the café and gave them free drinks, was sprawled out on a beach blanket, staring at the stars. They were waiting for the 'shrooms to kick in.

Ann wouldn't have approved of Poppy hanging out with stoners like

Kurt and Angie, and she already knew Michael hadn't liked them. Poppy thought they were cool; they got high for enlightenment. They wanted to experience stuff Ann wouldn't understand.

"When's your sister due?" Kurt asked.

"In two weeks, but it could be any day now," Poppy said. "She's starting to clean shit, like she literally cleaned the inside of the dishwasher last night. This morning she emptied out her backpack and put it through the wash. My mom says she's nesting."

"Is she going to give it up?" Angie asked. "That's what I heard."

Poppy was annoyed by the word "it" and this latest bit of gossip. "Ann never gives anything up."

Kurt lit a cigarette. "Your parents must be super pissed."

"Not really." Poppy was surprised it took Ann so long to tell them. It was a big deal, sure, but what had Ann been worried about? Did she think they'd kick her out, send her away to some reform school? It didn't take long for them to adjust to the idea, especially her mom, who'd been by Ann's side ever since she'd found out about the baby. She was even excited about it, coming home from shopping trips with a tiny pair of baby socks she'd found, or an adorable little onesie, and they'd ooh and aah. Her dad's response was more complicated. He flipped when he heard the news, got in his car and disappeared for a few hours every day. Later, he told Poppy that he'd driven all over the city trying to find Michael. He wasn't anywhere he'd looked; not in his old apartment building, the gym, running along the Oak Leaf Trail or Lake Drive or at any of his old haunts or friends' houses. What would her dad have done if he'd found him? He was just as likely to knock Michael's lights out as to give him a hug, depending on where he was in the arc of his anger—anger that settled into a deep hurt. "I really did think of Michael as a son," he'd said, his face in his hands. "I thought he was mine." This obsession with finding Michael never let up. Poppy saw him scan for Michael at the grocery store, under the trees in Riverside Park, sitting in the food court at Bayshore Mall, waiting for him to walk into the classroom—anywhere, everywhere. Poppy understood, because, confused as she was by what Michael had done, she looked out for him, too, refusing to believe he was truly gone.

Angie threw an empty can of Miller Lite into the fire. "I saw Ann the other day at Walgreens. She was huge."

Poppy agreed. Her sister *was* huge. She was all body now, hippy, chubbier, and big-breasted. Her golden hair had grown thick and plentiful during the pregnancy. Poppy had never seen Ann look more beautiful.

Kurt said, "You ever hear that Bill Cosby routine about childbirth, how it's as easy as pulling your lower lip over the top of your head?"

"You guys, stop it," Poppy said. She might have been more upset without the comforting sensation of the mushrooms. She liked the way they made her feel so . . . atmospheric, like hazy weather in her brain.

"I saw my dog give birth once," said Angie. "Nobody tells you about the afterbirth. It's like having a second baby. This sack drops out after the puppies are born, but that's not the gross part. The gross part is that she *ate* it. I'm telling you, it was, like, crunchy." Everyone was bent over with laughter, even Poppy, although her mind was starting to drift until she couldn't remember what she'd been laughing at in the first place. She tried not to think about Ann and the pregnancy anymore. She looked at Lake Michigan, the blue-gray water somehow lighter than the sky. The waves, so gentle compared to the waves in the Atlantic, weren't coming *to* the shore, they were pushing the shore away. How come she'd never noticed that pulling-away sensation when she'd ridden all those waves in Wellfleet? Kit told her a wave is just energy that never dies. It travels all over the world: one wave. She wished she could go back to the Cape and see Kit. She wished she could go everywhere, ride every wave. She couldn't stand the idea of being trapped in Milwaukee all summer.

"Let's explore," Kurt said, reaching for Poppy's hand. He wanted to screw around with her, she could tell. She wanted the same thing, only sex terrified her now that she lived with a cautionary tale. "I should have told you girls how easy it is to get pregnant," her mother said. "You were both a one-shot deal."

Poppy stood up and ran across the bridge. She raced after Kurt and Angie along a tamped-down dirt path between the old oak trees. They stopped, breathless, and began looking for patterns in the bark, marveling over a pinecone's symmetry, folding a dead leaf from last fall into small origami squares. Kurt reached down and grabbed fistfuls of dirt, sifted through it, and rubbed it all over her face. She did the same to him, and then Angie. They stuffed twigs behind their ears, held hands, danced in circles. Poppy forgot all about the baby and her missing brother.

"The moon!" Poppy said. "Just look at it!"

"Dude, it's bulbous," said Kurt. "Bulbous" was a word Ms. Martin, their English teacher, used all the time, until everyone at school said it the way she did, with a lisp. The moon *was* bulbous. She watched it expand and contract like it was breathing. The moon could breathe! She needed to get closer. She started to climb a tree, an old oak. How wonderful would it be to hold the moon in her hand, to pluck it from the sky and put it in her pocket? She climbed and climbed until she heard a crack. The sound didn't alarm her; it was in harmony with all the other sounds of the universe: the water lapping at the shore, her friends' voices, the hum of the cars that buzzed past on Lincoln Memorial Drive. Her fall was slow enough for her to appreciate the beauty of weightlessness, like when she was little and she and Ann used to jump off the roof of the garage and land in their father's leaf piles, back when she and Ann did everything together: compete at memorizing song lyrics, speed-reading, swim races across Duck Pond.

Then there was the ground, hard and real. Lightning shot out of her ankle, piercing through the haze. Kurt reached for her. "You dropped from the sky like a raindrop."

Kurt carried her home on his back. She almost forgot about her ankle, focusing instead on the smell of patchouli in his beat-up sweater, how his braids were coarse as ropes. Kurt stopped abruptly when he read the note her parents had left for her on the back door: "Ann's at St. Mary's. You've got to get there!"

THE HOSPITAL WAS CLOSE, LESS than a mile away. Her leg started to scream, and some little shred of sanity told her that putting weight on it would make it worse. Kurt left her at the hospital door. When she limped into the sterile lobby, she was struck by how much she didn't belong there, as if she'd emerged from another world, reeking of spring air, campfire smoke, beer, and pot while somewhere in that cold building her sister was having her baby.

Her dad was waiting for her. Her dad! She loved him so much, from his gruff voice to the cut on his cheek where he'd taken a dig from his razor that morning. He always had to tap out whatever song he heard with his fingertips. They were on the same wavelength. He wrapped Poppy up in his wiry arms and made her wish she were still his baby.

"How's she doing?"

Her dad just pulled her closer. She felt his body jerk with tears. She tried to sober up, be real, pretend she was the Poppy he wanted her to be. "Is the baby OK?"

"Now he is. His heart rate dropped, and the cord was around his neck. He could have . . . but the doctors were there. He didn't. He's fine. He's amazing, Pops. I wish you'd been here. That kid is a . . . he's a crescendo, you know? That sweet little fucker snuck up on me." His voice broke and he started to cry again. Poppy had seen her father cry before, but never when it was just the two of them in the same room.

"Did Michael show up?"

Her father shook his head no. Maybe it was the drugs, maybe it was long overdue, but she was rocked by a deep, hard seizure of sadness. She'd been convinced that Michael would come home before the baby was born; she'd fantasized all kinds of scenarios.

"Ann was all drugged up. She called for him. She wanted him to be there. Anyway, come see your nephew."

The baby's warm, pink body rested against Ann's bare chest, still curled up in fetal position, his bare rear sticking into the air. He was so new. Her mom sat at the edge of the bed wearing a red bandana. Her face was drenched in sweat, as if she'd had the baby herself. She was glowing, full of purpose. "Oh honey, he was sunny-side up. It got scary there for a while." Poppy couldn't believe she had been dancing with Kurt and Angie while the baby fought for his life. "Your sister was a trooper." Her mom ran her hand through Ann's matted hair. Poppy saw a closeness between them she'd never noticed, like they were wrapped in the same light. They even looked more alike. "It was incredibly painful, but you'll forget, you will."

"The drugs helped." Ann smiled, dreamy from whatever they'd given her. "Look, Pops."

His face was blotched and puffy, his skull misshapen from the forceps, his hair thick and black. Wavy, colorful vibrations spread off of him and out of his alien cool eyes, wet with the ointment the nurses put on them. She placed her hand on him; for so long he had been part of Ann's subterranean world. It felt so intimate, like she was touching her sister, too. And Michael, she supposed. "Oh, hey little man," Poppy said, crying now, overcome.

"His name is Noah," Ann said. "It means 'comfort.'"

Noah. What a nice name. "Hey little man, welcome to the universe," said Poppy. She spoke slowly. His fingers were so small! One, two, three, four, five. "Welcome to this cycle of life."

Ann pulled a twig out of Poppy's hair. "Why do you have dirt all over your face?"

Poppy shrugged. Her ankle throbbed and needed to be looked at.

Her mom stood up and put her fingers on Poppy's chin, trying to look into Poppy's eyes. "Honey, are you high? Your pupils are big as saucers."

"I think I busted my ankle."

Suddenly Ann started laughing. Her laughter was music, a wave to ride. Why didn't Ann laugh more? Poppy loved her sister when she laughed. She'd never loved Ann more than she did at that very moment. She was so tough, keeping this kid. She was in a different league.

"What's funny?" her dad asked.

"Just look at us. One of your kids is missing, the other is a burnout, and I'm a teenage mom. Great job, you guys!"

A nurse who'd been standing in the corner tried to hide her smile. Soon they were all laughing, and for a moment Poppy felt her family was complete again even with Michael gone. It was a feeling that wouldn't last.

Part Two

Milwaukee Journal-Sentinel

AUGUST 20, 2015

LOCAL COUPLE KILLED IN AUTOMOBILE
CRASH OUTSIDE TOLEDO

According to the Lucas County sheriff, a local Milwaukee couple traveling on I-90 through Toledo were involved in an early-morning accident when an inattentive semi driver crossed lanes and hit their vehicle head-on. The couple, Edward and Connie Gordon of Milwaukee, were en route to Wisconsin from Massachusetts, where they'd spent the summer. Connie Gordon was pronounced dead at the scene. Edward Gordon was rushed to a local hospital, where he died. The driver of the semi, Charles Radtke of Orlando, Florida, was also pronounced dead at the scene.

Edward Gordon taught history at Riverside High School. Connie Gordon was retired.

"This is just devastating," said Dawn Marks, a former colleague of Connie Gordon's. "They made that trip to Cape Cod every year."

EIGHTEEN

Poppy

Surfing used to be enough. Poppy once felt she was part of an epic, worldwide search for the best swells on the most perfect beach in a prized, undiscovered location. Nothing quite compared to the thrill of a jet taking off (especially when she was sleeping with a Hawaiian Air pilot who gave her free buddy passes) and the intoxicating sensation of living a life that was always changing, always moving. Newness was like a drug for her. As soon as she'd memorized the street names and got to know the locals in any given place, it was time to take off again.

Poppy started out in Central America; from there, she went all over. She'd surfed J-Bay, Pavones, Witch's Rock, and Uluwatu. There wasn't much thought or logic to where she'd go. If her friends were heading somewhere interesting and she could make it work, she'd pack her giant backpack and join them, staying only as long as it took to make enough "go" money.

The North Shore of Oahu was the first place she'd started to think of as home since dropping out of college. She was with her beautiful young boyfriend, Jens, a skinny German surfer she'd met in Indo. He looked like Pan with his shoulder-length hair, golden skin, full lips, and cinnamon eyes. The stripe of zinc oxide across his nose almost seemed tribal on him, and he wore his ripped-up wet suit so low on his waist that it practically hung off the hook of his penis. It wasn't love, but Jens was sweet and sensual and wonderfully indefinite. Maybe he'd go home, maybe he'd spend another month here or there, maybe he'd go to Bali, maybe New Zealand. Maybe she'd go with him. Maybe he'd go alone. It was all good.

Through their connections (the surfing underworld was all about connections), they were able to live in a tree house that was built into the bluff in a surf colony a few minutes from Sunset Beach, and she got a job working at Jameson's as a bartender. She owned a car, a five-hundred-dollar beater Volkswagen bug she could only afford to drive because, at that time, there were no insurance laws on the island.

The Banzai Pipeline was the best seven-mile stretch in the world. Poppy thought she could handle it. She was getting good enough that she even thought she might land some sponsorships and free gear, but just when she thought she was ready—when winter rolled around and the swells grew—she broke her jaw when she hit coral in a bad pearl. The break was fast, but the time she spent under the water had seemed to last forever. She would have drowned if the current had been stronger, or if she'd hit her head instead of her jaw. Her friends pulled her out of the water, semiconscious.

It was a painful break, more painful than when she'd broken her ankle. Her jaw was wired shut, and the ever-moving life she'd been living for over a decade came to a grinding halt. For six long weeks she sipped Ensure from a straw and got strung out and constipated from Percocet. She spent her days feeding the chickens and stray cats that wandered near her tent. Her only companion Burl, who owned the surf compound. He was a leather-skinned, silver-haired old-school surfer with an outie belly button so large it looked like it had been sewn onto his stomach. She wanted Burl to be a father figure to her, because she missed her own dad, but drugs had turned Burl's brain into scrambled eggs. He couldn't hold a thought. He just nodded and smiled, grateful for her company.

When the wires were finally removed from her jaw, she'd carefully go out on a body board, paddling safely beyond the breaks, or she'd walk the beach, dutifully videotaping Jens and the other surfers. The power of the water used to thrill her, but now it made her fearful. What if she'd snapped her neck? What if nobody else had seen her go under? Did she get injured because she wasn't that good in the first place? It was winter, and the best surfers in the world had converged at Sunset Beach. *They* didn't get hurt.

She'd never made a conscious decision to quit surfing; she thought she was just taking a break, but her hiatus went on and on, just like the hiatus from her former life. She found herself drawn to what was happening on land. Hawaii had become a melting pot of all ages and religions; the culture that formed was all about surfing, travel, spirituality, and healthy living. Things were happening on the North Shore back then that were just beginning to be known elsewhere, like capoeira, an Afro-Brazilian form of martial art performed as dance. After spending so much time balancing on the water, she found this kind of movement natural: easy, even joyful. She was still strong and flexible, and she had great balance. She was drawn to any physical activity that allowed her to lose herself.

One night at an ayahuasca ceremony, the Peruvian shaman passed around hallucinogenic tea. People flipped out, melted down, and became transformed. It was intense therapy for emotional stuff: victims forgave their abusers, alcoholics swore they'd stop drinking. Jens confessed that he'd been sleeping with a beautiful, blond Swedish surfer named Uma. Poppy didn't care much; she wasn't possessive. Her life was open and communal. She was attracted to elusive, adventurous men. She wasn't looking for commitment.

Poppy worried about what might happen to her when she took the drug. From what she'd heard, ayahuasca could unearth long-buried feelings, and she had plenty of those. Instead, she had a vision that changed her life. She saw herself with her palm pressed to a man's forehead. A red heat came out of her. The man's hands were clasped around her wrist in gratitude. She told the shaman about it.

"There's a light in you," he said. "You can do healing work. You're a healer. You've known this all along. Even strangers can see this in you. Give yourself to the experience. Just live it. *Be* it."

The next week she sold her VW and bought a one-way ticket to an ashram in Mulki, India. It was there that she learned about the Tamil *Divya Prabandham* and all the tricks of Iyengar, from liver-cleansing twists to handstands that improve fertility. She felt invigorated and reborn, full of new, useful knowledge and what she believed was healing energy.

From there she went to Bali and fell into a new "soul family" of teachers and gurus and guides. She was told that she was in the process of being re-created, but first she had to be broken down. She was warned to avoid the awesome, lurking power of dark energy. She learned about planets of water and planets of fire, of sweat lodges and love altars, of energy work, auras, vibrations, and chanting. She studied in caves with mentors who taught her about animal interactions, past lives, and the rise of the supreme feminine. She prayed to twin goddesses and started calling her friends mermaids. She wore a bindi on her forehead and tulsi wood bracelets on her wrists, and she constantly handled the mala beads around her neck that helped her to focus on the channels of her heart. Everything was soft and loving and light.

No greed. No hurt. No pain.

From there she spun around to yoga festivals and ashrams and lived for a while with a Buddhist family in Sri Lanka. Things seemed to be happening not to her but *through* her, she was so open. She didn't know what was going on; she'd forgotten who she was, and where she came from. She was so focused on her breath she could go for days without eating and slept only a few hours a night. She swore she could even levitate.

But then Poppy got a bad bladder infection, and one of her "mermaids" disappeared with what little money she had. Her guru told her that the gods love her, and it was time for her to go back. She assumed "back" meant the North Shore, so that's where she went. She returned to

Oahu feeling suddenly lost and stripped raw. Years had passed. Every-thing in Hawaii felt different: the colors, the earth, the water, the auras. She saw dark energy around all the party people, and felt that the island had become suddenly aggressive—and expensive.

Burl's surf compound had been sold to a software developer from Silicon Valley who had torn down not only the tree houses but also the trees, and turned it into a multimillion-dollar estate with a pool and gated entrance. Most of the people she'd known before were gone, in-cluding Jens and Uma.

With no place else to go, she lived in a tent behind a food truck. She wouldn't have minded the tent before, but the tiny, nylon confine snapped in the wind and rustled when animals skittered past. It made her feel unsafe and claustrophobic, and her back ached from the hard foam mat. "Don't attach to bodily concerns," she'd tell herself.

She wanted to heal someone—anyone—but she also needed to eat, so she started teaching yoga. She made simple flyers advertising "Beach Yoga with Poppy." She distributed them to the resort concierges, and sta-pled them to the bulletin board at Ted's Bakery, and on every lamppost and palm tree she could find.

Rain, sun, cold, or impending hurricane, she was there on Sunset Beach with her portable sack of mats and blocks. She had a battery-operated boom box that she set on a towel. When her students showed up for class, and there were somehow always students, she'd greet them with her sweet, open smile. She'd watch them congratulate themselves for finding an instructor who looked every bit the vacation yogi they'd expected. They loved her Oakley Big Taco sunglasses, deep tan, muscu-lar limbs, and golden-auburn hair pulled back into braided pigtails that somehow appeared sexy instead of childish.

She'd try to think of something inspiring to say from all she'd learned from her studies and travels, but it all seemed too involved and compli-cated to communicate to her students in a meaningful way. Instead, she read from a cheesy book of inspirational quotes her friend Monique had given to her when she'd broken her jaw. She tried to quote something that made her seem profound, like "Silence is an ocean. Speech is a river." She used her best poetry-reading voice, imitating her mother.

No matter what she said, her disciples would always nod in agreement, like she'd thought it up herself. She'd start to explain why a certain pose was important, or she'd explore a Sanskrit saying, but she'd forget the words and the meaning and talk herself into a corner while her students waited expectantly for her to get to the ideas that would help them change their lives.

That's when she got good at improvising. She'd make up names for poses, like "sitting cow," and tout health benefits that probably didn't exist, like "emulsifying the bile" and "pulsing kidneys." Poppy often forgot where she was in her progression, because she didn't plan her classes, and her jaw hadn't healed right, so yoga inversions caused her so much pain that she couldn't teach unless she was stoned. Her hamstrings, IT band, and shoulders were tight from years of surfing.

She'd look around at all those bodies, sunburned, twisted, and prone, and wonder: Did they just do their right or left side? What apex pose had she told them they were working toward? Crow? Tittibhasana? Did anyone even care? She could tell them to strip naked and hump each other and they'd do it.

Silence is an ocean.

Speech is a river.

At the end of class she'd collect her ten bucks from each participant. She hated that yoga was yoked to money, but she was barely scraping by. Maybe it was the money collecting that began to erode her love for yoga, or maybe it was her students. Travelers to the beach destinations were mostly wealthy middle-aged people who used the word "blessed" too much. The truth was they weren't blessed, they were privileged. They could afford to stay in fancy resorts and boutique hotels, while the people who actually worked in these places had to sleep in huts, the backs of vans, crappy apartments above souvenir shops, or in tents.

Poppy began to resent how hard it had become to find a place that was truly authentic, beautiful, and cheap—all the best beaches had been monopolized by the travel industry and catered to women in tight-fitting, eighty-dollar Lululemon tanks and butt-hugging Lycra yoga pants, and men in shirts with country club insignias. But it seemed that the more she resented her students, the more they liked her. They thought she was living the life they didn't have the guts to live, when what scared Poppy most was *their* lives of responsibility and commitment.

Who was she to tell these people to make space inside themselves with their breath, while she was wondering if this was really possible. Wasn't breathing just breathing? Did prana even exist? She'd talk about the light in herself connecting to the light in her students, even though she knew she'd be forgotten as soon as their plane touched down in Cleveland or Bismarck or San Antonio. It seemed navel-gazey to devote so much time and energy to self-improvement—this had nothing to do with healing.

The hard questions, the ones she used to keep at bay with weed, beer fogs, and meditation, grew more persistent. Could she do this forever, or would she end up like Burl? Should she call home? Visit her parents? Try to make peace with Ann and get to know Noah? Her dad said they weren't even in Milwaukee anymore; Ann finally got her wish and moved to Boston.

Go-time. Poppy decided to pack up her things and move to Panama. It seemed the more she moved, the more she felt like she was standing still. But if that was the case, how come she saw an older, startling version of herself whenever she snuck a peek at her reflection in the window of a parked VW van?

Could she give up the tides and the moon and the damp warmth and move back to Milwaukee? *Milwaukee:* the name of her hometown sounded funny, strange. She could return to the Wellfleet house. It didn't matter how far away she got from it; it called to her. All it took was the smell of a marsh or the sound of a catbird to make her want to go back. Was that what she should do next?

As if in answer to the question, she finally checked her "poppybythe-sea" email—something she hardly ever did, because it was a pain to get to the library. Mixed in with all the spam, she found about ten messages from Ann, who rarely wrote unless she had updates about Noah.

She opened up the last email Ann had sent:

> Where are you? I have no idea how to reach you. Look, I didn't want to say this in an email, Pops, I really didn't, but you need to know: Mom and Dad were in an accident. A bad one. They didn't make it. I'm sorry. It's already been two weeks, so I guess there's nothing you can do at this point. Everything's been taken care of—for now. Call me when you get this, send a smoke signal, something—please?

NINETEEN

Michael

It was so cold that February day that it seemed like a miracle the salt water managed to shove its way into Drummer Cove and escape back to the sea without hardening into ice. The Cape was so quiet, so frigid. The water was the only thing that moved.

It was high tide. From the roof, Michael took a break from his work and stopped to admire the view—there were so many trees around the Gordons' house that this was the only real way to take it in. The surface of the water sparkled royal blue against the light dusting of snow that had fallen earlier that morning on the bluff and the small islands of beach grass. The storm was off to sea now. Michael could see the thick layer of once-threatening clouds, like an army in retreat in the distance. It created a dramatic contrast between the hovering darkness on the horizon and the pure, high midday light of winter.

Michael loved the cove, a place that felt special and secret, especially this time of year, when it was hidden from the tourists' greedy eyes. He wished like hell that the Cape's economy and his own livelihood didn't depend on weekly renters who arrived on summer Saturdays in their minivans, armed with cell phones, floaties, flip-flops, and *People* magazines.

In winter, the tourists and all their crap were thankfully gone. The roads were clear, and the greasy sheen of sunscreen had vanished from the surface of the ponds, now frozen and still.

On days like this, it was so quiet that Michael could fool himself into thinking that the cove belonged to him alone. It felt like it did: he loved the whole Outer Cape, but this spot was especially sacred. The earthy smell of rotting peat and sulfur somehow made his whole confusing life make sense. He appreciated the danger of the silt, the privacy of the cove, the rhythm of the tides—a change that was predictable, the only kind of change he could stomach.

He wished his daughter, Avery, could be there with him, but she was at school. He'd never brought her to the Gordons' house or told her about them. But two or three times a week he took her to Blackfish Creek so they could walk along the crunchy straw path that wrapped around most of the cove. They'd stomp on the sand and watch the hermit crabs scamper back into their holes and inspect the carcasses of upturned horseshoe crabs. The small, young ones had golden backs as thin and clear as varnish, while the bigger crabs had thick shells like tree bark, and could live to be over a hundred years old. He liked to run his finger along the spiked toothy ridges of their backs. Avery knocked her small fist against their crab shells so she could create a drumming sound. She'd flip the dead ones upside down and yank off their sandy, barnacled legs like she was pulling petals off a flower. She could do that without hesitation; she was a child of the Cape, comfortable with the ocean and its creatures in a way he never would be, although his distance created a space for a sort of reverence that she'd never understand.

Michael pounded a nail into the side of the Gordons' chimney and wrapped wire around it. What started as a simple project had become more complicated when he realized the mortar between some of the bricks had started to crumble, and the chimney needed tuck-pointing. He'd taken care of that last week. Now he could proceed with the original task at hand: repairing the grate on the top of the chimney that kept the squirrels and raccoons out. This was something Ed should have checked when he left. It wasn't like he hadn't learned his lesson.

That second summer Michael came to the Cape with the Gordons, Connie opened the door and backed away, overcome by the odor in the closed-up house. They discovered a family of dead raccoons in the living room. Their nest had collapsed down the chimney, and the animals couldn't get out of the house. The signs of their desperation were everywhere: in the dirty animal prints all over the rugs, upholstery, and floorboards, the scratch marks on the windowsills and the nose prints on the windows. He should have seen it as an omen of how that summer would ultimately end.

Michael looked at the roof. The shingles needed to be replaced, but that was the kind of big job he couldn't tackle without being noticed. There were plenty of other big jobs he itched to take care of: spackling the cracks in the living room walls, sanding the floors, putting dormers in the second floor to make decent living space out of the attic—his old bedroom.

He'd wanted to fix the Gordons' house ever since the first year after he'd left Milwaukee, when he'd spent part of the winter living there undetected. That was the loneliest time of his life. No television, no companions, no job to go to, no school to keep him busy, no family, no friends: just Anthony's threats rattling around in his head, and the reverberating thoughts of Ann telling everyone that Michael was the father of that prick's kid. It crippled him to think of what Ed and Connie must have said about him, how wrong they thought they'd been to have adopted him. He was crushed and sorry for himself. By the beginning of March, he'd decided he couldn't hide out at the Gordons' place anymore. Sooner or later someone would find him. He closed the house down, careful to conceal every single trace of his presence, and he showed up at Jason's.

"Shouldn't you be in school?"

"I graduated early."

Jason could tell Michael was lying. "You're going to need to get your GED."

"Fine. Can you give me some work?"

"I knew you'd be back."

Michael could tell that Jason knew something was up, but he was grateful that his old boss—and now his only friend in the world—played along. "I could also use a place to stay for a while if you've got some extra room." It was all he could do to hold it together. As much as he hated asking for help, it was better than spending a dime of Anthony's dirty money.

"I've got a couch in the basement. It's not much, but sure beats sleeping on the beach."

"I'll pay you back."

"I've seen you work your ass off. I'm not worried about that. You hungry?"

Michael nodded yes. For months, he'd eaten only nonperishables. He was overcome with gratitude for Jason's company and warm food. He felt, for the first time in months, that it might actually be possible for his life to improve again.

Jason took Michael's bag off his shoulder and ushered him into the kitchen, where his wife, Angela, was pushing steaming food around in a frying pan. "Hey, Michael," she said. "You know you'd better like yourself a whole damn lot if you decide to live on the Cape in the off-season."

Jason paid him in cash; no background checks, no requests to furnish proof of who he was, no taxes to file, no way for Connie or Ed to figure out where he'd gone, not that they were looking. When Michael wasn't plowing driveways or checking on his clients' empty houses, he was studying.

When summer came around he asked Jason not to have him work in Wellfleet, convinced that Connie or Ed would spy him pruning a hedge or edging a lawn. Come September, once he knew the Gordons were back in Milwaukee, he'd slip away and spend a secret night in their Wellfleet house listening to Ed's LPs. Ed loved Dylan and the Eagles and all the stuff you'd expect a middle-aged, guitar-playing, sandal-wearing guy like Ed to listen to, but he also had a thing for blues and jazz. It was through Ed that Michael learned about heavy-hitters like Charles Mingus, Art Blakey, and Coleman Hawkins, but he also had albums by obscure musicians like Roswell Rudd, Jeanne Lee, and Alan Shorter. Michael didn't always love Ed's music, but he gave it a try, just like he'd read whatever books Connie had read. He studied the lines she'd underlined and paid attention to the notes she wrote in the margins. He wished he could talk to them, but getting that close to them, listening to their music, reading their books—that was as close as he could get to having a sort of conversation.

His overnight visits eventually stopped, like a childhood habit he'd outgrown. Still, he looked after the house whenever he could, the way he was watching over it that cold February afternoon.

He often worked in the barn, where he could use what Ed called his "medieval torture devices," an amazing collection of the kinds of rusty tools that had been passed down to him: a miter vise, a creeper, a Stanley plane—even a special hacksaw used to dehorn goats and calves.

The barn was where Michael found the die-cutting tools he needed to make what was, at first, just a toy for Avery. Later, it became a prototype that would help him launch Anibitz, his new side business based on that old game he'd played with Ann and Poppy, where they'd combine two, three, four parts of animals. A centipede, catfish, and crow: the "centifishow." A hyena, shark, and gerbil: the "hyarkbil." The thin wooden pieces snapped together like jigsaw-puzzle pieces, and the game was to try to guess and name the creations, and to find creations that represented who you were—your "spirit Anibitz." The concept had become so successful that he could hardly say it was a side business anymore, and sales had recently surged thanks to a few magazine articles and some active Anibitz fan sites. He could barely keep up with the orders on his own anymore, and soon he might need to cash out his share in the landscaping company to raise funds to invest in expansion.

His distributor was a freelance rep from Los Angeles named Sandi.

She was so into Anibitz that he swore she played with the toys herself when she wasn't talking to him about social media and the youth market. She had a million ideas for his product: a clothing line, coloring books, plastic figures that snapped together, an educational line for science teachers, and a bunch of other stuff Michael tuned out because she always called him at the most inopportune time, like when he was fixing an overflowing toilet for Shelby, or firing an employee with a heroin habit.

Sandi had called him earlier that week, excited. "The kids in Japan are going apeshit for them," she said.

"Great." Michael must have sounded unimpressed.

"Michael! Did you hear me? Japan! The kids are combobulating like crazy."

"Combobulating" was the process of selecting the animal segments that customers could choose from to make their own Anibitz creation. You could pick up to three, although Sandi was already imagining how they might expand to four, maybe even five, if they could find a plastics manufacturer that could come up with a decent prototype.

There was even talk of opening an Anibitz showroom somewhere. The past two years, during the low season, this was what Michael had been focused on. He'd always believed in his idea, although he'd rather work outside than deal with the business that needed to be done on his computer.

A truck rumbled down Route 6. It was easy to spend time at the Gordons' undetected. The neighbors on either side of the Gordons' house didn't notice Michael's presence. They were gone for the winter, and even if they'd been there, their houses faced the cove—they reminded Michael of chairs with their backs set away from each other. Michael drove a landscaping truck, and landscapers were hired to routinely check on houses during the winter—nothing suspicious about that. The police wouldn't care much, either. The force was thin after the budget cuts, and the few officers who remained were busy with bigger problems, the kind you wouldn't think you'd find on the Cape: thefts, drug abuse—stuff that kept Michael up at night worried over trouble that could befall Avery when she got older.

He finished his repair work, climbed down his tall ladder, and loaded it back in his pickup, which he'd parked on the service drive under the trees so nobody would know he was there. He figured he'd check to make sure the pipes hadn't burst. Ed and Connie emptied all the water, but sometimes they did a shit job, like three years ago, when they'd neglected to drain the water heater and Michael caught it just in time, before the heating element cracked.

As much as Ed and Connie loved their house, and as much as Ed liked to tinker, they weren't really house people, not the way Michael was. That was why Michael figured they probably hadn't ever noticed his small repair jobs. But he couldn't help leaving little messages behind, like the dried leaves he inserted between the pages of some of Connie's books, a shiny penny dropped head-up on the floor because Poppy used to be superstitious about pennies, or a jar of grilling spices he thought Connie might like tucked in the back of the kitchen cabinet. Last fall he'd set a pretty slipper shell under the pillow of Poppy's bed. When she was young, she told him the shells were cribs for babies. He noticed when he lifted the pillow up that her bed was covered in dust; he figured it hadn't been slept in for years.

But Michael never left a secret message for Ann. He didn't know how to communicate with her, not even in the smallest and most subtle way.

Anthony Shaw, on the other hand . . . for years, Michael had planned to someday send him a message loud and clear. Back when Avery was born and he and Shelby sorted through all their financials, Michael finally checked on "his" bank account and discovered that Anthony, who'd cosigned and had equal access to the account, had withdrawn so much that there was barely enough to keep the account open. That was money that was supposed to go to Ann. Michael knew Ann was getting screwed over, and even though she'd sold him upstream, he couldn't stand the thought of her struggling. He was so upset that he'd finally told Shelby the full story about the Gordons.

He didn't have much money then, not after he'd used the other check Anthony had given him to buy his partnership in Jason's business, but he suffered from lingering feelings of guilt for accepting Anthony's payoff in the first place. Michael worked it out with the bank and scraped together some of his own money to send to Ann, a little here, a little there, always in odd amounts that probably confused her since she'd been used to getting the same amount every month. Shelby was generally supportive, but during the financial crisis, when they were really struggling to get by, she told him that it was time to wash his hands of Ann and her "situation." After all, Shelby said, Ann was the one who'd fallen in love with a jerk, and she was the one who'd come up with the stupid plan in the first place.

Enough was enough.

Michael took off his heavy gloves and scooped the house key out of the bulb digger. The heavy, old key to the Gordon house slid into the lock. He heard the familiar click and opened the door, inhaling the familiar, musty odor. But this time something was different. Someone had been there. He spied a Starbucks cup with lipstick on the kitchen table. He picked it up and pulled off the lid. The little bit of coffee left inside had frozen solid. "Hello?" he said, although he could sense that he was alone.

The rooms were just as they'd been the last time he'd been there, the beds and all the furniture covered in sheets. He felt as if he were in the middle of a morgue. Then he saw something he also hadn't seen before: a business card with a photo of the ocean as the background. He picked it up: Carol Hargrove. Her photo was off to one side. She wasn't even smiling. She didn't look like any Realtor he'd ever met. She looked like she belonged outdoors, like she worked on his landscaping crew.

Perplexed, Michael stuffed the business card in his wallet and sat down on the sofa. That was when he felt something hard and heard a sharp crack. He lifted up the sheet and saw the photo of himself with Ann and Poppy that had always remained on the mantel. That photo meant everything to him, because, after what had happened, Ed and Connie had kept it on display when they could have stuffed it in a drawer.

Why, now, was it hidden under the sheet? The crack ran right down the middle, right through him.

How did it get there? He set the photo back on the mantel as it was. He felt spooked enough to drive back to the shop and pull the Shaws' house key from the pegboard. Jason still had the Shaws' key, and it dangled teasingly all these years.

Michael parked his truck down the street and walked quietly down the long driveway toward the brown house, careful to make sure nobody was watching him. The sun was going down, and he admired the slit of light on the horizon over the bay. There, in that eerie afternoon light, was the bluestone patio he'd once laid, visible in the gullies where the wind had lifted the snow. There were the rosebushes, although nobody had bothered to cover them with burlap. The key slid into the lock, and the door creaked when he opened it. He walked back into the place and felt as if he'd been body-slammed against the massive white walls. This was where his youth had died. It took him a moment to collect himself. What was it about houses, the power they had? The houses he'd once inhabited now inhabited him. They were witnesses to who he once was, to the people he'd loved—and hated. He could practically hear the fall of Anthony's footsteps, the jingle of Maureen's bracelets, the bored lamentations of the boys. And Ann, Ann, Ann. He could practically reach out and touch her ponytail, her bare feet, her smile.

Everything that had seemed modern and new now looked old and worn. The sheet on the couch was rumpled, the vase at the center of the dining room table was empty. He had to leave.

But first, he had a mission to accomplish, just a flick of a switch. Only Anthony might appreciate how a single gesture could cause such great destruction.

—

TWENTY

Ann

Ann pounded along the Salt and Pepper Bridge and made her way from the Back Bay to the MIT campus. She loved the view of the Boston skyline. She and Noah had moved here when Noah was eleven, almost five years ago. Yet she still felt like a newcomer in the city, still in awe of the old brick buildings, bay windows, turrets, and history, still proud she was able to insert herself, a single mom, into the bustle and flow of the intimidating Northeast, proud she'd found a life here. She could have easily never left Milwaukee, but Boston had always been part of her "Ann with a Plan" vision; it was where she'd always imagined her adult life taking shape. The city had seemed almost mythical to her, especially after her plans to study there had changed so abruptly. It was a city she'd always wanted to live in, near the Cape she loved. She was close, yes, but she always came up with excuses to not make the drive. Now she wished she could have refused to let that single memory of Anthony prevent her from spending more time with her parents.

Instead, she worked. As soon as she finished her MBA at Marquette, she secured a job at BNN, a strategic consulting firm in the Back Bay. Now she was in management, in charge of "top of funnel" channel messaging for an online housewares site. Lately, she was on youth and nursery, one of the "life stages." She analyzed search data—"industrial chic" was out, "boho" was in, and "glam" was on the rise. She selected pregnant celebrities who were social media influencers to promote their products, reaching out to offer them exclusive contracts and other product-for-publicity arrangements. Her work made her long to have another baby herself and participate in all the shallow consumer excitement that went along with it. When she had Noah, her parents hauled her own crib up from the basement, a crib that would be recalled for a thousand reasons today.

She was good at her job, and had a particularly shrewd eye for data analysis, but all of the management changes her coworkers whispered about had her feeling nervous. As a single mom, the prospect of losing her job terrified her. That evening, she tried to leave her concerns about conversion rates and job security at the office. She didn't think about her pace or the distance she'd gone, which was unusual, because Ann liked to measure things. She wore a GPS heart rate monitor on her wrist that was as big as a blood pressure cuff. She could upload data from her workouts to her computer and keep track of every step, interval, and heartbeat. Instead of a journal, she kept a training log and tracked it religiously, desperate to see improvement in her speed and endurance. She believed she could always improve.

It was getting dark. She'd meant to head back to the Cape and tackle the list of chores the Realtor had told her she'd need to take care of, but her assistant had screwed up a spreadsheet, her manager called to ask her to update a presentation, and then . . . Screw it. She hardly ever went back to Wellfleet, because returning meant remembering.

Don't, she thought. *Don't think about Anthony.* That was her mantra. She could have tattooed the words across her wrist as a reminder. When she thought of Anthony, she thought of how hollow his words were that everything would work out if she just followed his plans. She was so stupid back then, so overwhelmed. And look what happened: Anthony sent her some money, and her parents believed it was from Michael, happy that he'd at least managed to support her. Except after only a few years, the money, once a reliable thousand dollars a month, trickled to odd amounts, a little here, a little there, until it stopped completely.

Don't think about Anthony! Now, when she thought of Anthony, she thought of all that blood.

Ann realized her hands had clenched into angry fists. Her nails left half-moon-shaped marks in her palms. *Relax, relax,* she told herself. She was wound up so tight with worry and dread that she hardly had the slightest inkling what relaxation even felt like.

She'd been tense and distracted ever since Poppy told her she was finally heading back to Milwaukee, six months after their parents had died. Exotic Poppy, the great surfing, adventuring Robinson Crusoe. But damn, Ann missed her, even if she didn't understand the choices Poppy had made and she couldn't forgive her sister for leaving when she'd needed her most.

"What's Poppy like?" Noah would ask, the same way he'd ask about relatives that were long dead, and Ann would pull out old photos of the two of them from Cape Cod, or show him Poppy's pictures in their high school yearbook. "She's pretty," he would say, and Ann would have to agree. To everyone else, Poppy was charming, mellow, and impossibly cool. Ann had always admired Poppy, even when they were girls, although she hadn't liked to admit it. Like Noah, Poppy never tried to be like anyone else, never cared what people thought of her. She was her own person—so why was she the one trying to find herself?

Ann thought of the postcards and packages Poppy had sent to Noah over the years. They were wrapped in thin brown paper and decorated in unusual stamps from all the far-off places she'd stayed. She'd sent handmade wooden yo-yos, painted kazoos, knotted bracelets, strange currency, pretty stones from the beach. All those packages and scenic postcards—was Poppy trying to make Ann feel as if her own life was small and unlived?

Dear Noah, hello from Honduras! I hope you learn to speak Spanish while you are young, when it's easier to pick it up. There are parrots everywhere. Their eyes are black as stones, and they are so smart! They even know who I am. One of them, a green one named Mango, greets me every time I come home from work. Hello Poppy! I could swear he waits for me there all day long. He talks, but he doesn't say much I can understand. I'll try to teach him to say your name. I feed him beans and rice and bananas. He especially loves coconut Johnny cakes. I hope you are doing well in school. I'll bet you are smart like your mom. Give her a hug for me.

—Yours, Aunt Poppy

Dear Noah, a stray cat has moved in with me. I'm trying to think of a name for her. I'm calling her Little Mama for now. She's got a white star on her forehead. Any ideas for a better name?

—Yours, Aunt Poppy

Dear Noah, the surf here is very rough. Mother moon is full and the tide is so high that it washed out the dirt road to this side of the island. We can't surf or swim because the shore is rocky. It rains almost every day but it's warm. I love listening to the red howler monkeys scampering around in the mangroves at night. That's why I'm sending this monkey hand puppet. Have fun with it!

Dear Noah,

I hope you are learning to practice gratitude. I hope you are thankful for your beautiful face and your healthy body and your mother and grandparents and all the people who love you so much, like me. I can't wait to see you and connect. Hopefully soon!

May our spirits mingle,

Aunt Poppy

Now, at last, Poppy was coming home, and Ann worried about the ways in which their spirits would mingle. Ann couldn't quite forgive her for being gone so long, and Ann was especially hurt when she couldn't reach

Poppy after their parents had died. She'd never felt more alone in her life than she'd felt that horrible week, trying to stay strong for Noah while making arrangements with the crematorium, dealing with insurance, searching for the will, meeting with lawyers, sending notices to their creditors and banks, writing "DECEASED" on the mail that arrived and popping it back in the mailbox, unread. She was about to turn thirty-five and felt too young to lose both of her parents, too young to go to bed alone every night. She'd broken up with her only long-term boyfriend, Kevin, an investment analyst she'd met through friends. He was perfectly nice. Too nice. The kind of guy who wears tennis shoes with suit pants. Noah didn't like him. "He calls me 'pal,'" he'd said. "He gets excited about eating leftovers. He calls them 'LOs.'" Kevin was eating leftovers with a new wife now and living in Newton, with twins on the way. Ann's lack of jealousy confirmed that she'd made a good decision, although sometimes she wondered if she was getting too old to expect more from a romantic partner.

Now, all these years later, Noah couldn't wait to spend time with his aunt. He'd always wished they had a bigger family, more siblings, aunts and uncles, cousins, pets. At school, he tried to create that whirlwind of people and activity that he craved. He was incredibly social, the kid who volunteered as a math tutor, competed in forensics, organized a zine fest for the other students who were also into graphic novels. He'd even started a student film festival with two other high schools, and was interviewed by the television station. Noah was everyone's friend. They didn't care that he was on the heavy side, or that he wore mismatched vintage clothes from resale shops that somehow worked on him—argyle sweaters with tweed jodhpurs and black cowboy boots—and had painted nails and a shock of long bangs that he'd bleached and dyed purple, red, pink, blue. He was ambiguous about his sexuality. Ann didn't push. He seemed happy. At home, he'd befriended all the elderly people in their apartment complex. He took out their trash and picked up essentials for them at the store. Mary O'Grady in 3B was teaching him how to play bridge so he could fill in as her bridge partner, and he'd helped newly widowed Martin Cox set up a profile on a senior dating service.

Noah was actually a lot like Poppy. Sometimes he started his sentences the way Poppy started hers, like "Wouldn't it be great if . . ." or "Don't you think that . . ." He was always imagining possibilities.

The wind picked up off the river and blew so hard she could have been pushed over. *Stay loose, stay loose.*

Cars, bikes, and other runners zipped past her as she ran. It felt like everyone had a place they were supposed to go, including Poppy, who was planning to come to the Cape as soon as she had the house in Milwaukee squared away. Ann wasn't holding her breath.

Ann ran so fast that it felt as if she were fleeing the scene of a crime. She wished she could start running toward something instead of away, but what?

She would have to face Poppy's questions. There was so much Ann hadn't told her, so much Poppy didn't know. It seemed every question started with Michael, and every answer circled back to Anthony. *Don't think about Anthony!*

She tried to push away her last image of him, slumped in a wing chair, blood trickling out of his nose, his mouth.

TWENTY-ONE

Poppy

Dawn, Connie's best friend, met Poppy in the baggage claim of General Mitchell Airport, an airport Poppy hadn't set foot in since she'd come home for Christmas a decade ago, when Ann and Noah had waited for her just beyond security. Noah was jumping up and down with excitement, unsure which traveler she was. *Is that her?* she could still overhear him asking. *Is that her?* And Ann saying, excited, "That's her!"

Dawn wrapped her up in a warm, fragrant hug that smelled like department store perfume. They stood like that for a while, clinging to each other and crying, until Poppy's giant and worn backpack containing everything she owned, and decorated with a slew of colorful airport tags, slipped off the conveyor belt and landed with a thud against the bumper rail, like a dead body.

Poppy almost didn't recognize Dawn, even though she'd once been a steady presence in her life. She looked a lot older than she had the last time Poppy had seen her, heavier. Had it really been a decade?

Dawn took Poppy's hand and gave it a chubby pat. "Just look at you, as beautiful as ever. And so tan! I sure wish you could have brought the sunshine and warmth here with you. Where were you again? Hawaii?"

"Panama. On an island called Isla Colón."

"Panama! Well, how about that. There's a place I've never been."

"It's nice," Poppy said. "You'd like it."

"I'd like any place without this crud." She pointed at a chunk of snow outside the window. "I keep telling myself I'll retire somewhere warm, but who am I kidding? My whole pathetic life is here."

Poppy slung her familiar bag over her back. Dawn, who seemed happy to see her even though Poppy thought she might have been disappointed by her absence, spoke in quick, nervous bursts as they walked to her car. "You're here. You're here! It's so good to have you back."

"It's good to be here," Poppy said.

"I just wish you could have returned under better circumstances. And you know, I still think there ought to have been a funeral for your parents. I pushed and pushed. Funerals are for the living. For you. You and your sister. Even me! When things like this happen, we need closure. But Ann insisted. She said they absolutely didn't want any sort of service, church or no."

Or no. Poppy had forgotten how Milwaukeeans tack on *or no* or *yet* to the end of their sentences. *Nice day yet. Gone fishing or no?* Dawn's Milwaukee accent was thick with indulged vowels.

"They hated funerals," Poppy said. "My dad always said 'you die, the end.'"

Why *had* they hated funerals so much? Poppy wished she could ask them. In the absence of a public memorial, Poppy had honored them her own way. She'd made an altar for them at Carenero Beach. She lit two candles every night for a week. She'd prayed and cried and meditated and tried to invoke their auras. None of it made her feel any better, or any closer to them.

"Sometimes it feels like your parents just slipped out the back door in the middle of the night. And now, well, here you are. Here we are."

"It's surreal."

"Still no will?"

"Ann says she can't find one. She's the executor."

"I could see your mother not worrying about a will, but Ed. He would have left one. He wouldn't want you girls to have to sort everything out yourselves. What a mess. Good thing Ann is so good at managing situations like this."

Poppy wanted to say, "As opposed to me, right?," but she didn't. It was no secret that tending to major life-and-death concerns wasn't in her wheelhouse. She'd been too numb to function beyond autopilot since that horrible afternoon she'd read Ann's email. That had been six months ago. Now the probate judge said they could dissolve the estate, which was why Poppy was home: to help dissolve it. "Dissolve" was the perfect word—to reduce everything their parents owned, including the Cape house, to nothing.

Dawn led Poppy through the sliding doors toward the parking ramp. The harsh winter wind blew off the lake and hit her with a slap of reality. She'd forgotten how quickly the cold could get into her bones.

"Ann tried so hard to reach you, hon. She didn't say so, but I could tell she was worried. In this age of cell phones . . ."

"I don't want a phone," Poppy said. "I mean I have one . . ." She pulled out her ancient Nokia flip phone to show Dawn. "But I hardly use it."

"That's admirable I suppose, but why? I thought everyone your age loved their phones."

"I've seen too many tourists get lost in their devices. Half the time they don't even know they're in a beautiful place." That sounded good, but it wasn't the real reason Poppy didn't have a phone: she *liked* being disconnected. It made her feel weightless somehow to be anywhere and nowhere.

"Well, we were all very concerned. Could you imagine if something had happened to you, too? That's what we were all thinking—not that we don't believe you can manage on your own. You've always been a free spirit, that's what your mom called you. I think she was a little jealous, if you want to know the truth. Connie was a free spirit, too. I think that's where you got it from. She was one of those people who never cared if her earrings matched."

Poppy laughed. It was true. She followed Dawn to her Dodge Avenger in the airport parking lot, feeling like a kid again. It was Dawn who'd taken her out for pizza at Zaffiro's when she was a senior in high school so they could talk about drugs after Poppy had been busted at Mike Lassiter's house snorting coke in the bathroom. A few years later, it was Dawn who'd called her in Costa Rica and begged her, on behalf of her parents, to come back home and finish college. But Dawn's efforts to intervene had failed, and Poppy was glad about that. It wasn't always easy, but she wouldn't have traded her years as a vagabond. She'd found adventure and community and many moments of deep contentment, although now she realized that part of what made her adventuring possible and exciting was the knowledge that she always had a home to return to. Now that home was just an empty house.

Poppy's hoodie was thin and her jeans were ripped. The air was bitingly cold and made her jaw ache as though she'd just rebroken it. She was miserable, but she would have felt even worse without Dawn's constant chatter. It soothed her, and kept her from thinking about what she was in for.

"I can't imagine coming back here after, well, after everything. Such wonderful people, your parents. I couldn't have gotten through my whole breast cancer ordeal without your mom."

"You had breast cancer?"

"Not too bad. Stage two. No big whoop."

"I didn't know," Poppy said. "I'm sorry."

"Oh, I'm fine now. Lumpectomy and radiation. Connie was there by my side, even though she had her own stuff going on. I just had a follow-up scan. My oncologist says it looks like I'm out of the woods."

"That's good to hear." Poppy felt terrible. What else didn't she know? What did Dawn mean when she said her mother had her own stuff going on? She was too tired to ask, too overwhelmed to think about all the people she hadn't been there for. She'd spoken with her parents occasionally, and they emailed sometimes, but there had been long chunks of time when she'd drop out entirely, like when she was running from dark energy in Indonesia, or during her months in the ashram.

"I think of it as a blessing that your parents died together. They were so close, I don't think they could have lived apart. Everyone wanted what they had. I know I sure did."

Dawn started driving. Her conversation picked up nervous momentum along with her car's engine. She turned on Rawson and passed the airport runways. Icicles hung from the wings of the parked planes, and the snow on the ground was stained a toxic blue from the deicing fluid. There was so much snow and concrete, like a color photograph that's been turned to sepia, that Poppy wondered if all her time on golden beaches, with sparkling water and vibrant green palm trees, had been some sort of dream. How could both worlds exist on the same planet? Milwaukee in winter was a place that could make you believe that warmth and color didn't exist.

They crested the Hoan Bridge. Poppy was struck with a view of downtown Milwaukee that was strange and almost postapocalyptic: dunes of salt for the deicing crews in the industrial valley, and the rugged city in the distance, the blend of solid old buildings and sleek high-rises, looking clean, tough, and resilient under the stiff bank of clouds that hung above it. Lake Michigan was silver and still, like a pool of mercury. Incinerators belched out smoke in the distance, a dark reminder that her parents had been cremated.

In one of Ann's emails, she told Poppy that the crematorium had a waiting room. *Isn't that strange?* she wrote. *A waiting room. Everything is so weird now.*

Poppy pictured her sister on a vinyl chair, surrounded by grieving strangers, all alone. *When they handed me the boxes they were still warm. It was almost like they were alive.*

As if reading Poppy's mind, Dawn said, "I still can't believe they've left us." She lifted her glasses to wipe a tear that had settled into the pillowy crevice under her eye. She drove past the fancy new art museum and the 1950s War Memorial, where Poppy's prom had been held. Stately mansions perched watchfully on the bluffs over Bradford Beach. Poppy noted all the landmarks she remembered: Villa Terrace, the water tower by St. Mary's, the hospital where she'd been born. Dawn made her way up the hill at Lake Park, and soon they were back in the East Side, near UW–Milwaukee. Home.

Dawn passed Cramer, her street, and took a left on Oakland instead, the neighborhood's main drag, as if she knew Poppy needed a tour to get reacquainted. Some of the businesses she knew were still there: Oakland Gyros, where Michael had worked; Axel's bar, where Poppy and her friends used to get away with buying drinks with their bad fake IDs; and Shahrazad, the Middle Eastern restaurant her parents loved. Still, much had changed. There were new businesses without character, like the Goodwill and Walgreens, and a generic Irish bar stood where the German restaurant Kalt's used to be. She saw a sign on the edge of Riverside Park, where she used to sneak away to get high with her friends, for a place called the Urban Ecology Center.

The changes felt like betrayals. But why? Did she think her life could move on while everyone else's would stop, frozen in place?

Would she even remember which house was theirs? The Victorians on this typical East Side block near campus all looked alike, most of them owned by professors and idealists who rejected urban flight and were committed to the social causes of the city and public schooling. The block was studded with duplexes that had been trashed by students. She remembered empty beer cans in their bushes, students urinating on their lawn, and midnight games of touch football in the street, and potlucks, book clubs, and salons. They were walking distance to the businesses on Downer Avenue, the lake, and Riverside Park. This was the kind of neighborhood where you could let your porch sag, and where her mother could paint a giant mural with flowers and birds and a peace sign on the side of their garage. Here you could adopt teenage kids, raise daughters who remained unmarried and had children out of wedlock, who took off to explore the world. Maybe they would have been better off in a more conventional suburb like Whitefish Bay or Brookfield, where there were rules, and where gossip and reputations kept everyone in line—places where they would have been expected to follow a straighter path.

It was dusk. The house had no lights, no signs of life. Poppy could barely make out the outline of the turret against the darkening sky. Was it possible for a house to look sad? She wished Ann were there to greet her, even though Ann was pissed at her for having been gone this long, pissed that Poppy couldn't deal, pissed she'd had to be the one to take charge (even though Ann was always the one to take charge anyway).

"Let me help you with your things," Dawn said.

"I've only got my pack. I'm good. Thank you."

"Watch your step. I'm glad Brad shoveled the sidewalk."

"Brad?"

Dawn laughed. "You sure have been gone a long time, haven't you? Brad's been living in your house for a few years now, and thank goodness. He's taken good care of it. And your parents."

"But who is he? Ann didn't mention—"

"She didn't? Oh, he's wonderful. He was in band with your dad. Owns some kind of factory. He sleeps in the basement. It's very private, he has his own entrance and everything. You'll hardly ever see him."

"Does he know I'm here to get the house ready to sell?"

"I'm sure Ann told him. He knows he can't just live there forever."

"I thought I'd be alone."

"Oh, you will be. He told me he's going to stay with a friend for a few weeks. He figured you'd want some space. That's the way he is." Dawn leaned noisily across the seat in her big, squeaky coat to give Poppy another hug, and Poppy remembered that Midwesterners love hugs. "Promise you'll call me if you need anything. I live in Wauwatosa now, in a condo, but it's not that far, not really, just a hop, skip. Especially for someone like you who's been all over the world, right? What's *Tosa*, for Pete's sake? I'm here for you, honey. Call me. We'll get dinner. Oh, and speaking of, I left a casserole and some taco dip for you in the fridge." She handed Poppy the set of keys Ann had left for her. "Sure you don't want me to go in with you?"

"I'm fine."

She wasn't at all fine. Poppy was afraid to enter the home she'd left all those years ago, afraid of all the emotion she'd feel, all the regret and recrimination she was in for. Good thing this Brad guy had decided to make himself scarce; she needed to be alone to face her parents' absence and the grief she'd been wrestling like a wild animal since she'd first heard the news the previous September. Even if there had been nothing for Poppy to do, as Ann had insisted once Poppy finally connected with her, and no point in coming home earlier, it might have been better to have faced everything head-on. In the months since the news of her parents' deaths, she felt like she'd been pulled under and gotten caught in the current. She didn't know if she'd ever surface again.

POPPY SETTLED INTO THE QUIET HOUSE in a void of stunned sadness. It was like a dream: one minute she was bartending at a small hotel, sleeping near an orange-sand beach in the town of Bocas del Toro, and the next she was in Milwaukee in February.

How could her parents be dead? Their closets were filled with clothes waiting to be worn again. They still got calls from telemarketers. The mail kept showing up addressed to Edward and Connie Gordon: reminders for six-month dental checkups, letters from former students, and envelopes from prisons throughout the country with the inmates' next moves in the chess games they played with her dad.

There were also letters addressed to Brad: a vintage guitar magazine, a catalog selling nothing but industrial floor mats, and lots of credit card offers. The refrigerator was filled with cans of Pabst Blue Ribbon and dozens of tortilla packages. The kitchen cabinets were stocked with protein-powder shake mix and cans of refried beans and diced tomatoes. She poked around the medicine cabinet: nasal spray, floss picks, multivitamins, and a compact multi-tool Leatherman with hooks, saws, scissors, and wire strippers.

Who was this guy?

TWENTY-TWO

Michael

I t was another cold day. The sky was so heavy it felt like it was sitting on Michael as he drove Route 6 from Provincetown to his office in Eastham. Still, he preferred the cold to the impending summer heat and the migration of all the tourists, who drove slow and made it hard to get a seat at the Wicked Oyster for breakfast, and impossible to find a parking spot at the Beachcomber. "String bean eaters" was what Ed called them, a phrase passed down to him from his grandfather, who told him that the tourists arrived on the Cape when string beans were in season.

Ed had taught him lots of old sayings and sailing hymns, like "Pull for the Shore" and "There Shall Be Showers of Blessing." He knew to call a thunderstorm a "tempest," and that the morning fog that burned off was the "easterly mull." If a storm was coming he'd hear Ed say, "Long foretold, long last. Short notice, soon past." And after a period of rain, Ed would say, "Ain't going to clear up until the moon changes."

Michael could hardly think about the weather without thinking of Ed, which is what he was doing when he passed the Gordons' driveway and noticed a couch sitting next to the road. There was a cardboard sign that said FREE! taped to the armrest.

He knew that old couch. It used to sit in the sunporch, although it was meant to be outdoors. The base was made of shellacked wicker and the cushions were covered in vinyl. He'd slept on it whenever it got too hot in the attic. He remembered the creaking sounds the hard cushions made with the slightest movement, the way his sweat would pool on the vinyl, and how his back would ache in the mornings.

It was funny how a single familiar object out of place could also conjure up such a crystal-clear image of Ed. It had been ages since he'd really gotten a good look at him, but the sight of the couch triggered an image as vivid as a hologram, right down to his receding hairline and Adam's apple. For just a moment Michael swore he could feel Ed's presence in the seat next to him, hear the faint whistle in his nose when he inhaled. Michael had been close to Connie, too, and he missed her, but it was Ed who haunted him—he was a father figure, and Michael felt especially awful about how he'd let him down. There was so much Michael wanted to tell him, so much he wished Ed had known and understood about what happened with Ann. He figured that one day he'd have a chance.

FREE!

Michael couldn't stand the thought of the couch getting picked up by just anyone. He wanted to grab it himself, but he'd loaned his red truck to Jason, who needed it to tow his boat to the marina to get fixed. That's why Michael was driving Jason's '82 Camaro Iron Duke instead. Why would he even want the damn couch? It was as ugly and beat-up as the car he was driving, and the cushions had a bilious green cast to them. Still, he wanted it. "Want" wasn't the right word. You want something you don't already have. Michael felt it was his already, and he needed to retake possession, just like he'd always felt the house was his because he loved it. He dreamed of owning it someday.

He could picture himself sitting on that couch in the Gordons' sunroom, back when he was welcome there, looking up at the wrinkled poster of a clay Indian doll in a yellowing plastic frame. The poster said SANTA FE. Michael used to look at it and wonder why the Gordons would bother to drive all the way from Wisconsin to Cape Cod every summer only to conjure up the Southwest. They also had a Milwaukee Railroad poster in the kitchen that Michael always wished he could rip down. Maybe those posters were the reason he'd returned to the Cape and stayed here all these years, because they made him think: Why would anyone want to be anywhere else?

Michael didn't have time to mess with an old couch. He had to get to work. He needed to hire their summer landscaping crew and fill out all the tax forms and paperwork. The business had grown from the early days, when Jason could only have as many employees as he could fit in a truck. Back then, he ran it out of his backyard, and all his neighbors complained about the tools everywhere, the trucks in the driveway, the crew coming and going. Later, Jason bought one of the last industrial lots in Eastham and built a small office, and two garages large enough to fit the trucks, trailers, and snowplows.

He had plenty of competition, although he'd been around long enough to develop a solid arsenal of regular employees and clients. Michael had already agreed to rehire three of his regulars, and he'd lined up a few interviewees that morning to fill his open spots. He liked to think he was a good judge of character, but he'd accumulated his share of horror stories over the years: the oxy addict who stole an old widow's checkbook, and a pedophile who solicited a teenage boy. The one that gave him the most grief was the idiot who mixed up an address and tore up the wrong lawn. And there were always employees who would buy their own truck and try to poach his clients. How could you look at a person and predict what kind of damage they might be capable of doing? Is that what Ed thought when he reflected on his decision to adopt Michael? Look how that turned out.

Between interviews and two calls from Sandi about a copyright issue with Anibitz, Michael was nagged by questions about the couch. He wondered why Ed and Connie would be on the Cape already. They worked at schools, and it wasn't even spring break yet. He pulled Carol Hargrove's business card out of his wallet and stared at it. No, Ed and Connie would never sell their house. Never.

But something was wrong. He knew it. They never got rid of anything. But say they did? It was just like them to leave their crap by the
side of the road for someone to take instead of throwing it away.

And then there was the handwriting on the cardboard sign. Ed and
Connie didn't use exclamation points, and they didn't get excited over
material possessions, free or not. That sign could only mean one thing:
the girls, one or both of them, were back. But why now, before summer?
He could think of little else. He waited impatiently for Jason to bring his
truck back so he could snag the couch before someone else did.

When Jason finally showed up, Michael lied and said Avery was sick,
and he needed to pick her up from school early. They made good partners; Jason was on top of the accounts, taxes, and paperwork, while Michael had a keen sense of timing. He knew exactly when to plant from
the smell in the air and the direction of the wind.

"Nothing dies on your watch," Jason said to him. "You should work in
a hospice instead of a nursery." It was about as close to a compliment as
a salty New Englander like Jason could muster, and Michael's dismissive
shrug was about as close as he could come to thanking him.

But that damn couch got to him. It put him in a restless funk. He was
a mess over an old piece of furniture. Who put it out there? Why did they
want to get rid of it? He was almost afraid to touch it.

TWENTY-THREE

Poppy

The Milwaukee house had become a time capsule, especially in winter, sealed up from the elements. Everything was just as her parents had left it, from the tattered throw blankets on the armrests to the plants on the windowsills. The basement smelled like old cardboard. They were the kind of people who'd kept all the boxes that once held the things they'd bought: an old fan, a vacuum, a computer, a changing table.

Poppy wandered the house, restless. She finally mustered up the courage to enter her parents' room and lie down on their bed, feeling the dents in the mattress where their bodies left their impressions, smelling their pillows, crying her heart out.

Her own bedroom was just as she'd left it, although her tie-dyed curtains had been bleached by the sun. A poster of surfer Greg Cipes standing shirtless on the beach still hung above her bed, and a pile of faded surf magazines sat on her dresser, gathering dust. Even her one-hitter was still hidden in the back of her top drawer.

Ann's room was also neatly preserved. Poppy inspected her bookcase, which was lined with track medals and academic awards, along with framed photos of Noah as a baby. On the bulletin board, she saw a photograph of the two of them taken from behind. It was sunset at Mayo Beach, and they were squeezing each other. How Poppy had worshiped Ann! They must have been seven and eight, their legs still a little chubby, their hair more golden. Poppy sat on Ann's bed for a little while and guiltily looked through the nightstand, remembering how, in high school, she'd sneak peeks into her sister's diary to find out who she liked, and how surprised she'd been, once, to see an entry about Michael, how he was unlike other guys, and so cute!!! The diary was gone, but she discovered a folded-up drawing that lacerated her heart. It was a picture Noah must have drawn of Poppy when he was around six, when Poppy had visited home for Christmas. It was a trip she didn't remember well, aside from feeling like Milwaukee was cold and boring. She'd taken everything for granted. Her mother must have spent hours preparing Poppy's favorite dishes, and she'd blown off her father's invitation to see a band at the Jazz Estate. She got high before her parents took the family to see the Milwaukee Ballet perform *The Nutcracker* and slept during the entire show. After only a few days she left, strung-out and in a huff because Ann had gotten on her case about being more *responsible.* Noah must have made the drawing the next day when he'd woken up to discover she was gone. He pictured Poppy standing on a surfboard, her face as big and round as the sun on the corner of the page. The Milwaukee house with the turret stood behind her. He'd written in painstakingly careful letters, some backward, "Ent Popee you fgrot to soy good bie from NOAH."

She *had* forgotten. She'd been so thoughtless, leaving the way she had, at night, when Noah was sleeping, without ever taking his feelings into account. The worst part was that Ann had kept the drawing in the intimate space of the nightstand, so Poppy knew it had mattered to her.

It took emotional fortitude to enter Michael's old room, too. It still felt like it was *his.* She would stare up at the glow-in-the-dark stars he'd attached to the ceiling with her dad, who bought them for Michael shortly after he'd moved in with them. She couldn't believe nobody had ever gotten rid of Michael's stuff after what he'd done. His T-shirts were still folded in the drawer. The bookshelves held his track trophies, the desk was stuffed with old math quizzes he'd aced. The giant aquarium that used to fill up the room with its comforting hum and eerie, wet light sat empty on the table.

Michael's rolled-up balls of socks reminded her of when she'd teased him because he always wore his socks inside out. He explained that his mother, shortly before she died, told him that whenever he was sad, all he had to do was wear his socks inside out and he'd feel happy again.

Michael, Michael . . . She had so many questions for him, so much she wanted to say, so much anger. But alone in his room, a room she knew her parents had left untouched because they wanted him to come back, like all of their bedrooms—she only wished that he were there to mourn with her. Sure, he'd left, but she'd left, too, only for different reasons.

So much had changed, yet Poppy still felt stuck in that hard time when Noah was a baby, when the atmosphere in the small home often grew tense, loud and anxious. Sleep-deprived, her parents had snapped at each other. Poppy withdrew and started sleeping at her friends' houses, escaping to their cottages, tripping at music festivals on the weekends, using drugs to escape. Everyone was too stressed and exhausted to worry about her.

The longer she stayed in the house, the more she pieced together her reasons for leaving, and why she hadn't come back, save for that one awful visit. She'd once felt integral to her family. After Michael's adoption and the trauma of his exit, along with the birth of Noah, she'd been rendered invisible, insignificant, especially by Ann, who'd never confided in her except to share details about her body.

Normally private and self-conscious, Ann was surprisingly open about childbirth. She told Poppy about the stitches from her episiotomy zigzagging all the way to her ass, explained how her breasts hardened into hot, hard boulders. When the milk came in, Poppy made warm compresses to set on her painfully infected nipples. She nursed so much she walked around the house with her nursing bra unstrapped, the flaps up, right in front of their father.

Ann had a hard time burning off the baby weight. Poppy inadvertently set off a fit of tears when Ann saw her walking from the bathroom to her bedroom wearing only her bra and underwear. "What's wrong?" Poppy asked.

"Look at you. You're so thin," Ann said. "Check this out." She pulled up her shirt and grabbed a handful of flesh from her stomach. "It's so gross. Like raw chicken."

Noah was amazing and precious. Poppy loved the way he smelled, loved to clip his fingernails while he was sleeping, loved the way he sucked his bottom lip. She played peekaboo and blew into his stomach so he'd laugh. He was so soft and juicy and sweet. But he was also difficult in the way that babies are difficult. She understood why sleep deprivation was used as a method of torture on prisoners, and during long crying jags from teething or gas she felt sudden sympathy for mothers who shook their babies. She begged Noah to stop crying. "Please," she'd say. "I'll do anything. Just give me peace and quiet for five minutes."

Even though it was hard, Ann was a good mother, shouldering the burden of love and worry for this tiny living thing she'd brought into the world while still somehow managing to take classes at the college in the fall. Poppy had vowed she'd never have a child of her own, partly because having a kid meant having a family, and her once-close family had changed from the stress. She couldn't wait to move out.

But when she did, she thought of Noah all the time, and ached to be with him, remembering how his sweet face lit up whenever he saw her. Most weekends through college, she took the Badger Bus home from UW–Madison. One fall day she'd arrived home and found Noah banging his hands on the tray of his high chair when she walked into the kitchen, baby food all over his face. "Pay-ay."

"He knows your name," her dad said, his big hand resting gently on Noah's soft curls. Most people seemed older when they became grandparents, like her mom. She'd doted after Noah, talking in baby talk, knitting pumpkin hats for him and showing baby photos to all of her friends. Her dad, on the other hand, seemed younger now, as though he fed off all Noah's endless baby energy. "Hey, sport, who am I?" He pointed at himself. Noah said, "Dooo." Her dad beamed. "I'm not ready for 'Grandpa,'" he said. "I want him to call me 'Dude.'"

One weekend when Poppy watched Noah, she gave him a bath and trimmed his hair with her mom's sewing scissors. Ann came home, took one look at him, and broke down in tears. "That was his first haircut! How could you do that? I wanted to save his first lock."

Poppy didn't know Ann had a soft, sentimental side. The baby had changed her. "That's so, like, Victorian. You really care about stuff like that?"

"Of course!" Ann reached into the bathroom garbage looking for hair. It was easy to set Ann off.

"You're welcome for babysitting."

"That's all it is to you: babysitting. Don't do me any favors," Ann snapped.

Soon, Poppy learned that talking about college was a hot button. She saw Ann's face turn bitter with jealousy when she told her about helicopters dropping joints on the State Capitol lawn during Mifflin Street days, and her excellent political science professor and the bands she'd seen on the Union Terrace, or how she'd partied at the Kollege Klub. Ann was too proud to admit she was jealous of Poppy's freedom. Instead, her jealousy manifested itself as meanness that only pushed Poppy further and further away until her visits became less frequent. One afternoon Ann exploded when Poppy came home, breathless with excitement, and told her she was planning to go to Costa Rica on a study-abroad program. "Costa Rica?" Ann said. "You don't even care about school. You just want to surf and hang out with a bunch of dropouts and losers."

"What's your problem?"

"I'm raising a kid on my own and going to school. What the hell are you going to learn about in Costa Rica? Study abroad is total bullshit. You can learn something right here in Milwaukee."

"You don't have to be a bitch about it."

"Whatever. Just leave, go to Costa Rica. Go anywhere, see what we care." Ann held Noah in a tight grip. *We:* she was speaking for both of them.

"Fine," Poppy said, deeply hurt. "I'll do anything to get away from you."

And she did. Poppy left for Costa Rica, seeking a less complicated life somewhere, anywhere else.

Poppy tried to escape her memories the way she usually did: by heading outside. The wind was sharp and cold, and the city was covered in a blanket of dirty snow that looked even darker under a flat, gray sky. Instead of VW vans and palm trees, Poppy had to readjust to a world of Jiffy Lubes, Home Depot, and frozen-custard stands.

Green Bay Packer T-shirts were on clearance at Walgreens because the Packers just lost the last round of the playoffs. Everyone seemed aimless and deflated now that football season was over.

She sought the solace of water. She walked through Lake Park to Lake Michigan in her dad's ancient L.L.Bean parka, which still smelled like his beard. She was freezing, even with the parka and several layers of her mother's old sweaters. Maybe it was true that her blood had become too thin. She didn't mind, because the cold reinforced her inner numbness. She walked until her cheeks were raw and red and her eyes watered.

She found herself at the funky deco terrace at Bradford Beach, where she'd shroomed the night Ann had Noah. She squinted and read the waves on instinct. The wind had blown the snow into drifts, and there were mounds of ice where the waves had crashed and frozen before they could retreat. She'd heard that people surfed here, the way her Cape Cod friends, the "townies," had surfed in the freezing Atlantic during winter.

All those years she was away, she'd grown accustomed to thinking of Milwaukee as ugly, a tired old industrial city, a place where time stopped. But the longer she was home, the more she began to appreciate the ways in which it hadn't changed, and the city's quiet, sturdy beauty. When it snowed, the oak trees in Lake Park looked like they were made of white lace, and the cold steam that rolled over the icy lake at sunrise took her breath away. She loved how she felt her parents here, walking where they'd walked, appreciating nature and the dramatic winter sunsets. It was an unexpected comfort to be in a place where everything was familiar and solid, and people didn't just come and go. Even Dick Bacon, the legendary Milwaukee man who sat on the beach in a reflective tinfoil contraption to tan himself all year long, was still there in his Speedo, catching rays in the cold.

She called Ann sometimes to catch up, but Ann's voice sounded clipped, businesslike. "Have you contacted a Realtor yet? St. Vincent's will pick up furniture if you call them. A coat of paint will work wonders." She cut Poppy off whenever she asked about the missing will and the distribution of her parents' assets.

There was so much distance between them. If it weren't for Noah and real estate, would they have anything to talk about?

She was lonely. She thought about calling some old friends from high school, but she'd been gone too long to casually reconnect. The people who stayed in Milwaukee had kids and busy, purposeful lives.

Desperate for company, she took a few Anusara yoga classes, because the focus of Anusara was on celebrating the heart, goodness, and worthiness, and she really wanted to believe in those things again. The classes were in Cedarburg, a quaint old mill town half an hour north of the city where the main street was lined with ice-cream parlors, antiques stores, and a coffee shop where ladies her mother would have been friends with met to quilt together. Everyone seemed to know each other there, which made Poppy feel even more alone. She was a strange species in the Midwest: a single woman in her thirties without kids or a job. She rolled up her mat and took off as soon as class was over. She wanted to avoid conversations so that people wouldn't ask about her life story.

She put everything into her practice, hopeful that something, anything could help her work through the grief she felt over her parents and her confusion about what she should do next with her own life.

After one class, the instructor walked up to Poppy and said, "I know I tell you to open your ribs, but you need to keep them a little tighter. I can see you give too much of yourself away in your poses. Careful, or you'll end up empty." Poppy broke into tears and never went back.

One day, almost three weeks since her return to Milwaukee, she was doing yoga alone in the living room, surrounded by piles of books and her parents' worn Scandinavian-style furniture, working on poses that were supposed to help with depression. She tried to quiet her mind and rebalance her sympathetic nervous system. Nothing worked. She'd listen to Habib Koité, do a hundred sun salutations, and go into wheel pose, only to collapse on the floor. She screamed out loud to the ceiling and whatever higher power was above it, "I'm opening my fucking heart and it's not helping!"

That was when she met Brad. He was standing in the entrance to the living room holding two beers. "Maybe this'll help?"

"Yeah," she said, embarrassed. A beer sounded perfect, almost as perfect as the hard stuff she'd sworn off a few years ago.

"Brad Sobatka. You don't remember me, do you?"

Brad Sobatka, Brad Sobatka. She studied his face, his cropped copper hair. Nothing clicked. "I don't. I'm sorry, I've been gone a long time."

"We were at Riverside together. I was in your class."

"I'm surprised I don't recognize you. You're so good-looking." She wasn't flirting. He *was* good-looking, even if he wasn't the kind of guy she was usually drawn to. His hair was beginning to recede, and he didn't have a surfer's lithe, athletic frame. Brad was more a part of the land. He was tall but stout, a little thick in his neck and gut. His nose was straight and blunt, and his chin and jaw were covered in coppery razor stubble. He had perfect teeth.

He held up the stiff fabric of his heavy twill work pants to reveal the rubber lift on his big, black shitkicker of a shoe. "I have a club foot. Kids could be pretty brutal about it. By the time I got to high school I learned how to make myself invisible. That's probably why you don't remember me. I was that guy in the back row."

"High school was a long time ago, and my last year there was, you know, a bit of a blur."

"You partook," he said, pretending he was inhaling a joint.

Poppy smiled. "Yes. I partook."

Her eyes traveled back up his leg to his broad, square chest. His coat was partially open, and on one side she could see the clips where the tan Carhartt bib overalls attached. Overalls, a leather tool belt, and oil under his fingernails: this guy was the real deal. "You remember me?"

"Sure I do."

Poppy smiled at his awkwardness. She was used to attention from men, but Brad's interest seemed more straightforward and sincere. She pretended to be distracted by the sanitation truck that rumbled down the street, and the dog barking in the neighbor's yard.

Brad said, "I can get my stuff out of here as soon as you need me to leave. I don't want to be in your way. I know this is a hard time."

"Ann tells me I'm supposed to get the house ready to sell."

Brad shook his head. "Ann is a force of nature."

When Poppy thought of forces of nature, she thought of hurricanes, tsunamis. The kind of power that could cause complete destruction. "She is."

"I spent some time with her after, you know, helping her with some of the arrangements. She's tough. Tougher than I was. I told her I could move out but she wanted me to stay, keep an eye on things."

"She didn't even tell me about you. I think she's pretty pissed that I haven't been around much. At all, actually."

"What were you supposed to do? She wasn't here that long, anyway. Just long enough to take care of logistics, look for the will, talk to lawyers, meet with the judge. She seemed like she was in an awful big hurry."

Poppy looked around the living room. "There's so much stuff to get rid of, and this is just one of the houses we have to clear out. I don't know what I ever thought about death. I thought it would be neater, like everything just goes *poof!* Gone. But there's so much. And what's the deal with the bathroom upstairs?"

Brad said, "I was helping your dad with that renovation project. It was sweet, actually. Your parents—" He blushed and looked down.

"What about them?"

"Well, they liked to take baths together."

Poppy put her hand over her mouth and laughed. "Oh, God. That's so them."

"Your dad wanted a bigger tub, and he had the space for it. We'd just gotten started with the demo when he, when they—"

"A bigger bathtub. I'm not at all surprised."

"I loved your parents. He was my favorite teacher. We were in a Dylan cover band at Linneman's, and we bowled together. And your mom, she was the best. We'd shoot the shit for hours. She knew something about everything. Aristotle, the special biscuits they made for Cold War fallout shelters. It's funny what she could still remember."

She wanted to ask—*still* remember? But there was too much to focus on, like the way his hair curled over the top of his ear, and his green eyes, like the unbroken green waves she'd have to paddle out to surf.

"Anyway, I can take off if you want, or if I stick around, I can help you get the house cleaned up, finish the big sextub. That's what your dad called it." He smiled. "I've held off because I wasn't sure what you'd want done, and I got busy with my welding—I own a welding shop, it's more like a hobby but whatever. The shop is slow right now. So I guess I'm trying to say I've got the time and I work for free in exchange for lodging."

"Yes! God, yes. I'm so glad you offered. This place is like the Land of Unfinished Projects."

"This is a great house. I've thought of buying it myself if I can make it work. They don't make 'em like this anymore. I love these old Victorians."

"I'm up for selling it to you. I'd give you a good price. I don't plan to be here long."

"Where to next?"

"The Cape house. One last summer." She wanted to get there soon, while the winds were still good, before the swells disappeared. "I thought about moving in there, but Ann wants to sell that house, too, and I'm not in a position to do much about it."

"Then what?"

"Oh God, I don't know. There's always someplace to go to," she said, although she was so weary from winter and grief that the thought of going back to her old lifestyle exhausted her. "Ann says I need to start investing in my future."

Brad laughed. "Sounds like Ann."

"I tell her she needs to learn how to live in the present."

Brad said, "The present is a hard place to be sometimes."

In her yoga classes she'd tell her students in warrior two not to reach for the future or the past. Finally, her advice made sense, even to herself. The future? She really had no idea what was in store for her. And the past? Well, that was complicated. For Poppy, the present was all she had.

Brad said, "I don't mean this in a creepy way or anything, but would it be OK if I just, like, gave you a hug? You seem like you need one and I guess I could use one, too. It's been really lonely here without your parents."

Poppy nodded yes. She did need some human connection, he was right. She felt his warmth, and also something else, an electric jolt. She buried her face in his coat. It smelled like snow, metal, and musk. He smelled real.

TWENTY-FOUR

Ann

The Shaws' Marblehead house was eerily familiar to Ann. That fateful summer she'd worked for them on Cape Cod, Maureen had hired a Wellfleet artist to paint a portrait of the house based on a professional photograph. Ann couldn't understand why someone would pay good money to turn their house into art they hung inside of the place they went to *escape* their house.

The portrait reminded Ann of the home in *The Amityville Horror*, a cold-looking barnlike structure with a grand porch set atop large red stones, and winking eyebrow windows peeking out of the slate roof. But Maureen had loved that painting—she loved anything that made things seem better than they were.

Shortly after her parents died, Ann drove up to the Marblehead house and saw it for herself for the first time. She was focused and strangely calm after all the anticipation and anxiety she'd felt about Anthony over the years. That anxiety had been replaced with a loneliness that became more obvious to her now that she couldn't call her mom twice a day or go for walks with her dad when they visited her in Boston, or when she and Noah spent long weekends with them in Milwaukee. It was strange how losing her parents made her brave. Her grief was without end; what more could happen to her now?

The cement walk that led to the front door was covered in cracks and patches of ice, and dead ivy snaked up the stone walls. When she walked up the steps of the massive porch, she noticed that the slate-blue paint on the stairs was peeling in broad strips, and had worn down entirely in the centers of the treads. A pile of yellowed newspapers sat in a corner, and a faded cushion had fallen off the porch swing. If it weren't for the name SHAW on the mailbox, she might have thought the family didn't live there anymore.

She steadied her nerves with a single thought: *Noah*. Just the thought of him gave her strength. She wanted to be able to sign him up for classes and camps. She wanted Noah to feel special and exceptional the way Toby and Brooks had. Why shouldn't he get to go to whatever college he wanted without worrying about student loans? As for herself, she wanted a bigger apartment in Boston, and she had her own student loans to pay back. She didn't worry about Anthony's threats anymore. She wasn't a scared teenager. Now she was a scared adult.

She walked to the big door, painted a cheerful yellow. What would Anthony look like now? In Boston, she thought she saw him standing on every corner. She did a double take at every businessman walking down the street with a leather attaché case, every homeless guy picking through garbage in the South End. She imagined him sitting at the restaurant table next to her or taking up a seat in the same Brookline movie theater. All these years she and Noah had lived in such horrifying proximity to this man who had changed her life forever, a man she wondered if she would even recognize. Was he fat and bald or fit? Was he repentant for what he'd done, or still smugly protective of his personal empire? Would he want to meet Noah? And what about Maureen?

Oh, man. Maureen. She would be deeply hurt. Devastated.

But *Ann* had been hurt. Devastated.

She'd survived.

She peeked through the thick glass window into the foyer and saw an enormous pair of cheap, plastic sandals under the bench, the kind you might buy at the CVS. Anthony's? No, no. Anthony wasn't the kind of person to wear cheap plastic shoes, and Maureen wasn't the kind of person to buy them. Perhaps Maureen had divorced and taken up with someone simpler—Ann wished that were true. Maybe they belonged to Toby or Brooks, grown now.

She knocked on the thick door with a shaking hand.

She knocked again, this time harder. Nobody answered.

What was she thinking? She looked up at the wainscoting on the ceiling of the big old porch. The light fixture holding the yellow lightbulb was covered in spiderwebs and dead bugs. Ann found some relief that nobody was home. She'd come back another day, figure something else out. She'd turned around and begun to descend the stairs when she heard the lock click, and the giant door opened with a loud, spooky creak, as if the door hadn't been opened in years.

Maureen.

The first thing Ann noticed was that she was wearing jeans. Jeans! And a loose-fitting Smith College sweatshirt. Her auburn hair was rusty gray, and pulled back into a ponytail. Given the condition of the house, Ann half expected to see her stumble out in a housedress with a bottle of Jack Daniel's in the pocket, curlers, and fluffy slippers. Instead, Maureen's lack of upkeep wasn't a fall from grace but a slip into a more comfortable, casual life.

"Ann? Ann Gordon? I can't believe it! You haven't changed a bit."

Ann couldn't help but smile. Maureen made her feel young and special again.

"Good Lord, it's been ages. You're all grown up. Just look. Come here!" Ann slowly walked back up the steps. "Don't be shy."

Maureen's warmth startled Ann. She put her hands on Ann's shoulders and looked her in the eyes. "What on earth brings you to this neck of the woods? I've wondered about you all these years, how many, ten? No, twelve? Fourteen? Good Lord, my whole life is a blur. How are your wonderful parents? Did you know I used to send them notes? I was so embarrassed when you quit, all because I'd had too much to drink. I was positively mortified!"

Ann, trying hard to stay focused, stiffly leaned into Maureen's hug. Already she was overwhelmed. Her parents never told her about Maureen's notes. Anthony said she'd quit because Maureen had been drunk? It wasn't bad enough to do what he did; he had to embarrass his wife, too.

"I'm sorry, I thought I'd—"

"Tell me, how is Michael?"

Michael's name had been off-limits for so long that it sounded forbidden. "We've lost touch."

"But you were so close. I don't understand. He was so dear, and the hardest worker I'd ever met. He'd finish the day covered from head to toe in dirt."

"We're estranged now." Ann's voice was clipped. She didn't want to invite any more questions.

"I'm sorry to hear that, I really am. I found him, and you, remarkable. Although if you want to know, he never paid us back the money we'd loaned him for college. That's always surprised me."

This was new. "You loaned him money for college?"

"Well, Anthony did. Anthony has always been one for large gestures. He saw a bit of himself in Michael. Wanted to help him out."

So, Ann thought. Another story. "I'm not surprised he never repaid you," she said.

"Funny we should speak of Michael. Just this morning I was rehearsing a monologue for *Duchess of Padua.*" She put her hand to her chest and looked off into an imaginary audience. "Here's how it goes: 'I read love's meaning, everything you said touched my dumb soul to music, and you seemed fair as that young Saint Michael on the wall in Santa Croce, where we go and pray. . . .' Saint Michael indeed! Let me get you something to drink. Come in, come in."

Ann followed Maureen inside the home, so classic and elegant compared to their house in Wellfleet. The living room was stuffed with deep, masculine leather chairs, a fat couch, and antique side tables. Yet the cashmere throw was left in a heap on the hardwood floor, the bouquet had gone limp in the vase, and dead blossoms littered the coffee table, along with piles of mail and take-out containers. Maureen said, "As you can see, this place isn't fit for company."

"You weren't expecting me, it's fine."

"No, but I've always felt a home should be guest-ready when nice surprises like this spring up. You've graduated from iced tea to something stronger, I hope? I've got a fridge full of beer from the cast party last week."

Ann couldn't drink, much as she would have liked to. Her nerves were jangled, and she was disarmed by Maureen's sweetness.

"I joined a community theater and the members are an absolute riot! We had a party here last week. It was a wonderful time. Do you remember I started acting that summer you worked for us? It saved me, Ann. I couldn't tell you then, but I'd reached a dark period in my life. I needed a new direction. It all started because of you, do you know that? I never could have snuck away to take those classes in Provincetown. I wouldn't have left just anyone alone with the boys. The boys! Can you believe how big they are?" She pointed at a framed photo on her kitchen counter. Brooks and Toby stood next to each other in matching sports jackets, their ties loose, khakis wrinkled. "That was at Toby's wedding last summer in Bar Harbor. His wife Celia is a nurse. She's a keeper."

Toby? Married? "What about Brooks?"

"He's a—what do they call it these days? A *player*. How about you, are you married?"

"No," Ann said, before Maureen could ask the next question she knew was coming: kids? She lifted the photo to inspect it more closely. "I'm still single." The boys resembled Noah, and she was surprised by the tenderness she still felt for them. They'd finally grown into themselves, taller and fairer than Noah, but just as solid and broad. They could definitely pass for brothers, although Noah wouldn't be caught dead in those outfits. He'd be more comfortable in a vintage bowling shirt.

"They're handsome," Ann said. "Brooks still has that little grin."

Maureen busied herself putting dishes in the dishwasher. "Brooks doesn't know how to work a comb. He was just here, in fact." She opened the door of her refrigerator. "And as I recall, we were more fully stocked before he showed for the weekend. I've got nothing but Sam Adams. Not what you're used to drinking in Wisconsin."

"Oh, I live in Boston now."

"Just down 128? How long have you been there?"

"A while." She didn't want to say years—more than a few at that point, long enough that Boston felt like home. Long enough that she could have confronted Anthony sooner.

"Good! Now it will be much easier for us to stay in touch. I've always felt a special connection to the girls who babysat for us, and especially you. When else do we get into other people's homes and see how they live? It's such intimate work. And it was so nice not to be the only woman in the house."

Maureen gestured for Ann to take a seat at the kitchen table in the breakfast nook overlooking the backyard. It was still decorated in vintage Maureen: bright Lilly Pulitzer fabric on the seat cushions and curtains.

"I'm so glad I heard your knock. I was in the basement folding laundry when you arrived."

"You fold your own laundry?"

"Look around, my dear. I do my own everything these days. My cleaning lady is long gone. No more ironed linens. Let's face it, nobody buys clipboards anymore."

"Clipboards?"

"You didn't know? That's what the business made. My father even patented the spring clip. With computers and all that, who needs 'em? Anthony tried to think of a way to diversify into laminate, cookbook holders, that sort of thing, but it's hard to diversify a clipboard. Enough about that. So, I have to ask. What brings you here? It's lovely to see you of course, but so entirely unexpected."

Ann wasn't sure what to say, or where to begin. "I was in the area."

Maureen was instantly skeptical. "My dear, nobody is ever just *in* this area. You either live here or you come here to visit someone who does. Why, just last week our neighbor called the cops because she saw a strange man sitting in a car. Turned out it was a housekeeper's husband just waiting to pick up his wife while she cleaned. Of course they were black. It's awful what goes on right here in this supposedly liberal place. I'm not sad I'll be gone soon."

Before Ann could ask what she meant—gone where?—she felt her stomach twist at the sound of footsteps above her. "Someone's here?"

Maureen frowned. "Oh, that's Tony."

Ann's body flushed with heat and fear. "He's home? During the day?"

"All day, every day. He's sick, Ann. Depressed. I used to be embarrassed to say that word but I decided I didn't want to be that proud person any longer. Through acting I've learned to pay attention to how I'm acting all the time. I became a character in my own life. I decided not to be that character anymore unless I'm on the stage. I'm being *me* for a change. Tell me, does your family still have that wonderful old house in Wellfleet?"

Ann decided not to tell Maureen about what had happened to her parents. Any sympathy could derail Ann's efforts, and her emotions were still so raw, who knew if she could keep from breaking down. "They sure do."

"That's a real Cape Cod house. So much character. I'll bet they'd sooner die than sell it."

Ann shook her head again and choked back the sob in her throat. "That's true."

"What can I say? Our place was built during a bad time for architecture. We hardly go there anymore. We've tried to sell it off and on for years to no avail. Nobody wants a house like that anymore. Thirty-some years old and already it's dated. Your house, it's timeless."

The sound of water flushing through the pipes from the upstairs bathroom practically coursed through Ann.

"I should go," she said. She wasn't ready for an encounter with Anthony—then again, she'd never be ready for him, never.

"Oh, stay! You just arrived! I can make some egg salad. I want to hear about what brings you to Marblehead and catch up!"

The footsteps were on the stairs now. Slow, one step at a time. Ann's stomach churned. That night on Duck Pond came back to her in little snapshots. Anthony's calves, his wet hair, the moles on his back, his grunts, her protests. Her painted toenails. How many times had she blamed those painted toenails for everything that happened?

"Don't let him scare you. He's not accustomed to visitors anymore, I'm afraid, all cooped up in this house."

"Who's here?" Anthony's voice was unmistakable. It brought out a feeling of sheer contempt. Her veins felt like they were filled with fire.

"Tony, you'll never believe!"

Ann gripped her beer bottle in her hand so tight she might have been able to shatter it. She looked for the door. If she ran fast she could make a quick exit—

Anthony appeared in the doorway. He wore a V-neck undershirt and a pair of flannel pajama pants, barely the Anthony she remembered. His belly hung over his waistband, and his hair, what was left of it, was a wiry mess. He had dark bags like black pincushions under his eyes. It was hard for Ann to imagine she'd ever been attracted to him, hard to think he'd ever had power, harder still for Ann to imagine what it must have been like for Maureen to live with him in this condition.

"Look! Why it's Ann, honey."

"I have eyes."

All these years, and here he finally was. Ann was shocked by his appearance, overwhelmed by his decline. She couldn't look into his eyes, so she fixed her gaze on his bare feet. They were fat, with pads of hair on his toes and thick horns of nails that needed to be cut. It was hard to believe she'd once fantasized about him, swum naked with him. His genetic material had become braided with her own. She'd hated him for all these years, but now that he was standing in front of her, the hate felt different, like it had congealed into something more like pity. He was weak, damaged, pathetic, and she was glad.

"Well," Anthony said. "Well, well. This is a trip down memory lane."

"It's his medication," Maureen said. "His therapist is trying—"

"Please stop talking about me like I'm not here, Mo. I'm here. I'm so goddamn here I can't stand it."

Maureen frowned. "Of course you are."

He looked at Ann. "She says I'm going through a 'bad patch.'" He used his fingers for air quotes.

Ann let her gaze rest on the coffee stain above his belly. "I see that."

"She also says she wants to divorce me, did she tell you that?"

Maureen, embarrassed, reached for Anthony's arm and tried to steer him out of the kitchen. "This is of no concern to Ann. Let's not—"

"Ever since she started acting she's turned into just another artsy kook."

"Stop it, Tony," Maureen said. Her voice was strained, pleading. "Please."

Anthony's chest hair stuck out from the V in his shirt. "You still look good, Ann Gordon." He stared at her breasts. "You always looked good. Healthy. Wholesome. You could have walked off the set of *Little House on the Prairie*."

"Tony!"

"*Tony!*" He screeched, imitating Maureen. "Just think of it, Ann. Mo wants out. She's cut me off. Now you can have me all to yourself. Remember when you strutted around our bedroom naked? God, you gave me a hard-on like a torpedo!"

Maureen looked at Ann in disbelief. "What is this about?" Ann didn't reply. After a brief silence, Maureen added, "Ann, why are you here?"

"Yeah, Ann. Tell my wife what this is about. Go ahead. Nothing matters now. She knows I'm no saint, but I'll tell you something: you were no saint either. You wrapped yourself around me like a snake."

Anthony walked to the sink and filled a glass with water as if this were the most normal gesture in the world. He took a drink and made a loud gulping sound.

"Ann?" Maureen sounded painfully hopeful for a different story. Ann wished she could tell her this was a lie, a mistake.

"You want to come here and tell my wife I knocked you up, go ahead." Anthony sounded like a suspect confessing to a crime after realizing the gig is up. "I feel bad, I do."

He could have stopped right there. That might have been almost enough for Ann: honesty and remorse. But Anthony set his glass down hard on the granite counter, looked Ann straight in the eyes, and said, "But I still think that kid belonged to someone else."

"Oh yeah?" Ann reached into her purse and pulled out a copy of Noah's yearbook photo. His smile was so sweet, so innocent, it hurt Ann to look at it here. She hated to admit that he was the spitting image of Anthony. Anthony without the bluster. Anthony without the edge. Anthony without Anthony. She shoved it in his face. "Just look."

Anthony pushed the photo away. It fell to the floor, and Maureen grabbed it. She looked at it long and hard, her hands shaking. "Oh, Ann," Maureen said. "How could this be?"

"It didn't happen the way he says," Ann said. "I really need you to know that."

Maureen's expression sank. Suddenly every freckle stood out, and every line in her face seemed visible, worn deep from a lifetime of trouble. "Oh my God." She showed it to Anthony. "She's right. Look at this, Tony. Look! There's no doubt."

"What's with his hair?"

"That's how he likes it."

"You agreed to stay away," Anthony said. "I had it all worked out with that orphan."

"How is Michael part of this?" Maureen asked. She looked at Ann in disbelief.

"Now you know why we're estranged," Ann said. "He said he was the father."

"No," Maureen said, shaking her head violently. "He wouldn't do such a thing."

"Sure he would." Anthony stepped closer to Ann, so close that his nose almost touched hers, so close she could smell peanuts and whiskey on his breath. "There are people you can buy, and he's one of them. I gave that little junkyard dog more money than he'd ever seen in his whole life."

"You said that money was for college," Maureen said. "I'm such a fool. That was *my* money, from *my* trust. Anthony, how could you?"

"I did it for you. So you wouldn't know. And aren't you glad? Think of all these years of blissful ignorance you've enjoyed."

Maureen sank back. "Everyone keeps coming out of the woodwork for money. That's why you're here, isn't it, Ann?" She was crying, and wiped her face with her sleeve.

A rage built up in Ann. She looked Anthony in the eyes. "You *raped* me."

Maureen gasped. It was the first time Ann had ever said that word out loud, and it felt both awful and cathartic. Noah and his friends talked about triggers, of not saying words that might upset you at school. But saying that word out loud allowed her to call it what it was. It gave her power and strength after all those years of blaming herself, for thinking she'd asked for it. She could scream it through a megaphone and it wouldn't be loud enough.

Maureen sank to the floor and rested her head against the wall. "Oh, Tony. She was our babysitter! She was just a girl."

"She wanted it."

It occurred to Ann that the person they were talking about—this "she"—was someone else, someone other than who she was now. "I said *no*."

"You said it too late. You want me to say I'm sorry? I am. I got carried away. I got carried away with a lot of things in those days."

"It never stops," Maureen said. "It never, ever stops, not ever! All these secrets you keep. I should have divorced you ages ago." She picked up a beer bottle and threw it at his chest, and it hit him, but not hard. The beer sprayed all over the room and the bottle shattered on the floor near his feet. The abruptness of the sound changed something in

Anthony; suddenly it seemed he wasn't even in the room with them anymore.

"I've seen the kid, you know that? I watched you walking with him to school."

"What?" Ann wanted to clean out her ears. "Where?"

"In Milwaukee. I saw his Teenage Mutant Ninja Turtle backpack. His blue hat. I followed you the whole way. It was all I could do not to say something. I just wanted, you know. I just wanted to see—"

"You had no right. No business."

"I was different then."

Ann thought about what Maureen had said, how people can become actors in their own lives.

"I felt bad, I did," he said. "I never forgot."

"You promised you'd leave me alone."

"And I did. You promised the same thing, and here you are in my kitchen."

"Stop it," Maureen said. "For the love of God. Stop."

"You want me to stop?" Anthony said.

Maureen nodded her head. "Yes. Yes, I do."

"How about you, Ann? You want me to stop?"

"I wanted you to stop a long time ago."

"OK, I tell you what. I'll make both of you happy. I'll stop."

He left the room and pounded up the stairs. Each thud of his feet on the steps sounded like an asteroid hitting the earth. Ann wanted to run away but she was so shocked she couldn't move.

"I'm sorry," Ann said to Maureen, not sure exactly what she was apologizing for. Flirting with Anthony, letting it get out of hand? For not telling Maureen a long time ago? She was sorry she'd hurt Maureen, but she was also deeply sorry for her. She had to live with Anthony. At least Ann hadn't been stuck with him.

"Why?" Maureen asked. "Why didn't you tell me before, a long time ago, when it . . . when it happened?"

"I was scared," Ann said, still shaking. "He threatened me. I was young. Young and stupid and scared. And pregnant. And then Michael came up with this plan. He'd say he was the—"

Maureen interrupted her. "My boys. They've had a brother all these years. They don't even know, they never knew. *I* never knew." It seemed to Ann that Maureen was speaking to herself instead of to her. Maureen snorted and wiped her nose with the sleeve of her sweatshirt. "Nobody takes me seriously."

"I'm so sorry. You've always been kind to me. I can tell it's been hard. I should go."

"That's what I've been saying for twenty-five years: *I should go.* And then he gets better, you know? He can be charming. For all his faults, for all his gruffness, he really could sometimes be a good dad. The boys adored him. I'd try to leave and they'd beg me to stay because he needs someone to look after him. He makes all these threats. The doctors can't do much. Now here I am."

At that very moment the house was rocked by a loud crack that made the walls shake. It stunned Ann and Maureen, who could only look at each other with questions in their eyes. The crack was followed by a heavy silence.

Maureen's face turned white. "Oh dear, I thought I hid all the guns."

TWENTY-FIVE

Michael

When Michael returned home from work, Deedee took one look at him and knew something was wrong. That couch had thrown him off balance. The couch, and before that, the Starbucks cup and the broken glass over the photo.

Deedee pointed at the small kitchen table covered in invoices and gestured for him to sit.

"Avery," she said, "go upstairs and do your homework."

Avery looked from Deedee to her father. "I thought you were going to take me to the harbor." She was a stunning child, everyone said so. She had his thick, dark hair and Shelby's pale skin. Her features were delicate, and her eyes were big, soft, and brown. At eleven, she was just beginning to shape-shift, like a human anibitz—not exactly a child, not exactly a teenager.

"I need to talk to Deeds," Michael said. "I'll take you to the harbor when you finish your homework."

Avery could see that Michael was in no mood to mess around. "Fine," she said, and she ran upstairs, her small footsteps light and quick.

Deedee pulled two Coronas out of the fridge. Deedee was short and skinny as a rail, with olive skin, small black eyes, and long, dark hair that had turned silver only in the front, where it hung to the sides of her face. She looked cool, Michael thought, wearing her Yoko Ono circle eyeglasses, leather necklaces, and big rings made with natural stones. She also had a sexy way of moving, crossing her legs, tossing her hair back, sucking on a cigarette when she was drunk. He could see why Shelby was into her. If Deedee were straight, and if she weren't his ex-wife's partner, Michael would be into her, too.

"Can you take a look at the toilet in 2B when you get a chance? It's leaking. The flange or something is the wrong size."

"I'll take care of it."

Deedee reached across the table and playfully tousled his hair and sang a few bars from "Handy Man."

When Shelby and Deedee asked Michael to move in with them, they said he could be the caretaker. He lived for free, fixing the occasional leaking faucet and cracked window and working on the gardens. He ran the bed-and-breakfast when Shelby and Deedee went on vacation. It was an unconventional arrangement, but it made sharing custody a hell of a lot easier. Deedee and Shelby encouraged Michael to go out more, meet someone, but he was perfectly happy to spend his time with Avery, and with the women. It was hard to explain to people, him living with his ex and her girlfriend. All that mattered was that it worked.

"Where's Shel?"

"Client."

"It's late for a client," Michael said. He winked at Deedee. "You know what happens when she works late."

"You know I've got nothing to worry about."

They were both Shelby's former "clients" at the day spa where she worked as a massage therapist. Michael was referred to her by his chiropractor, who said massage would help get rid of the constant pain in his lower back. Shelby was five years older than Michael. When she found out she was pregnant a few months after they'd started dating, they were both excited about having a kid, although their relationship had already settled into a platonic friendship. Michael wasn't upset when he heard about Deedee. He couldn't deny that Deedee and Shelby were together in a way he and Shelby never were.

Deedee said, "What's up, Michael?"

"Nothing."

"Nah, something's up. You've got a look in your eye. There's a bug in your rug. A crab in your crotch. A tick in your prick."

Michael picked at the soil under his fingernails. His sweatshirt was covered in dust from the pavers he'd moved for a patio job. He hated that he always came home dirty. He could feel the dried sweat on his face and back and the grease in his hair. "I think something's going on at the house."

"What house?"

"The house in Wellfleet. Where I used to live."

"Your family, Michael."

"They're *not* my family. You guys are."

Michael regretted that he'd ever told Shelby and Deedee about his past with the Gordon family. He stood up and walked to the window. He looked out over the miniature waterfall and hyacinth bushes in the small courtyard surrounded by the rental units. Shelby had painted them a blue-green that reminded him of the color of toothpaste. He hated the color, but he wasn't in a position to complain, and he didn't care very much anyway. Someday he'd have his own place, but for now, his unit was fine. It was small, mercurial, and had nothing to do with him, from the lace curtains to the floral-print bedspread and old-fashioned washstand. He didn't care about the décor or the fact that he had to share a bathroom with strangers. The guests weren't a problem; they were courteous and fun, happy, on vacation, and some of them came back every year and became friends.

Deedee threw a spoon at his shoulder. "Would you look at me so we can have a conversation?"

Michael took a long drink of his beer. "I've got something for you guys." He pointed out the window at the green couch.

"The hell you do."

"It's from their house."

"I don't care if it's from the Palace of Versailles. That's an ugly beast and we don't have a place for it."

"Yeah you do, the courtyard. It would be perfect out there. It's for the outdoors."

Deedee stared out the window at the couch, perched upside-down in the bed of his truck. "It's for a dump."

"It's not a puppy I'm asking you to take care of. I live here, too. I want it."

"Why do you suddenly want something? The only thing you own is the shirt on your back. You live like a monk. And now you want an ugly-ass couch you found on the side of the road? Forget the couch. Buy something nice for yourself."

"It's mine."

"It's going to look awful against the blue paint."

"Anything would look awful against that blue."

Michael saw Shelby walk past the window, the sunlight glinting off the tiny sapphire stud in her nose. Her hair was so fine and fair that in the light it almost looked see-through. She entered the house smelling of eucalyptus, wearing her ugly cork nursing clogs that were comfortable for a long day of standing over prone bodies.

"Hiya!"

Deedee and Michael didn't respond.

"Let me try that again. Hello!"

Still no response.

"What's going on?"

Michael didn't say anything.

"Tell me."

"I think something happened."

"To what? To whom?" She began to look panicked. "Avery?"

"She's fine," Michael said. "Someone was at the Gordons' house. Something's up."

"If you'd just stop by in the summer and talk to them like I've always told you, you might know what's going on."

"Nobody's there now."

Shelby walked up to him and poked the cell phone in his front pocket. "Jesus, Michael. Call them in Wisconsin. All these years I've been telling you to just call. Stop by when they're here during the summer. Clear the air."

"They don't want to hear from me."

Shelby stood behind Michael and gently rubbed his shoulders, even though her hands must have been tired. "Remember when Avery was born and you called, and Ed answered, and you just held the phone and didn't say a word? I'm sure they aren't holding a grudge. What happened with Ann is in the past."

Deedee took a seat in front of her iPad. "I'll Google them."

"Don't." Michael felt funny having Deedee search for his old family. He'd thought about looking them up a thousand times, the way he might have tried to find an ex. But every time he'd start typing their names in that awkward way he used the dreaded computer, he'd get a sick feeling in his stomach and stop. He couldn't do it. Now the sick feeling he had was different. Before, he worried what they might think of him. Now he was worried *for* them.

"Don't tell me what you find out." He stood up to work something out of his system and accidentally knocked a glass to the floor, and it shattered. "Goddamn it!"

Avery came running down the stairs and into the kitchen. She looked scared. Jesus, he knew what it was like to be a scared kid and swore he'd never put her in this situation. He felt that old anger and fear and frustration build up in him, and he heard Connie saying, *Jump, Michael!*

He looked at his daughter and jumped, and all the dishes in the cabinets rattled. Connie's advice still worked better than anything he'd learned in therapy and meditation. He'd gotten so good at managing his anger that he could pull over to the side of the road and meditate for ten minutes when he felt it coming on, searching for silence and stillness.

But this feeling he had building inside of him was bigger than that—bigger than anything he could jump or meditate away.

"You need to cool it," Shelby said. She knew all she needed to know about Michael's moods.

Shelby took Avery's hand. "C'mon Avery, let's go get an ice cream at Turner's while your dad gets some exercise."

Deedee kept typing. "Gordon. Milwaukee, right?"

Michael didn't answer. He shot out the back door, ran into his unit, changed into his running clothes, and hit the road toward the abandoned air force station in Truro. He remembered when Ed and Connie brought him here with the girls. Ed blindfolded them in the car, and when they got there he led them to the front of an empty barracks and took the handkerchiefs off their eyes. It was the strangest place, so wrong for the Cape, ugly and empty like a ghost town, especially this time of year, with chunks of snow littering the parking lot. Connie had said, "Walk around. Try to come up with a story. What happened here?"

What happened here?

He bent over to catch his breath. When he stood up, he wiped the sweat off his eyes with his sweatshirt and noticed that the place was still as big and as lonely as it had been back then—even lonelier, because it wasn't summer, although summer always filled him with painful nostalgia.

Calmer now, he turned around and ran back to Provincetown on Route 6 instead of the back roads. There was hardly any traffic, just a few trucks rumbling by. That was how Michael liked it.

When he got back to the house, he knew something was wrong, because Deedee turned off the water and Shelby, who'd been cutting carrots, put her knife down. They didn't usually stop anything for him. He liked being part of the flow of the house, part of the rhythm.

Avery was at the table doing homework. Deedee said, "Can you do me a favor, Aves? Can you run to the store and get me some milk?"

"I'm doing math."

"Now." Deedee handed her a five-dollar bill and everyone fell silent.

Avery rolled her eyes. "Fine." She sounded just like an adult, and why shouldn't she? She was constantly surrounded by grown-ups.

As soon as she was gone, Shelby walked up to him and put her hands on his shoulders. He shrugged them off. He knew what was coming. He remembered when the Gordons' old dog Fender had died, shortly after he'd moved in with them. Poppy sat on the stairs crying. He sat next to her and watched as she pulled at her fingers, which was what she did when she was upset. "It hurts *too* much," she'd said.

Shelby said, "So about Ed and Connie."

He hadn't heard their names out loud in so long. They sounded strange coming from Shelby, who didn't even know them. "I don't want to—"

"Baby," Deedee said, "they passed away."

"They?" Michael said. He thought of the one-two punches his dad had taught him. "Both of them?" His lungs were burning from the run and he could still feel his heartbeat in his eardrums. Sweat dripped down his back and it felt cold. But it made sense. If it was just Ed, or just Connie, they'd never let the house slip into other hands.

Shelby looked him in the eyes as if she needed to be direct in order for him to believe her. "They were on their way back home last fall. A semi."

Deedee said, "They died together. In Ohio."

"No."

As awful as it was to get such horrible news, he was grateful that Shelby and Deedee were the ones to tell him. Who, he wondered, had told Ann? Who told Poppy? Had they been alone when they'd found out?

Shelby tentatively reached for his hand, unsure if he'd take it or push it away. He gripped tightly, the way a patient might clutch a nurse's hand while undergoing surgery without anesthesia. This pain he felt was real and intense, inescapable. He couldn't even cry, although he wished he could, because crying might have offered him the slightest relief.

Deedee held his other hand, and the women moved closer to him, pillars for him to lean against.

TWENTY-SIX

Poppy

Poppy had sex with Brad in every room of the house except her parents' bedroom, and on every surface: the dining room table, against the refrigerator, in the foyer. They came together quietly and without discussion. Their lovemaking—the naturalness of it, and the urgency—frightened and confused her. She'd been with enough men to appreciate his straightforward approach to intimacy. He didn't think about what he was doing, didn't try any tricks. Their sex was natural and grown-up, and it was also scary because it wasn't just for fun, and that's how she was conditioned to think about sex. She tried to keep her emotions separate, tried not to worry about commitment, tried not to feel that deep connection when she'd reflect on the sound of his laughter or the current that ran through her when he placed his hand on her hip.

She tried to keep it casual. That wasn't a problem for the other men she'd been with, but Brad wasn't like that. She could tell by the way he kissed her, and the way she caught him watching her when he thought she was sleeping. Casual sex might become a problem for Brad. It might become a problem for her, too. Maybe it already was.

Poppy gave up her bedroom and started sleeping in the basement with

Brad. It all happened without discussion, as natural as a change in the weather. They planned meals together, cooked, and spent long hours at Boswell Books, the neighborhood bookstore, leaning against each other as they read on the big, comfy canoodling couch. They laughed as they stumbled home from drinking at Von Trier, the neighborhood German bar, and talked constantly when they went on long walks.

He was smart and confident, and he didn't smell like a wet suit. She liked that he didn't put pressure on her to be any different from the way she was. Most unsettling was her feeling that they were becoming her parents. They lived together in the house with the same closeness, the same ease. They were spread out on his bed, lit by the dim green light of her father's antique desk lamp. His foot bent inward at the ankle. He wasn't self-conscious of his foot anymore, or anything else, which made her wonder if he'd had lots of lovers or just one who had been particularly accepting. She liked the softness of his red chest hair, the rough calluses on his fingertips, and his sturdy presence. She felt he could absorb her.

Poppy said, "Don't you ever want to leave?"

"Leave where? Your house?"

"No, Milwaukee. I spent my whole childhood wanting to get out of here, and you've never left."

"I like it. Besides, where would I go?"

"Anywhere. There are lots of places."

"Yeah, but my business is here. My parents. My friends. People know me, I know people. Beer's cheap. I make a point of seeing the lake every day. The people are nice. This is a great city. I can afford to live here, and Chicago is just a train ride away. It's home. It's easy."

"Isn't that the problem?"

"What?"

"That it's easy."

"Why make things hard?" He slowly ran his finger down the bridge of her nose.

"It's hard to explain." Poppy tried not to think of Brad's complacency as a problem. Was it really so bad to feel that way, to be released from the restless energy she felt?

Brad said, "I don't feel like I need to run around the world chasing after something I've already got."

"I'm not chasing anything."

"Chase *me*." He kissed her. "I'm all the adventure you need." He eased his hand down the elastic waistband of her pants and started to work his magic. Her back arched and, before she knew it, their mini argument was all but forgotten. Sweaty and relieved, they lay side by side. Poppy put her hand in front of the bare lightbulb in the lamp and waved her fingers around, casting shadows on the far wall. A rabbit, a fox, a bird. Animals in motion, running away. She remembered the game she and Ann and Michael used to play where they'd put all the animals together. What did they call it? Ani-something. Bird, rabbit, fox: a "babbitox."

Poppy said, "So when you hung out with my dad, what did you guys talk about?" She couldn't look at Brad when she asked. It was too hard; she was afraid she might start to cry.

"I don't know, we shot the shit about a lot of stuff."

She laughed. "He was good at talking about a lot of stuff." She found a path in the hair on his chest, and ran the tip of her finger through it, along the dip in his sternum, over the gentle mound of his emerging beer belly. "Can you be more specific?"

"I don't know. You know what he was like. He'd go off on music, politics. One minute he'd talk about colonizing Mars, the next he'd tell you about some show he liked on reality television. He liked to hang out at the shop. He'd pick up old bike parts and bring them to me and I'd weld them for him. He has an awesome bike. You should check it out. I saw it in the garage."

"Sounds like you knew him pretty well."

"Yeah, I guess. But he was also one of those guys that could talk your ear off about anything without talking much about himself."

"Did he . . ." Poppy smiled, embarrassed. "Did he talk about me?"

"Sure. Yeah, sure he did."

She drew back a long slug of beer, bracing herself for what Brad might say. "And?"

"And he thought you were great, of course."

She pounded his shoulder. "Come on, what did he really say?"

"I think he wished you and Ann lived closer. He was a teacher, he spent his whole life devoted to kids, but his own were pretty far away."

"Ouch."

"I didn't mean for that to sound bad. It's OK. He understood. I think he admired you for being so independent, like your mom. He was probably even jealous of your freedom to move around. He said he kept track of you on a map in his classroom, did you know that? He put a pushpin in every place you ever lived. It made him proud."

"I should have called more. I should have visited more often."

"You were living your life."

"But I only came home once in over ten years. One time. And only for a few days."

"He raised you to live your life. Besides, he didn't want you to worry about your mom."

"My mom? Why would I worry about my mom?"

Brad rubbed his hand over her shoulder as if she were a precious wood instrument he was about to play. "It was hard on him."

"What?"

"You know." Brad pointed at his forehead. "That she was starting to lose it."

Poppy sat up and pushed Brad's arm off of her. "What are you talking about? My mom wasn't losing it."

Suddenly, Brad's face took on the expression of someone who'd accidentally let someone know about their surprise party.

"My mom was smart. Scary smart. She could speak four languages and play the viola. You should have heard her recite poetry. She read every book in the library. She wasn't losing it."

"I'm really sorry. I thought you knew."

"There was nothing to know."

"She got lost once, for two days. I helped your dad look for her. They found her under the North Avenue Bridge wandering the Oak Leaf Trail."

"You don't know what you're talking about. You're making this up."

"Why would I do that? God, I'm so sorry. I didn't think I would be the first person to tell you."

Her mother, who knew every twist and turn of the Milwaukee River, who walked all over the East Side, couldn't possibly have gotten lost there. No, no. "She was fine."

"That's why I moved in, Poppy. Your dad wanted me to help keep an eye on her. It came on fast."

"No!" She wished she could cover her ears.

"Haven't you noticed all the prescriptions lined up on the kitchen shelf? What do you think those were for? Donepezil, galantamine."

Yes, Poppy had seen the prescriptions, but she hadn't checked the labels, in case they were pills she'd be tempted to take herself.

"There are crossword-puzzle and sudoku books on every surface. Poppy, she hadn't worked in almost a year."

Poppy tried to recall their phone conversations, but her dad always said her mom was out on a walk or at book club or working in the garden. She thought of all her dad's excuses for why they couldn't come visit, tried hard to remember how long it had been since she'd spoken with her mom. She didn't know, couldn't remember.

"Hey, I know this is hard. My grandfather, he—"

"I'm sorry, but I don't . . . I can't . . ."

Brad was quiet, waiting for what he'd said to sink in.

"Why wouldn't my dad say something?"

"What good would it do? What would it change?"

"Oh God. He'd asked me to come home last summer but I was in the middle of moving to Panama. Maybe he meant to tell me." She rose onto her knees and sank back down into child's pose as though she'd been dealt a body blow. Brad folded himself over her, and rocked with her as she cried. "Didn't he know I would have come back to help if I'd known?"

"Maybe that was the problem. Maybe he was worried you'd feel obligated."

"They were my parents!"

"What could you do?"

"Do you think Ann knew?"

Brad didn't say anything. Ann *did* know, she could tell from Brad's expression. How could she not have told her?

What else didn't Poppy know?

TWENTY-SEVEN

Michael

Michael could see that the listing agent, Carol, was one of those Cape Codders who seemed out of place in an office, but he understood why she was there: you have to pay the bills somehow. She'd been completely unruffled when he stormed into her office. He guessed she bartended on the side. She had a bartender's confidence, like she could deal with anyone's bullshit. He could tell from her Dennis bracelet and the WFLT tattoo on her wrist that she probably went three, four, five generations back—one of those locals who don't even think of the Cape as part of America.

This time of year, the windows of the tiny real estate office were covered with tattered and yellowed printouts of last summer's listings that still hadn't sold. Some of his friends were Realtors, but it wasn't as profitable now that people used sites like Airbnb and HomeAway to rent their houses, instead of relying on agents to manage their rental listings.

"I was told the title was clear," Carol said.

"Clear as mud. I'm an heir." The word "heir" seemed too fancy for a guy like him, but he said it with confidence, even though it had been over a decade since he'd publicly identified himself as a member of the Gordon family or had any reason to say their name out loud.

"Mr. Gordon, if you are—"

"Davis. I'm Mr. Davis." The title "Mr." sounded foreign to his ears, as if he were saying his father's name. Hardly anyone out here went by their titles, like teachers. "Michael," he said.

"I've seen you at the Pig. Trivia nights. You're friends with Deedee?"

"You could say that," Michael said. The Outer Cape in the winter was a small place. "How do you know her?"

"Kayaking."

It was no surprise that they knew each other through kayaking. What did anyone do out here before kayaks were invented?

"Still," Carol said, "if you aren't in the immediate family, you don't have a claim at this point."

"I *am* a member of the immediate family. I was adopted. It's a long story."

"I'll bet it is." She opened a drawer and pulled out a file marked GORDON. "I was very careful to ask about other interested parties. I'm surprised, frankly. I didn't see this coming. Do you have proof?"

"That I'm adopted? Yeah, I can show you proof." He kept his adoption paperwork in a safe-deposit box in the Cape Cod Five Cents Savings Bank.

"If you can demonstrate you're entitled, you'll need to go to the clerk's office and file a notice of an interested party, unless you just want to approach your sisters yourself?"

"I might," he said. "Look, I've always loved that house. I don't want to raise trouble. But if they plan to sell it anyway, I want to buy it. I'm entitled to do that, no matter what Ann says. Or doesn't."

He *knew* that house. He still knew that the latch to the old cellar often got stuck, and he remembered which steps to the attic creaked, and which floorboards buckled. The girls took the house for granted, letting it sit empty the way they did. Not Michael. He'd buy them out if he had to—it would be a stretch, but he just might be able to afford it. He wanted Avery to grow up there. "What else do I need to do?" Michael asked.

"I'm not your lawyer. I'm just the Realtor. And I'm apparently getting screwed on this deal."

"That's not my fault," Michael said. He scooted his chair closer to her desk. "We're both getting screwed. Please, can't you just tell me what to do?"

Carol yanked the ponytail holder out of her hair, shook her hair loose, and gathered it all back up again into a new ponytail. She twisted it around, secured it again, and just like that she had a mound of hair on top of her head that looked exactly like the one she'd had before. "You'll want to meet with a probate attorney. You'll need to furnish evidence."

"Like I said, that's not a problem."

He was agitated. For years anything that had to do with the Gordon family felt like a secret. Now he was telling her, a complete stranger—well, maybe not a complete stranger, if she knew Deeds—about the house he loved, the family he belonged to. He wiped the sweat off his dirty forehead. He was always sweating dirt.

"I swear, nobody cares about these old summer houses until it's time to sell and then suddenly relatives come out of the woodwork like termites."

"Termites. Thanks a lot."

"You know what I mean. Look, if you're really an heir, you have two options. You can sign onto the deed on the property or release your claim."

"Why would I release my claim? I'll buy them out." He could tell Carol thought he didn't have two nickels to rub together. He wore a ripped-up fleece, a pair of old jeans, big boots. His hands were covered in dirt.

"Either way," Carol said, "I'm out of the picture. Nobody wants the property if someone else claims to be on the deed."

"I really want that house."

"I can see why you would. I had half a mind to buy it myself. It's a special place." She flashed him a smile. She seemed harsh, like so many of the year-rounders. But he could tell she was kind.

"So, it was Ann who told you the title was clear?"

"I'd really prefer not to get involved. I think you should ask her yourself."

"But I'm right here and I'm asking you."

"Like I said, I'd really rather not get involved."

"You were lied to."

Carol paused. She shuffled through some of the paperwork and passed a form across her desk. She pointed at Ann's signature on the bottom line. "See?"

"I see." Michael pushed his chair away from the desk and stood up abruptly. "I'm sorry about your listing."

"Maybe it was an honest mistake."

"Nah. Ann's mistakes are never honest." He walked toward the door to leave but hesitated.

"You can't cut a house into three parts," she said. It was charitable of her to offer advice. "You can buy out the other interests, or come up with a way to share the property. That's easiest. Actually, it's easiest when there's a will, but there's no sign of that."

"I'll bet Ann's made sure of that. Ed was the kind of guy who would have left a will. He taught history. He documented stuff."

"Ann said she's looked everywhere."

"What does it mean if Ann says something? She might have found it and destroyed it if my name was on it."

"Maybe, but I don't know. Seemed to me she would have preferred a will, like she felt bad about selling in the first place."

"Any other options?"

"Worst case, I suppose you can file a petition to partition."

"What does that mean?"

"You force the sale. The house usually ends up at auction. It's not your best option. You might end up bidding against each other. It could end up going for more than you'll be willing to pay. And you risk it going to some other party."

"Nobody is going to get that house but me."

"Good luck, Michael." He thought about asking her out—there weren't many people to date on the Cape—but he had too much to think about.

Michael pulled the door open, and a gust of cool air blew into the office.

"Can you do me a favor and not say anything about seeing me? I need to figure out the best way to work this out."

"She needs to know sooner than later. Look, these things can get messy. I see it all the time."

Michael appreciated her concern. "Oh, it got messy a long time ago."

TWENTY-EIGHT

Ann

Ann buried herself in work to avoid her trip to the Cape—or, really, to avoid Poppy. The house. Her grief. Everything.

But she really *was* busy, and Ann was terrified by the talk of layoffs. Evaluations were coming up in a week, and her assistant, Mindy, had sent her yet another screwed-up spreadsheet, but the mistake landed on Ann's shoulders.

As she tried to make sense of Mindy's work, her phone buzzed. Poppy again. She let her sister's call roll into voice mail. She'd check it later. The last time they'd spoken, Poppy told her that Brad was buying the Milwaukee house. Brad—of course! Why hadn't Ann thought to ask him if he wanted to buy it?

Now Poppy was headed for the Cape, and Ann had given her a list of to-dos that had to be taken care of before the house could go on the market: leaky gutters; a well test for arsenic, radon, and bacteria; and questions about the plat map that needed to be resolved with the town. Apparently, the shed encroached on the neighbor's lot and needed an easement. Ann didn't want to talk to Poppy about the house, didn't want to think about it. However, she wasn't sure whether they could act like sisters again.

Later, she thought. *Maybe later.* Had her dad ever told Poppy about Anthony and Michael? She doubted it. Ed and Connie had only learned about it themselves shortly before they'd died.

One night last summer, when Noah was away at camp, Ann decided to drive to Wellfleet to see how her mom was doing, and also to see how her dad was holding up. The constant care she required wore on him. Ann entered the house without so much as a knock, startling her parents. Her dad was laid out on the floor stretching his back, and her mom sat in her usual chair, a book on her lap, her readers balanced so low on her nose they might have slipped off. "Annie?"

The house smelled reassuringly familiar, like old wood and sea salt, although it seemed so empty with just the two of them in it. They looked old; how did that happen? Her dad stood up and gave her a hug. His hair was fully gray, and so thin that he'd cut it, because it no longer fit in the usual low sprig of a ponytail. Her mom, in her sleeveless nightdress, seemed soft. She'd gained weight. Her biceps showed no sign of muscle or bone. "What brings you out here?" Her voice was sweet and warm as always. "Where's Michael?"

That was a question her mother asked with heartbreaking regularity as her dementia grew worse. This time, the question almost broke Ann. She dropped her overnight bag and slumped against her father's chest. "Oh, Daddy." She hadn't called him "Daddy" since she was a little girl. "I wish Mom could come back to us." She cried softly, allowing herself the rare luxury of weakness, of being parented, of letting go.

"It's better now that she's not as aware of what's happening to her. It made her so frightened. Now here she is."

Her mother's pale skin was translucent, her blue eyes glassy. Her memory slipped away like a pulled thread from a sweater, unraveling backward, leaving her in the past, when their family was still together. The doctor had described it as a cassette tape being erased from the end to the beginning. As far as she was concerned, Ann, Poppy, and Michael were still young, still at home. She was happy in those memories—why upset her? Ann let her mother fuss over her, making her a bowl of macaroni and cheese (powdery, because she forgot to add milk), freshening the linens on her bed. Her mother went to sleep, and her father checked on her a few times. "You look tired, Dad."

"I'm OK," he said. "But I sleep with one eye open now. She's taken to wandering, and, well, you know. We've got a state highway on one side and a tidal marsh on the other. This would be the last place you'd build an old folks' home."

Ann held his hand and ran her fingertip along the thick network of veins.

"Want to go for a walk?"

"What about Mom?"

"This is the time of night she sleeps best. She's out, and we won't go far. Tell you, I sure could use some fresh air."

It was a warm night, and the moon was full and bright. The tide was coming in, and the surface of the cove glimmered in the blue-white light.

"So, what's on your mind?"

Ann hesitated. Her father had so much to deal with, did she really want to burden him?

"Anna Banana, talk to me."

Ann smiled. She'd always hated it when he called her that, only now it sounded sweet. She began haltingly, nervous. "It's about Noah. Dad, there are things I should have told you."

"I know," he said. "I knew you'd tell me in your own time. It's OK. Speak your truth."

"Michael isn't Noah's dad," she said.

He didn't say anything, although she could see relief wash over him, the same relief she'd felt saying those words out loud. Soon, the rest of the details of that sordid summer came out like a blast of water from a fire hose: Anthony, the pond. When she finished he didn't speak for a long time, and she was grateful. The moonlight lit a streak in the cove like a searchlight.

Finally, he said, "I always knew something was off." Her father was thoughtful, concerned, sad. He wrapped an arm over her shoulder. "I wish you'd told me. I don't know why you didn't."

"It was a lot. And I didn't know what you'd do to Anthony, or what he'd do to you, or what he'd do to me, and you'd taken in Michael because I asked you, and—it's so stupid. I mean, I tell you all this now and I could have handled it better, but at the time I was doing what I thought I had to do. The story was out. It was easier to just go with it, I guess."

Her father looked out at the tufts of beach grass sticking out of the small islands in the water. "I understand, I do."

"I felt so . . . responsible."

"No more blaming yourself. I know this isn't your way, but you need to learn to lean into people." He wiped a tear from his eye.

"That's what I'm doing now. It's just taken me about sixteen years." Ann laughed, and so did her father. She loved his gravelly laugh.

"And now we have Noah." Her father smiled at the thought of him. "That kid, he's exactly right."

A baby red fox rustled in the bushes along the bluff. The stars twinkled the way they always had. It was so nice here, so peaceful. Why had Ann felt she needed to run from the bad memories when the good ones were here, too? They walked a long time without speaking, their feet crunching along the path. They could have walked all night, walked all the way up to Provincetown. "We need to find Michael," he said.

Ann stopped in her tracks. "No!"

"But he—I just don't get it. It's not like him. Any of this."

"He took money, Dad. Anthony gave him money to send to me. Michael set up the account. The checks were in his name. When they stopped I couldn't go after Anthony, because he said he'd sue for custody. And I didn't know how to reach Michael, and frankly, I couldn't stand the idea of even talking to him after what he'd done."

"He was a son to us, Ann." Her father's voice broke. "Losing him was so painful. I felt I'd failed. Your mother and I both did. I feel we ought to at least have a conversation."

"No!" Ann wanted to leave Michael behind the locked door of her past. "He exploited my situation. I loved him, I did. He knew it. And he took advantage. Promise me."

Her father didn't promise. He just put his arm around her and nodded.

She returned to Boston feeling wonderfully unburdened, happier than she'd been in a long time, determined to finally confront Anthony. Little did she know that would be the last time she'd see her parents alive. They'd stopped in Boston just before their fateful trip, but only Noah saw them, because she was at a furniture conference in Chapel Hill. She figured there'd be another time. Christmas, the next summer, whenever.

Now she was haunted by her father's silence when she'd asked him to promise not to reach out to Michael. Only once in all these years had she tried to find him herself. Once, during her last job search, she typed his name into LinkedIn on impulse. Who knew there were over two thousand Michael Gordons? She didn't even allow herself to scroll, and cleared her browser history as if she'd been searching for porn, scolding herself. Now this search gave her comfort. Suppose her father *had* tried to reach him? Wouldn't he also have hit the wall of Michael Gordons, and even more Michael Davises?

Was it possible that Michael knew her parents had died? He'd already profited from her. Surely he wouldn't try to get a piece of the pie?

The will, the will! She'd looked everywhere for it, in both Milwaukee and Wellfleet—between her parents' mattress and box spring, in the secret hiding space next to the fireplace, in every drawer, cupboard, and filing cabinet, even folded between the pages of books. She just needed to sell the houses quickly and get it over with so he couldn't come out of the woodwork. She had absolutely no intention of sharing the proceeds of the estate with him. When she filled out the forms the lawyer gave her, she didn't include his name, didn't signal that anyone else might have a claim.

Ann looked up at the potted plant on her shelf, and at the padded cubicles in the now-empty office. A cleaning person was emptying the garbage. Just beyond her window she saw the sun setting over the Prudential

Tower. Somewhere out there was Cape Cod—and Poppy. All these years of not knowing or even being able to imagine where her sister was, and now she was home. Once the houses were sold, what would happen to her family? Would they become just a memory with no physical ties to place, no history? Is that what houses really were, containers for families? And once the containers were gone, the people inside were just set loose in the world, particles.

She saw people walking down Commonwealth and Newbury. Wouldn't it be nice to be carefree, to meet up with friends, go on a date? She imagined herself sidling up to the bar with a guy she was excited to be with. She'd catch the bartender's attention. "I'll have a martini," she'd say, and a warm hand would rub her back. This nameless, perfect man always appeared in her fantasies as Michael, but why? Perhaps because he'd once been her best companion before she pushed him away. A companion, that's what she wanted. She wished she could tell him about her day, about Mindy's spreadsheet, about Noah's latest exploit, about Anthony, about selling the house in Wellfleet, about how nervous she was to see Poppy again. "Can you imagine?" she'd say. "I'm nervous to see my own sister!" And, familiar with the contours of her life, he'd nod in understanding.

She shut down her computer. She couldn't stand the idea of being alone like this forever.

TWENTY-NINE

Poppy

Brad stood in the alley next to Poppy's mother's Civic, his callused fingers gripping the edge of her rolled-down window. It was only four in the morning, and his hair glowed copper under the streetlight. He leaned in to kiss Poppy. She could tell he wanted it to be a slow, meaningful kiss, but she wanted to get it over with, get on the road, get through Chicago before rush hour, get to Cape Cod, get away. She was in "go" mode.

"Come back soon," he said.

"I can't promise anything."

"I'll wait for you," he said. "And I can come visit you. I'd love to see the Wellfleet house. Your parents talked about it all the time."

"That would be great," Poppy said, but she knew she sounded half-hearted.

"What's going on with you?" Brad asked.

Why did everything about him have to appeal to her? The blunt shape of his nose, the intelligence in his eyes. What was wrong with her? She left all the time. But she didn't want to hurt him. "You need to live your life."

"We've got something special. You know it."

"I do know," she said. "This has been great."

"This?" He seemed sad, exasperated. "What's 'this'? Are you breaking up with me?"

"Brad—" She put her hand on his, looked into her lap. His fingers were cold under hers, warm from the travel mug of coffee.

"Look, don't say anything more. Just think about us. Call me when you get to Syracuse—don't just keep driving. You need a break for a night. Let me know you got there safe."

"OK, OK."

"I hate to think of you driving that far by yourself."

"I've been all over the world by myself." What did he think, that she needed a man? Was this patriarchal BS or—

As if reading her mind, he said, "I know you're going to be fine but it's also OK for me to be concerned."

"I don't need your concern."

"Goddamn it, Poppy. Can't you see I love you?"

There it was: love. She was afraid that was coming, afraid of commitment. But why? There was nothing scary about Brad. Everything about him was easy, good. Something about him snapped in place. "I've got to go."

"I know you feel it, too. At least I hope you do." He kissed her one more time, and she enjoyed it, and she wanted him. She had half a mind to . . . *Love?* Did he really just tell her he loved her? She was as terrified as she was thrilled. "Don't forget about me."

"I won't."

"I'll be right here, you know. And I can come there, help you out. We're good together."

"We are. I'm just—"

"But you need to know that I'm not going to put pushpins on a map to keep track of you."

"I never asked you to."

"Jesus, Poppy. What are you so afraid of?"

What was she so afraid of? That was a question she asked herself as she made her way onto the freeway, her eyes blurry with tears.

She had twenty hours of driving ahead of her. She tried not to think about Brad, or the house, or the way Brad's hair curled at the nape of his neck, or the way he'd stood there with his hands stuffed deep in his jacket pockets as he watched her drive away. She was afraid to look in her rearview mirror, fearing he might still be there, no matter how far away she drove from her old house. Soon it wouldn't even be hers anymore. She and Ann had accepted Brad's offer: a reasonable price, no Realtor fees, no inspection, no hassles. The closing would happen in about two months.

Take that, Ann.

She made it through Chicago, and just as she drove through Toledo she realized she'd gone past the spot where her parents' accident had happened. She turned around and headed back in the opposite direction, looking for some kind of sign to mark the spot where the truck had hit them. The driver, it turned out, had had an epileptic seizure, and had died, too. It was hard to be mad. It was tragic, that was all.

She pulled to the side of the freeway and broke down so completely while cars whipped past that she felt as if her veins had been scraped out by grief. It wasn't just her parents she cried over: she cried for Brad, for the end of an era with her house in Milwaukee, for the feeling she had that she'd never be able to return to her old life, for the loss of family, for not having a center, for being a fucked-up, commitment-phobic betrayer of family and friends. She was so caught up in her crying spell that she didn't see the cop pull up behind her, and startled when he rapped on her window.

"You OK?"

Poppy wiped her face with the back of her jacket sleeve. "No."

He was an older cop, probably in his sixties, and he seemed awkward about confronting a tearful young woman. "It's not safe here. You should use your hazards. Better yet, pull off at the exit."

"Sorry." Her tears caught in her throat. "I'll leave."

She thought he was about to hand her a ticket, but he passed her a tissue instead. "Your registration is expired, did you know that?"

"No. Really? I don't pay attention to any of the right stuff. I don't know what's wrong with me."

He patted the top of the car as if he could pat her on top of her head. "I'll let it go for now. But in the future, find a safer place to cry. And get those tags renewed."

She was facing west instead of east now, and thought about going back to Milwaukee, but the pull to the Cape was too strong. She felt it every spring, no matter where in the world she was living. She could practically hear the terns, plovers, and barn swallows, smell the heady scent of sulfur and peat of the cove, feel the damp sand at the shore of Gull Pond, and taste the oysters and lobster rolls. This impulse to migrate back to a familiar place was troubling. She'd always defined herself as someone who could continually expand outward, never needing to return.

EXHAUSTED FROM DRIVING, SHE stayed overnight in Syracuse. The next day, she got a late start. The area outside Albany was lovely, with barns tucked into rolling hills, like in Wisconsin. She felt a surge of energy as soon as she hit the Mass Pike. The closer she got to the Cape, the more she remembered—all the positive things she thought she'd forgotten, like the way her father would turn up whatever stupid song was playing on the radio as soon as they went over the Sagamore Bridge, and her travel-weary family, including Michael, would roll down their windows and start singing at the tops of their lungs, magically transformed from weary to revived. When Poppy saw signs for Plymouth, she turned up the classic-hits station. "Walking on Sunshine" by Katrina and the Waves came on. It seemed like the perfect song at first. She didn't even like it; it was cheesy and old and familiar, but when she started to sing she became acutely aware of the sound of her own voice and the fact that she was the only person in the car.

She was nervous to reunite with prickly old Ann, who she was sure must have withheld information from her on purpose as a kind of punishment. She hadn't warned her that Brad was living in their house, hadn't mentioned their mom's deteriorating mental state. So why was it hard to stay mad at Ann? Poppy felt lonely for her instead. They'd shared this childhood trip, and the memories, and this horrible loss. If Ann were with her, they could reminisce about the music, and how her mom would insist that they stop at the Friendly's just off the rotary. She said the ice cream was a reward for good behavior on the drive out, but really it was also a kind of sweet torture she exercised to delay their arrival and amp up their anticipation.

Friendly's was gone. How could Friendly's be gone?

Was it possible that the Cape could no longer deliver the way it did when she was a kid? She hadn't been back since she was sixteen. In all those years, had it become just a place?

Before she knew it, she was on the bridge over Buzzards Bay that didn't seem nearly as high over the canal as it used to. She saw signs for towns like Osterville and Sandwich, towns that meant nothing to her because her family had only ever cared about the Outer Cape, where the peninsula was chewed away to a resilient sliver of sandy earth. Poppy couldn't wait to get past Hyannis, where Ann had once sworn she saw John F. Kennedy, Jr., in Ray-Bans pumping gas into his convertible at the Mobil station. The real turning point came when she went through the rotary at Orleans, just past the elbow of the Cape. After Orleans, she could see salt ponds and marshes instead of scrub pine, and she began to feel that magic tingling of anticipation again. Driving past all these towns made her feel like she was driving through time, not to a place, but to her past. The Lobster Shanty, National Seashore Museum, Audubon Center, mini-golf barn, and drive-in movie theater were still there, although now there were Mexican, African, and Thai restaurants. Since when could you buy ethnic food on the Cape? What other changes should she brace herself for?

She wasn't ready to experience the house yet, and the flood of emotion she knew was waiting for her there, so she pulled into the parking lot in front of the General Store and went inside. Even that had changed. It had been remodeled. Now you could buy kombucha and six-dollar smoothies. She missed the General Store she remembered, where you could enter in your bare feet. The floors were never swept, doughnuts were fifty cents, and she and Ann would use their paltry allowance to buy Mad Libs and quiz books with invisible-ink pens while her parents bought *The New York Times*.

She went into the liquor store, quaintly called the "package store" in New England, or "packie," as her dad had called it. She bought a six-pack of beer that cost more than ten bucks, the most obvious sign she wasn't in Milwaukee anymore, where beer was practically free.

Across the street was a fancy boulangerie where there'd once been a clam shack. A boulangerie in South Wellfleet?

She got back into her car and drove to the long dirt drive that led to her family's house and came to a stop in the clearing. Poppy had never been to the Cape this early in the season, and she found the landscape strangely lush from rain, not dry and brown the way she remembered it. This time of year, mist rose from the lawn instead of dust. She parked next to the old barn her father had converted into a workshop and looked between the clusters of scrub pines on the bluff. In the distance, she could see the expanse of flat brown silt in Drummer Cove and wondered if arriving at low tide was a bad omen.

The rusty hinges moaned when she opened the door of her mom's dinged-up car. She unfolded herself from the seat she'd been pressed into for what felt like a lifetime, stepped outside onto the crushed oyster shells on the driveway, and inhaled the achingly familiar scent. She'd lived all over the world, but at that moment she felt like she'd never left Wellfleet, never known anything or anyplace else. She even felt *known* by it. This was where the feeling of her parents lingered.

She popped open the trunk with the decal that read BELIEVE IT, DREAM IT, DO IT! and another one she'd sent her for Christmas one year that read OM. I. GOD. She smiled when she looked at the bag of cat litter her dad kept there to add weight to the rear wheels during the long Midwestern winter. It was such a practical gesture. Her smile disappeared when she surveyed the rest of the contents. Wedged between the spare tire and her tattered backpack were the robin's-egg-blue boxes from the crematorium. They hadn't budged during the long ride out. Poppy had felt their presence on every bump and turn, and when she got lonely and tired of listening to her own thoughts she imagined that her parents were really there in the car, alive and engaged in their usual banter, arguing about politics, food, art, and household chores the way they always did.

Now, looking at the stickers with their names on them, she saw that the boxes were deathly quiet and still. When she picked them up she was again surprised by the weight of ashes. Ann's plan was to dispose of the ashes and put an end to their grief. Ann said they needed to *move on,* but that didn't make sense to Poppy. She resented the way Ann made it sound like grief was a simple problem when she knew full well that Ann's problems were never simple.

She threw her backpack over her shoulder and headed for the door. The old saltbox looked the way she remembered it, although the weathered gray clapboard shingles, moss on the roof, and sagging shutters made it seem private and sad instead of welcoming the way it had when she was a kid, when she felt like she was reuniting with an old friend.

She walked up to the back entrance they always used because the front door had been sealed off ages ago, just a floating door that someone had nailed shut long before she was born. The steps had rotted away and been removed. Nobody knew why. It was one of the house's many mysteries, something she'd always considered part of the antique charm. Now, according to Ann, whatever Poppy found charming was an "issue." Ann had emailed her with a whole list of "issues" that would need to be fixed over the course of the summer.

Poppy fished around in the giant woven bag that she'd bought in Honduras and wrapped her hand around her mother's BOOKLOVER key chain, which she'd found hanging from the bulletin board in Milwaukee. Everything she owned came from somewhere else. Had she ever used a key? They'd always left the door unlocked. It was a heavy bitted key with an ornate bow, the only fanciful element of the no-nonsense Puritan design of the house. When she slipped it into the lock, she remembered the summer when she and her mom painted the door bright green, but it was red now. At least the paisley curtain was still there, hanging over the window. Her mother made it herself, at home in Milwaukee.

She opened the door and smelled the familiar scent of trapped air. She walked to the Formica kitchen table she and Ann used to cover with blankets and newspapers and hide under with flashlights and books. A pamphlet that said "Preparing your home for sale" sat on top of it. If only she could figure out a way to keep the house.

Poppy looked around and thought about all the things she had to do. Her parents had always attended to the business of opening the house for summer. They turned the water valves, lit the pilot light, and cleared away spiderwebs and evidence of mice. Now it was up to her to figure out how to make the house inhabitable, and she had no idea where to start. She didn't even know how to turn on the electricity, and remembered the summer when she and Ann were little, when, just as an experiment, the family lived without electricity for almost a week.

She heard a noise on the other side of the house, near the sunporch. Was she imagining it? Was this what happened after spending too much time alone? She wished Brad were there. Footsteps. Then she swore she saw someone outside in the back lot, or was it just the tree moving in the wind? A neighborhood cat? A mouse? A squirrel? Ghosts? What was that?

"Hello?" Poppy said.

She ran to the kitchen and picked up the old mustard-yellow phone on the wall. Nothing. The service had been shut off for the winter.

She needed to be comforted by the sound of her own voice. "Noah?" she shouted. "Ann?" She looked at her Nixon watch. It was only five o'clock. Ann said they'd come down for the weekend, their first face-to-face encounter in more years than Poppy wanted to consider.

She lifted the curtain to peek out at the driveway: nothing. She'd felt someone, she was sure of it. She still did. She stood still in the quiet of the house watching the dust particles light up in the day's last light and float in front of the windows, waiting for the figure to appear again, listening for more footsteps, waiting for the door to burst open.

Nothing happened.

It was getting dark, so she went to the basement and found the breaker so that she could turn on the lights. She went outside, and walked around the property. Had she imagined the intruder after such a long drive and so much time alone? She couldn't see anyone, but she felt like she was being watched. In the creepy, invaded quiet, she became even more acutely aware of her parents' ashes waiting in the car. She went back outside to get them and headed back indoors. "We're back," Poppy said, startled by the weight, "where do you want me to put you guys?"

There was the giant fireplace mantel, but setting them there could be mistaken as an attempt to be decorative next to the old conch shell Michael found his first summer on the Cape. *You can hear the waves,* she told him, and he looked at her, amazed when he held the shell next to his ear. She saw the family photo, the glass broken. Michael . . . Who knew where he'd landed. Maybe Milwaukee. Maybe anywhere. He'd only spent two summers in the house but his presence was heavy, like the lingering feeling of the ghostly intruder.

She went into her parents' bedroom, which was lit through the slits in the old wood shutters. She set her father's box on his tallboy, and her mother's box on the wide, squat mahogany dresser. No, she thought. Still not right, too far apart. She moved them to the bed they'd shared for all those years and set her father's box on his side and her mother's box on hers.

A wind kicked up and the entire house seemed to shudder. Poppy took that as a sign of approval from her parents. She touched her finger to her lips and pressed a kiss onto the stickers with their names. She walked quietly out of the room and shut the door, as if to give them privacy.

She walked into the sunporch and heard the mournful, unearthly squeal of the fisher-cat who'd taken up residence somewhere along the cove. The alien cry went right through her. It was the sound of trouble she knew was out there, but couldn't see.

THIRTY

Michael

Michael's clients came out of hibernation all at once, as if they'd spent the entire winter dreaming of nothing but their precious summer-home lawns. His phone lit up with calls from Boston, New Jersey, Connecticut, and New York. His clients wanted everything yesterday: new annuals, thicker grass, stone patios, and, of course, puffy blue hydrangeas as big as pompons.

Unfortunately for them (and for Michael), their wish lists were piling up because of the weather. It had been a brutal spring, with a couple of freak nor'easters that locked the Cape in ice and pounded the bluffs, leaving the ground as hard as concrete. Some of his clients wanted him to risk it and put the plantings in early, but Michael patiently refused. There had been some unusually warm days, but he'd lived on the Cape long enough to believe in the "Three Icemen" Ed had told him about long ago. Ed said that just when you thought winter was over, there would be three more bouts of bad weather, or "visits" from the icemen. Michael waited, and just like every year, Ed's theory was rock solid. The third iceman hit late in March.

Now the ice was finally gone, the earth was soft, and the weather was warmer, but the forecast called for heavy rain that would wash away whatever grass seed the birds hadn't eaten. Michael didn't have time for rain. Shelby, Deeds, and Avery were in Santa Fe for a well-deserved vacation before the summer season kicked into full gear and the renters descended in droves. Michael had to deal with their inn—taking reservations, assembling a cleaning crew, and fixing the broken window in the corner unit—and, of course, he had plenty of his own landscaping work. And then there was Anibitz. His company wasn't unlike a bright but troubled teenager with the kind of potential to become either a heroin addict or a Harvard grad. There was some kind of bullshit trademark dispute he needed to address, lawyers he had to call. He'd gotten used to having a partner at the landscaping business; he wished he had a partner in Anibitz. It was too much.

But what really bothered him was Poppy.

A few days ago, he'd been poking around the house the way he usually did. He wanted to see if any more furniture had been cleared out, and he'd brought a bag with him so he could take a few things he wanted to keep for himself, just in case. He filled it with a few of Ed's records, some of Connie's books, and the Yahtzee game they'd played so many times that first summer he'd lived with the Gordons. The score sheets still had Poppy's doodles and Ann's careful math.

He was looking through Connie's bedside table, hoping to find a piece of her jewelry to pass along to Avery—nothing fancy or expensive; Connie's jewelry was the stuff you'd buy at a craft fair. She had lots of leather, rocks, and beads. He cringed with embarrassment when he saw an almost-empty bottle of lubrication gel. He heard a noise, and when he looked outside he saw Poppy standing next to a beat-up old Honda Civic.

Poppy!

She stared off into space, deep in thought, like always. Her reverie bought him some time. He snuck into Connie and Ed's closet, where he inhaled the musty smell of Ed's big Pendleton wool shirts and Connie's cardigan sweaters. The smell alone was almost too much for him. In the dark, he listened to Poppy's footsteps, the thunk of her suitcase. He heard her call out for Ann and Noah. Who was Noah? Was that Ann's kid, or did Ann have a husband?

When he heard the door shut, he made a run for the sunporch. Just before he ran outside, he paused and considered that this might be the last time he'd ever be able to enter the house. He looked around and jumped up, grabbing one of the ace playing cards nailed to the wall above the door. It came off easily, the nail clattering to the floor.

He stuffed it in the large pocket of his windbreaker and darted outside, wincing when the screen door bumped against the frame when he shut it. He hid behind an old oak tree, sweating and light-headed, watching as the lights went on in each room. He saw Poppy looking out of the windows—she'd heard him, he could tell. After a few minutes, he darted for the barn, figuring she wouldn't ever look for him there. The door slid open and he gently closed it behind him, his heart thumping wildly in his ears. He felt crazed—what was it about this house, this family? About seeing his old friend Poppy again?

The barn was almost completely dark. It was now dusk. Michael peered beyond the small window and saw Poppy pull some boxes out of her trunk, hesitate, sigh, look around—did she see him? He ducked. When he rose again, he saw the back door close properly thanks to the hinges he'd replaced a few years earlier; that door had never hung right, so he'd used Ed's plane on the bottom edge. That was perhaps his boldest and most obvious home improvement.

He slumped to the floor. Once his eyes adjusted, he noticed all the familiar tools on the pegboard, the old ham cans filled with screws, nails, and bits, jars of oil, and dirty old rags. He remembered what Ed had told him: "After I kick the bucket, these tools will be yours."

In the corner, he saw the old white refrigerator from the 1950s with the sleek, long perpendicular handle that looked like an exclamation mark, and proud, silver letters spelling out A-D-M-I-R-A-L across the front. "No wasted space!" That's what Ed had said whenever he opened it up to grab one of the Point beers he'd brought with him from Wisconsin. Michael could vividly remember the afternoons he'd spent with Ed in the barn, and the story Ed told him about how his mother had begged his father for the refrigerator after she'd seen an ad touting all the food-storage potential in the door. "No wasted space!"

The machine was unplugged and felt dead. He looked inside, and in the light coming through the window, he saw the two cans of beer that might have been there for a decade tucked into the door. It was strange: that was when the news of Ed's death really hit him, when he realized Ed would never return to drink them. Michael backed away from the refrigerator the way a boxer might back off after a blow. Without bothering to shut the door, he slipped out of the barn and disappeared into the trees.

Now, still wounded, he parked his truck in front of a pile of pavers behind the landscaping building and took a sip of coffee from his thermos. He had a nervous twitch in his right eye from thinking that soon he'd have to confront Ann and Poppy and insist his way back into the family.

Jason was in a fit when Michael walked in.

"What's wrong?" Michael asked.

"Oh Jesus," Jason said. "The Shaws' house. I just checked on it." He had a way of saying "Shaw" that made the name sound much more complicated than it was—*Shawerer.* "Should have gone sooner. Damn pipes froze. Place is a goddamn disaster."

"Thermostat?"

"Nah, I change the batteries out every fall. Furnace is only a few years old. Beats me what happened. Place is ruined, man. That asshole's going to rip me a new one when I tell him."

"That's what insurance is for."

"I guess."

Michael took a bite of an apple. It tasted sweeter than usual. "Karma's a bitch," Michael said, careful not to look Jason in the eyes.

Jason began to laugh. Michael knew that was how he'd respond.

He turned and pretended to reach for something in his drawer in order to allow himself a small, private smile. Mission accomplished.

THIRTY-ONE

Poppy

Denial was Poppy's best option. She decided to pretend this would be just another summer, and the house would always be there, and her parents were on a quick trip to the Stop & Shop in Orleans and would be right back. Only it wasn't even summer yet. It was the first week of April, and the damp cold went straight to her bones. That first night at the Cape house she did manage to find the breaker and turn on the lights, but she didn't know how to turn on the heat, and when she went to the bathroom she discovered that the toilet bowl was drained, empty. Fortunately, her father had left heaps of wood in the woodpile outside the back door. She sat under a sleeping bag in front of the fireplace, dreading the moment she'd have to emerge from her cocoon and go to the bathroom or actually *do* something. She could hear mice scampering between the walls; maybe that was the life she'd felt in the house when she first arrived?

Ann ditched her, but the next morning Noah arrived to spend the weekend with her.

"Aunt Poppy!" he said, his voice lower than she'd imagined it would be. He was awkward at first, and so was she: How could this be the same little guy who'd squealed with delight when she'd given him a bath? She hadn't seen him since he was six. He had Ann's precise features—her sculpted, thin nose and wide-set eyes—but he was sturdy in a way that neither Michael nor Ann was, barrel-chested and thick, with long, luscious blue-dyed bangs and dark brown hair.

Their connection was instant—two free spirits who cared little about what other people thought of them. Blue hair? Awesome—and even more awesome that Ann could raise a child so comfortable in his own skin. Noah told her he had spent as much time as he could with his grandparents every summer, and she could see her father's influence when she watched Noah work the house. In no time, he got the water running and the old boiler chugged to life. They watched classic films and sat next to each other on the couch playing games on Noah's laptop. He showed Poppy how to use Garage Band and he'd parse out the separate tracks for the mournful-sounding songs he'd recorded. Poppy thought his music was brilliant, like everything else he did. But what really united them was their love of the house.

"I don't understand why my mom would want to sell," Noah said. "This place is perfect. And it fits us. It's, like, us."

"I know," Poppy said. "I can't even imagine anyone else living here."

"I *hate* them."

Poppy laughed. "Me too. I've already imagined who they are. The woman—she has an elegant name. Something like Evelyn or Jacqueline. She buys organic and sleeps on one of those acupressure mats. She has a rule: no makeup on vacation."

"Except lipstick," Noah says, "because lipstick isn't really makeup."

Poppy laughed. "Her husband, his name is Travis."

"Totally! And he's a banker."

"He likes to talk about deals. At parties, he tells everyone we're due for a correction soon."

"He's on his phone all the time."

"He can't go to the beach because the sand irritates his feet, and the sun makes his psoriasis flare up," said Poppy. "Instead, he sits around and reads Malcolm Gladwell books when he isn't following the market."

They went on like this about everything.

As soon as Poppy got used to Noah's company, he had to go back to Boston, promising to return the next weekend. Poppy fell to pieces during the week. She missed her parents, Noah, and especially Brad. She even missed Ann, and was irritated that she hadn't bothered to visit.

One morning, while Poppy was resting on the couch, someone knocked at the door, which startled her. Nobody knocked on doors in Wellfleet.

More efficient tap-tap-taps. "It's me, Carol. Anyone home?"

Not Carol, the evil Realtor. Ann went on and on about all the stuff Carol wanted her to do around the house—Carol says this, Carol says that. She was like a stepmother.

Poppy looked around and thought about the messes she'd made. She'd let her clothes sit in rebellious heaps on the floor next to her bed. The frying pan with dried eggs had remained unwashed in the sink for days. Empties. Damp towels. Dust. Poppy could have done everything Ann asked her to do, but she didn't—not because she was lazy. There was more to it; a simmering anger, a willful effort to defy Ann, who had been terse and cold when they spoke on the phone. Instead of talking about anything that mattered, she went over to-do lists at a clipped pace, cold and practical. What did it even mean that they were sisters? Ann treated their relationship as an inconvenience.

Another knock. *Don't answer, don't answer....* She heard the key turn in the lock—of course Carol had a key. Poppy abruptly tossed off the throw blanket, stood up in the harsh chilly air, and smoothed out her hair. She felt guilty, busted. The door swung open, followed by energetic footsteps. Poppy said, "Um, hi?"

"So, someone *is* here." Carol's voice was cold, even angry. "I saw the car in the drive. I have some paperwork, and since I was on my way to a show-ing in Brewster I figured—wait." She stopped in the doorway. "Poppy?"

"Yeah."

"Is that really you?" It was remarkable to see her transform at that moment, from Realtor to surfer, professional to friend, like a play of the light.

"Kit?"

"Oh God, I haven't heard that name in years. I go by Carol now."

"Why would you go from Kit to Carol?"

Carol—no, Kit—laughed, a low, grumbly laugh that reminded Poppy of all the times they'd gotten high together at Dirk's. "That was a name I gave myself when I started surfing. Typical teenage-girl thing to do, trying to change my identity. The surfer persona. I thought it would catch on, but I guess I wasn't cool enough for Kit."

"*I* thought you were Kit. And cool. Seriously, you changed my life."

"Oh stop."

"You did! I became a surfer because of you. You'll always be Kit to me."

Carol looked around the house. "I can't believe you're Ann's sister. The 'itinerant.'"

"Is that what she called me?"

"Sure did. She's a ball-breaker."

"Tell me about it."

"You guys are really related?" She looked at the Wisconsin Badgers mug on the table. "I should have put it together. You were, like, the only person I'd ever known from the Midwest."

"I'm so exotic."

"God, I can't believe this is your house. Hey, sorry about your parents. I was afraid to ask Ann what happened. I heard from the librarian in town. Everyone loved your mom and dad."

"Thanks."

"This place is a wicked mess."

"Yeah—I know."

Carol frowned. "You're depressed."

"I probably am."

"Swells are supposed to be good tomorrow. Offshore. Storm coming. Let's go."

Poppy crossed her arms tight in front of her, defensive. "I don't really surf anymore. It's been a long time. And I'm used to warmer water."

Carol smiled.

"I don't even have a wet suit."

"Some things don't change. You never had any gear, Wisconsin. I've got an extra, I'll bring it by. See you in the morning at your home beach. Let's get you out of your funk."

Carol was about to put a folder on the kitchen table but hesitated. "I have some paperwork for Ann."

"She's never here. She's avoiding me."

"She'd better avoid me now, too." Carol set the folder on top of the bookshelf. "Can you give this to her when she finally shows up? She won't answer my calls."

"She won't answer mine, either."

THERE HAD BEEN SO MUCH EROSION over the years that the parking lot at LeCount was half the size it had been when Poppy was a kid. The lifeguard stand was blown on its side. There weren't just trucks in the lot but cars—nice cars, the same cars she'd seen in the parking lot at the boulangerie. Poppy stepped out of Carol's car with her wet suit halfway up, the top hanging limp from her hips, nervous. The sun broke over the dunes and fractured over the steel-gray water. The wind was cold, but it was a good cold, unlike the chill in the lonely house.

She expected to see the same hard-core crowd and join in the super-tight camaraderie. Instead she saw clusters of surfers who looked at her with suspicion, making *her* feel like the outsider, although she could tell they were mostly newbies and old guys in their fifties and sixties with longboards and stand-up paddles. At least half of them were girls. She was used to this in other places, but it threw her off on the Cape, where she expected everything to remain unchanged, where she and Kit used to be among the only girls in the inner circle of OGs, or "originals," and everyone treated them like younger sisters.

The surfers acknowledged her. Poppy could tell they thought she, too, was a newbie. She didn't care what they thought, and she didn't participate in the surf world one-upmanship that happened on land. What mattered was how well you could read and ride the waves. She wanted to lose herself in the water and the rhythm and the rush. She wanted to forget about Brad and Ann and the sale. She wanted to forget that her parents had died.

"Ready?" Carol said, looking more like Kit with her messy morning hair and broad smile. "Keep your eye out for sharks. They're bad now."

Poppy zipped up, got into the water, paddled out so she could take off deeper, and started reading the waves. She'd forgotten how heavy the water was in Wellfleet, how salty and thick with a stew of seaweed, how *real*.

The cold made her ankle and jaw begin to ache, and she felt the tug of insecurity that chased her out of the water a few years ago. *Forget about it*, she told herself. This wasn't the pipeline, it was her home break. She paddled out to the lineup. The surf was good and Poppy was in great form. She started hitting the lips and cutbacks and got the little barrels. She surfed like she was in a dream, letting her thoughts recede the way they did. It felt great, amazing even, to be alive like this, all animal instinct and muscle memory. She was in the moment, standing on top of the water like she owned it.

She overheard some surfers talking.

"That girl is charged."

"She rips."

"Who is that?"

Their jealousy turned into respect mingled with resentment when Gary, one of the OGs paddled close and said, "Hey, I remember you. You've picked up some skills. Tell me you didn't learn to ride like that on Lake Erie."

"Lake Michigan."

Poppy was conscious of the strange sound of her own laugh, a laugh that once came easy to her.

"So, where you been?"

Poppy shrugged. "Everywhere, just about."

"But there's no place like here, that's for sure. Once a dunebilly, always a dunebilly."

GARY AND CAROL TOOK POPPY under their wing, introducing her to the other OGs. Gary's family had a shell-fishing grant; grants were priceless. You had to be grandfathered in, and you had to stay active to keep it. The guys who had grants might drive crappy rusted-out trucks over the flats, but they could buy out anyone on the Cape with all the money they made. Some of the guys scored two to five thousand bucks a week working both tides, day and night. These were the real Fleetians, and Poppy knew they'd accept her, but only to a point.

Carol convinced Gary to score a coveted town permit for Poppy. "You need something to keep you busy," she said. "And this is the best job on the Cape." She'd put on waders and hit the mudflats with the equipment Gary loaned her: a rake, a culling knife, a bushel basket, and a ring to measure the oysters. Shell-fishing was hard: she had to bend over for hours at a time, lugging a bucket and ice through the muck, culling and clearing off baby oysters spat from the adult shells. Picking wild was good, lucrative work—perfect for a surfer, because it offered what she was already used to: solitude, and the tides.

Gary explained that some guy at Oysterfest a few years back had eaten a bad oyster and blamed it on the bacteria. Now there were laws that required the pickers to ice the oysters, and log every oyster they picked, where it was picked, what time they iced. Her friend "Andy Clam" said, "They even make you record your shits."

Some of the more experienced pickers could pull as many as three hundred and fifty oysters in a tide, while Poppy felt good if she could get to two hundred. She'd sell them to Wellfleet Harbor for forty to sixty cents each. In two to three hours, she could make four or five hundred bucks. She was new at this, but after only a few days she felt the money take on weight. With every oyster, her plan for her future came into focus. She'd put Ann off for a few years. She could save up, rent out the rooms to the seasonal workers who couldn't afford to live anywhere else. But after all those years of "go" money, it was hard to think of her savings as an anchor instead of an airline ticket.

When she wasn't in search of oysters over three inches, she was on the water with Gary and the rest of the crew. The surf was decent thanks to a series of squalls offshore. At night, they'd hang out at the Bomb Shelter, or the "Bomby," a bar under the Bookstore Café that reminded her of a typical Milwaukee corner bar, and it made her homesick for her old city, and for Brad. She was actively trying to forget him, but found herself drunk-dialing him when she returned home. He always answered, and the sound of his voice made her hungry for him.

One night, Carol bought Poppy a beer and sat on a stool next to her at the bar. "It's good to have you back," she said.

"Actually, I didn't really feel like I was back until you showed up."

"Listen," Carol said, her expression serious. "When someone asks me not to say something, I don't say it."

"Did I ask you not to say something?"

"Not you. Someone else. Pops, you're my friend. I have to tell you something." Carol tore at the label on her beer bottle with her fingernail. Whatever she wanted to tell Poppy, it wasn't good. "It's about your house."

Poppy had never thought of the house on the Cape as *hers*. It had always been *ours*. "Oh no. I hate this house stuff. I keep trying to forget you're a Realtor."

"You and me both."

Carol smiled, revealing the bright white crowns on her front teeth. This was nothing new to Poppy; so many of the surfers she knew had messed-up teeth.

"So," Carol said. "You know when I came over with some paperwork?"

"Yeah."

"You haven't looked through it, have you?"

"No," Poppy said. "I just put it in a pile for Ann. She's the one who deals with this stuff. Why?"

"I kept waiting for you to say something. Those papers? They terminated my contract. I can't sell your house."

"Why?"

"Because I got a visit from your brother a few weeks ago."

Brother. An image of Michael popped into her head—his sheepish smile, his easy manner. She got the chills. But Michael hadn't been her brother for a long time.

"You mean Michael? He's on the Cape?"

"You didn't know?"

"I never thought he'd—I mean, no. I didn't know, but that's nothing new." Poppy was so shocked she could hardly speak. "It didn't ever occur to me he was right here, so close, although now that I think of it, it makes perfect sense."

"He said he lives in P-town. Didn't get a gay vibe, but who knows. He's cute."

"I still can't believe this. Why did he see you?"

Carol took a swig of her beer. "Good old Ann misrepresented the sale."

"She did what?"

The bartender set another round on the bar and pointed at some guys in the corner. "They sent this over."

This happened to Poppy all the time, only now, because the beers arrived just when she needed them most, she felt like they'd been ordered not from the men in the corner, but from a higher power.

Carol said, "He's entitled to his share of the house from what I can tell."

"His share? Ann said he wasn't—that we didn't have to worry about him."

"She's wrong. You do. And she knows it. That sister of yours was supposed to list him as an heir, but she didn't. I knew something was up from the first time I met her. She seemed like she was holding back. I revoked the contract."

"I'm sorry, but damn, I'm so confused about what this means." Michael was alive and well? And the house—maybe it could stay in the family after all. She didn't know what to think. She resolved right then and there to call Brad as soon as she got home. She needed him, she didn't want to deny it any longer. She couldn't get through this without his support.

Carol said, "You've got a lot of shit to work out. Shit that's above my pay grade. Lawyer shit, right? But you're lucky. I could have put a lien on the property and sued for misrepresentation. Believe me, I thought about it. That's what I was planning to do the morning I stopped by, I was so pissed. But then I saw you."

"What do we do now?"

"We? Honey, I'm out of it. I just want to be your friend. My advice? Keep looking for the will. You've got a mess on your hands without one. Michael wants the house, and from what I can tell, he's got a right to it." Carol reached into her purse and dug around. "Here, he gave me his card."

Poppy couldn't believe it when Carol put the card in her hand. It was Michael's. He really was real, and he was here, on the Cape.

"I'm sorry to be the one to tell you this. I know you've been through a lot."

The men who'd sent the beers over slowly started to make their way to the bar, but hesitated and turned back around when they saw Poppy look at the card, grab Carol's arm, and tell her she had to go.

THIRTY-TWO

Michael

Michael looked up and saw Poppy standing in the doorway.

"What's up?" he asked, a stupid, casual-sounding question that belied the way his heart seized at the sight of her. In the dim light of his office he could see that she looked older, and resembled Connie now. A bomb of emotion exploded inside his chest. Her face was more weathered from the outdoors, with permanent creases around her eyes. She looked like the landscapers he worked with, not older in the sense that age depleted her beauty. She still appeared youthful, only now her looks were more defined, more particular to her.

The string from her sweatshirt hood was wrapped tight around her finger, her expression pained.

He cleared his throat. "I wasn't expecting to see you."

"No, no. You weren't. You don't expect to see the people you run away from." Her sarcasm was startling. He couldn't remember her ever being sarcastic.

"Come in." He liked to keep things clean, but his office was an exception. It wasn't a place where he had many visitors. There were piles of paperwork, seed catalogs, and contracts on every surface. He stood up and picked up a pile from the chair in the corner and set it on top of his file cabinet. She looked as though she might leave at any second.

"How did you find me?" he asked.

"Carol," Poppy said. "She gave me your card."

"I asked her not to say anything."

"It would have come out eventually, Michael. She said you're making a claim on the house."

He'd planned to approach them in his own way, in his own time, when it felt right. Maybe this was easier. Poppy had always been his ally, although he had no reason to think she'd stand by him now—why should she? What must she think of him after the lie he'd told?

Poppy's eyes fixed on a framed photograph of Michael and Shelby on a fishing boat that he'd never taken down. "Your wife?"

"My ex."

"God, you've been married and divorced."

"We didn't marry or divorce."

"She's pretty."

"Yeah," Michael said. "She is. How about you?"

"What about me?" she asked.

"Are you married?"

"No. Geez. Everybody asks me that. I don't have to be married to be happy."

"OK, no argument from me." They fell into an uncomfortable silence. Michael didn't know what he was supposed to say. He still thought of her as his kid sister. He hated that she looked so sad and alone and confused, and that some of her sadness and confusion was because of him, and what he'd done and not done. "I have a boyfriend, I guess. He's here now. On the Cape."

"Lucky guy." He meant this. "Your parents—I can't—I just found out not too long ago. It's terrible."

"It is." Poppy nodded like everything he said was no big deal, trying hard to seem cool. Her faux-toughness made him ache for her.

He leaned back in his chair and put his hands behind his head. It was a gesture that was meant to show his physical openness, a trick he learned when he went through family therapy with Shelby and Deeds when Avery was little, and they faced coparenting challenges. The women accused him of closing himself up when things got tough. The therapist said he should strive for transparency above all else, and that body language has everything to do with the success or failure of a conversation. Really, he wanted to curl up into a tight ball.

She walked to the other side of the room and picked up another framed photo, this one of Avery. What a way to explain your life to someone, photo by photo, the way they did on social media. In that snapshot she was only two, playing at Race Point Beach in a broad sun hat and daisy-print bathing suit. He didn't understand then how much it would hurt, years later, to look at photographs of his daughter as a little girl. Days are long, years are short, as Ed liked to say. He wished he could stop time.

"Is this your daughter?"

"Yeah. Avery. She's older now."

"Just look at her. She's gorgeous. She looks just like you, especially in the eyes." She paused and turned her gaze back to Michael. "Ann's son," she said. "Noah. He doesn't look like you. Not at all."

"There's no reason he should."

She froze. "What did you just say?"

"He's not mine, Poppy. He's just not, OK?" God, it felt good and clarifying to say that out loud after all these years. He wanted to scream it from a mountaintop.

She sat down, breathless. "But all these years . . . I mean, why'd you say he was? Why, Michael?" Her voice cracked. "You didn't even say goodbye. How could you do that? Did you ever even think of me?"

He hadn't anticipated Poppy's pain. What a time, with Poppy sitting right in front of him, to realize what a selfish shit he'd been, and what a shitty job he'd done trying to navigate that messy situation with Ann and Anthony. Poppy was the victim of collateral damage. "It's such a long story."

"Who's the dad?"

Such a straightforward question, but the answer had been a secret for so long that it felt like it was still locked away. "Ann should explain that to you."

"Oh, come on." She slapped her hands by her sides and stared at him, imploring, waiting for him to break. He looked right back at her. Even after all these years, she knew he was stubborn and wouldn't back down. "I've been pissed at you all these years for something you now say you didn't do. Why did you lie?"

"Did you ever hear me say that was my kid? Did those words ever come out of my mouth?"

"No. Nothing did." Poppy looked angry, as if she wanted to put up a fight but then, in almost that same moment, she looked sad and defeated. He'd forgotten about Poppy's incredible emotional range. She was nothing like Ann, who rode her emotions like an arrow. "You left."

"You're right," he said. "I left. You can be pissed at me for that."

"I guess I've done my share of leaving." Poppy walked over to the window and stood with her back to him. Michael watched her stare out at the gravel parking lot through the yellowed plastic shades, all pent up.

Michael walked over to her and put his hand on her shoulder, afraid she'd push him away. "Want to get out of here?" Michael asked. He knew Poppy needed to move around, the same way he did. "Go for a walk or something?"

Poppy nodded. "A walk would be great."

MICHAEL PARKED HIS TRUCK NEAR Wireless Road. They followed a fire road that eventually led to White Cedar Swamp and Marconi Station, where the first transatlantic signal was sent.

He remembered how much Poppy loved to explore the fire roads. She was always up for an adventure, always looking for a new place, some amazing discovery she could make. She showed him how to get to Dyer Pond and access the remote houses on the far shore that he'd only seen from the water. Before she showed him the way, he couldn't figure out how people got to those houses. The Cape was nothing like Milwaukee, where the streets were part of a neat grid, the houses announcing themselves, lined up and orderly.

It was still cool and damp outside. Poppy wore a white fleece jacket that made her look innocent and set off the amber streaks in her hair. The white also made her easy to find if she got too far ahead, something that seemed likely to happen in her current state of mind. She blew past all the education signs that Connie and Ed used to make them stop and read. That was how he'd learned about the shapes of leaves, how ferns grow in the shade, and how trees, like people, crowd each other out and battle for dominance.

"This was always my favorite part," Poppy said as soon as they got to the elevated wooden footpath through White Cedar Swamp.

"Mine too," he said. The cedars had a prehistoric quality about them, rising out of their mossy mounds, everything dripping. "Feels like I'm in a cathedral."

Poppy stopped because she saw a bird that interested her. Poppy never missed a bird.

"I bet you wish you had your binoculars," he said. He remembered that she'd had two pairs, one so old that the leather was worn off and the lenses had turned green, and a smaller, better pair that Poppy always insisted he use when they'd gone bird-watching together.

She looked at him, genuinely touched. "You remember."

"I remember *everything*," he said. "That's my problem."

Poppy looked up again, into the branches of an oak tree that Michael could tell had top rot and wouldn't last many more years. "My mom was losing her memory."

"Connie? That's impossible. Her brain was a steel trap."

"I know. Nobody told me about her dementia. It set in fast, I guess. I think about it all the time now. I wonder what she forgot first. I'll bet it was hard for her to be here, knowing all her memories of this place were slowly being erased."

"You don't need to remember being here, though," Michael said. "You can just experience it. I can't think of a better place to be in the moment."

"But can we really just be in the moment here? Isn't it the past that makes this place so meaningful?" This was new: the last time he'd seen Poppy, she was sixteen and said whatever popped into her head. She was older now. More mature. She saw some movement in the branches and squinted to get a look. "I've seen two Eurasian wigeons since I got here."

"Remember all the goldfinches that used to crowd around your parents' feeder?"

"And you'd laugh when you saw them fly, because they moved around like they were drunk?" It was remarkable to watch her mood change before she'd ended her sentence. She smiled, then slapped her arms to her sides in frustration. "I can't believe I'm standing here at Marconi Station with you and we're talking about goddamn birds! They're dead, Michael. Dead!"

Michael winced. The Gordons weren't the only parents he'd lost; now he was—what? A double orphan? He remembered when he'd stood at his mother's side, holding her hand, his ear on her bony chest, willing her heart to keep thump, thump, thumping. She wasn't alone; the hospital was filled with people with HIV. He watched as they dropped away from the poisoning, one by one. It felt like it still should have been news, an outrage, a national crisis. Instead, it was a quiet die-off. Nobody seemed to care anymore. When his mother finally took her last, raspy breath, the nurse, obviously sorry for him, looked from the IV bag to Michael. He knew from the way the room changed as soon as she'd died, the way it felt like a little bit of air had been sucked out of it, that the entire universe would always feel different. The nurse—he still remembered her name was Yvonne—was the only person who seemed to care. "She's with the other angels now, honey." Michael didn't cry. He just shook his head: no, no, no. Now he was doing it again, only this time he wasn't entirely alone in his grief, and that—well, that was some kind of comfort, he supposed.

"I've been in this fog for months," Poppy said. "I miss them so much.

We, like, have conversations in my head and I find myself narrating my life for them. Or you know what's weirder? They have conversations with *each other*, like I'm not even there! I know it sounds crazy, but they're like the people who sit in the booth next to you at a restaurant and you can't help but listen in on what they are saying."

"That doesn't sound crazy," Michael said. But he was thinking about how, all these years, he'd silently narrated his life for Ann.

"You think I'm nuts. Everyone does."

Michael smiled. "You're just more aware than most people."

"Maybe." She twirled some of her hair around her finger. "It's funny how I think differently now. The other day I found a long, gray hair stuck to a bar of soap when I was in the shower. My *mom's* hair. I tried to pull it off but it had already come loose and before I knew it, it slipped down the drain. I felt like, if I could have just held on to that hair I could, like, get her back. It's stupid, the stuff I think. Like if I use up the roll of toilet paper they started, or finish the olive oil, or if I take the socks and towels they forgot to take out of the dryer, that they'll really be gone. All their unfinished things will be finished—*forever*. It's so irrational. Nothing has prepared me for this. I've spent the last decade learning yoga and mindfulness and delving into the spirit world and mysticism and it doesn't help me feel better. It's like I've failed at everything, even thinking."

She seemed so alone at that moment that he was glad to be there for her the way a brother might have been there. She trusted him enough to say these things.

"And then I keep discovering all these secrets!" She hit Michael on the arm, a bit harder than she'd probably meant to. It was a punch that wasn't meant to be entirely playful. "Nobody bothers to explain anything to me. Like, I mean, I was really happy my family wanted to adopt you, I really was, but nobody bothered to even tell me. And then . . . you left. One minute you were my best friend . . ."

"You thought I was your best friend?"

"Sure! We did everything together, especially, well, especially before I . . . you know."

"You found a new group."

"I was a dumb teenager. It was all so sudden. One minute you were helping me understand derivatives, and then you were gone. Just gone. *Poof!* I'm still trying to figure out how it happened. I had so many questions. The world was one way, with the family I thought I knew, and then we were strangers with these major secrets. Do you know that I found out from kids at school that Ann was pregnant—she didn't even tell me. Those were the same kids who told me you were the father. It blew my mind. You were my friend. My *brother*."

The word "brother" might as well have been a knife in his gut. Not until she said it did he ever really believe she thought of him that way, and not until that moment, with the pines towering overhead and that incredible stillness in the marsh.

"I always thought your family was too perfect for me."

Poppy seemed shocked by this. "Why would you think that? We were like any family. We argued. We had secrets. We could hardly shut the junk drawer."

Michael nodded. "No. You always took for granted how special you were."

"It doesn't feel like we're a family anymore, like we never were again after you left." She was really crying now, a deep, heavy cry that wasn't at all self-conscious; it was raw and real, and the truth of her emotions touched him in a place he usually kept protected, shielded. "Why didn't you say goodbye, Michael?"

He told her the truth: "I couldn't."

"But we loved you! Even if you really *had* gotten Ann pregnant we would have worked it out."

"I thought I was protecting her."

He could tell by the way she rolled her eyes that things were not good between the two sisters. "Oh, please. Ann can take care of herself."

There was too much to say, too much to explain. "Everything was so fucked up."

"It still is. But I don't know, seeing you again, I can't help but feel like it's starting to feel a little better." Poppy stared at him in a way that made him feel vulnerable and transparent. She knew him, she did.

"Let's walk to the station," Michael said, needing to move, or at least escape that look.

Poppy grabbed him by the sleeve. "What went on with you two?"

Michael threw his hands up in the air. "Nothing."

"Ann always had a thing for you."

"No way."

"Everyone knew, Michael. Everyone saw. I even heard her say it!"

"You heard nothing."

"It was when we were in the process of adopting you. I overheard her talking to Claire Caldwell when she slept over one night. I always eavesdropped on Ann. She said she was worried her feelings for you weren't exactly, you know, the kind you might feel for a brother."

"She did not." He could feel his face get hot.

"She *did*! She said she wondered if what she'd really wanted was for you to be her boyfriend."

"That sure would have been a lot easier."

"I'm not so sure about that. And then when that lady she babysat for called and told my parents you kissed her? Like her kids saw it or something? That's part of the reason I believed the story about you getting her pregnant."

Mo told Connie about that?

"Look at me. You loved her that way too, Michael. You did, didn't you? Just say it."

Michael stuffed his hands into his pockets and felt for his "worry stone," a milky white quartz pebble Connie had given him all those years ago. "Rub it whenever you need to calm down," she'd said. He was surprised he hadn't rubbed it down into fine grains of sand over the years—hell, he felt like he could rub it to sand at that very moment. "I don't even know what you're trying to get me to say. That was a long time ago."

Poppy was growing impatient with his evasiveness, he could tell. Why couldn't he just be honest? Instead he bit his lip, rubbed the stone, looked down at his feet as they kicked at the sandy ground.

She let out an exasperated sigh. "So, Carol says you want the house?"

Oh, God. The house. He'd almost forgotten that this was what all this was about. "You and Ann were going to sell it anyway."

"*Ann* was going to. She railroaded me. We never even talked about it. But now that I'm back, I'm having second thoughts. She keeps telling me I can't afford it, it's so much work, it's just a house, blah blah blah."

"It's not just a house, and I'm a legitimate heir." A breeze picked up, a warm breeze from the south, carrying with it the surprising smell of summer.

"But why?"

"Why what?"

"Why do you want it? Even if you're entitled, you could get some of the money from the sale."

"I don't give a damn about the money, you know that. I've always loved that house. It's the only place where my life ever felt like it made any sense." This felt like such an enormous confession that Michael couldn't just stand there and let his words settle in the air around them. He started to walk because he had to move, had to escape his own weakness, had to resist everything Poppy wanted to say to him. He walked with a brisk pace through the empty parking lot until he got to the open shelter, perched on the edge of the bluff overlooking the Atlantic, where it had to be moved because of erosion. The whole damn Cape was getting chewed up on all sides the same way he was. The wind was so strong closer to the water that bits of sand blew into his face, and when he licked his lip, it tasted like salt. Poppy stood next to him, her hair tossing wildly in the cool ocean breeze. She tugged his sleeve again.

"Maybe we can think of something, the two of us. There must be some way for us to keep it."

"But you said Ann is hot to sell, and you know she doesn't want me to have it."

"I don't even know what she thinks. We haven't talked much yet. She's been avoiding me."

Michael was grateful for the wind; perhaps Poppy thought his eyes were just watering. "How did we end up like this?"

"I wish we could do everything over again," she said. He'd thought the same thing a thousand times.

Poppy stepped closer to Michael and leaned lightly against him. "At least I found you. I've missed you, Michael. I've missed you so much." She was crying, too. "Don't you know I've looked for you everywhere I've ever been?"

THIRTY-THREE

Ann

Ann and Noah argued the whole ride down to the Cape. He assailed her with a litany of reasons not to sell. "We've gone over this again and again," she said. "Old houses are a lot of work."

"*I'm* the one who does the work. I got the whole place running when Poppy arrived. I can do it. I'll open the house. I'll close the house. I'll fix the house. Dude taught me everything."

"Is that really how you want to spend your time? What about when you get an internship? What if you want to be like Poppy and travel? You don't want to be tied to a house. Houses tie you down."

"Like kids? Kids tie you down. You knew that. You didn't get rid of me." Ann smiled. "Maybe it's not too late."

Noah banged the car dash with his cast—he'd broken his arm at the skate park, and his friend painted the YouTube star Miranda Sings on it, with her pouty red lips and center part, and the words *Hi Guys! It's me. Miranda.* "I'm serious! I like being tied down to that house. It's ours, Mom."

"Have you seen the tax bill? Hurricane insurance isn't cheap, either. And it needs a roof. Carol calls it 'deferred maintenance.'"

"Poppy and I have thought of a million ways to make it work out."

Ann laughed. "The two great business minds in our family."

"You gotta fight for what you love! Stop the car."

"No. Please would you stop being dramatic."

Noah twisted around and reached for the emergency brake with his good hand. "I said stop the car. I'll walk the rest of the way there."

Ann kept driving; she knew Noah was bluffing, or at least she thought she knew until she began to feel the pinch of brakes against her wheels. She swatted at his hand, alarmed, remembering how her own parents had died. "Noah Gordon! That's dangerous."

Noah was crying. His tears moved her deeply, but she couldn't let him see that. "Please, Mom. Don't sell. Keep the house for me even if you don't want it."

"I wish it were that easy."

She didn't tell him that Carol had left a curt voicemail saying simply that she'd canceled the contract. Why would a Realtor give up a commission? Ann was afraid to talk to Carol because she worried this had something to do with Michael, but how would he find out about the house? He was probably back in Milwaukee or Chicago or who knows where. Carol didn't answer, and she didn't return her calls. It was fine, fine. Ann didn't care. She'd find another Realtor. She had to let go of the stupid idea that she'd feel better about her parents' deaths once the house changed hands. She'd started to believe that her grief was part of the transaction.

Poppy wasn't home when Ann and Noah arrived. He was still upset and walked into the girls' bedroom, set his bag down on one of the beds, and shut the door.

She took a deep breath and looked around. The place was messy, so Ann went straight to cleaning, resentfully scrubbing the dishes that her sister had left in the sink, wiping the counters, taking out the garbage. The more she cleaned, the more messes she encountered—clumps of hair in the drain, wet towels on the hardwood floors, empty beer bottles on the end tables. She was putting the playing cards laid out for solitaire back into the box when Poppy blew through the door.

There she was, at long last. Her sister's face was chapped and red from the outdoors, and her long hair was pulled back into a fishtail braid. She looked the same as always: fresh, soft, sweet. For a second, all the pent-up anger Ann felt disappeared. Despite everything, it felt good to see Poppy—better than good. She saw not just Poppy but also her mother, whose features were now more visible in her sister. She was overcome with an unexpected gush of warmth. Ann said, "Where've you been?"

All the energy drained from Poppy's face when she looked at Ann. "Out." Poppy kicked off her rain boots and breezed right past the spot where Ann stood, stirring up the dust pile she'd just swept. Ann might as well have been a piece of furniture in the wrong place. Poppy walked into her parents' bedroom and threw her coat on the bed. It wasn't just unmade; the sheets were so twisted it looked like people had been wrestling on it.

Ann was so surprised by Poppy's dismissiveness that all of her emotions jammed up in her mind. Why was Poppy mad at her? She was the one who'd taken care of things—she should be grateful. Ann was trying to think of what to say next when a man walked through the kitchen door carrying a bag of groceries.

"Hello?"

"Oh hey, Ann."

He set the bag on the kitchen counter and shook Ann's hand.

"Brad? *Milwaukee* Brad?"

"The very same."

"I wasn't expecting to see you here."

"Just got in last week." He pulled a head of cabbage from the bag and set it on the kitchen counter. "I wanted to see your place here, and Poppy, of course. When she called and asked if I could come out, I booked the first flight."

"It's great you're buying the house in Milwaukee. My parents would have loved that."

"Yeah, so about that—"

Before he could say more, Noah emerged from the bedroom. "You're here!"

Poppy gave him a fist bump followed by a warm hug—nothing like the cold shoulder Ann had received.

"Hey, man." Noah's face was lit with a smile. *Hey, man.* Since when did he talk like that? What had Noah and Poppy done together? Did they get high? Listen to Bob Marley? Chant? So, they were buddies now. Poppy could just sashay into his life and fist-bump her way into his heart.

"This is Brad," Poppy said. "He's the guy I told you about."

"Your boyfriend," Noah said teasingly.

For someone so natural and easy, Poppy seemed oddly thrown off by the word "boyfriend." "Yeah, I guess."

Brad came up behind her, wrapped his arms around her waist, and kissed her on top of her head. There was no denying the chemistry between them. "You *guess*?"

"You know I don't like labels."

Ann thought of the dates she'd gone on over the years, the guys she'd imagined introducing Noah to. Aside from safe Kevin, they never measured up, never seemed worthy of the emotional trauma she might inflict on him. He was possessive of her, sensitive, needy. Ann envied the ease with which Poppy could bring a man into Noah's life. Everything seemed easy for her. She was in Milwaukee, what, two months? And here she'd sold a home and met someone willing to travel halfway across the country just to see her. Now she and Noah were thick as thieves.

"No surfing for us tonight," Poppy told Noah. "Rain coming in. How about I teach you tomorrow? OK if Brad joins us?"

"Yeah, sure."

"You were going to surf?" Ann asked. "You never told me that. No way. It's freezing. And aren't there sharks?"

Noah rolled his eyes. "Mom, Poppy promised to teach me. A friend loaned her a wet suit for me to wear."

"I'm down for surfing too," Brad said. "I'll fend off the great whites."

It was obvious Ann was the only person who wasn't invited to come along. "No." She wasn't about to let Noah get into surfing, but not because of the danger. She was worried that if he loved it, he'd disappear the same way Poppy had.

Brad started cooking dinner, a Polish dish called *haluški* that Brad said was a secret family recipe. Soon the kitchen was filled with the smell of cabbage and pork. Noah put her dad's Gene Krupa album on the record player, and Poppy lit candles and turned on the string lights. The house, which had seemed so empty and abandoned this past year, felt warm and golden, almost like a home again, only Ann felt unwelcome.

"Noah, c'mere," Brad said. "I'm going to teach you how to make this the way my *babcia* taught me." Noah was eager for a cooking lesson, and hungry for attention from Brad, who drove a motorcycle, played a mandolin, and ran a machine shop. He told him stories about the characters he'd hired to work for him and the rats on the shop floor.

With nothing better to do, Ann started wiping down the walls so she could get them ready to paint. Poppy sat at the table in the area between the kitchen and the living room drinking wine. Occasionally, Ann would find her gaze cast in her direction. Ann thought about trying to strike up a conversation, but Poppy quickly looked back at her crossword puzzle. Poppy's silence was out of character. So was her anger. *She* was the one who'd been gone all these years, the one who was AWOL when their parents died. Poppy knew something, and so did Brad, and that was why they were so cool to Ann. But what did they know?

"I'm worried about all these cracks in the walls," Ann said. "There might be a problem with the foundation."

"The foundation is fine," Poppy said, her voice scolding, as if Ann were some kid who was worried about a monster under her bed.

"It can't be fine. The house is over two hundred years old. There are problems, you know there are."

"It looks OK to me," Brad said, "and I know a thing or two about houses." He'd set some plates on the table. "The walls are amazingly plumb for a structure this old." He gently lifted the album off the record player and leafed through her dad's album collection as if it were his own. "How about some dinner music? Look at this Grant Green. The LT Series. This is better than the Blue Note edition. I wonder where your dad picked this up." The song "Solid" began to play, a song far too tinkling and light for Ann's dour mood. Ann's father called songs like that one "Sunday morning music." For a moment, it felt as if he'd walked into the room to join them. Ann could picture him exactly, right down to his soft T-shirts, paint-stained carpenter shorts, and tattered sandals, his big toenail always split like a piece of old wood.

Poppy walked over to the bookcase and pulled out a yellowed, motheaten dime-store paperback of *All Creatures Great and Small*—Connie had loved that series about the British veterinarian. She'd forgotten how her father had used scraps of toilet paper as bookmarks. They floated to the floor, and Ann panicked: she'd never again know which pages he'd marked.

Noah set the water glasses down. Ann counted: one, two, three, four . . . five. "Why are you setting five places? Who else are you expecting?"

"A friend," Poppy said. "He should be here soon."

"What friend?"

"Just a friend. Someone I met out here."

Ann wasn't sure what to do next. The windowsills were rotting. So much to do, so much, and now Carol was out of the picture. Noah, always alert, sensed her tension. He stood behind Ann and rubbed her shoulders. "You should try some of Poppy's lavender oil."

"Her what?"

"She says if you rub it on your feet it'll relax you."

"The only thing oil on your feet does is make you slip and fall."

"Your feet are incredibly receptive," Poppy said. "If you stand on an onion for half an hour you'll start to taste it."

"Who has time to stand on an onion for half an hour?"

Brad laughed.

"God, you haven't changed," Poppy said.

"Dinner is a long way from being done," Brad said. "I'm not sure the oven works the way it's supposed to."

"It worked in 1979," Poppy said, and hit Brad's ass with a dish towel. Poppy lit some candles and opened the game cabinet next to the fireplace where the family stored taped-up boxes holding ancient versions of Boggle, Parcheesi, Chinese checkers, and Pollyanna. There were at least a dozen decks of cards held together with crusty rubber bands, scattered dice and orphan game pieces. Poppy dug around. "Where's Yahtzee?"

Ann knew the game cabinet would be the last—and the hardest—space to clean out. If a house had a heart, that's where it was.

"I guess we'll do a jigsaw puzzle." Poppy held the box in front of Noah, smiled, and shifted into a graceful, well-practiced warrior three position while dumping the puzzle pieces into a dusty mound on the kitchen table where Ann had picked up the cards. Ann thought Poppy was showing off, forcing the world to acknowledge that yes, she taught yoga and yes, she was still in great shape. Yes, yes, yes—there was always an imperative to admire Poppy for her easy good looks, her sweetness, her athleticism, and her free spirit.

Poppy opened another bottle of wine and poured three glasses almost to the rims. "Here," Poppy said, holding the glass in front of Ann like a peace offering. "You need this."

"Now you're talking," said Brad, who lifted his glass to initiate a toast. "To this awesome place."

". . . that will soon be sold to strangers." Noah made a face at Ann.

"OK," said Poppy. "Here's to being together again."

The puzzle was so old that the cardboard rose like phyllo dough and the photograph was peeling off the pieces. Without discussion, the sisters began to divide up the land and sky and started with the edges, the way they always had. It was like muscle memory. Noah pulled up a chair and sat between Poppy and Brad. Ann felt outnumbered.

"You do the lighthouse," Poppy said.

"Oh sure, give me the hard part."

Poppy tousled Noah's thick, brown hair, and Noah's face lit with a smile of satisfaction that both pleased and angered Ann. She wanted to say to her son, "You hardly know her! Or Brad!" But she held herself back, because even if she was upset with Poppy, she wanted Noah to have a decent relationship with her. She was all the family she had left.

Ann looked at the clock on the wall. The battery was dead, and the hands had frozen in place at 2:34. "When is your guest coming?"

Brad and Poppy looked at each other, an inside look. "Wasn't he supposed to be here ten minutes ago?"

"What's going on?" Ann asked. The room was filled with energy.

"Nothing," Poppy said. "I've got the corners."

They got to work on the puzzle as if its completion really mattered. Noah snuck sips of Ann's wine so he'd look cool for Poppy. Ann didn't mind, not really. He was sixteen. Who knew? Maybe Poppy had gotten him drunk or high when they spent the last few weekends alone together. Now they had shared secrets and inside jokes.

Noah propped his chin on his cast. Ann noticed that Poppy still bit her lip when she concentrated. She had to admit that Poppy was kind of adorable. Ann found the familiarity of her gestures oddly endearing, and somehow reassuring. Brad was also staring at Poppy. Oh man, he had it bad, poor sucker. Didn't he know Poppy would desert him, just like she had deserted everything—and everyone?

The wine and physical exhaustion set in. Ann allowed herself to relax. The soft rain on the windows and the flickering candlelight made the space feel intimate, like it was the only place in the world that mattered. She allowed herself to imagine that she and Poppy were kids again, and that it was Michael instead of Noah who sat at the kitchen table, and their parents were sitting next to each other in their respective spots on the couch in the next room, their reading glasses perched on the ends of their noses, her mother intent on a book, her father's head tipped back, asleep, a gentle snore.

Ann put her hand over Noah's. "You used to call her Puppy." Ann gestured to her sister. "Do you remember that?"

"I did?"

Ann nodded. "Poppy would visit from college. When she went back to Madison, you'd would walk around saying 'I want puppy, I want puppy.' Everyone thought you wanted a dog."

"That's sweet," Poppy said. "I didn't know that."

"No," Ann said. "You didn't."

"But I *did* want a dog," Noah said. "I mean I do. I've always wanted one."

"You'll be in college in a few years. I don't want to be stuck with it."

"God forbid you should be burdened with a dog or a house." Noah looked at Poppy. "How about *you* get a dog? We can pick one out at the shelter. We could give it a real Wellfleet name, like Dune or Whydah."

Poppy said, "It should have an oyster name, like Spat." She put another piece in the puzzle. "Or Shucker."

"Nobody's getting a dog," Ann said. She tried to force a spade-shaped piece into the corner. It didn't fit, but it looked like it should. "Besides, Poppy, you won't stick around."

"How do you know what I will or won't do?"

Ann began to feel some alarm; she never counted on Poppy really wanting to stay.

"I was thinking," Poppy said. "We could rent out the house and live in the barn while people are here."

"Nobody wants to rent this place," Ann said. "It's a disaster."

"I've slept in worse places."

"I'll bet you have. Don't worry about the house. You don't want to be tied down. You know how many crossed-out entries I have for you in my address book?"

Poppy was quiet. She and Brad exchanged another knowing glance.

"I don't know how you can live like this," Ann said.

"What do you mean, 'like this'?"

"You don't even have any savings, do you? Not even an IRA?"

"So what?"

"You need some security."

"You need to stop being so judgmental." Poppy pushed her chair back and looked up at the ceiling.

"I'm being realistic. Tell me, what's the longest you've spent in any one place? A year? Two?"

"Mom," said Noah. "Don't. Please just don't. Poppy's great the way she is."

"I'll stay," Poppy said. "I've been working, you know."

"Working?"

"I always work, Ann. Everywhere I go I have a job, sometimes two. My life isn't totally free of responsibility. Sue me if I don't want to waste my life in a cubicle in some corporate office."

"I don't just have myself to think of."

"That's a choice you made."

It was all she could do not to say that it wasn't a choice, *it wasn't a choice!* Instead, she took a deep breath. "So, what kind of work did you find out here? Are you at that yoga place by the lumber store?" Ann tried hard, for Noah's benefit, to strike a tone that was calmer, kinder, but instead she knew she sounded fake, falsely cheerful.

"Oysters," Poppy said. "I'm oystering. I like it. And the pay is pretty great."

"I'll bet it comes with a terrific benefits package."

She could hear Poppy's breathing slow down, as if she were trying to calm herself. "Do you have to be a bitch?"

"Seriously, what if you get sick?"

"Sick?" Poppy said, her head tilted. "Like, if I get, say, Alzheimer's?"

The word slipped out of Poppy's mouth as unexpectedly as a dove from a magician's hat.

"I had to hear it from Brad. He's the one who told me Mom was sick."

"So now you know," Ann said. "And what difference does it make? Really, Poppy, is it my job to tell you everything?"

What Ann really wanted to say was: "I didn't think you'd care." She had to be careful, though. She needed to tread softly with her sister, at least until the house was worked out.

"You could have said something," Noah said.

"Well," Ann said, "I thought Dad told you."

"He didn't."

"He probably didn't want to upset you, or make you feel like you had to come back." Ann tried to be clinical, matter-of-fact. She used her work voice. But she couldn't stand to see the crushed look on her sister's face. She could tell tears would come next, and Ann didn't want to deal with Poppy's tears, not after everything. It was all she could do to hold it together herself. "It set in fast," Ann said, her voice softer. It was hard to think about the panicked phone calls from her dad. "Like really fast. They weren't even sure it was Alzheimer's. There's nothing you could have done."

"I just wish I knew."

"But why? You were an ocean away. I was the one who talked to them every day. They told me every little thing, like how warm their showers were."

"You love making me feel guilty, don't you?"

"I'm not making you feel anything." But Poppy was right. It was horrible and petty, Ann knew, but she *did* want Poppy to feel guilty—or something, because, deep down, her extended absence felt like an extended rejection.

Poppy said, "This is *our* house. It belongs to us. All of us."

"Amen!" said Noah.

Ann said, "Suddenly you're nostalgic."

"Well, suddenly Mom and Dad are fucking *dead*. Excuse me for having feelings about that."

"They died over half a year ago and you're just home now. Those are your feelings."

"Wait a minute: you're the one who told me not to bother coming home right away. There was nothing to be done until probate was over. Your words. *Yours!*"

Poppy was right. What could Ann say? She pushed her chair away from the table. "I have to go to the bathroom."

That was a lie, but she needed to get away, be alone for a minute. She sat on the edge of the claw-foot tub and stared at the damp wood floor around the base of the sink. Another problem, a leak. All these problems with the house: How could she deal with them on her own? Houses like this, old family homes, aren't meant to be owned by just one person.

Finally, she emerged to face her sister again. Only there, standing right next to her in the kitchen, was Michael. He wore jeans and running shoes. It was as if, when she'd imagined him there earlier, she'd invoked his presence, made him real.

"So, you're the mystery guest," Ann said. This was the voice she used at work when she was the only woman in a meeting full of men, or when she asked for the raise she didn't want to seem desperate for, or when she turned down a request for a second date from a perfectly nice guy for no good reason. It was a practiced, cold voice that belied her raging emotions.

Poppy stood next to Ann. "We thought it was a good idea to talk."

"No, this is a bad idea." Ann could feel her jaw clench. Her hands balled up at her sides. Her body grew stiff. Liquid anger coursed through her. "You're all in on this."

"Isn't it better to discuss the house face-to-face?"

"No. It's not. This is sneaky and manipulative."

Poppy said, "Sneaky and manipulative is leaving Michael off the estate. Now we've got a mess on our hands."

Noah was standing up in front of the table where they'd been working on the puzzle; what must he think? Why did Poppy feel it was OK to say this in front of her son?

"This is a mess he created." She refused to speak directly to Michael. "He doesn't deserve a thing, not even my time."

"Ann, please," Brad said. "He's got a claim—"

"Stay out of it!"

Poppy stood with her hands on her hips. "He's just trying to help."

"I don't need help." Ann went into her room, threw on her coat, and slipped into her shoes. She walked back into the living room, head down, and made her way to the door.

"Where you going?" Noah asked.

"I'll come get you Sunday. I need to go back to Boston." She took a deep breath and stepped outside.

Michael followed her. Even his footsteps sounded the same. "Please, Ann. Can we talk? This doesn't need to go badly."

"It's already gone badly."

The motion sensor flicked on above them on the back stoop. He grabbed her arm and she swung around. "Please?"

The light above Michael's face made him appear so ghostly that she wondered if he was real. She had to admit he looked great; she'd always thought he looked great. His features seemed more distinct now—his cheekbones more defined, his nose more angular. In her mind, he'd been frozen at the age of eighteen. But here he was, and he was older, a real man now. Everything had changed, and yet—nothing. He still had that wildly misbehaving cowlick on the right side of his hairline, only now his thick, jet-black hair glimmered with a few silver strands—or was it the porch light and the rain?

Ann felt Michael watching her in his steady way. She'd almost forgotten what it felt like to have his eyes on her; he'd always watched her, hadn't he?

"I need to go," she said. It was too much, seeing him here after all these years. She had to fight this strange and unexpected impulse to collapse in his arms. He'd been not just part of her life, but her family's life. She had to keep reminding herself of what he'd done, although now, with so much happening, it was hard to even remember what, exactly, that was.

"You just show up like this after all these years?"

"Hello to you, too." He tried to force a crooked smile. He seemed embarrassed by his own gesture, or perhaps overcome? He fixed his eyes on the rotted porch board he nudged with the toe of his shoe. Ann almost wanted to feel sorry for him—but that was what had gotten her into all that trouble in the past, wasn't it? She'd thought of herself as an object lesson in what happens when you go soft. And yet—what was it about him? It was like listening to a chord change in music that plucked on her most vulnerable emotions. A part of her wished that nothing had come between them, that they'd always been there for each other.

"So, you're the reason the Realtor canceled the contract."

"I'm a legitimate heir. Poppy knows it," he said. "And come on, Ann. You know it, too. I don't care about the house in Milwaukee or any of your parents' other assets. All I want is my third of the house. This house. I'll buy you and Poppy out of your shares. Or if Poppy wants to share it, we can work something out."

Ann crossed her arms even more tightly across her chest. A straitjacket, arms that were doing their best to keep her from coming completely undone. "Two years you lived with us, and you call yourself an heir?"

The drizzle intensified. It felt good, actually, and she knew Michael thought so, too. They used to love running together in the drizzle and fog, both on the lakeshore path back home, and along Ocean View Drive here. Once, when it was raining really hard, Michael stopped running and stood on the Humboldt Bridge over the river, his hands in the air like Jesus, his head tipped back, drinking the rain as it fell from the sky.

"I'm not trying to take anything from you." He looked at her, sincere, trying to draw her into his gaze, his argument—

No, no, *no!* Ann ripped her eyes away from him, staring into the fire pit where the family—including Michael—used to sit in their better days, her dad with his guitar on his lap, her mom using a pocketknife to sharpen sticks for s'mores.

"Here's the thing: I don't want you to buy us out with your dirty money, the money you took from Anthony. Did you tell Poppy about that, too, or did you conveniently leave that part out?" This anger was so familiar to Ann that it felt like it held her up, a second spine.

Michael cleared his throat. "I talked to my lawyer." His voice was deeper than she'd remembered it, more gravelly and wise. He sounded like what he was: an adult now. They were adults.

"You're a big man now, huh? Your lawyer? You love saying that, don't you?"

She could tell she was hurting him. Good. She wanted him to hurt the way she'd hurt all these years. "I won't let you buy this house."

"My lawyer says I'm a cloud on the title."

"You're a cloud on my life."

"God, Ann. Don't say that."

She'd hit a nerve, so why did it make her feel guilty instead of victorious?

"Listen to me: you have no right to this house. I don't care what you and Poppy spoke about, and I don't care what your fucking lawyer says. Just go away. Please. Just leave me and my family alone."

"I *am* your family."

She hadn't expected that. "No. We all just felt sorry for you."

He winced again. She was reminded of how she'd felt all those years ago when her father finally got out his pellet gun and shot the woodpecker that had been tormenting them for months. Relieved, yes, but the woodpecker was just doing what woodpeckers do. The silence that followed the bird's death was more relentless than the noise it had once made.

Michael said, "You used me."

"*I* used *you*? Pot, meet kettle."

"Whatever." Michael threw back his shoulders and took a deep, jagged breath. A hardness passed over his face, a hardness that took Ann by surprise because she'd never seen him look like that. He'd always been open with her; open to her. Now he was cold, firm. "I'll force the sale. I can do that. And when I do, the house will go to the highest bidder. You can bid on it for what it's worth to you, which might be more, or less, than you were asking. But I want you to know that the person you'll bid against is me." He reached into his pocket and took out his keys. Ann noticed that the key ring was silly—a picture of a cat and the words HAPPY CAT. She knew that wasn't a key ring he'd picked out for himself. For the first time, she considered that he had other people in his life, people who gave him gifts. People who loved him.

"I'll never let you buy it."

"You might not have a choice."

"You're bluffing."

"I've already filed a petition to have you removed as the administrator of the estate." He crunched the keys in his hand so hard they had to have cut into the flesh of his palm. "You've acted in bad faith."

"Just listen to you, talking about acting in bad faith. You would know."

Ann began to walk toward her car. She couldn't take it anymore. She had the wet door handle in her hand when Michael said something that stopped her.

"Does your kid know?" *Your kid.* The idea of Noah seemed so casual, so distant. Just some kid. "Say he needs a kidney or something."

"He knows. I told him after Anthony died." She knew she was dropping a bomb. She needed to destabilize Michael.

"I heard about that." Michael stood with his arms at his sides as if he didn't know what to do with them.

"Right. You two were thick as thieves."

"No, I mean my business partner told me. He'd called—" Michael started to say something more, but Ann wouldn't listen.

"I don't want to talk about Anthony. Look, Michael. Do whatever you think you need to do. I don't understand why you're making this so difficult. You took his money."

"I did, but can't we just talk?"

"No!" Ann stomped her foot like she was shooing a raccoon from a garbage can.

"We have nothing to say to each other. I'm getting out of here."

Ann stepped into her car, slammed the door, and threw it into reverse. It was a two-hour drive back to Boston, and she was still fuming with anger when she returned to her apartment, an anger made worse when she collected her mail and saw a letter from some attorney's office in Provincetown. "Oh, no," she muttered when she ripped the envelope open and saw the words "My client, Michael . . ."

It was such a relief to see Maureen waiting there for her. She was curled up on the couch under a fleece throw with a book in her hands.

The women became friends after their shared ordeal, and Mo occasionally took up residence on Ann's couch when she couldn't stand to be alone.
The three of them, and even Toby and Brooks, had become close, and
a new sort of family had emerged from the tragedy of Anthony's death.
Maureen was like a mother, sister, and friend to Ann, and to Noah she
was grandmother, stepmother, aunt, and a bridge to his real father. She
was honest with Noah about Anthony's faults, yet she also told stories
about him that were funny and sometimes moving. He'd liked to dance.
He was terrified of mice. He loved Bruce Springsteen.

"Oh, Mo. I've had the worst day."

Maureen stood up, grabbed a bottle of wine from the refrigerator, and
poured two glasses. The women sat down on the couch. Maureen nudged
Ann with her foot. "What's going on?"

Ann relayed the day's events, from Poppy's dismissiveness, to Brad, to
Michael's reappearance and their argument.

"Michael?" Maureen gasped. "In the flesh? He was on the Cape this
whole time? That must have really been something."

Ann nodded. She couldn't talk about Michael without fighting tears,
without seeing this new, sturdier, quieter, handsomer version of him
standing on the stoop in the rain, with the slightest crow's-feet etched
into the skin next to his almond-shaped eyes.

"What can I do?" Ann asked. "At first, I didn't think I even wanted
the house. Even before the Realtor canceled the contract I'd thought of
holding off, renting it to Poppy, turning it into an Airbnb or something.
Noah was beating me down. And now I want it more than anything.
It's *our* house, it belongs to us. But now the one person in the universe I
can't stand to see it go to—the one person who really let me down—well,
Michael's got a lawyer and a claim, and he says he has money to buy me
out. It looks like he'll have his way, because I've been dishonest. I don't
want him to end up with the house. I really don't."

"Well," Maureen said. She took a sip of her wine. "I think I might
have a plan."

There was nothing Maureen could do, Ann knew this. Yet the little glimmer of hope made Ann feel better. "Let's hear it," Ann said. She'd indulge her, even though Anthony's debts had cleaned her out. Now Ann had more money than Maureen did.

Maureen tapped her glass against Ann's. "You won't believe it, my dear. The most wonderful thing happened recently. Terrible and wonderful, which is how wonderful comes to me these days, but this is such terribly wonderful good news. I think I can help you, Ann. Help both of us. If you'll let me."

THIRTY-FOUR

Poppy

Poppy walked along the shore of Duck Harbor Beach. It was nice to be there so early in the day. She was reminded of the morning she'd gone surfing with Dirk, when she was in her wet suit before the sun had come out. That's when she first learned how special it was to commune with the ocean in the dark, the water black, endless, lumbering, and mysterious, shimmering in the moonlight.

She'd walked for half an hour or so, and already the sun had begun to rise from under last night's heavy cloud cover. The beach and sky were bathed in a dusty, rose-colored light. Seeking calm and a clearer head, she'd chosen to walk the bay instead of the back shore. The water here was less aggressive; the waves were gentler. Her mother had always preferred the less dramatic bay side for picnics and beachcombing, and even though Poppy surfed, she suspected she preferred the bay side, too.

When she looked up the long beach, she could see Pilgrim Monument in P-town way off in the distance. She noticed the ribbons of seaweed marking the highest crest of the last very high tide. Terns picked at the sand, while gulls swooped overhead. She took a deep breath of the salty air and tried to relax. It helped to think of Brad. That morning he got out of bed to make coffee for her. She explained that she needed to spend some time alone, and he handed her an old Campbell-plaid thermos, the one her father used to take with him when he'd gone fishing, and kissed her on the forehead. "I understand," he said. "I'll hang here with Noah. He promised to show me some of the tools in the barn. Good thing your dad told him what they were used for back in the day. They look like they belong in a surgical museum."

Poppy thought of the last thing she'd seen before she left that morning: Brad standing in the kitchen in his sweatshirt and flannel pajama bottoms, his hair messy, cleaning the dishes from the dinner he'd made the night before—he even cooked and cleaned! He seemed so right for the house in Milwaukee, and right for the Cape house, too. Jesus, was that love she felt when he'd looked up at her and smiled? The pang of tenderness, coupled with desire, was so powerful that she had to look away, almost shy.

Not love. She couldn't.

She reminded herself of *aparigraha,* the virtue of nonattachment. She liked to think she was capable of practicing this in all aspects of her life; she ate moderately, and when she thought of buying something, she'd think: Will this bring me peace? Longtime happiness? The answer was usually no, which was how she could travel alone and lightly, just her and her pack. But Brad—even his toes were perfect. She smiled.

No! Do not attach! Do not become bound to a person or a thing. Do not get caught up in outcomes. Do not get weighed down with energetic baggage. Do not, do not, do not. Aparigraha.

She wished she could suggest this fifth *yama* to Ann and Michael, whose angry voices were still rattling her head from the night before. But then she thought that maybe, just as Brad brought her peace and happiness, so did the house—after all, she'd been coveting it herself. But there was something different about her siblings' greed; it had more to do with each other. Their desire wasn't rooted in possession but in jealousy or betrayal, implying the other couldn't have it. What went on between those two? Poppy suspected that even *they* didn't really know.

She needed to meditate.

She lowered herself to sit cross-legged on the beach, detaching first from comfort, trying to ignore the cold dampness beneath her. She straightened her back, set her hands palm-up on her knees, and concentrated on her third eye. It had been a while since she'd done this, but her mantras were still accessible. She invoked an old meditation to clear energy and began to hum in *kirtan,* touching her index finger to her thumb: *sa-ta-na-ma-da-sa sa-say-so-hung.* She inhaled and waited for the ancient sounds to work their magic. Again, on an exhale, she touched her thumb and hummed: *sa-ta-na-ma-da-sa sa-say-so-hung.*

She heard Michael's and Ann's voices. She replayed the events of the night before in her mind, her complicated feelings for her sister. Admiration. Guilt. Love. Tension.

The idea of Ann making another appearance the next day, when she would return to pick up Noah, made Poppy's gut clench. She thought of how they'd all probably lose the house in the end. It could really happen; they'd all have to let go of their grip on the place. She tried to convince herself that was fine.

Don't attach!

She sang out loud: *Sa-ta-na-ma-da-sa sa-say-so-hung.* And again, louder, her voice skipping out over the water, rising in the breeze. Brad, the house, Brad, Michael, Ann, Brad.

Sa-ta-na-ma-da-sa sa-say-so-hung!

She was screaming now, and it felt great. Tears ran down her cheeks. She felt something cold against her neck and startled. When she turned, she saw the yellow Lab that had pressed its nose against her. The owner, an older woman in a knit cap and big sweater, wasn't far back. "Are you OK?" she asked.

"I'm meditating!"

ON HER WAY HOME, POPPY stopped at Carol's house near Indian Neck. Like her own house, Carol's had been in her family forever, and, because she shared it with several siblings, nobody had the money or the will to make any major changes to it. Their home, like her own, made Poppy feel like she was stepping back in time.

Carol rented the other bedrooms out to seasonal workers and divided up the proceeds with her siblings. It was a good arrangement, from what Poppy could tell, although now she worried how long it would last. On that morning, she saw it as a delicate balance, just one family rupture away from disaster.

The home was at the end of a sandy stretch of road, a true beach house with a more spectacular view of the water than the Gordons' home. Cape Cod Bay stretched out on almost all sides. The house was painted white with green trim, and featured a Victorian-style wraparound porch wide enough to accommodate several dilapidated couches. Whenever Poppy came to visit, someone or other always seemed to be on the couch taking in the view, reading a book, checking their phone. On that morning, it was Carol.

"Hey," Poppy said, making the *shaka* "hang loose" sign with her hand.

Carol returned the gesture and smiled weakly. "I was going to call you."

"Ann and Michael got into it last night."

"I know." Carol gestured at the cushion next to her. "Have a seat. I need to tell you something."

Poppy could tell from Carol's voice that whatever she had to say would be hard to hear. She was grateful she could at least look out at the water. The tide was high now, almost up to the stack of kayaks at the edge of the beach. A red rowboat bobbed up and down in the choppy water. Carol sucked on her vape. As she exhaled, she said, "Michael called me last night."

"And?"

"And Pops, he's forcing the sale. He's really going to go through with it. My friend in the clerk's office said he's already begun filing the paperwork to have Ann removed as executor. That's the first step."

"He can't. I mean, we talked, and I didn't think—but then again, what do I ever know? I mean, why would he do that without telling me?"

"I guess he's really got his sights set on that house." Carol passed the vape to Poppy, who grabbed it with greedy hands.

"Fuck." Poppy let the news sink in along with the THC, hoping it might loosen up the knot in her gut. Part of her wished she'd stayed in Panama. What would have happened if she'd never returned, not ever?

"He wants the house, and he's legally entitled to do this," Carol said. "But here's the thing. Before I pulled the listing, I was working with a developer. He wants to buy the property so he can create a service road. He's been circling your house like a vulture."

"A what? A service road?"

"Right through the property. Where the barn is. See, if he can put a road there, he can develop condos along the water because the lot is large and pie-shaped—"

"No!"

"He's got investors and deep pockets. Guys like him don't care about places like yours. I haven't even told him I gave up the listing to keep him at bay. If Michael forces the sale, he'll be outbid. Poppy, the house will be destroyed."

Poppy leaned back against the couch, the weight of the world on her chest. *Aparigraha* did nothing for her. "Did you tell Michael?"

"I'm telling *you.*" A seagull alighted on the armrest of a plastic armchair in the sand. For some reason, when Poppy looked at the bird, she thought of her mother. A message? "You know, you always complain about not ever being told anything, of being left out. But don't you see? As far as I can tell, you're the only person in your family who can fix this. You're the glue."

WHEN POPPY RETURNED TO THE HOUSE, her face was red and puffy from crying. The sight of the home at the end of the driveway, still intact, still theirs, brought on another jag of tears. She imagined the violence and noise of bulldozers tearing it down, the chimney tumbling one brick at a time. She saw a pile of shingles, shattered beams, broken glass, downed trees, the barn reduced to the slab of pavement it sat on. This would be no place for her parents' ghosts to return.

She ran into the house. "Brad!"

The kitchen was spotless and smelled of bacon and pancakes. The beds were made. Nobody was home. How could Brad and Noah go away at a time like this? She checked the birthing room, the sunporch, the attic. The house was empty. Vulnerable. She closed the blinds, threw herself in the bed she shared with Brad, and curled up into a fetal position. She remained like that for the rest of the day. When Brad and Noah returned from wherever they'd been and checked in on her, she told them she had a migraine. She could barely even talk. "Please," she said, "just leave me alone."

THE NEXT MORNING, STILL WORRIED and heartsick, she took a long shower and prepared for Ann's return to pick up Noah, trying to think of the best way to approach her. If only Ann had listed Michael as an heir, if only she'd been honest.

Poppy could tell by the curt texts Ann had sent that she was still smarting: *tell him to be ready by three* and *no surprises this time*. Poppy dressed, careful to choose an actual outfit with zippers and seams instead of her usual sweats. Once she was dressed, she realized the house was empty again. Hadn't Brad come to the Cape to see her? He and Noah were two peas in a pod. She couldn't stand it. She didn't want to be alone anymore.

She had slipped on her sandals and walked outside, calling Brad's name again and again, when Noah peeked out of the garage and darted across the lawn to meet her. "Aunt Poppy!" He was breathless. "You have to come!"

Noah's smile was such a wonderful, refreshing surprise; it almost cut through her feelings of dread and concern. Then her heart broke for him: he didn't want to lose the house any more than she did. He'd die when he heard about this developer, and about the mysterious "brother" who'd seemed so sweet. She still didn't know why Michael had lied about being Noah's father, and now he was forcing the sale without even telling her? She thought of how good it had felt to see him again, and now, just a few days later, she was upset that he was strong-arming the sale. She had to stop Michael. She had to!

"What's going on?"

"Seriously, you just have to see what Brad found."

"Tell me it's not a dead animal."

"It's the greatest thing ever. Come! Just come see!"

After a lifetime of summers on the Cape, Poppy wondered what new discovery could make Noah so ecstatic. He grabbed her hand, pulling her toward the barn. He was practically skipping. "Hurry!"

She walked through the sliding door into the musty dimness of her father's workroom. Noah was hunched over, his hands together in a perma-clap, a broad smile on his face. Brad was smiling, too. How could they smile? Didn't they know the barn would soon become a road?

"What's going on?"

Brad pointed at a sheaf of papers sitting on top of a manila envelope on the plywood countertop. "Just look," he said.

She picked up the papers. She gasped, not at the words "Last Will and Testament," but at her father's block-print handwriting spelling out his own name, Edward Gordon, just before the words "of sound and disposing mind and memory . . ."

"I told you to look in the freezer," Brad said. "That's where everyone keeps their wills. It's been here the whole time."

Poppy looked at the old refrigerator, the door swinging open. "That old thing hasn't worked in years. I totally forgot about it. I mean, it didn't even occur to me, but of course it was here."

Poppy tore through the pages, reading and rereading the fine print, barely able to focus, tears of relief running down her face. She'd sent her intentions to the universe just yesterday, and already the universe answered.

Noah said, "I can't wait to tell my mom when she gets here."

"Hey, can you do me a favor?" Poppy asked, remembering what Carol had said: *You're the only person in your family who can fix this.* "Can you let me tell her?"

Noah seemed to deflate, but just a little. "Why? Look what it says!"

"I know, I know. But just trust me, OK? I think we need to handle this carefully. Maybe this afternoon when she gets here you two can get lost. Go kayaking or something." Poppy shoved the papers into the envelope and tucked it into her coat. "I think it would be best if she heard about this from me."

THIRTY-FIVE

Ann

Ann walked through the door without knocking—why should she knock? Soon the home would be hers, all hers!

Poppy was in the living room, shoving wood into the big fireplace. She startled when she turned and saw Ann.

"Where's Noah?" Ann asked.

"Hello to you, too."

"Sorry. Hello. Do you know where my son is?"

"He took Brad kayaking."

"Fun!" Ann tried to seem bright. She forced herself to smile, but deep down, she was still seething with anger over what Poppy had done to her on Friday night. Kayaking on a cold spring day didn't sound fun at all to Ann, but it was just as well: she needed to talk to her sister about the house now that she had a plan. "How about we go to Wicked Oyster?" Ann said. "Get something to eat. Talk. Catch up."

"I'm sorry about what happened. It seemed like a good idea."

"It's OK." It wasn't OK, and it was hard to lie about it. Ann had tossed and turned the whole night, wondering what Poppy knew. Had Michael told her that he'd intended to sue them? Did she know he wanted to force the sale? Was she in on it? What else did Michael tell her? Whose side was Poppy on? What was Ann up against? Whatever it was, she felt certain she had the upper hand now.

"Let's just stay here," Poppy said. "The fire is finally going, and I've got leftovers. Brad's a great cook. There's still an open bottle of wine."

Ann looked around. The place really was inviting. Clean, even. The beds were made, and the sink was free of dirty dishes. More than that, the house felt like it had . . . what? Life. It smelled of food and showers and smoke from the fireplace.

"About Michael—" Poppy said.

"Let's not talk about that." Ann forced herself to smile. "I want to hear about *you*."

"What about me?" Poppy seemed suspicious—or at least leery. Sure, time had gone by. Not so much that Ann couldn't read her sister's skepticism. "What do you want to know?"

"Just, you know, normal catching-up stuff." Ann tried hard to sound bright, although she knew she probably sounded more like she was trying to give a bad performance review to an employee she liked. "So, where all have you lived? How've you been?"

"How've I been? Let's see: Good. Bad. Confused. What the fuck? I don't have a SparkNotes version of my life prepared for you. God, I don't even know how to talk to you anymore, Ann. You're so mad all the time, and I don't know why." Poppy pushed her hair away from her face and tied it into a ponytail, a practiced move. She looked especially lovely, and Ann wished she could say so. "I've been learning things, Ann. About you. About Michael. About Noah. About the house. I thought we could work things out if we all had a chance to sit down together. I wasn't trying to hurt you or piss you off. All I wanted to do was talk, and you shut me down. I'm your sister, not your enemy. All you care about anymore is . . . real estate."

Ann thought of something a friend had told her when she'd left for Milwaukee shortly after her parents had died. "Everyone grieves differently," she'd said. "The grief can come out in all different ways, like anger." Was that what was happening to Ann? Maybe Poppy was right: maybe she was hiding her grief behind the houses. And now, thanks to Maureen, Ann had a lovely solution for what, for so long, had seemed like an insurmountable problem.

But before she could say anything about her plan, before she could apologize and try to marshal Poppy's support, Poppy leaned close to her and said, "Michael isn't Noah's father. Is that true?"

Ann was so shocked she didn't respond.

"Is it?"

Ann shook her head. "Yes. That is the truth."

There it was, the same relief she'd felt when she'd told her father—if only her younger self had known how cathartic the truth was.

"If he's not the dad, why do you hate him so much?"

"I don't hate him," Ann said, and realized this was true. What an inconvenient revelation!

Poppy bent down for a second, letting herself hang in one of those Raggedy Ann yoga poses with her hands on her elbows, her ponytail scraping the wide floorboards. Ann had taken a few classes over the years but her hamstrings were so tight from running that she felt like she had steel rods in the backs of her legs. Without looking up, Poppy said, "Does Noah know that Michael isn't his dad?"

"Now he does. I told him after . . . well, I told him when I needed to."

"How come you never told me?" Poppy spoke in barely a whisper.

"What was I supposed to do, Poppy? Should I have sent you a text? An email? A vibe?"

"Ann, please. You've got to stop making fun of me. It hurts. It's always hurt."

Ann collapsed onto the couch and felt something against her back. She pulled out a needlepoint throw pillow that read, OLD TEACHERS NEVER DIE, THEY JUST LOSE THEIR CLASS. Poppy and Ann had chipped in to buy it as a birthday present for their mom back when they were in what—first and second grade? They'd bought it at the Christmas Tree Shops, the Cape's knickknacky version of a dollar store. "It's not the sort of thing that just comes up. 'Oh hey, the weather here has been cool and overcast and by the way, my kid's dad isn't who I said he was.' " Ann threw the pillow across the room in frustration.

Poppy sat next to her, in the spot where her mother always used to sit. She was careful to leave a safe distance between them. "Will you tell me who is?" Her chin quivered. "I know we haven't been close, but we've only got each other now. Tell me. Talk to me."

Ann took a deep breath and put her hand on Poppy's leg as if to attach a rope line to a buoy. "I had this . . . this *thing* with the father of the family I babysat for."

"Mr. Shaw?" Poppy cringed. "The golf shirt guy?"

Ann felt so embarrassed and ashamed—that look, that was what she'd wanted to avoid all these years, and especially when she was younger. Sure, he'd forced himself on her, and he'd threatened her. She blamed him, she did. But Ann was proud. Too proud. She couldn't stand to think she'd let her guard down, couldn't forgive herself for getting into that situation, even if, on the deepest level, she knew it wasn't her fault.

"It seemed exciting at the time. We flirted. I thought it was fun. Harmless. I was actually into it at first. Then he took me swimming one night. It was hot, and nobody else was there."

"Wait, where? Where did he take you?"

Ann swallowed hard. "Duck Pond."

Some of the best moments from their childhood had happened there. An old-fashioned slideshow of images flickered through her mind: the blueberries, handstands in the shallow end, tadpoles, her parents resting on beach blankets in a free spot on the narrow beach, the pine trees lining the path. "Things went too far. Not in a way I wanted them to."

"Oh, I know what you mean," Poppy said, and Ann wondered if maybe Poppy had stories of her own, stories Ann wasn't around to hear. "That fucker."

"He said I was asking for it," Ann said.

"Sure he did. That's what they all say."

"I said no, I did. I said no."

"I believe you, Annie. I need you to know that." Poppy could have been twelve years old at that moment, so loyal and true to Ann the way she'd once been, her eyes big and focused like laser beams.

"He didn't listen. I said no." Ann's whole body shook. Her hair swayed over her face. She felt like she was telling her story for the first time. "No, no, *no*! And then, wouldn't you know, that first time, I end up getting pregnant. Just my luck. I couldn't believe it."

Poppy put her arm around Ann's shoulders and drew her closer to her. "You don't need to convince me. He was wrong to do what he did. He should have known better."

Ann stood up, walked into the bathroom, and returned with a box of Kleenex. She offered Poppy a tissue and sat on the edge of the couch, wiping her eyes. "You know that house on Duck Pond, the only house on the far shore? The one we used to swim to? We'd make up stories about the people who lived there, and what we wanted them to be like?"

Poppy nodded.

"I used to think that house was so perfect and peaceful, almost like a dream. But when . . . when it was happening . . . I looked at it. I looked at it the whole time—you know, like when they tell you to stare at one spot in yoga?"

"A *drishti*."

"A *drishti*. And now I see that house in my head every time I close my eyes. I want to see it the way I used to see it. To see *everything* the way I used to." Ann started to cry again.

"It's OK."

"I wanted to tell you, I did. You were the first person I went to when I got home, but you were gone, so I went upstairs to talk to Michael. I couldn't say it—I couldn't even talk, the words just didn't come. I just wanted to be with him. He was my other best friend. I didn't want to be alone."

Poppy started to put it all together. "That's when Dad saw you guys and freaked out."

"And you came home, high out of your mind. You thought the books were dancing in the bookcase. You called Mom Britney Spears."

Poppy laughed, but grew serious. "I'm sorry I wasn't there for you."

"But you were getting into your own kind of trouble, and I guess I wasn't there for you, either. That was one hell of a summer."

"It sure was."

They lapsed into a warm silence. The fire snapped and flickered, and the rain fell against the windows. Ann looked up, her eyes red. "He's dead now. Anthony."

"Well, good riddance. I hope you killed him."

Ann winced.

"What?"

"I feel like I did. He killed himself while I was there. I think I pushed him over the edge. I saw him die, Poppy. It was horrible, worse than in the movies. The smell, the way his eyes stopped, you know, they stopped looking. I know he did a terrible thing. I'm not condoning it. But he was a person, and he had a family, you know? Everyone's so haunted by him, including me. I feel like it's my fault." Ann's voice broke. "Everything is always my fault. I handle things so badly."

"Oh, Ann," Poppy said. "I know it's been hard for you."

"I'm OK. I am. I feel like I'm getting better at least. One thing about dealing with all this stuff—it's made me stronger."

"And you know there are good guys out there, right?"

"You mean guys like Brad?" Ann said, smiling. "Swear to God, as soon as I saw you guys together I had this feeling that Dad sent him to you, like he's part of a master plan."

Poppy got the chills. She'd thought the same thing. "I guess we're a good fit." She expertly steered the conversation away from Brad. "Dad, he was the best. And look at how sweet Noah is." Poppy hesitated. ". . . And Michael? I don't know what to think about him. He's the part of this story that still doesn't make sense. I was so happy to see him, but I still can't figure out why he lied."

"Oh, Poppy. It was such a mess. He overheard me say I was pregnant. He contacted Anthony and told him he'd say the baby was his if Anthony paid him off—and paid me off, too. Michael set up an account, and for a while, I got some of the money Anthony gave him. And then the rest of it was just gone. He spent it. He benefited from my situation."

"He wouldn't."

"He sure would. I've got checks in Michael's name to prove it. All these years I've been putting myself through school, eating tuna out of a can for every meal, never going out, barely able to pay rent much less cover the cost of Noah's school supplies. That's why I freaked out when you pounced him on me the other night, and why I don't want him to have the house. Poppy," Ann said, "you can't let Michael have this house. Promise me."

Poppy drew back. "I can't do anything about that. Did you know he's already filed to remove you as executor? He wants to force the sale. And Ann, it's bad. Carol told me—"

"Oh, don't worry about that," Ann said. "Michael says he can buy me out, but I think he's bluffing." Ann sprang from the couch, bright, energized. "I know you don't want the house to leave the family, and even though I thought I wanted to sell, I just can't stand the thought of giving it up anymore, but I couldn't afford it on my own. But then Maureen, Anthony's wife, well, his widow I guess—anyway, we're close now. We were both there when he—" Ann made a gun with her index finger and thumb and pretended to put it in her mouth.

"Oh, Ann. I'm so sorry you saw that."

Now that the truth was coming out, Ann felt impatient to tell her sister everything. "But I was racking my brain trying to think of a way to keep this place, and when I told Maureen, she said her house here was totally destroyed this winter. She got some insurance money, and she wants to buy another one. She said she'd front me the money and we could go in on this place. Isn't it horrible, having to buy your own house? But do you see? Thanks to Maureen, we can buy Michael out. The house can be ours!"

It was perfect, so why did Poppy seem so hesitant?

"What?" Ann asked. "What's wrong?"

"Well, Brad is totally obsessed with Dad's old tools."

"He can have them! Oh my God, is that what you're worried about? He can have every last one of those rusty hunks of metal. I made sure Noah had a tetanus shot at his last appointment."

"No, listen . . ."

"Or he can sell them on eBay. I'll bet he could get some good money for the spokeshaves and bevels. Some we should actually keep though, like Dad's first hammer and . . ."

"No. Ann. Would you stop and just listen?"

Ann put her hands on her hips.

"Remember the refrigerator in the barn?"

"What about it? Oh God, Brad can have it, too. It hasn't worked since I can remember. Some people turn those old refrigerators into coolers, bookcases, couches. I'll bet Brad could . . ."

"Ann!"

What was going on? "What's your problem?"

"Freezers are where people hide their wills. You know, so they won't burn up in a fire." Poppy walked over to the desk and pulled out a legal-sized manila envelope. "This is what we found."

"A will? You found it?"

"Brad did. And Noah."

"I can't believe Noah didn't tell me sooner."

"It happened just this morning, before you got here. We know what Mom and Dad wanted now. Ann, we don't have to fight over the house anymore. Michael can't force the sale. The evil developer can't buy the property and build a road."

"What evil developer?"

"Carol told me about some guy who wanted to put a road through the property."

"No way. Are you kidding me? What does the will say? I've looked everywhere for this."

Ann greedily ripped the large envelope out of Poppy's hands and pulled the papers out. Her eyes wildly scanned the pages. "Wait a minute," Ann said. "The house is in a trust."

"Right. We can't even sell it or buy it from each other or whatever. It's set up to skip generations."

The logistics began to sink in. "*We* don't inherit it. The grandchildren do." Ann set the envelope on her lap and smiled, elated. "So, that means the house belongs to Noah now! Michael can't have it. Oh my God, that's the best news ever!" Ann started dancing around the room, so relieved she thought she might cry. She reached for Poppy's arms, trying to pull her up to join her in her celebration, but Poppy wouldn't budge. "What's your problem? Don't you see? I don't even need Maureen. Michael can't get his dirty hands on this place. How perfect!"

"Ann, there's something—"

"Does Noah understand what this means for him? He must have been out of his mind. I need to call him."

"Wait!" Poppy said. "Slow down. Please."

"What? What's wrong?"

Poppy took a deep breath. "Ann, Michael has a kid."

"He has a what?" She was sure she had misheard.

"Avery. She's eleven or twelve. She looks just like him. I saw her picture in his office the other day."

"That could be someone else's kid. Are you sure it's his?"

"I'm sure."

Ann rolled the envelope around the pages and walked over to the fireplace. "Let's forget we ever found this."

"We already made copies. Ann, this is what Mom and Dad wanted. Noah will have to share the house with Michael's daughter."

THIRTY-SIX

Michael

Michael's lawyer successfully fought Ann when she tried to contest the will. Finally, after months of legal wrangling, the judge issued a sharing agreement between Michael and Ann for the house on the Cape, if sharing was what you could call it. To Michael it felt more like two people "sharing" a rope in a tug-of-war. But he had to make the best of the situation, at least until Avery turned eighteen, and then who knew what would happen.

Every two weeks, occupancy changed hands between Michael and Ann. For someone who seemed so eager to sell, Ann rarely missed an opportunity to drive down from Boston to take advantage of her allotted time in the house, even in the heart of winter.

Things were just as strained between Michael and Ann as they were between himself and Poppy. Shortly after that awful night, Poppy showed up at his office again. It was a bad time. He was on the phone with Sharon Gold, who was upset about the bluestone patio he'd installed earlier that week, because one of the bigger pieces was already cracked. Sometimes that just happens, he explained, and he was happy to replace it. Jason stormed into his office and dropped a seed catalog on his desk.

"They raised their prices again." Jason left, Mrs. Gold kept screaming, and there was Poppy.

He smiled, happy to see her, anxious to debrief after that fight with Ann, but she didn't smile back. "I just have one question," she said. "Did you really . . . ?"

He raised his finger—just a minute.

It was finally warm out. She wore a tank and shorts that showed off her muscles. She still had the build of the sixteen-year-old he remembered.

"Hang on," he said to Mrs. Gold.

"Don't tell me to hang on!" Mrs. Gold was one of his biggest customers, and usually she was OK to deal with.

"Did you or did you not take money from Anthony Shaw?"

"I can explain," he said.

"Yes or no?" Poppy's voice was unexpectedly shrill.

Mrs. Gold said she wasn't sure she even liked the bluestone to begin with. "Are you sure it's real?" she said. "Not some stone made in China that's supposed to look like it's real?"

"It's real."

"Answer me," Poppy said. "It's a simple question."

Michael put his palm over the mouthpiece of his phone and said, "Yes, but—"

"You planned to force the sale of the house without telling me?"

"No, all I'd done was try to remove Ann as executor. I hadn't even—"

And then Poppy was gone. Really gone—later, he'd learn from Carol that Poppy took off for Portugal the next day. She was an ocean away. He couldn't stand to think of Poppy feeling badly about him. He wished he'd just hung up on stupid Mrs. Gold that afternoon. She'd ended up having the whole damn patio torn up and replaced with brick.

He never saw Ann, but she made sure he knew she'd been there. He found evidence of her stay every time he returned, which was at five o'clock on the dot every other Sunday, when the court-ordered change-over took place.

Michael made his presence known, too. He took it upon himself to sand, paint, and rehang the battered shutters against the windows. He pruned the trees, treated the pitch pines for bark beetles, cleared the brush, and cut down the leggy yews that had grown too close to the foundation.

Even in their silence, they'd somehow found a way to divide and conquer, with Michael and Ann addressing separate but balanced kinds of work. While he tended to the nuts and bolts of the house, Ann purged the junk drawers of crumbs, expired coupons, brittle rubber bands, and acid-burned batteries. The plastic Tupperware containers and rusted baking sheets were quietly decommissioned. New hand towels hung from the hooks in the bathroom.

Michael filled the cracks in the walls with Spackle, while Ann transformed the space with paint. He had to admit that he liked the bold colors Ann picked out, especially in contrast to the fresh coat of white he'd painted on the trim and windows. Avery thought the colors were fantastic. She gasped with delight when she saw the eggplant purple in the birthing room, and she was taken with the vibrant periwinkle in Connie and Ed's old room, where Michael now slept—he wasn't about to go back to the attic. This was where Ann slept, too.

Ann also rearranged the furniture and bought bright rugs and throw pillows to brighten up the space. The décor was tasteful, not showy, and complemented the rustic antiques, adding visual interest and warmth to every room. She'd somehow managed to skirt the line between classic and contemporary, lived-in and new, beach house and family home. The Gordons were never into decorating. He wondered how Ann had developed such a refined design aesthetic.

Like Michael, Ann was a neatnik. If he had to share a home in a less than ideal arrangement, it might as well be with someone who labeled her storage bins, returned things to their rightful places, and left every corner free of dust bunnies. Upon arrival, he found the dishwasher empty, the bed stripped, the counters gleaming.

Everywhere he looked he saw evidence of a human being who ate, slept, flossed her teeth, and clipped her toenails just like anyone else. It was strange after all these years to stand in the same spot where she showered, sink into the same comfortable chairs she sank into, to eat his cereal out of the same bowl she'd used. He could smell her shampoo in the pillows. He stumbled across her box of tampons in the medicine cabinet. The nightstand drawer next to the bed was filled with lip gloss and ponytail holders.

Once, he found one of her earrings on the floor, and left it for her in a small bowl on the kitchen table. It was gone the next time he stayed there. That was their first real act of communication.

The Post-its marked ANN's that Ann had affixed to half the cabinets and drawers were starting to fade and lose their adhesive. It was hard for Michael to avoid these forbidden spaces. Late at night, he couldn't help himself. He'd open her closet and see her sweaters, T-shirts, and running clothes stacked neatly on the back shelves. He opened a drawer in Ann's dresser and pulled out her bra. He ran his fingers over the soft satin cups and fingered the discreet lace on the straps. It was the kind of bra a woman wore not for herself, but for someone else. Who saw it on her? Did she have a boyfriend? Did she bring him here? Did they make love in the same bed he slept in?

He held the bra up to his nose and inhaled her still-familiar scent. He knew she hated him, and he resented her, so why was he smelling her damn bra? He stuffed it back in the drawer where he found it, feeling like a seventeen-year-old kid again. He told himself for the hundredth time that he ought to start dating again even if the inventory on the Cape was severely limited.

But Ann, still tempting and illicit, was everywhere he looked, like an invasive species. She took root in every drawer, cabinet, towel, pillow, and book. It made him mad, horny, frustrated. He couldn't stand it. It didn't help that Avery couldn't stop asking about the mystery woman, this strange poltergeist who changed things around when they were gone. *Is she pretty?* she asked. *How old is she? Is she nice? Why do you share the house with her? How come we don't ever see her? Who is she?*

How could he even begin to explain Ann to his daughter? If he started to answer one question, he knew it would provoke a landslide of more totally understandable questions, so he didn't say much at all. Ann was just some "lady" who shared the place, someone he'd known when he was younger. He said the house was a place they'd "invested" in. He brought Avery with him whenever he could because he wanted her to love the house, even though she had no idea that she had a stake in it.

Michael tried to pass the situation off to her like it was the most normal scenario in the world, the way it was normal for him to live with his ex-wife and her partner. This was just another odd arrangement that worked out for them, he said, and that was all there was to it.

THE SILENCE BETWEEN MICHAEL and Ann started to feel suffocating and intense. Connie and Ed's ashes sat atop the bedroom dresser, untouched, while the rest of the house was subject to almost relentless progress. There was something Michael found disturbing about the emerging aesthetic. It was starting to feel too perfect, like a rental that would appeal to anyone instead of the people who lived there.

He tried to get under Ann's skin. He put fresh flowers in the vase on the kitchen table shortly before the end of his stays there, because he figured a nice gesture would annoy her. But then she tricked him and did the same thing.

He began to fix Avery's school portraits and some of her drawings to the refrigerator with magnets. Avery was an amazing artist like her mother, mostly because she had inherited Shelby's incredible attention span and could focus on a single drawing for hours, and because so many artists stayed at their inn. They all seemed willing to nurture and develop his daughter's talents. She carried her drawing pad with her everywhere she went. Provincetown was an ideal place for a budding artist, with interesting landscapes like busy Commercial Street, the harbor, the dramatic bluffs at Herring Cove Beach, Race Point Lighthouse, and the iconic Days' Cottages, little houses that sat like beads on a necklace along the shore of Cape Cod Bay. Avery frequently raided the inn's lost and found for odd trinkets the tenants had left behind and arranged them in configurations for still-life paintings. She did the same thing at the Wellfleet house. Avery had an eerie knack for finding objects that carried psychic weight, like Connie's old wind chimes and chipped mugs she'd bought at one of the many pottery places in Wellfleet, or the ship in a bottle that Ed said his grandfather had given him.

It felt good to brag about Avery through her artwork this way, because Michael wanted Ann to know that his daughter was beautiful and bright, and that she wasn't the red-haired stepchild or pushy outsider Ann likely thought her to be.

It took a while, but Ann began to return in kind, and the refrigerator slowly became a metallic Switzerland. Michael saw that Ann had posted a photo of Noah eating an ice cream at Emack & Bolio's, and a clipping from the *Cape Cod Times* of Noah leading a kayak expedition as part of a youth group at sea camp. Michael couldn't get over how much the kid looked like Anthony, but still different. Anthony's hair had been straight, while Noah's had some wave to it. They were both stocky, but Anthony's build had been more solid. Noah wasn't chubby, not exactly, but he looked like he still had some baby fat he hadn't grown out of yet. Anthony was intimidating, while Noah seemed approachable. Noah looked like someone who wanted to make friends, while Anthony was on his guard. Michael wanted to meet this kid, and he was grateful Noah hadn't grown up with Anthony in his life, because he was the kind of kid Anthony wouldn't have wanted to deal with.

MICHAEL KNEW HE'D HAVE TO TALK to Ann eventually. So far, thanks to their lawyers, he hadn't had to say a single word to her. But that couldn't last. They weren't permitted to do any major remodeling or repairs unless they were in agreement. Fortunately, nothing major had come up so far, although the old oil furnace probably wouldn't make it through another winter, and Michael was starting to think about a kitchen remodel. He had a feeling Ann was, too. With that awful mushroom-print wallpaper, how could she not? The drawers swelled shut in the summer and hung loose in the winter. The Formica countertops curled up at the edges, revealing moldy particleboard underneath. The old faucets leaked, and the linoleum floors were pocked and chipped.

He could subcontract the job himself, but he knew Ann would have good ideas about the layout and a strong opinion about the details. It was a big project, one they'd need to sit down and discuss, and they'd need to agree on a budget.

He thought he'd show up early for his two weeks on the off-chance that Ann might still be there. It was a sultry mid-July day, over a year since their confrontation, and he was a nervous mess. Thank God he had Avery with him, at least for part of the ride. He was going to drop her off at her friend Jess's house in Truro. She kept him occupied with her chatter about school and her friends, and the odd facts she accumulated in the Velcro of her young brain. "Did you know a whale's heart only beats once a minute?"

"That can't be true." He thought of his own heart racing in his chest.

"It is. My science teacher told me."

"One beat a minute, huh? That's like ringing a big bell."

"Whales are cool."

"They sure are." Michael and Avery went to see the stranded pilot whales whenever they heard news of beachings in Wellfleet Harbor, a disorienting place for the animals. They swam in at high tide, and because of the distance between the shores and the shallow slope, they frequently got confused and couldn't find their way out.

"Almost all animal hearts will beat about a billion times," she said. "No matter how big or small."

"That so?"

Avery nodded. She watched the blur of pitch pine, white pine, and oak that lined Route 6. She wore a T-shirt from the Kidz Dash triathlon she'd competed in last year, and already it was getting small on her—uncomfortably small for Michael, who noted that she needed to start wearing a training bra. He wished Shelby or Deedee would bring it up with her, but they refused. They thought bras were a choice, and Avery should make the decision about wearing one when she was ready, but he didn't want the boys at school to notice anything about Avery but her brains. Whenever Michael thought of boys who might be interested in Avery, he thought of Anthony preying on Ann. Look how that had turned out.

"I wish I could go with you to the old house," Avery said. That was what she called it: "the old house."

He couldn't talk to Ann with Avery there. "I'm just going to spend the whole time working."

"On the house, or Anibitz?"

"Anibitz," he said. The company was big now, so big he'd finally sold his interest in the landscaping business to Jason, so big he was considering buyout offers from larger toy companies. Sandi called him with talk of offers. He didn't want to let go, but couldn't keep it going on his own. He worked night and day, doing everything he could to avoid trips to New York to meet with the sales reps and marketers. He'd have to travel to China to meet with the fabricator soon. He didn't want to go to China. He didn't even want to go to Boston.

"Jess is boring," Avery said.

"She's been your friend for a long time now. You should be loyal to friends."

"She only cares about boys. She's always taking pictures of herself with them so people will think she's hot."

"That's probably not a bad strategy. Guys are dumb."

"Not Noah."

Michael wanted to slam on the brakes. Noah? "Is that a kid at your school?"

"No, *Noah* Noah. The boy who shares the house with us."

"You know him?"

"We're friends, actually."

Friends? What was going on? "But you've never met him. How could you be friends? Isn't he older than you?"

"We leave notes for each other in the secret space next to the fireplace. We call it the portal. He started it. He was, like, hey, who are you? And I was, like, hey, I'm Avery, who are *you*? And then we started leaving entire notebooks for each other, and writing back and forth. You know him, right?"

"Not really. I've seen his photo on the fridge, same as you. He's not telling you things he shouldn't, or asking the wrong kinds of questions?"

Avery rolled her eyes. "You're so gross. Nothing like that. You and Deeds watch too much *Law & Order: SVU*."

"I'm your dad. It's OK for me to ask questions."

"Don't worry. He's not like that."

Michael *was* worried, but not in the way Avery thought. "What else does he tell you?"

"Nothing really. He's a junior. He's into *Game of Thrones*. He likes to do old-people stuff like collect rocks and do crossword puzzles. We make puzzles for each other. He's writing a book about us, actually."

"You haven't even met and he's writing a book about you?"

"A graphic novel. I'm helping. It's about these two kids who find out they live in the same old house, like us, but then they discover that they are actually trapped in two different times. His character is from the fifties. Mine is from the Civil War. My parents free the slaves that come in through the cove. Noah said they snuck in on banana boats. He knows everything about the house and all this stuff that happened there. It's his family house."

This got under Michael's skin. "It's your family house, too."

"Not like his. Noah says his great-great-great-great-great-great-grandparents used to live there."

"That many 'great's, huh?" Avery would have loved Connie and Ed, her own grandparents. How sad it was that they weren't around to meet her.

"Well, we're there now, so the house is *your* family house, got it?"

"Whatever. Noah was supposed to leave a new chapter for me but now I have to go to Jess's dumb sleepover, and she'll make me smell Jasper McNally's T-shirt that he left on the bench after gym."

"That's gross."

"Jasper McNally smells like a sunfish. I left an anibitz for Noah in the portal."

"You did?" Now Michael felt like Avery had shared one of his own secrets. "What'd you pick?"

"A bee for staying busy on our project, and an owl, because Noah is wise."

"Sounds like 'bowel.'"

"And a lion for strength. A 'beeowlion.'"

"That sounds like a winner."

"I think he'll love it."

THE TOURISTS HAD INVADED THE CAPE. His dread over the encounter with Ann was exacerbated by his annual displeasure, a vacation frenzy as unavoidable as a high tide: two long months of Volvos with kayaks strapped to the roofs and bikes of all sizes hanging off the racks, long lines of cyclists in Lycra stretching outside the French bakery, jammed-up parking lots at the beaches, and impossible throngs of tourists clogging the streets and roads. Couldn't *The New York Times* stop writing stories extolling the virtues of this place? Couldn't they help him keep it a secret?

When he turned onto the dirt drive, he felt nervous again, the way he used to feel when he snuck into the Gordons' place. After all the years as an intruder it seemed incredibly strange to him that he had a legitimate stake in the home. He wasn't trespassing—well, not exactly. He was trespassing now, arriving an hour earlier than he was supposed to.

The water in the cove gleamed in the sun: high tide. The driveway was empty. If Ann had been there, she was gone now. He wasn't sure if he should feel relief, because her absence just pushed off the inevitable. He parked and unloaded the bleach he'd bought to clean off the cellar walls and set the jugs next to the outside doors. He returned to his truck and pulled out his familiar overnight bag and a sack of groceries. Shelby and Deeds were coming for dinner later that night. They loved the house the way he did, and laughed at Ann's Post-its marking her space: ANN'S, ANN'S, ANN'S. Deedee made Post-its that said BEYONCÉ'S!, TOM BRADY'S!, MELANIA'S!, and attached them to Michael's drawers. They made Ann seem ridiculous, and she was, so why did Michael feel like he needed to defend her?

He walked quietly toward the bedroom with his bag, stopping in the living room to watch a gentle wind ruffle the old yellow lace curtains that reminded him of Connie. Thank goodness Ann still hadn't replaced the curtains. He stood in a patch of golden light from the low afternoon sun and watched the dust motes swirl around in the sacred air. He inhaled. That smell, that smell.

He shook off his moment of self-indulgence and walked to the bedroom. Even before he got to the door he could feel another presence, the way you can smell rain before it falls. Quietly, he pushed the door open and saw Ann curled up on the bed. Her hair was longer now, the way it was when they were kids, and it fanned out on the quilt. The curtains fluttered in this room, too, the only movement aside from the gentle rise and fall of her chest. She slept with her head resting over one raised arm. She was sweating, and the hair close to her face and along her neck was dark from moisture. Her cheeks were flushed. She wore a pair of shorts and a tank, more casual than the clothes he pictured her wearing. Her skin glowed. She might have been seventeen.

Michael was caught off guard. Here she was, Ann, and she wasn't intimidating or full of bluster—she was human, vulnerable, beautiful in this light, a natural fixture in this house she was part of.

Michael began to close the door but the squeak of the old rusty hinges woke her. "Noah?"

What should he do? He had half a mind to run out of the house, get in his car, and leave, but he'd brought in too much stuff to make a quick, quiet exit.

Her eyes fluttered open. She looked at him. "Oh."

Oh. Why hadn't she attacked him? Instead she said *oh*, like she already knew the answer to a question.

She sat up, wiped the drool from her cheek with the back of her hand. "What are you doing here? Is it after five?"

Michael looked at his watch. "Close. I got here a little early. I wanted to, I thought—I had some questions about the house. I'm sorry, I didn't think you were home. No car."

Her hair was matted on one side. "Noah took it to Lieutenant Island. I'll bet the tide covered the bridge and he got stuck. I just wanted to close my eyes for a few minutes. I dozed off."

"Sorry I woke you."

Ann looked around the room like she was just beginning to realize where she was. "I had a dream about my parents. I only dream about them when I'm here. It's so strange, like they come to visit me." She looked at her hands and paused. "I dreamt my mom sat right here on the edge of the bed and looked out the window. She didn't say anything. She was just here, present. It was beautiful. Nice. Then I asked her if I could hug her. She said, 'Sure, you can try. Let's see what happens.' I reached for her, and she was gone."

Michael said, "I dream about them when I'm here, too. I can't really remember my dreams, just that they were in them. When I wake up I feel like they tapped me on the shoulder or something." Michael cleared his throat. "We're talking. Weird."

Ann grinned; she knew something. It made him uncomfortable. "When I opened my eyes and I saw you standing there in the doorway, I don't know. You looked just like the Michael I used to know. The old Michael."

"I *am* the old Michael." He smiled.

"You don't look much older."

"Neither do you." Michael cleared his throat.

"Thanks." She sat up and adjusted her long legs so that she could sit cross-legged on the bed. The anibitz that Avery had left for Noah sat next to her: lion, owl, bee. Until that moment, his project hadn't felt real. But there it was, in Ann's hand, as if he'd made it not for Avery and all the kids in the world, but for Ann. He knew at that moment that he wasn't ready to sell the company. "Anibitz, huh?"

"You remember."

"Remember? I was the one who made that game up, Michael. Now it's yours, I guess."

Michael worried that Ann was about to go after him for stealing her idea. "It started out as a toy, something fun, and then people started telling me I should make more. I thought—"

"Relax. I didn't get a trademark. You did. The toys are great. They are. I'm impressed. I wish I'd thought of it myself. I've always wanted to start my own business."

"Did you know they write notes to each other?" Michael said. "Avery and Noah?"

"Yes," she said. "I saw Noah's notebooks. His drawings. They're pretty good. And Avery's got quite an imagination."

"She told me they leave stuff for each other in the secret compartment by the fireplace."

"Yes, I heard."

What was it about Ann? Now that he could finally look at her again he found himself stumbling over every little detail: the freckle in the iris of her eye, the tuft of hair in her eyebrow that bent a different way from the rest. It was as if he'd been born preprogrammed to find her exact form of beauty his singular ideal. Her image was burned into his brain like acid on metal. He'd loved other women, but it was always Ann he measured everyone against, and here she was, in the flesh.

Ann's phone rang. "Hang on." She started talking in her mom voice. Noah. She said something about the tide, the bridge, the island, about getting back soon. Her eyes were on Michael the whole time she spoke. She hung up and looked at him. "He's stuck until the tide goes down. Is it OK if I'm here beyond my time?"

"Well, I got here early for mine, so we're even."

"Great," she said. She stood up and threw a daffodil-yellow cardigan over her shoulders. "Because we should talk."

"I was thinking the same thing." Michael scratched his head. "I don't even know what's going on. Why are you being nice to me?"

Ann smiled and pointed at the periwinkle wall. "Do you like the paint colors?"

"Yeah. I do, actually."

"I thought they might be too bold. Maureen picked them."

"Maureen? Maureen Shaw?"

"Mo. We're friends now. She's practically a godmother to Noah."

Michael looked at Ann in disbelief. "Shut up. You two are friends? After everything? That's like, I don't know. Super adult."

"We grew close after Anthony's suicide."

Michael winced. "That's good, I guess. Not about Anthony, but—"

"I know what you mean." Ann smoothed the wrinkles out of the sheet with the flat of her hand. "Did you know the Shaws' house out here was torn down? The pipes burst last winter and the place filled with black mold."

Michael coughed. "I think I heard something about that."

"You did, huh?" He still knew her well enough to recognize that she was teasing him. Had she really figured out that it was Michael who'd cut the heat? "Maureen sure was grateful for the insurance money."

"That's good. I always thought she was a nice lady."

Ann said, "She never liked that house anyway."

"Speaking of heat," Michael said, anxious to change the subject. "About the boiler . . ."

"What's wrong with the boiler?"

"It burns oil instead of gas. The thing is a beast. Wastes energy. I think we should replace it now, before all the pipes burst if it stops working. I had someone look at it last year. He said the gasket is rusted—"

"That's fine. Call him. Let's have it replaced."

Fine? What was going on? He thought this would be difficult. Everything that had to do with Ann was difficult. Now she was doing a one-eighty on him.

"But," Ann said—he knew there would be a "but." "You should get a second opinion."

"Not a lot of people to give second opinions around here."

"True." Ann stood up and walked over to the window that looked out to the cove. The afternoon light lit up her hair so it looked like a golden halo. "Noah knows better than to get caught on Lieutenant Island at high tide. I swear he stalls so we can spend more time here. He never wants to leave."

"Same with Avery. She loves this house as much as I do."

Michael smiled, almost drunk with surprise. He felt like he'd slipped through a net and found himself in a parallel universe that seemed just like the one he knew, only Ann didn't hate him, or at least she didn't act like it. "Look," he said. "While I've got you in a good mood, I may as well give this a shot: I was thinking we should fix up the kitchen."

"The kitchen is OK the way it is."

Michael rolled his eyes. "Oh, come on." He walked out of the room and gestured for Ann to follow him, and she did, her bare feet almost silent, padding across the wood floors. He walked into the kitchen and tried to pull out a drawer. "Stuck," he said.

"It'll come loose in winter."

"It's tighter than a clamshell." He jiggled it again before it finally flew loose, rattling the cooking utensils. "We could get drawers on glides." He pointed at the ground. "And look at this linoleum. It's all beat-up. There's asbestos under it. I don't want Avery breathing that in, or you and Noah."

Ann crossed her arms across her chest. "We breathed it in our whole lives. We're fine." This he could handle; he'd come prepared to disagree.

"The stove," Michael said. "Come on, Ann. You've got to agree it needs to go."

Ann looked at the avocado-green stove with the tilted electric coil burners and started to laugh, a sound that was as beautiful and unexpected as hearing a call from a rare bird. "I'm messing with you. The stove is a complete piece of shit," she said. "It took Noah two hours to cook a frozen pizza."

"Want me to pick one out?"

"It's fine. I'll do it."

"Look, I think we should do the whole kitchen."

"I think so, too."

"I know it's expensive. I can pay for it if money is the problem."

Ann drew in a breath, and with it, the relaxed atmosphere in the room. "Because you've got money." There it was, that edge he'd expected.

"I've got some." He stuffed his hands in his pocket and waited for Ann to lay into him. "The business. The Anibitz thing? It's starting to do well."

"We need to talk about your money, Michael," she said, although the iciness he'd thought he'd heard in her voice was gone. "Can I show you something?" She walked past him into the living room and pulled a manila envelope out of the desk. "Let's sit on the porch. The light is better."

What was this all about? Michael followed her out to the three-season porch that looked out into the woods. The room was the last to be fully updated. The white paint on the clapboard wall was chipped, and the rusty screens pulled away from the edges of their frames. Ann had replaced the old couch with a small loveseat that Michael had to admit was a lot nicer, with upholstered cushions that were, well, cushiony. Ann gestured for him to sit right next to her. He must have looked like he didn't believe her. "Sit," she said, patting the cushion harder.

He sank down, careful to keep some distance between them.

She set the envelope on her lap.

"What is it?"

Ann tilted the envelope so that Michael could see what was written on it: *Please give this to your mom.*

"That's not Avery's handwriting," he said. Then he looked again.

Shelby? His stomach knotted up. That was her writing. What was she up to?

Ann smiled and opened the envelope, pulling out a pile of papers held together with a binder clip. "There's a little note." She pulled off a sticky note that said FAILED NUN—he'd given those notes to Deeds as a stocking stuffer last year—and held it close so he could read it. *Michael is a good man!*

"I had nothing to do with this. I didn't put Shelby up to whatever this is, I swear."

"It's OK, really. She's great. We met for coffee this morning. She's shared lots of helpful information." She tossed the papers so that they landed on Michael's lap. The one on top was a statement. He immediately recognized the bank logo. "The account," he said. He felt like he'd swallowed a stone.

She ran her finger down a column. "Here's where it started, with fifty grand, the same amount Anthony told me you'd extracted from him."

"I didn't extract—"

"And here are the monthly payments to me—here, here, here, here. Anthony said you'd set this up. He said it was your idea. But it was his, wasn't it?" Ann pointed at Anthony's name on one of the pieces of paper. "Anthony was on the account, too. It was all set up to look like the money was coming from just you."

When Michael had discovered that a chunk of the money was missing, he'd asked the bank to send photocopies of the statements. There they were, straight out of his file, including the withdrawal slip with Anthony's signature, signed so hard the pen almost broke through. It was painful for Michael to see Anthony's handwriting. The thought of Anthony still bothered Michael in that primitive, raw way, only now it was harder for Michael to summon the anger and revulsion he'd once felt. He'd pulled up the news stories after Jason told him he'd died—news Jason had received when he called Maureen to tell her about the house. He saw the photo of police tape on the porch steps, another of Maureen with her hand over her face, trying to avoid reporters. He hated to see her so upset.

"Anthony took that money, not you." Ann turned her head to get a good look at him.

Michael stared at his feet. He still wore his battered Red Wing boots even though he wasn't landscaping anymore. He liked the way they made him feel like he was really working. He let out a deep breath. Here was something he'd wondered again and again: How could one man sneak into their lives the way Anthony had, and mess everything up? He'd been a crowbar of a man, wedging open every seam he could pry loose.

"Thirsty?" Ann asked.

"Yeah," Michael said. "I guess I am."

When she left the room Michael wondered if she'd ever really even been there in the first place, or was it just a dream? She returned holding two glasses of lemonade, poured into the old Welch's jelly jars decorated with *Muppets from Space* characters. One with Kermit in an astronaut suit holding his helmet like John Glenn, the other with Gonzo just before blastoff.

"Lemonade, spiked with vodka. I think we both need it." She took a long drink and reached for the papers, which had fallen to the floor. "So, here's what I thought was fishy." Her bangs fell forward, and she gently tucked them behind her small ear the same way she'd tucked her hair behind her ears when she was young. When a thick strand slipped out, it was all Michael could do to resist fixing it for her. "The account was drained to almost nothing. But then look, suddenly there's a deposit, and a check issued to me for seventy-eight bucks. Such a random amount. Two months later? A hundred and twelve. And here, nineteen dollars. November was a good month: six hundred and eleven." She looked up at him, waiting for Michael to say something.

He didn't. He couldn't.

"You made those deposits. That was your money."

Michael looked out beyond Ann, out into the yard, the cluster of oak trees, the barn that needed to be painted. He felt like he was getting busted. Why was he so embarrassed? "I did what I could. Just a little here and there."

"That's not the point," Ann said. "You helped. You used your own money to help me, and it came at a time when I really needed it." Ann's voice broke.

"Yeah," he said; then he lowered his voice so he almost couldn't be heard. "I've always cared about you, Ann." It was as close as he'd ever come to telling Ann he loved her. He could tell that Ann was moved by what he said. If things had been different between them, if they had an easier rapport, he swore she might have hugged him. Instead, she kept her distance. What was that definition of hell that Connie had taught him from Dante? Something like proximity without intimacy, the kind of hell he'd known with Ann when he'd lived with her as a teenager. Later, he would suffer the opposite: intimacy without proximity, feeling so close to Ann and the whole family, even though they were far away.

Ann said, "You convinced Anthony to give you money in exchange for saying Noah was yours, so why?" He felt like he could melt under the heat of Ann's intense gaze. "Why, all those years later, did you care?"

"Wait, what? You think *I* convinced Anthony? He blackmailed *me*, Ann, not the other way around. He said if I didn't take the money and sign the forms to open the account, he wouldn't support you."

"He said that?" Ann set her glass down so hard that the lemonade spilled over the top. "Anthony bribed *you*? Not the other way around?"

"He said you'd get nothing if I didn't lie and get lost. And he'd try to take your kid away from you. He said the account was *your* idea."

"Stop!" She walked closer to where Michael stood, her eyes wild. "You thought *I* came up with that?"

"Yeah," he said. "You're Ann with a Plan, after all."

Ann hit him on the arm. "You idiot!"

He jumped, not because she'd hit him hard—it was more of a playful tap—but because he was unprepared for physical contact with her. It was disconcerting after so much time apart. She was flesh and blood. He could even smell her.

"He told me you two were in love." There it was: the real reason he'd let Anthony get to him; the real reason he'd believed all those lies. Michael could see it so clearly now, so clearly it made him feel ashamed. He'd been jealous.

"Love?" Ann looked like she was about to throw up. "No. No, no, no. There was no love. Why would you believe him?"

Why had Michael believed him? Because Ann was right: he was an idiot. "That guy was the absolute worst," Michael said. "Nobody's ever made me feel like such a worthless piece of shit, and believe me, a lot of people have tried."

"You know he'd say anything to get what he wanted," Ann said. "Do anything."

"And we let him, that's the worst part. We just let that dude plow us down, drive right over us. We should have figured this out. Should have assumed the best about each other, not the worst."

Michael stood up and walked over to the edge of the room, so frustrated that he wasn't sure how to handle the rage building up inside him. Before he knew it, his fist went straight through the screen. Ann gasped.

"I'll fix that," Michael said, worried that he'd scared her. "A busted screen is no big deal, really. I can fix it in ten minutes."

"I know you can," she said.

They stared at the fist-shaped hole in the screen for a long while, long enough for a fly to find its way through. "You know what?" Ann said. "I'm done being mad at him. He's dead. I need to move on. Poppy tells me I need to practice *ho'oponopono*—something like that, some kind of healing practice that she says will clear a path for the divine. She learned it in Hawaii. I have no idea what it means."

"Sounds like Poppy."

Ann excused herself and walked out of the room. Michael figured she wouldn't come back. He'd blown it. He waited to hear the door slam. Instead, her soft footsteps padded across the living room. Then he heard a door open and close.

When she returned, she held another envelope in her hand, this one smaller. She handed it to him. "I found something else for you."

"What is it?"

He answered his own question: a letter addressed to Anthony, from Ed.

"You'll see. I think you should read it later, when you're alone. Maureen found it when she was going through Anthony's things."

The letter burned in his hands, competing with his view of Ann leaning against the doorframe, one leg bent, her toes curled like a dancer's. The sun was beginning to set. The light entering the home was low and rose-colored. Red sky at night, sailor's delight. A gull squealed out in the cove. On the other side of the house the traffic rumbled, a low, steady din. "I need to tell you something else. About what really happened between me and Anthony. It wasn't consensual."

Michael winced. He waited a long time for Ann to say more. Maybe she'd tell him the whole story someday, but she was quiet now. "I'm so sorry. I should have figured it out. That was a really shitty thing he did, and a lot for you to go through." He stood up and reached for her hands. Her fingers were long and delicate, her palms warm. She didn't pull away.

"I couldn't tell anyone. I don't know why. Instead, I pulled away. I let Anthony lie to me about you. I lashed out at all the people closest to me. I swear I chased Poppy off to the other side of the world. And look at you. You ended up all the way here."

"I wouldn't want to be anywhere else. I wouldn't have ever known about this place if it weren't for you. Now I never want to leave."

Michael looked through the doorway into the house. He could see the wide fireplace, the transom windows above the skinny doors, the iron hardware, the wide planks in the old wood floors.

Ann said, "Don't you think it's time you return the fourth ace?"

Michael smiled, embarrassed. He reached for his wallet and pulled out the old playing card with the hole in the middle. Ann snapped it from his fingers with a playful smile. She squeezed Michael's hands and leaned closer to him, resting her forehead on his sternum. He would have been happy if they could have stood like that for the rest of time. On the wall behind Ann, Michael noticed, the red arrow on Ed's tide clock was pointing toward the words HALF TIDE FALLING. Noah would be back soon, and they'd leave for Boston. Who knew what would happen next? He'd worry about that later, just like, later, he'd worry about the content of that letter Ann gave him.

He could smell the sulfuric smell of the peat in the cove, a scent that mingled with the sweet aroma of Ann's shampoo and the musky smell of the old house.

It wasn't the house he wanted; it was Ann. It had always been Ann.

August 12, 2015

De—

I thought of beginning this letter Dear Mr. Shaw, but hell, you aren't dear to me. And Mr. Shaw is the name my daughter called you because you were in a position of authority and she was your employee. A position you exploited. I have names for you, bub. I sure do, but that's not why I'm writing.

I wish I could forget what Ann told me a few weeks ago. It was you, huh? I knew in my gut it wasn't Michael, but you? You weren't even a fly on my radar.

You probably think I'm writing to chew you out for what you did, and believe me, there are things I'd like to do to you, but after all these years I guess what you did is between you and your creator. I got a damn fine grandchild out of the deal, and you? You've got nothing, and I'm sorry for you. I won't waste my energy on hate or pity. I'm old now. I feel older than I am. And I'm watching my wife forget everything that has ever happened to her.

I don't understand how exactly you puppet-mastered the deal. I'm trying to put together the pieces. Ann says Michael was paid off. That he blackmailed you. I know that's bullshit. You were behind everything.

They were just kids. The damage you did. Man, there was damage.

Still with me? I'll get to my point. I'm writing because I want to find Michael. He's my son. He has always been my son. I don't know where he is. All my leads are dead ends. Perhaps you know where he's gone off to. Tell me. How can I find him? Please help. Earn back some goodwill. I want to see Michael, but don't do it for me, do it for my wife. She's missed him so. I want Connie to look into Michael's eyes and recognize who he is before she can't anymore.

Please, will you help?

Sincerely, and I am sincere,

Ed Gordon

THIRTY-SEVEN

Poppy

2017

Poppy loved the town of Nazaré in Portugal. It was fun to watch the surfers of Praia do Norte, the beach where the largest wave ever had been surfed. And it was still cheap. She could eat a huge piece of turbot and some vegetables for under ten euros.

The reason she'd chosen Nazaré was because it was on the westernmost point in Europe, almost directly across the Atlantic Ocean from Cape Cod. It was her way of staying connected to Wellfleet without actually being there, providing her with the global traveler's illusion of proximity.

She savored her time here in a way she hadn't savored the other places she'd been. She loved watching the fishing women in their colorful skirts sit by the beach sewing their nets while the seagulls picked at the junk the beachgoers had left behind. She wished she could talk to the women, and learn from them. But, hard as she'd tried, she couldn't learn Portuguese, a language that sounded especially foreign to her ear. When they spoke, it sounded like someone had filled a blender with words and turned it on.

Poppy didn't need to know the language when she taught yoga, a practice she'd begun to enjoy again. She'd nod, give hand signals, and make gentle adjustments. Her tourist yogis were mostly tall, sunburned Germans who smiled a lot at her growing belly.

The house in Milwaukee belonged to Brad now, and the money she'd made on the sale had ironically set her free, whatever "free" meant. Brad said he wouldn't follow Poppy around the world by putting push-pins in a map the way her father had. He didn't need to follow her. Soon she'd go back. She wanted to deliver their baby in the same hospital where she and Ann and Noah had been born, and return the baby to the same wonderful home and city she'd grown up in. Brad couldn't wait. He'd sent her photos of the crib he'd put together and the mobile he'd made in the welding shop out of odd pieces of metal. It was beautiful. *He* was beautiful. Not long ago, she realized he was the man who'd clutched her arms in that vision she'd had during that long-ago ayahuasca ceremony, telling her she was a healer. Funny that that image had sent her searching all over the world for a man in Milwaukee; funny they'd healed each other.

Maybe this would be her last long trip abroad. Maybe she'd stay in Wisconsin, and they'd spend their summers on the Cape in the house her child would someday become part owner of. Brad had plans to renovate the barn so they'd have their own space.

So many maybes.

The only certainty was the kick she felt against her ribs, the pressure on her bladder, the heartburn that kept her up at night.

She stepped into the ocean and imagined her parents' ashes swirling in the surf. Not wanting to miss out on another family event, Poppy had returned home to the Cape for a week to attend what Noah jokingly called a "DIY funeral." They'd walked down to Drummer Cove at high tide and stood in a semicircle. Brad played "I'll Fly Away" on Ed's mandolin. Noah read lines of poetry in Connie's poetry-reading voice. It was funny at first, until he stumbled on some lines by Edna St. Vincent Millay: " 'Gently they go, the beautiful, the tender, the kind; / Quietly they go, the intelligent, the witty, the brave. / I know.'" He hesitated. "'But I do not approve. I am not resigned.'"

Poppy admired Noah's comfort with himself. He reminded her of her father, weeping openly while everyone else tried to hold it together. Avery, soulful and wise, had become Noah's sidekick. She held his large hand in her small one. And Michael was sensitive to Noah the way a father might have been.

Poppy said, "They've always been and still are part of this universe. They're on a new journey now, a progression of their souls, taking the growth from this life into the next one."

Ann had tried hard not to laugh out loud—so hard that she snorted. Her relationship with Poppy was still tender, though—tender enough that Poppy saw a brief look of concern cross her sister's face. How far was too far? What was appropriate anymore? Where were their borders? "Do you really believe that, Pops?"

"Sure. I mean, I like the idea of living forever, and of reincarnation," Poppy said. "What's the point of learning all this stuff and then just, you know, having it all end?"

Brad leaned against her. "I can feel them here with us. I see them in all of your faces. They're here, they are." The wind picked up as he said this, a warm breeze that felt like an embrace.

Michael wiped his eye with the back of his sleeve. "I feel them too. I've missed them for such a long time. Now I'll miss them forever."

When it came time to toss the ashes in the ocean, they realized nobody had thought to bring anything to put the ashes in, so Noah found the empty shell of a horseshoe crab and they took turns sprinkling them into the cove, one by one, careful not to allow the ashes to blow back in their faces.

"I wish we could always be like this," Avery said. "I wish we could, like, sew our arms together."

"I *think* that's sweet?" Ann said. "Or creepy?"

They made their way up the bluff. Just as they got to the top, Ann stopped and set her hands on her hips. There the house stood as familiar to them as their own bodies in the mirror: the old red-brick chimney, the weathered shingles, the narrow, multipaned windows. "Isn't it funny?" Ann said. "I used to blame this house for blowing up our family. I thought everything would have been different if we could have just stayed in one place. But now . . . I don't know. Without it, what would have happened to all of us?"

That very night, Poppy hid a small, wooden fertility doll between the mattress and the box spring of the twin bed she'd slept in her whole life, pulled up the covers, and invited Brad to squeeze in with her. She knew the doll worked, a secret that made her smile while she packed to take off the next day. Brad begged her to stay, but she knew she had to leave (and return) on her own terms.

Nobody in her family had ever been good at leaving.

At night, the Portuguese women spilled olive oil into the water and said prayers for the fishermen to come back to them alive and well. Poppy watched them at the shore in the moonlight, thinking of how much had changed in the past year. Michael, Ann, Avery, and Noah now lived in the old house on the other shore. It was hard to believe that Michael was part of the family again, and Ann was now working with him on his toy business. Noah and Avery, she'd said, were practically siblings, while Ann and Michael were far more than that. At the funeral, Poppy had spied, peeking out from under the collar on the back of Ann's shirt, a tattoo of the British farthing her father had found under the support beam of the house when they were kids. The original builder of the house must have placed it there for good luck. Poppy almost said something to Ann— "You got inked? Really?" Ann was the last person she'd imagine with a tattoo. But she didn't say a word, because she'd spied the same tattoo on the back of Michael's bicep.

Her family had been stressed and reconfigured, but it still held, just like the house across the ocean. It was still theirs, still in the family, still vulnerable to the elements, still requiring upkeep. It was an anchor, yes, but one that held her in place.

Acknowledgments

They say you should write what you know, and I couldn't write about the importance of family without knowing the deep and sustaining love of family myself.

Thanks to my late grandparents, Warren and Lee Seyfert, for introducing us to South Wellfleet and my original "second home;" and to my amazing mom, Pat Geiger, for making sure we stayed connected to it and for knitting so many beautiful sweaters for me over the years, especially one to match the novel's cover.

To the best sisters and friends ever, Sheila Cardenas and Karen Geiger-Niedfeldt, with whom I'll never have to argue over the fate of a second home. Big, proud love to my amazing kids, Olivia and Tim (don't worry Tim, Olivia says you can have the cottage). To my aunt Mel and uncle Bo Van Peenan for being early readers and cheerleaders, and for keeping our special Wellfleet house in the family. Love also to my aunt Val Piper and my cousins Wendy (Cutie) Van Peenan, Kristen (Scuz) Wild, Laura Van Peenan, and especially Bob Piper, who read the book many times and answered all my landscaping and year-round Cape Cod questions. Thanks also to all my nieces and nephews and to the extended Clancy family, who have embraced me as their own even though I'm short. And a tremendously heartfelt thanks to my husband, John Clancy. I couldn't ask for a more loving, thoughtful, and patient friend and partner.

I wish to shower my steadfast agent Marcy Posner with eternal sunshine and warmth. Thank you for believing in this book, and for connecting me to Sarah Cantin at St. Martin's Press. I knew from our first phone call, when we talked about the Gordon family as if they were our mutual friends, that Sarah was the perfect editor for this novel, and that the Gordons were in good hands. She even wears an original Dennis bracelet! I'm so grateful for Sarah's enthusiasm and smarts, and for the assistance of Rachel Diebel and Sallie Lotz.

The publishing pros at St. Martin's Press have welcomed me into the family, and I'm grateful to Jennifer Enderlin, Sally Richardson, Andrew Martin, Lisa Senz, publicist extraordinaires Katie Bassel and Dori Weintraub, and marketing dream team Erica Martirano, Brant Janeway, and Alexis Neuville. For their creative talents, I'm thankful to Kim Ludlam, Tom Thompson, and Olga Grlic, who gave me my dream cover. I loved talking to the audio experts, Mary Beth Roche, Robert Allen, and Dakota Cohen.

Thanks to Don Laventhall, Hannah Brattesani, and Melissa White at Folio Literary Management for help with film and foreign rights. Thanks also to Christina Jokanovich at TriStar.

Independent booksellers have been so supportive early in this journey, including Kayleen Rohrer at InkLink Books in East Troy, Daniel Golden at Boswell Books in Milwaukee, Joanne Berg at Mystery to Me in Madison, Pamela Klinger-Horn at Excelsior Bay Books in Excelsior, and Mary Webber O'Malley at Skylark Bookshop in Columbia. Jason Gobble and Stacie Michelle Williams have been so generous with their time and advice. I am awed by the care and effort booksellers put into finding the right books for the right readers.

For help with my research, thanks to Lynn Southey, for keeping me connected to her lovely, memory-filled Wellfleet home; Kate Paddon, for her Cape Cod real estate knowledge; and Jen Hannon at Godfrey & Kahn, for trust and estate help at far below her hourly rate. Thanks also to Molly Snyder, Monica Rausch, Marilyn Duarte, Sigrid Ohnesorge, Airin Aquarius, and Katy Weeks from Sugar Surf; Bonnie McIlvene from the Wicked Oyster; and Julie Prochnow and Margie Freeman for the yoga assists.

Special gratitude to the best writing group in the universe: Lauren Fox, Liam Callanan, Aims McGinnis, Anuradha Deshmukh, and Jon Olson. My writing friends and partners have been so generous with their time and expertise: Sarah Eisner, Janelle Lindsay, Judy Bridges, Phong Nguyen, Chris Fink, Jean Thompson, and Christine Sneed. Thanks also to the Ragdale Foundation, for offering me the time and space to write; LitCamp, for connecting me to an amazing writing community; and UW-Milwaukee's English department for nurturing my craft.

Love to my early readers, who absolutely helped make this a better novel: Lisa Blue, Betty Porter, Joan Kappas, Karen Jarrard, Stephanie Lyons, Sheila Cardenas, Bob Piper, Olivia Clancy, Diana Goldberg, Tim Kiefer, Francine Inbinder, Joan Wickersham, and Kristen Park.

I'm humble and teary-eyed with gratitude for the many constellations of kind people who have offered me support over the years and wish I could name all my former students and colleagues at Beloit College, my book group, the spinners who have endured my spin classes, my wonderful friends in Milwaukee and Madison, and my East Troy "chickpeas": Linda Dodge, Dave Dodge, Sue Enright, and Barb Jones.

Finally, thank you to all the people I've yet to come into contact with, including marketing and promotion experts, booksellers and librarians, and of course you, the reader. I'm so genuinely happy that this novel has found its way to you.

Reading
Group
Gold

THE
SECOND HOME
by Christina Clancy

About the Author
• A Conversation with the Author

Behind the Novel

Keep On Reading
• Recommended Reading
• Reading Group Questions

Also available as an audiobook
from Macmillan Audio

For more reading group suggestions
visit www.readinggroupgold.com.

*A
Reading
Group Gold
Selection*

ST. MARTIN'S GRIFFIN

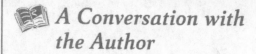

A Conversation with the Author

You cover a lot of ground in this novel—both the secrets we hide from and the joys we share with our siblings, the way place leaves an impression on us, and what it's like to lose our parents in time. Did something in particular inspire this very expansive and emotional story?

My grandparents retired to a home in South Wellfleet that had been in my mom's side of the family since the 1890s. Because my mother had no aunts, uncles, or cousins, they were the pillars of a very small clan, and all the grandkids (including me) loved to visit them each summer. It was a real shock when they died less than a week apart from each other. In the wake of this sudden loss, I remember my mother saying that she and her sisters, who lived in distant cities, were the next generation, and it was up to them to *decide* to remain a family. I was fascinated by that sentiment because, until then, I'd always thought that family was just . . . family. Over the years, I've seen how the house they'd lived in, which my aunt now owns, has facilitated our feelings of connection. I wanted to write about how vulnerable a family is to change, and how purposeful we need to be about maintaining familial bonds when it's healthy to do so. I also wanted to explore the nature of family itself— the families we are given and the families we choose, or are chosen by.

What scenes were the most painful—or pleasurable—for you to write?

As you would probably guess, the scene between Ann and Anthony was incredibly difficult and delicate to write. I really like Ann as a character and wanted to protect her, but I could also see how naive she was, despite her confidence. She was tantalized by Anthony's power and bravado, and didn't see the real danger in their flirtation. I'd actually stopped working on the book for a while because I'd overheard someone say that they never read novels that deal with rape as a plot device, but then the #MeToo movement happened, and I couldn't go a day without discovering that a politician or celebrity had assaulted or raped someone. For many women, rape is their story, and it affects the people who love them. I'm so grateful for all the women who came forward with their stories; they emboldened me to write that hard scene and the scene where Ann finally confronts Anthony about what he'd done. I admire Ann's can-do attitude; she was dealt a hard hand, but she still manages to go to undergrad and graduate school, and she raises an awesome kid.

The most pleasurable scenes to write were the ones that brought characters together, like when Poppy and Brad meet, when Ann and Maureen become friends, and the scenes where reconciliations occur between the siblings. I especially loved writing the scenes where Avery and Noah find a way to communicate by passing notes to each other in their "portal."

You cover several decades in the novel. Why was it important for you to have us meet Ann and her siblings in their teen years, and then again in their thirties?

They say that early drafts of a novel are for the author, not the reader (yet), and I definitely had to tell the story to myself first. Initially, Poppy, Ann, and Michael were adults, and time moved only forward. I'd challenged myself not to write backstory, but the more I wrote, the more I felt I needed to understand what had happened to cause the family to fall apart and to understand their attachment to the house and the horrible feelings of loss they experienced when their parents died. I gave myself a writing exercise to explore the characters in their teen years, and they absolutely insisted their way into the novel. I decided to try splicing the chapters so that the reader would be jolted backward and forward. That started to feel schizophrenic, so I reorganized the book into two parts with a prologue, and it felt, at last, like that was the right order of telling for the reader.

Why Wellfleet and Milwaukee? What spoke to you about those locales that have such diverse characters and landscapes? Were you drawn to either in a very personal way?

A friend from Milwaukee recently confessed that she thought Cape Cod was "out of her league." I could totally identify with that sentiment. Although our family had a long history in Wellfleet, as a Midwesterner, I always felt like an outsider on the Cape and on the East Coast. I thought everyone I encountered there came from old money and ate their food with monogrammed silver.

When I'd say I was from Wisconsin, they'd
either look confused or mention *Laverne &
Shirley*, cheese curds, bowling, or beer. Their
reactions reminded me of that old *New Yorker*
cartoon with the view of the world from Ninth
Avenue, with a map that shows the middle of
the country as an inconvenient strip of land
between New York and the Pacific Ocean. But I
absolutely love Milwaukee! It is such an authentic
place, and home to wonderful, smart people,
gorgeous architecture, Lake Michigan, and ethnic
neighborhoods with rich histories. I suppose this
novel is an opportunity for me to take readers
there and to show how the characters internalize
the ways in which other people regard, or
disregard, place.

**What was your "second home"? Is there a summer
escape or family vacation setting that has rich
memories attached for you?**

My "second home" was Wellfeet growing up, but
now I have a second home of my own: a rustic
three-season cottage on Lake Beulah in East Troy,
Wisconsin. My husband's family is from that
area—I joke that he's East Troy royalty because
his grandfather and great-grandfather served as
mayors, and his family owned the hardware store
on the town square that is now the home of a
wonderful bookstore, InkLink Books. I'm as happy
on the lake as I am near the ocean. Our kids are
divided: my daughter says she's more interested in
Cape Cod, and my son loves to water ski, and he
was a camp counselor at YMCA Camp Edwards
on the lake, so he's more the lake guy. I guess this
means there will be no fighting over our own
second home! East Troy is the setting for my next
book, *Shoulder Season*.

What do you hope readers take away from this book? What issues or scenes do you imagine book clubs will spend ample time discussing?

When I tell people about the book, they seem to really connect with the idea of the second home. It seems there are lots of "third spaces" for families, whether they are grand estates, cottages, or even a campsite in the woods. I hope readers will connect with and discuss the power of special places where our memories and even our identities are formed, and the ways in which they can become contested. I'd love for readers to think about what family means to them. Even if they have unhappy family lives, they might find that they can find and form new, reconfigured families with people who are important to them, just as the characters have. I would imagine that readers will be disturbed by the scene between Ann and Anthony and can have nuanced discussions about the shame and damaging implications of sexual assault. I think they'll also discuss how and why Ann and Michael were manipulated by Anthony. Finally, I hope the novel compels readers to think about and discuss the feeling of being at home with themselves, wherever they are—whether that's in a home, a second home, or on an airplane traveling to their next adventure.

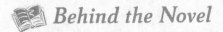

Behind the Novel

After I published *The Second Home,* a reader asked me a great question: "Is it really that specific Cape Cod house that matters, or could it be any house?"

I knew what she was getting at: a house is a powerful metaphor. Yet I was taken aback. I responded, probably a bit too forcefully, that yes, it is that very house that matters, the one with birthing rooms, captain's stairs, and wide-plank floors, the one that smells like dust and old wood. I could picture the Gordons' house in Wellfleet down to the lace curtains fluttering in the breeze and the cracked bar of Dial soap on the ledge of the bathroom sink. I knew this because the Gordons' house was inspired by the first home I ever fell in love with.

My grandparents had retired to Wellfleet, and we visited them every summer. This was not your traditional beach vacation. My sisters and I had chores and volunteered. On Sundays my grandmother made a formal midday supper with roast lamb, and my grandfather, a retired secondary school headmaster, would send us away from the table if we didn't hold our silverware properly. My sisters and I were told that this was our mother's vacation, not ours. I'm sure this is why so many characters in the book question and challenge the idea of vacation: what's the right way to vacation? When is vacation actually relaxing? What are you supposed to do on vacation?

In an effort to make ourselves scarce, we ended up next door at Mrs. Andl's house. She was a widow from Connecticut who wasn't strict at all. We spent hours playing the battered games we found in her cabinet next to the massive fireplace: Tiddlywinks, Yahtzee, Parcheesi, and Pollyanna. Mrs. Andl loved to tell us about the distinctive architectural features of her pre—Revolutionary War home and regale us with stories of Clarence, the ghost of the prior owner who'd made money running rum up Drummer Cove during Prohibition (as a child, my grandmother stood on Route 6 with a lantern on the lookout for cops). Clarence died very suddenly after he fell and became impaled on a fence while painting the house.

After his death, his daughters searched everywhere for the cash he'd made running rum. There were loose floorboards and holes punched into the stair risers and walls. They had good reason to believe the house was studded with hidden treasure, because Clarence and his friends had stolen the Wellfleet town cannon as a prank. He swore that whoever revealed its whereabouts would be cursed, but after seventy years, his daughter snitched and led a crew of preservationists to the yucca tree near my grandparents' garage. The cannon is now on display in front of the Wellfleet Town Hall (Ann points it out to Anthony as they make their way to Duck Pond on that fateful night).

Because the Andl house has lingered in my
memories so warmly—and vividly—I'd always
wanted to write about it, yet it seemed like a
radical act to set a book in an actual house. Why?
I'm not sure. Perhaps because I felt as a fiction
writer that it was a failure of my imagination not
to make everything up. I was in the throes of an
early draft of the novel when I heard Joyce Carol
Oates read a short story called "Pumpkin Head,"
featuring a woman who invites a strange man into
her living room. During the Q&A, an audience
member asked about the vividly rendered setting,
from the books in the bookcase to the painting
on the wall. "I could write with such specificity
because that's my own living room," Oates said. I
got the chills. That's when the Andl house became
the Gordons'.

My characters are often inspired by people I know,
but the more time I spend with them, the more
real they become. Sometimes I even forget who
the person was who inspired the character. I was
about to say that the same thing happened with
the house, but in fact the opposite is true. Setting
the book there allowed me to burrow in, luxuriate,
and become so familiar with my memories of that
special structure that it became more than a house;
for me, it also feels like a home. When I visited
after years away, I was overwhelmed with emotion.
I could feel Clarence, but I was also aware of the
wispy presences of Ed, Connie, Ann, Michael,
and Poppy.

Ann Patchett said that she included less than a dozen physical descriptions of the home in the novel *The Dutch House,* yet readers always tell her that they can envision the house perfectly (as I could). Even though I've shared far more than a dozen details of the Gordons' second home, I wonder if it looks the way readers imagine it. Here are some old photos of the Andl house the way I remember it.

Photo 1: Exterior of House
Doesn't the house look peaceful? I love everything about it, from the hammock to the worn shingles. You see the door that leads to the bean pot cellar.

Photo 2: The Barn

The old barn had to be torn down and rebuilt.
I remember all the strange, rusty tools that were
kept there, including one for de-horning goats.
As a Wisconsinite, it's hard for me to imagine
that this was once a working farm. I miss the old
lobster traps on the roof.

Photo 3: The Keeping Room

This is the "keeping room" with the transom
windows for spying and birthing rooms off to
each side of the massive fireplace. To the left of
the fireplace is where Noah and Avery would
have hidden their letters to each other. The game
cabinet was to the right.

Photo 4: The Bedroom

I imagined this room with the twin beds as the room Ann and Poppy shared. The windows had wavy old glass. When I was a kid, you could look through them and see the cove, but now trees block the view. I always suspected that Clarence had perished just beyond those windows.

Photo 5: The Attic

It might have seemed mean to relegate Michael to the attic, but for me, that was the most enchanted space, perhaps because it was the most forbidden. We were only allowed upstairs a few times, and it felt like a secret fort. Mrs. Andl was convinced that she'd hear Clarence up there, pacing the floors.

Photo 6: The Captain's Stairs
If you're a New Englander, these stairs may look familiar to you, but for the rest of us, stairs this narrow seem strange and precarious.

Photo 7: Drummer Cove
This is the view from my grandparents' house. It's high tide in this photo, but usually the cove looks like a mud flat. My grandmother said that when she was a kid, it was a freshwater pond. She can remember swimming in it. I shudder to think about swimming in it now.

📖 Recommended Reading

When I taught creative writing, one of my favorite exercises was to have my students write about something that couldn't exist anywhere but the place where they were from. One of my students wrote about a guy who sat in a tree in the park and dropped knives from the branches. Years after he'd disappeared, the tree was still referred to as "the knife-dropping tree." This leads me to think about stories, like *The Second Home*, that grow out of the places where they are set.

Karen Dukess, *The Last Book Party*

This coming-of-age novel also takes place on the outer Cape, but in the town of Truro, right next to Wellfleet. Dukess writes about a young woman's encounter with the literary set when she takes a job as an assistant to a writer for the *New Yorker* (spoiler alert: she assists him in lots of ways). I've become friends with Karen, and we marvel at how much our books have in common, especially the way the characters are aware of status in these venerated communities. Insiders have long histories on the Cape, and they're special not because they are rich, but because they are smart.

Marilynne Robinson, *Housekeeping*

Fingerbone, Idaho. That's the town where sisters Ruth and Lucille, left in the care of their eccentric aunt Sylvie, explore what it means to accept or resist what conventional life has to offer. The house at the center of the novel isn't "kept." As it falls into neglect, it complicates Ruth and Lucille's understanding of what a house really is or should be, and the relative benefits and drawbacks of rootedness and transience.

Willa Cather, *A Lost Lady*

I'm originally from Denver, so I'm a sucker for stories set in the West. Here, Cather charts the end of pioneer days with her story of a young man's obsession with Mrs. Forrester, whose much older husband is a town patriarch. The novel begins with a description of Sweet Water as "one of those grey towns along the Burlington railroad, which are so much greyer today than they were then," yet a few paragraphs later it's described as "a town of which great things were expected." That's enough to keep me reading. What changed? Why didn't the town live up to its potential?

Louise Erdrich, *Love Medicine*

Erdrich made me feel as though I'd inhabited the fictional Ojibwe community in the upper Midwest that she so vividly depicts. Her character June Kashpaw is a down-on-her-luck prostitute who decides to walk all the way home to the reservation she'd left years earlier. She dies along the way, and, through the voices of people who knew her, we learn about who she was, and the people and the place she left behind.

Jamaica Kincaid, *A Small Place*

I once taught a literature class with the theme of "elsewhere," and found that Kincaid's nonfiction novel about the island of Antigua really challenged my students' ideas about what it means to get away, and also what it means to be "here."

Colonialism, she argues, upended every aspect of culture and rendered native Antiguans orphans with "no motherland, no fatherland, no gods, no mounds of earth for holy ground, no excess of love which might lead to the things that an excess of love sometimes brings, and worst and most painful of all, no tongue." Other "elsewhere" readings included Shakespeare's *The Tempest, Being There* by Jerzy Kosinski, and *A Complicated Kindness* by Miriam Toews. Rebecca Solnit's *The Faraway Nearby* was our core text.

Rebecca Makkai, *The Great Believers*

I was so engrossed in this novel that I literally threw it across the room when one of the characters experienced misfortune. I love how Makkai shines a light on the AIDS crisis in Chicago, specifically the Boystown area, near where I used to live. Until I read this novel, I associated AIDS narratives with the East Coast. I can't walk down Clark Street without summoning the ghosts of her characters and feeling the tragedy of all that was lost.

Jeffrey Eugenides, *The Virgin Suicides*

Eugenides takes direct aim at suburbia in this novel about the deflated promise of post-war America, and how it plays out in towns where people—specifically the Greek chorus of men who narrate the novel—are so watchful that the only way the Lisbon girls can escape is through suicide. My concentration for my PhD was in suburban literature, so you can imagine how much I love this smart, quirky, and innovative novel.

Reading Group Questions

1. "Cape Cod felt like a hazy dream the rest of the year, a place suspended forever in beach days filled with sunshine and warmth" (p. 1). Do you have a place from your younger years that inhabits your memory in this way? How does the youthful memory compare to the reality?

2. Upon returning to their home in Wellfleet, Ann "felt her parents' radiant energy in everything she saw as she paced the house to stay warm: in the chipped wineglass left in the sink, the sloppily folded beach towels and stained pillowcases, in her mother's cookbooks, her father's telescope, even in the bulb digger where they'd always hidden the heavy iron key that unlocked the back door" (pp. 1–2). Imagine walking into a house—what would "tell" of your own parents; what would signal that they were the most recent inhabitants? When you are gone, what objects might reflect your presence?

3. "It smelled like rotten eggs at low tide, but that was a smell she loved in the same primal way that she'd loved the smell of Noah's sweet bald head when he was a baby...every molecule in her body seemed to change" (p. 3). What senses are activated by a special place or person? What powers can smell have?

4. How do each of the Gordon children explore and deal with the loss of their parents? Did you consider any of their reactions healthy or unique?

5. Michael's background is very different from that of Ann and Poppy. What intense experiences has he already had before joining the Gordon family? What misconceptions did outsiders hold about what Michael might bring into their lives?

6. "She loved Michael, so why did she feel so selfish? She wanted to tell Michael that the house was *theirs,* and summer was *her* time with her father" (p. 45). Can you track Poppy's emotions in this adolescent outburst? What is she wrestling with here? How do Ann's complicated feelings toward Michael manifest over the course of the novel?

7. What role does family—the ones we're born into and the ones we create—serve? What are some assumptions we might make about families like the Shaws?

8. "He signed quickly...before he could change his mind. And just like that, he became nobody" (p. 138). What does this mean, for Michael to become a "nobody"? Did you feel empathy for Michael's choice? Which adults could have handled the situation differently?

9. "Just look at us. One of your kids is missing, the other is a burnout, and I'm a teenage mom. Great job, you guys!" (p. 153). What did you make of the Gordon family? Are their secrets and struggles commonplace?

10. The Shaw family is, on its surface, quite different from the Gordons. Do they share any similarities? Did you feel sympathy for Maureen? What about for the Shaw boys?

11. Discuss the role and impact of secrets in this novel. Are they inherently destructive, or are some secrets worth keeping? Why do Ann and Michael hold on to their secrets, and why is Connie's illness not openly shared with Poppy?

12. How is Anthony able to manipulate both Ann and Michael? What kind of power does he hold over each of them?

13. "She felt like a part of her drowned in that pond" (p. 110). As a reader, what was it like to read Ann's rape scene and the unraveling that followed? Why does Ann blame herself for what happened that night, and everything that came after?

14. "Poppy was the victim of collateral damage" (p. 267). Discuss Poppy's trajectory from unsupervised teen with risky behaviors to globe-traveling yoga teacher and commitmentphobe to mother. What makes Poppy resist responsibility and returning home? What changes for her?

15. In what ways do children and grandchildren change the dynamics of a family?

16. How does Ann's confrontation of Anthony affect her? Discuss the emotion and drama of this scene, and the impact on you as a reader. Did this meeting play out as you expected?

17. Explore what Wellfleet means to each of the main characters in the novel—what did it represent for Connie and Ed, for Michael and, ultimately, for the sisters? Why are they drawn to it? What are they nostalgic for?

18. "We should have figured this out. Should
    have assumed the best about each other, not
    the worst" (p. 330). Why is Ann so late to
    forgive or welcome Michael back into her
    life? In what specific ways did they each feel
    betrayed?

19. "Is that what houses really were, containers
    for families? And once the containers were
    gone, the people inside were just set loose
    in the world, particles" (p. 239). A theme
    throughout the novel is that houses hold our
    histories. How does this play out on the page,
    and has it proven true in your life?

20. "It was still theirs, still in the family, still
    vulnerable to the elements, still requiring
    upkeep. It was an anchor, yes, but one that
    held her in place" (p. 337). How is a house an
    "anchor," and what does that mean for these
    characters moving forward?

Turn the page for a sneak peek at
Christina Clancy's new novel

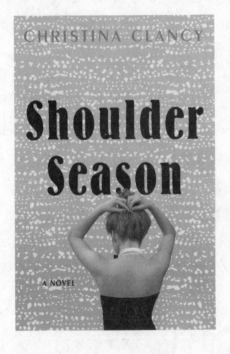

Available Summer 2021

CHAPTER ONE

East Troy, 1981

Roberta was late.

Sherri waited for her friend outside of the family store on the town square, shivering, her stomach in knots, her ears tuned for the sound of approaching cars. Under her parka she wore her favorite Junior House outfit, which she'd purchased on clearance at Waal's Department Store in Walworth, a burgundy velour skirt with a pink tie and a matching pink blouse. She'd loved it when she first bought it, but that morning she worried that her clothing made her look like a priss, and the heavy fabric felt stained from sadness because she'd worn it to her mother's funeral the week before.

In her bag she carried a pair of narrow shoes with smart heels that she wore when she played the organ, and a red string bikini that wasn't exactly stolen, but borrowed. She'd slipped it out of her friend Jeanne's sister's drawer and into the front pocket of her jeans when nobody was looking, as inconspicuous as a wad of Kleenex. Claire was bustier than Sherri, and the fabric was stretched thin across the chest and rear, but where else could Sherri find a string bikini in January in the middle of Wisconsin?

She hated wearing a hood, but she pulled hers over her head

because she was freezing, and she'd spent hours trying to tame her crazy, curly hair, deciding finally to pull it back into a ponytail the size of a small hedge. She checked her makeup for the hundredth time in her reflection in the store window. If Roberta didn't arrive soon, the light mist of sleet would make her foundation and mascara run, and ruin the cerulean eyeshadow that she'd swabbed all the way to her eyebrows; she'd read in *Tiger Beat* magazine that light blue was the best color for hazel eyes like hers. Her lips were smeared with CoverGirl's Shimmering Shell, an opalescent nude shade she thought was more sophisticated than coral or pink. She hoped the sparkles would make her look iridescent, like she'd emerged from a gauzy dream instead of a small town that was notable for its rich soil. It felt strange—wrong, even—to wear so much makeup in East Troy on a cold, gray Tuesday morning.

She could have waited inside, but the apartment she'd shared with her mother had grown claustrophobic. Sherri felt so drained from taking care of Muriel while also holding herself together that she had nothing more to give. She looked beyond her reflection into the abandoned wreckage of her late father's watch repair shop below the family's apartment and felt another pang of sorrow. Losing her mother was a body blow, and the loss of her father three years earlier still managed to shock her system with grief, like a cracked tooth exposed to cold.

Her father, Lane, had been a confirmed bachelor until he met Muriel. He was much older than her friends' fathers, and he was also quieter and slower. Unlike the sturdy German and Eastern European farmers in the area, he was small and balding, with bushy white eyebrows and an Adam's apple that pointed out of his neck like an elbow. He'd been better suited for intricate machines and the steady beat of time than the erratic natures of people. Sherri used to love working by his side while the chorus of clocks hanging on pegboard walls dinged and chimed behind them. He didn't talk much, but he did love to read poems out loud to Sherri, especially the ones that made him sad, as if sadness were a form of pleasure for him. Rilke was his favorite:

"Everything is far and long gone by," he would say at the end of the day, and "harry the last few drops of sweetness through the wine." By the time Sherri was twelve, she could dismantle, clean, and reassemble the whole movement on a watch and recite the first section of *The Sonnets to Orpheus* from memory.

The shop had been silent since his death. Between the slits in the shades, she could see the empty cash register yawning open, and boxes of yellowed paperwork and his remaining inventory of crowns, gaskets, rotors, hands, and wristbands gathering dust. The Chamber of Commerce was always after her mother to wash the porous cream city bricks and rent out the neglected storefront space, fearing it made the town of East Troy appear less prosperous—what a joke. They finally hung a FOR LEASE sign in the window and hadn't had a single bite in over a year.

Sherri's mother had suggested she open a "this and that" store in the space, selling stationery, pinecone wreaths, painted pots, and other useless stuff she referred to brightly as "bric-a-brac." "People will come from all over," she'd said, but Sherri had no desire to hawk useless junk, because she had other plans—plans that hinged on Roberta's arrival.

She turned to face the square. There had been several fierce blizzards that winter, and the snow was piled so high around the perimeter that she could only see the American flag hanging like a frozen sheet on the pole beyond the squat, red brick bandstand in the center. Part of her wished she were a kid again so that she could climb the snow bluffs and sled down the small berms on her mother's vinyl placemats. She'd loved playing in the square until she'd overheard Roberta's mom say that hooligans with nothing better to do hung out there. Sherri hadn't wanted to be thought of as a bad kid, and she wasn't, not with her mom to take care of. Unlike Roberta, she'd never had the luxury to misbehave. It was *Roberta* who ended up smoking cigarettes and drinking cheap wine at the picnic tables, Roberta who lost her virginity in the bandstand, Roberta whom their classmates thought of (respectfully) as a "bad kid."

The businesses around the square were slowly limping to life. Giles was serving breakfast, and the air smelled of sausage and their famous cinnamon rolls. The desk lamp in the window of Haskell's Insurance glowed green, and on the other side of the square, probably in front of the tavern, she could hear someone shoveling snow and ice from the sidewalk.

Marshall's department store on the corner wouldn't open until nine o'clock, the same time her interview was supposed to start, which was in, what . . . twenty-five minutes? Sherri checked the time again on her art deco antique watch. Like the bathing suit, it wasn't exactly stolen. An old lady from Whitewater had brought it in for repair and never picked it up. After a year or so, her father had told Sherri she could keep it. Sherri didn't generally like old things, but she loved that watch. It had a delicate gold chain for a band and an elongated, angular bezel that suddenly reminded her of the shape of her mother's coffin. It was 8:38, and it took twenty minutes to get to Lake Geneva. Sherri began to hope that Roberta had overslept so that she could avoid this fool's errand, but just then Roberta veered off Highway 15 at breakneck speed and pulled up in her rusted-out Chevy Chevelle. She came to a loud stop and reached across to unlock the passenger door.

"Think we'll get there in time?" Sherri asked before getting in.

"We're fine." Roberta threw her cigarette out the window. "Let's go. It's just down the road a piece. Traffic in Milwaukee was the shits. Should have only taken half an hour to get here."

With her red blush, thick eyeliner, and blue mascara, Roberta looked like she was ready for a night on the town. They'd been best friends their whole lives, a friendship that felt predestined and sisterly because their mothers had delivered the girls on the same day. When they were younger, Roberta had buck teeth so severe that she needed to wear headgear to school, while Sherri had massive curls like Slinkies for hair, and a loud laugh.

The girls had been lost in their own private world. They'd wear their clothes inside out and their shoes on the wrong feet, and they'd walk backward down the hallways, their ponytails on their foreheads. When the kids looked at them funny, which they always did, Sherri and Roberta would say, "Didn't you hear? It's backwards day!," and squeal with laughter. They were boy-crazy. In winter, they'd spend long afternoons in Roberta's bedroom composing love notes that they'd never send to their latest romantic interests. In summer, they'd have picnics in the square, eating peanut butter and jelly sandwiches and drinking milk out of Roberta's dad's empty whiskey bottle because they thought it made them look cool. They'd lie on their backs and stare at the sky, planning their weddings at Linden Terrace and picking names for their children. One summer, Sherri and Roberta both had a crush on Trent Eagan, the lifeguard, and they'd go to the deep end of the public swimming area at Booth Lake and practice the dead man's float, holding their breath almost as long as the Japanese pearl divers they'd read about in Social Studies, trying to trick him into thinking they needed to be saved.

In middle school, Roberta's brown hair was always greasy, parted down the center in permanent wilt, and her face bloomed with acne. "You have a great face for radio," Jan Stone once told her, leaving Roberta in tears. But then, in high school, Roberta's skin cleared up. She cut her hair and feathered it like Pat Benatar's. And when her braces were removed, she emerged a regular butterfly with a perfect, toothy smile. She got a job in the kitchen at Camp Edwards and started dating Ian, a British guy who worked there. Everyone in East Troy listened to rock and roll because Alpine Valley, the outdoor music amphitheater, had opened when Sherri and Roberta were sophomores, and it transformed the town from a sleepy farming community into a place that was actually cool. Alpine was just down the road, drawing all the big acts to the area in the summer, from James Taylor to the Doobie Brothers. When the Grateful Dead played, the fans took over the whole town. They'd hang out in the square with their tie-dyed shirts and long braids, and use people's hoses to shower in their yards. Most kids sold tickets to shows or worked as ushers, and come fall they'd return to school bragging about the famous musicians they'd met, showing off their autographed tickets and albums. Roberta had been the biggest rock-and-roll freak Sherri knew, especially for the Allman Brothers, but all that changed when Ian introduced her to British music that people in East Troy had never heard of, like Siouxsie and the Banshees and the Sex Pistols. She'd gone from being a first-class dork to one of the smokers that all the other girls were afraid to even walk past. She took up menthol cigarettes, sported a black leather bomber jacket that must have weighed as much as she did, and wrapped a Union Jack bandana around her wrist.

Roberta's ascent to tough-girl popularity was hard for Sherri, who felt left behind. Sherri had always been pretty enough, but she was too socially awkward to get much attention for her looks, and her free time for the last three years had been spent taking care of her mother. Even though they both understood that Roberta couldn't be seen with her anymore, Roberta watched out for her old friend, making sure nobody teased her or made her life too miserable. The kids stopped asking Sherri if she'd stuck her finger in a light socket to make her hair so wild and giving her a hard time for checking books out of the school library from the "Coping With" section with titles like *Coping with Cliques* and *How to Be Your Own Best Friend*.

After they graduated from high school, Roberta moved to Milwaukee to work at the Wooden Nickel store selling jeans in Southridge Mall, while Sherri spent the next year taking care of her mom. Sherri was touched that her friend had returned home to pay respects at Sherri's mother's funeral. Roberta genuinely cared for Mrs. Taylor, who had taught her how to play the piano. Sherri's mom had known that Roberta's father got rough with them sometimes, and even though Muriel could be bossy and adamant with Sherri, she was always available to offer Roberta quiet support without interfering.

After the service, Sherri stepped out of the receiving line, shattered.

Roberta, her eyes red from crying, gave her a big hug. "Sorry, Sher. This must be hard."

"It was a long time coming," Sherri said, exhausted from trying to say the right thing to the funeral attendees, as if she were comforting them instead of the other way around. She didn't want people to feel sorry for her, or to worry. She did her best to appear poised and appropriate. Sherri thought she'd done well; she had a gift for remembering her parents' friends' names and the connections between the family's few and distant relatives. Her father had been an only child from neighboring Burlington. She'd met a few of his aunts, uncles, and cousins over the years, but Sherri didn't know them very well. They were farmers, and her father, the black sheep, preferred to stick his head in a book. He had no interest in animal husbandry or big tractors. He didn't like to get his hands dirty—he couldn't even stand to get Jismaa oil on his fingers when he repaired a watch. Her mother had been a loner for different reasons. At thirty, she'd left her parents behind in Albany, New York, when she'd heard about the church organist job in East Troy. When Muriel was in her teens, her parents converted from Catholicism to Christian Scientist, and had refused medical treatment for her beloved brother when he came down with TB. She'd never forgiven them for rejecting her entreaties to seek medical attention as he grew sicker. *Just call the doctor!* Muriel often noted the irony that in the last years of her life she'd seen one doctor after another, and they'd all been useless.

Sherri held each attendee's hands and looked them in the eyes when they spoke to her, her smile caring and authentic. "Honestly, we were just waiting for her to pass so she'd be relieved of her pain." She used "we" to make herself feel less alone, although it only made her more aware of her new status as an orphan. She repeated what she'd said a hundred times that day to Roberta, this time with sarcasm.

"Still." Roberta could see through Sherri's act. She knew there was more to it.

"Yeah. Still." Sherri tried not to cry. "It's just. I had to do every-thing for her. Literally *everything*." Her mother had battled against a mysterious neurological disease that made her dizzy. The doctor called it cerebral atrophy—her cerebellum had turned into scrambled eggs. She had a sound mind, but her body slowly became a cage for it. As an only child, Sherri was the only person to care for her. The last year had been especially brutal. Her mother couldn't even go to the bathroom without help. Though Sherri got along with her just fine, Muriel had been stubborn and strident even before she got sick. She had strong ideas about how things *should* be: music should be played at tempo, daughters should be obedient, and Muriel should be able to do all the things she used to be able to do.

"I had to watch her like a hawk," Sherri said, thinking about the accident that led to her mother's final decline, when she fell down the stairs. Sherri looked around the church. "She's just *nowhere*. I know it sounds crazy, Roberta, but now that she doesn't need me anymore, I'm all alone, and I'm—I'm useless."

Sherri needed to vent, and aside from her friend Jeanne, there were very few people in her life she could confide in. Roberta, she felt, could absorb some of her emotions. "I can't believe she's really gone, even though I have a death certificate to prove it. The coroner typed out the technical term for the disease. I couldn't even tell you what it is, but I counted. It was twenty-three horrible letters long."

Roberta fixed Sherri's collar and kept her hand on her shoulder. "Have you thought about what you'll do next?" Roberta asked. "You can do anything now."

Roberta was right: Sherri could walk right off a cliff if she wanted to. This new freedom she'd guiltily anticipated during her mother's decline was at once frightening and exhilarating. Everything was changing. The people she'd gone to high school with had moved on to jobs or to college. She had the building on the square, she supposed, but she felt too young to be saddled with real estate. She couldn't even afford to pay the taxes without someone to lease the space downstairs.

It seemed everyone else had a plan, but what was Sherri supposed to do? She'd been so busy taking care of her mother these past few years that she'd never had the luxury of thinking much about her future. She was smart, but she had no money for college, and she didn't know what she'd even major in. She knew one thing for certain: she didn't want to become a nurse.

"This might sound crazy," Roberta said, "but my friend Ellen from the store told me that they're interviewing for Bunnies at the Playboy resort. I already mailed in my application, and they called me for an interview."

"You did?" Sherri had a hard time imagining Roberta without her leather jacket on.

"Sure, why not? They pay serious money, more than I make at the mall, that's for sure, and it sounds fun, doesn't it? Think of all those men."

"I wouldn't know what to do with them. I've never even had a boyfriend."

"What about Tommy?"

Sherri rolled her eyes. She'd dated Tommy briefly when they were sophomores. He played the clarinet and made patterns in the spit that fell on the band room floor. He took her to a dance at the youth center, and then on a date to see *Exorcist II*. He put his arm around her, but he might as well have placed a dead cat across her shoulders. When he leaned forward to kiss her good night, she saw his greasy forehead and thought of all the drool that came out of his mouth. She closed her eyes and winced as his lips, like two earthworms, landed on her own. She hadn't enjoyed it at all. That was the only time she'd ever been kissed, and it was nothing like the passionate kisses she'd seen on her mother's soap operas.

Roberta said, "You don't want to date anyone from around here. Besides, you already know everyone. The men at the resort have good jobs. They open doors for you and chew with their mouths closed. You could find someone decent to marry."

Sherri felt like her life was just getting started. "I don't want to get married."

"Not yet, but someday you will, so you might as well find someone handsome and rich."

"At the Playboy resort? Aren't the guys there a bunch of perverts?"

"No, are you kidding? The guys there, they have an *outlook*." It had always struck Sherri as strange that someone as tough and seemingly independent as Roberta would worry so much about having a boyfriend and a husband. She'd already designed her own wedding dress. Sherri figured it was because her family was more "normal" than her own. Mr. Fletcher worked in management at Trent Tube, and she had siblings. They always ate dinner together as a family, drew lines on a special wall in the basement where they marked each kid's growth on their birthdays, and they went on beach vacations to Florida every other year. If it weren't for Mr. Fletcher's short temper, Sherri would have given her eyeteeth to be part of their family.

"Berta, are you crazy?" Nobody called Roberta "Berta" anymore except Sherri. "You really want to work at the Playboy resort?" Sherri said these words softly, because they weren't meant to be spoken in a church. The resort opened more than a decade ago and there were still some people in town, mostly older ladies, who couldn't even talk about the place out loud, while the men would brag openly about owning membership keys to get into the club. They'd take out-of-town visitors there for dinner and drinks, and make it sound like they were friends with Hugh Hefner himself. Between Alpine Valley and the Playboy resort, there were people in town who felt that they lived on the edge of the center of the universe. "You seriously want to work at that place?"

"You know how much money you can make? Thousands—not a month, but in a *week*. You can save up for your car. Didn't you always want to move to California?" When they were in middle school, they'd sneak into the Community Hall and play "California Dreamin'" on the jukebox over and over, dancing until they could hardly stand. That was Sherri's favorite song, because she couldn't believe there was a place where the weather was nice every day, all year long.

Roberta said, "My interview is next Tuesday at nine. They said to bring heels and a bathing suit. I can call and see if you can come with me."

"No, that's OK. That's not for me." What Sherri meant was that becoming a Bunny would permanently change her reputation in a small town where your reputation was all you had. Everyone knew you, and they knew your aunts, uncles, grandparents, siblings, and second cousins. Even her relatives in Burlington would get wind of it.

"Oh, come on. What have you got to lose? You can always say no if they want to give you a job. And they have a dorm."

"You mean we can live there?" Now, *that* appealed to Sherri. She couldn't imagine spending another day alone in the apartment she'd shared with her mom. She'd already talked to Jerry Derzon, the town Realtor, about finding someone to buy or lease the building.

"Don't you want to see what it's like? What else are you going to do? Let me just ask."

A few days later, when Roberta called to tell her that she'd arranged for Sherri to join her for the interview, she couldn't say no—then again, she could never say no to her old friend. The idea of the resort, while "pie in the sky" as her mother would say, offered a nice psychic refuge from the sad work of cleaning Tupperware dishes from the noodle casseroles the church ladies had dropped off and writing thank-you notes for flowers and memorials.

Sherri tried to imagine how she'd answer the interview questions they'd ask her. Could she really be a Bunny? *Sherri Taylor?* No way. But maybe they'd hire her to work in the laundry room folding towels and ironing sheets, or cutting vegetables in the kitchen. She remembered in seventh grade when Greg Thielan told their teacher with a perfectly straight face that he wanted to be a photographer for *Playboy* magazine. Greg's aspirations seemed about as realistic back then as Sherri's did now, only *she* was actually going to try.

Just before Sherri got into Roberta's car, she heard a little girl's voice. "Hey, Sher!" Sherri looked up and there, in the apartment above the flower store, she saw Raylee's face hanging out the window. She was the pesky neighbor kid, with thick glasses, a smattering of freckles, and massive gerbil cheeks. She was just as lonely as Sherri was. Her dad was a long-haul truck driver and her mom, Donna, worked the second shift in a nursing home, where there were lots of emergencies. Donna was always asking Sherri if she could do her a "little favor" and watch Raylee. The kid was always desperate to talk to someone—she'd even talk to Muriel as though she were able to hold up her end of the conversation. "Did you know glass is made from melted sand? Mozart could play the piano upside down and backwards. Could you do that before you got sick? Could you? Could you do a backflip? I heard about a man who could eat forty hot dogs in a minute. Do you think the sky is blue on other planets?" Sherri heard her voice and felt the girl's eyeballs on her everywhere she went. "Where are you going?" Raylee asked.

"It doesn't matter. Shut the window, it's freezing! Your dad doesn't drive for two days straight to pay to heat the outside." That was exactly the kind of thing her mother would have said, and this made Sherri impossibly sad. But Raylee did everything Sherri told her to do, so she slammed the window shut with a startling *bam*.

Roberta's car smelled like exhaust, cigarette butts, and the Little Tree air freshener hanging from the rearview mirror. She turned onto Highway G. The ride from East Troy to Lake Geneva was pretty, even in the heart of winter. Off in the distance, Sherri could see the lifts on the ski hill at Alpine Valley, worn tracks from ski runs, and the domes of giant floodlights. Bare old oak trees lined the roads. Dilapidated barns, silos, and weather vanes were tucked into the rolling hills. The black cows looked like semicolons against the snow.

It had always been a big deal to go to Lake Geneva. There were only about three thousand residents in the winter, a number that swelled in summer, but people in East Troy considered it a real town second only to Milwaukee. It was only an hour away from Chicago, and the area had a certain mystique, because it had been a playground for mobsters like Al Capone and John Dillinger in the 1920s. There were nice restaurants, bars, and a little shop she liked called Barden's on the main drag, but the real attraction was the giant, deep lake. When Sherri was ten years old, her father had splurged and taken her and her mom on a tour on a converted steam yacht called the *Louise*. Everything seemed huge to Sherri back then: Lake Geneva, yes, but especially the Gilded Age mansions that the Chicago industrialists had built around it, like Stone Manor with its rooftop swimming pool, and the Alta Vista, Edgewood, Wrigley, and Black Point estates. Decades later, Hugh Hefner had built his Playboy resort nearby so he could have a country playground escape from his Chicago mansion, which gave Chicagoans yet another reason to visit.

They passed near Bower's farm and the old schoolhouse, and suddenly Sherri felt herself come loose. She didn't know what was wrong with her. She'd kept it together all week since her mother's funeral, so why fall apart now? Maybe it was leaving East Troy for the first time in months, the exhaust making her feel light-headed, or seeing Berta, her old friend. Maybe she felt bad about yelling at Raylee, who was just lonely and lost—all she'd wanted was Sherri's attention. Why had she barked at her to shut the window instead of just saying hello and asking nicely?

When Roberta gunned the engine at the bottom of the hill, Sherri's stomach dropped, and suddenly she was in tears. She leaned forward and began to cry, really cry, for the first time since her mother had died. She sobbed without feeling embarrassed, jerking with grief.

Roberta reached her arm across the seat and rubbed Sherri's back. "It's OK, Sher. It's OK. Here." She grabbed an A&W napkin out of the glove compartment. Sherri appreciated that Roberta knew her well enough to just be there; she didn't offer the stupid platitudes Sherri had been bombarded with since her mother had gotten sick, and especially since she'd passed. The worst was *God doesn't give you what you can't handle.* Sherri especially hated that one.

She wiped her face, dabbing under her eyes, knowing her makeup would be ruined, and her pale china doll skin would be splotchy with tears. She blushed easily, which made it hard for her to conceal how she felt. She knew this was why it was so easy for the girls to make fun of her; unlike Roberta, who'd learned how to let their teasing roll off her back, Sherri's hurt blared like a neon sign. Everything got to her.

Soon her sobs, like thunder after a storm, grew less frequent, and Sherri slowly sank back into the cold, hard bucket seat, exhausted but also feeling better, cleansed even. She pressed her face against the window in hopes that the coolness would restore her complexion. When she pulled away, she saw she'd left an ugly smear of tan foundation on the glass.

"Hey Sher," Roberta said, "remember? Two all-beef patties, special sauce, lettuce, cheese, pickles—"

Sherri mustered a smile. "—onions on a sesame seed bun!" They said this last part together. The girls used to sing the McDonald's jingle over and over again, and in rounds. By the time Roberta turned off Highway 50 Sherri felt better, but the knot in her stomach tightened again when she saw a little booth with an attendant and the massive wooden sign advertising the Playboy resort with the familiar, giant white profile of the bunny head with the blank eye carved into it, and she remembered why she was there. Roberta stopped to tell the guy their names, and he waved them in. Sherri flipped down the mirror on the visor. "I'm never going to get this job." Long black streaks of mascara ran down her face. "Look at me. I look like I just finished a shift in a coal mine!"

"You'll be fine, you just need to get cleaned up. You're so pretty, Sher. Just wash your face when we get there. If anyone can get away with a natural look, it's you."

Sherri didn't believe Roberta meant what she'd said. Roberta was always the pretty one; she liked having Sherri as her sidekick, not her competition.

The road up to the resort was almost a mile long, and it wound up and down gentle hills. Sherri had always imagined that the main building would be closer to the lake, but when she turned and looked through the rear window, she could hardly see the icy expanse glinting in the distance.

"This place is posh *posh*," Roberta said. "They have their own airplane landing strip."

"You've been here? You never told me that."

"Just once. My dad has a key. They give them to all the managers at Trent. He brought me to see Gabe Kaplan perform in the Cabaret. All I remember is his stupid joke about teaching a monkey how to shave."

"You saw Gabe Kaplan?" Sherri was impressed. She loved *Welcome Back, Kotter*. She loved all the shows; whatever happened to be on TV was her mother's only form of entertainment, so Sherri left it on in the background for hours at a time. But her mother's true pleasure had been to listen to Sherri practice the organ, nodding along to the music she knew by heart, a look of concern crossing her face when Sherri missed a note.

As they crested the hill, Sherri saw the building. It was modern and earthy, with massive overhangs and stucco walls. It was sprawling and as flat as a sheet cake. It was easy to look at; it didn't compete with the landscape but managed to appear as if it had grown out of it. Most of her life she'd imagined the Playboy resort as a dirty place, forbidden. But up close it was almost disappointingly normal, not tacky at all. Tasteful, even. What had she expected, some brothel like the ones in the movies about the Wild West?

Roberta had to drive around to find a parking spot. The resort was pretty busy for a blustery Tuesday morning. "Hurry," she said. "The interview starts in two minutes."

"You go ahead," Sherri said. "I don't want to make you late."

"But the woman I contacted, she's expecting you."

"I don't even care if I work here."

Roberta was visibly annoyed. "Then why'd you come?"

"Because you asked!" Sherri started to cry again, and a fresh round of tears began to flow. "I wanted to do something with you. We never do things together anymore. You were my best friend."

"Oh, Sher." It was clear that Roberta was moved. "I'll always be your best friend. Just do this for me, OK? I really want this job or I'll have to sell jeans at the fucking mall forever. Please don't make me look bad by skipping out now. Just interview. It won't take long."

Sleet began to gather and thicken on the windshield. What could Sherri do? "Fine. Go on ahead, you go first. I'll be there in a few minutes." It didn't matter; they'd never hire her, not with Roberta for competition, and not the way she looked that morning after crying her guts out.

When she finally approached the building, the doorman opened the thick glass doors. "Welcome to Playboy, dear!" He said it as if Playboy was more than just the resort; like it was a way of life. Maybe for some people, but certainly not Sherri.

She half expected a bolt of lightning to strike her dead the minute she crossed the threshold. The entrance was grand, and the sound was muted because the walls had millions of small pebbles pressed into them. The ceiling was covered with wood beams that were stained almost black. A woman in a brown vest sat at a switchboard with a headset on. A happy Bunny with blond hair and a bright yellow outfit worked a table covered with Playboy merchandise—mugs, pens, stacks of magazines. "Here for the interview?"

"I guess," Sherri said. She didn't want this woman, so perfect and poised, to see her blotchy face, so she looked down at the navy carpet. Even the carpet was decorated with the bunny logo—bunnies everywhere.

"You're going to need to show more enthusiasm than that," the Bunny said, although her voice was kind, concerned.

"Where's the bathroom?" Sherri asked. She looked up, and the Bunny frowned when she saw streaks of mascara on Sherri's cheeks.

"Tell you what, I'll walk you there. Follow me." She led Sherri by the arm down the hall. "I'm Bunny Tina."

Sherri felt so dowdy in her parka and velveteen, her face stained and mottled, while Tina could have walked right off the cover of one of the

Playboy magazines. Embarrassed, she stared at the black leather furniture and the floor of the main area, which, unlike the lobby, wasn't carpeted but covered in fieldstone. Between the stones was a sheet of plexiglass, and beneath it ran a river that streamed from a waterfall. It made Sherri think of her father reading Coleridge's "Kubla Khan" to her:

> *In Xanadu did Kubla Khan*
> *A stately pleasure-dome decree:*
> *Where Alph, the sacred river, ran*
> *Through caverns measureless to man*
> *Down to a sunless sea.*

"What's your name, hon?"

"Sherri," she said, still thinking of the next lines she knew by heart. She looked up and noticed the sunken indoor pool behind a glass wall, right there in the middle of the resort. Little bistro tables surrounded it, and there was a bar in the distance with a wall glittering with bottles of liquor under the lights. The air smelled faintly of chlorine.

"We just lost a Sherri."

"She died?"

"No, silly, she quit! But that means that when you get the job, you'll be able to keep your own name—you'll be the only Bunny Sherri for miles around."

"I'm not going to get this job."

"Don't say that! Come on now."

"Are you really Tina?"

"No, my real name is Mary, but forget I ever told you that. Here I'm Bunny Tina. We say 'Bunny' in front of our names the way you say 'Doctor,' even with each other. Did you know that Sonny and Cher bought Hugh Hefner's jet? And when they did, they had a party out there on the landing strip." Tina pointed beyond the big floor-to-ceiling windows. "Frankie Valli and the Four Seasons played. Just for us Bunnies! There's always something fun here—well, in the summer at least. Back home everyone just watches the corn grow." They entered the bathroom, and Tina handed Sherri a towel. "Start washing up. Don't go anywhere. I'll be right back."

Sherri did as she was told, grateful for Bunny Tina's calming chatter, her kindness. She soaped off her makeup. The mascara, like ink from a busted pen, swirled down the drain. She ran the water until it was cold and pressed it on her eyes with the hand towel to get rid of the puffiness.

Bunny Tina returned with a purple Chivas Regal bag made of soft velvet. She pulled out foundation, fake eyelashes, lipstick, and blush. "I can do this in record time. Trust me, I've had lots of practice."

"But those are *your* eyelashes."

"My drawer is crawling with these little caterpillars! I've got plenty to spare, and you're going to need to learn how to do this."

She stepped closer to Sherri and told her to look up. Bunny Tina smelled good, like cotton candy. It was hard not to stare at her ample breasts sitting on the shelf of her uniform, so Sherri fixed her gaze on the black bow tie at the base of her neck instead.

"You have to be pretty to be a Bunny, and you are, but there's more to it. The Bunny Mother wants each of us to have our own look. You've got that, did you know? A look. Real distinct. Plus, you seem sweet, and Gloria wants girls who are wholesome. She wants happy girls, friendly girls. So when you interview, trust me, smile until your mouth breaks. No drama, no tears. Here, let me put some blush on those cheeks." She bit her lip as she dabbed puffs of pink with a giant makeup brush and lined Sherri's lips before filling them in and asking Sherri to blot them on a paper towel. "I'm so jealous of your heart-shaped mouth."

"I have a heart-shaped mouth?"

"Sure you do. And a heart-shaped face, with your wide cheekbones and cute pointy chin. That's part of your look, see? What do you think?"

Tina placed her hands on Sherri's shoulders and adjusted her stance so that she could see herself in the mirror. The eyelashes made her eyes look huge, and her cheekbones appeared more angular and distinct. She looked better than she ever had, she really did.

"Now let's free up that gorgeous hair and unbutton your shirt. You look like you've come to interview at the library!" Tina set Sherri's hair loose and puffed it with her fingers. "You're a regular Bernadette Peters with those ringlets, has anyone told you that?"

"Oh, I hate my hair," Sherri said.

"We always want what other people have, but trust me, it's amazing. Look at you, Sherri. You're beautiful! What on earth made you so sad? Did you and your friend get into an argument?"

"No. My mother died."

Sherri could tell that Bunny Tina wasn't prepared for something *that* bad to have upset her. "Oh, you poor thing." Instead of brushing her hair, she started to pet it. "I'm sorry to hear that, I really am, but listen, don't mention it. Gloria won't even hire a girl if she hears her parents are divorced. Remember, no drama. This is a family resort. You need to ooze sweetness and smiles. Just tell her what she wants to hear, even if you have to lie. Trust me, it doesn't matter to her if you're telling the truth—all she cares about is how you look and how you *seem*." Bunny Tina led Sherri out of the bathroom and down the stairs and pointed to the door for the locker room. She gave her a big hug. "When you get the job, I'll look out for you. Remember, Sherri. If you've got an edge, don't let Gloria see it, and don't let her scare you. She scares the crap out of all of us, but you won't make it here if you show it. Good luck!"

When Sherri entered the locker room, she was overwhelmed by all the activity. The walls were covered in full-length mirrors except for one wall that had a door and a big window with the shades closed, and there were a few women in hot rollers applying makeup and shimmying into their costumes. The air was thick with perfume and hair spray. The women paid no attention to Sherri. Where had Roberta gone?

She stood with her bag hanging off her shoulder, unsure what to do. She took off her coat and folded it over her arm, and yanked off

her ugly winter boots and hid them in a corner. After a few minutes the door opened, and Roberta walked out wearing her bikini,
a frightened expression on her face. Sherri had never seen Roberta
look so small or so vulnerable with her pale skin and rib bones. She
was followed by a woman who must have been the Bunny Mother,
based on the silence that fell over the room when she entered it. She
was older than the other women by a decade or so but still beautiful.
Her cinnamon-colored hair was styled in a fashionable bob, with her
bangs cut bluntly across her forehead, and her lipstick was bright red.
She wore a loose, ivory silk kimono with orchids embroidered on the
neck, and her eyeglasses were propped at the bottom of her thin nose.
"What's your name?"

"Sherri," she said. She could feel everyone's eyes on her. "Sherri
Taylor. I'm Roberta's friend."

"Well, Sherri Taylor, which part of nine o'clock did you not understand? I usually have the interview before I see you in your suit, but I
don't have time for that today. Get changed, pronto. I've been waiting.
Come to my office when you're ready."

Sherri remembered what Bunny Tina told her: smile, be wholesome
and sweet. So Sherri forced herself to smile even though she felt like
dying. "Absolutely!" She was so rattled she didn't know what to say. Was
she really supposed to change in front of all these women? Then she
saw a topless Bunny standing with her breasts hanging out for all the
world to see, not a care in the world. Sherri stripped, fumbling with
her snaps, zippers, and ties because her hands were shaking and cold.
Finally, she was in the borrowed bathing suit, which seemed grubby and
worn. There was still sand in the crotch from last summer at the lake.

She stuffed her feet into her narrow organ shoes with modest heels
and Mary Jane straps and tapped the door to Gloria's office. "Stand
there, against that wall, so your knees and ankles touch," Gloria said
without looking up. Gloria got up and shut the door so that it was just
the two of them in the room. She bent down and inspected Sherri's legs;
Sherri realized that she was counting to see if she could see three tri-

angles of light shining through between her feet and ankles, between her ankles and knees, and between her thighs. Fortunately, Sherri had lost her appetite with her grief, and she was skinnier than she'd ever been. When Gloria saw her shoes, shaped more like dress shoes for men, she frowned with displeasure. "What are these?"

Sherri didn't want to tell Gloria that she played the organ. "It's my only pair."

"Well." Gloria stood up. "Take a seat."

Sherri lowered herself onto the chair next to Gloria's desk. She crossed her legs and set her hands on her lap, feeling more naked than she'd ever felt before, covered in a rash of goose pimples. She could tell that Gloria was inspecting everything about her as if she were a hog at the state fair: her skin, her hair, her bust, her waist, her teeth. "Why were you late?"

"Oh, I got here as quickly as I could. I was waiting for my ride, and—" She just blamed Roberta for making her late. She wished she could push the words back into her mouth. She decided to change the subject. Sherri smiled and fixed her eyes on the bracelet watch on Gloria's wrist. "I can put a new battery in that for you if you like. That's why your second hand is skipping."

Gloria seemed taken aback. "I thought it was broken."

Sherri repeated something her father had taught her: "Swiss watches don't break."

Gloria scribbled some notes. "You have work experience?"

"I brought a résumé. It's nothing much, but I've waitressed—"

"You don't need a résumé. And we don't call this '*waitressing.*'" She said it like the word was dirty. "Where'd you work?"

"Inn the Olden Days. In Mukwonago." Sherri had picked up a few shifts a week while a church deacon stayed with her mom. She worked hard and was lucky to leave with twenty bucks in her pocket after a four-hour shift. There, she'd waited on old ladies who farted and played bridge, and farm-equipment salespeople passing through town who called her "doll." She never wanted to smell chipped beef on rye ever again.

"And what do you like to do? Hobbies? Interests?"

At this point, Sherri figured she had nothing to lose by following Tina's advice—*even if you have to lie*. She channeled Tina's people-pleasing personality. "Well," Sherri said, smiling the way Tina did, and pulling her hair back behind her ear. "I guess you could say I'm your typical small-town girl." She giggled. "I love to play volleyball and golf and tennis, and I volunteer at the Salvation Army camp as an aide—I just adore kids. And I'm in 4-H, like everyone in my town. Lop-eared rabbits are my specialty." This was partly true. Sherri *had* been in 4-H, but her rabbit, an American Dutch named Radio, had bit the judge on the knuckles and was disqualified.

"I know it might sound funny," Sherri said, "but I just love spending time with my family. My mom is in charge of the annual cookbook for the East Troy Lioness Club, and she knows everyone in town." Ha! Sherri's mother would never have joined the Lioness Club, not in a million years. She thought the local women were busybodies with nothing better to do than gossip and exchange recipes. In turn, they considered Muriel a foreigner because she was from New York. "Between my dad's Rotary friends and my mom's potlucks, and all my brothers, our house is practically as busy as this resort!"

After everything she'd been through, it felt so good to be someone else for a change, good to imagine herself surrounded by a close-knit, unmarred family. Sherri tried to think of more lies to tell Gloria, but before she could say anything else, Gloria asked, "You're not planning to go to college, are you? You don't strike me as a college girl."

"No." Even though she had been trying to be someone else, Gloria's comment made her feel exposed; it was directed right at her, the *real* Sherri, and it hurt. Sherri was bored easily, but she'd been a good student, and she had a keen memory and proficiency with numbers. She could balance her father's books when she was just eleven years old. At the restaurant, she could tally her tickets and tax without an adding machine. She received perfect scores in her business simulation accounting classes, but the teachers only praised the boys for their good work. She liked how numbers made sense, and she loved that feeling of correctness when they clicked, but everyone assumed Sherri was a dip because of her loud laugh and awkwardness—and so did Gloria, apparently, right at first glance.

"We aren't so busy now, but by summer it'll be a madhouse. I need someone who can live here and work year-round, someone reliable to pick up shifts and work doubles, even triples sometimes."

"Oh, I can do all that. I'm a hard worker, I am. And I want to work here. The resort is so beautiful and classy." Just saying it made Sherri realize this was true—she really did want to work there. Suddenly it seemed as if the job was the answer to everything. She smiled and said, "I have the heart of a Bunny."

Later, on the drive back to East Troy, Roberta would die laughing when Sherri told her she'd said this, but Gloria seemed moved by the sentiment. She'd slipped off her watch and handed it to Sherri. "You'll get a letter from me in a few days. When you come back, bring this with you, and don't you dare lose it."

Sherri couldn't help herself. She reached out to Gloria and tried to give her a hug, which would be the first and only time she would ever try to touch the Bunny Mother. Gloria recoiled. "I didn't say you got the job," she said, her voice cold and firm. Sherri felt more stupid than ever—even more stupid than the time she tried to take the steno machine down from the top shelf at school and dropped it on her head in front of everyone.

Gloria opened her office door and ushered Sherri back into the dressing room. She frowned when her eyes fell on a Bunny in a pink costume who wore a cowboy hat with a turquoise stone and feather. "Bunny Carmen," Gloria said to a messy-looking Bunny with a shaggy Dorothy Hamill bob haircut, "let's talk about what happened last night." The pink-costumed Bunny's face fell. She ran into the office and the door slammed shut.

A few days later, Sherri got a letter offering employment. Training would start the following week. It seemed impossible. For someone who didn't plan to take the interview seriously, she suddenly felt like she'd won the gold wrapper on the Willy Wonka candy bar.

She called Roberta and blurted out her news. "We're going to work together, Berta!"

"You got it?" Roberta asked, dismay creeping into her voice.

"Didn't you?"

"No," Roberta said.

"Sure you did. Check your mail."

"I *did* check my mail, Sher. I got a letter of rejection yesterday. They don't want me."

Sherri was shocked. Was it because she'd mentioned that Roberta made her late? Or because Sherri didn't have a chance to share Bunny Tina's advice and tell her friend that she should act wholesome and never show her edge?

"I'm so sorry. I didn't even think I'd ever, you know, it wasn't even something I'd wanted, and you're so gorgeous."

"I didn't want to work at that trashy resort, anyway." Sherri knew Roberta well enough to know she was lying and she didn't think the resort was trashy. A ripple of guilt braided with pleasure ran through her when she realized how good it felt to step in front of Roberta for a change. It was the first sensation of a new life. She clutched the Bunny Mother's repaired Provita watch like a talisman.

James Bartelt

CHRISTINA CLANCY's work has appeared in *The New York Times, The Washington Post, Chicago Tribune, The Sun Magazine,* and in various literary journals, including *Glimmer Train, Pleiades,* and *Hobart.* She holds a PhD in creative writing from the University of Wisconsin-Milwaukee. *The Second Home* is her first novel.